Paperboy

STAN CRADER

Paperboy

Published by Wheatmark®
610 East Delano Street, Suite 104, Tucson, Arizona 85705 U.S.A.
www.wheatmark.com

ISBN: 978-1-60494-476-1
LCCN: 2010928707

rev201101

Dedication

I dedicate this book to paperboys, past and present.
Every morning, rain or shine, I open my front door
and see my newspaper on the driveway.
Roxie, my golden retriever, runs and fetches it for me.
I don't take my paperboy or Roxie for granted.

Contents

Contents

Acknowledgements

A BOOK IS SIMPLY THE product of everyone who has had a hand in teaching, influencing, encouraging, or raising the author. Reading is a prerequisite to writing, so I am grateful to my elementary teachers who suffered through my attention deficit days and taught me to read. The disorder was yet to be identified at the time, but I'm sure I had it. Others would agree.

I'm thankful for my grandparents, who raised my parents, who raised me.

Raising our three sons helped keep my memories of my own childhood crisp and clear in my mind. It's amazing how many personality traits are passed on to the next generation. Although none were paperboys, they all have a knack for observation, storytelling, and appreciate the unique nature of living in a small town.

Sometimes an author can be difficult to live with ... or so my wife, Debbie, says. She had to endure my hours of staring into space and not responding during conversation. She knows it can't be helped and is patient, most of the time. Since she's my best friend, she also has the responsibility of offering constructive criticism, which she did a number of times during the edit of *Paperboy*. I always value her opinion, even when I don't like it. And it's when I don't like it that I usually need it the most. And editing a book is mostly about making corrections, not celebrating accuracy.

There are countless others who helped in the edit process. Lawanda Rhodes thinks she's cruel, but she's not. "You want me to tell you what I think?" she'd ask. I'd brace for something really bad, and then she'd offer some minor critique. Her editorial assistance was of almost as much value as her perpetual encouragement.

And then there's the Hopkins, clan—Gregg, Bill, and Sharon. They're a clever lot and they have a great eye for story development. I'm very much grateful to them for sharing their time and talent.

Pamela, Debbie's sister, advised me on the redundancy of some of my adjectives. After looking up the meaning of redundancy and adjective, I made adjustments. A thesaurus is a very handy tool.

To the countless people at Cape Bible Chapel who asked, "When's your book coming out? I'm looking forward to reading it." Your words may have helped the most. Writing a book is a long and hard process. Bill Ringpfel and Charlie Thurman are forever on my favorite persons list. Thank you, Bill and Charlie, for always asking about *Paperboy*.

Thanks to Wayne Smith, an old friend, and I mean that in every sense, who couldn't wait to see a draft copy. Wayne has been a constant source of encouragement.

A special thanks to Dodi Conrad, whose artistic talent graces the cover of this book. Her painting was done of an actual building in Marble Hill, Missouri, using a live model. The building is the inspiration for Gooche's Grocery.

I owe an enormous measure of gratitude to the people of Bollinger County, Missouri; that's where I grew up, or at least got older. It wasn't until I spent some time away that I realized what a special place and time it was to grow up there. Coming of age in Bollinger County was a privilege that I no longer take for granted. All of the people in this book are fictional, however many of them possess characteristics of those I knew, grew up with, and observed while delivering newspapers so many years ago.

Prologue

THIS BOOK WAS WRITTEN BECAUSE the story had to be told. It was bottled up inside me for too long. Now that the story is on paper, I can relax, at least for a day or two. What is the story that had to be told? Glad you asked.

I consider growing up in rural America to be a blessing. Few things compare to the freedom to ride a bicycle anywhere in town, speak to everyone, know practically every person, and do all of this without fear of anything. With that freedom comes responsibility and accountability. Do something unacceptable and the word spreads quickly. Fall on bad times and help arrives instantly. My memories of my paperboy days are good ones. While writing this book I have come across many former paperboys (and one paper girl) who also have fond memories of the days when they rushed home from school, grabbed a shoulder bag and delivered the afternoon paper—rain or shine.

Although I can read my daily paper online, I still enjoy holding the paper and turning the pages. The delivery of newspapers may soon be a thing of the past. And that's too bad.

Back in the day when the paper was delivered by pre-pubescent boys, communication was different. If someone wanted to know what was going on in the community—they just asked the paperboy. The paperboy saw inside more houses and businesses than anyone else. He or she got invited into homes where even the preachers weren't welcome. Seeing is believing and paperboys saw it all. Believe me.

Older folks who hadn't had company for a spell took advantage of a fresh set of ears and were difficult to get away from. They frequently plopped onto the virtual psychiatrist couch, got into full disclosure mode and literally followed the paperboy out the door, to the edge of their lawn, lamenting health, religious, civic, and political concerns.

Ladies sitting under the hair dryer at the beauty salon carried on oblivious to the young perky ears of the paperboy. Men at the filling stations continued with their colorful language regardless of the presence of a curious adolescent paperboy. The crusty old men who frequented the courthouse bench, and had lost their social filters, revealed more about life than could be understood at the time by the boy handing them their daily newspaper.

The most incredible aspect of being a paperboy is learning that everyone has an untold story. Paperboys get to know the people of the town they serve like nobody else can. Those who have been a paperboy know what I mean. Those who haven't will need to read *Paperboy*.

The Band of Boys

TOMMY RUSHED HOME FROM THE bus stop, running as fast as his lungs would allow. He was still aching from a brutal seventh hour PE class conducted by a new and overexuberant football coach wannabe. He had less than thirty minutes to squeeze in a ride on the Mini Trail with Melody before meeting Booger at the stone. During band he'd described to Melody how the trees that canopied the creek were at their fall peak. She'd listened intently with dancing eyes and eagerly agreed to a ride to Craggy Creek Bridge. His fancy speech had worked!

Thinking about a first kiss with Melody energized him. But after several unsuccessful attempts at kick-starting the Mini Trail his right leg quivered from exhaustion. The chance for a first kiss with Melody slowly faded. He slumped and rested his head on his folded arms, which were draped over the handlebars of his lifeless Mini-Trail. He could see himself reflected in the chrome gas-tank cap. Sweat dripped from the tip of his nose.

Putting a halt to the pity party, he mustered the energy to sit up, wipe the sweat from his nose, grab the neatly folded tool bag from under the seat, and remove the spark plug. He knew what he'd find. A minuscule piece of carbon had lodged in the gap between the center and ground electrode. It had happened before—that's how Tommy knew to check the plug. And he had learned that the chronic carbon deposit problem was caused from riding primarily on gravel roads. Using his fingernail, he removed the microscopic piece of carbon. After replacing the plug, the Mini Trail roared to life on the first crank. By then he'd lost fifteen precious minutes.

Tommy had worked all summer, earning enough money to purchase a Honda Mini Trail. During those long, hot days of mowing lawns, his daydreams had often been of getting the Mini Trail and taking Wendy, his previous adolescent heartthrob, for a ride. Tommy's adolescent passion had been further fueled when his mother had made him take piano lessons from Wendy's mother. And to make matters worse—or better, depending on one's point of view—Wendy's mother, oblivious to Tommy's crush on Wendy, had arranged for them to perform a duet at the end-of-summer recital.

Tommy and Wendy had spent several hours sitting side by side on the piano bench practicing. Tommy found the experience both exhilarating and nerve-wracking. He had constantly worried about his hair, body odor, and breath. He'd fervently prayed for whiskers and had gotten two. A recurring nightmare he'd had during that time was discovering after the piano practice that he'd had a flapping booger in his nostril. After getting the Mini Trail, he'd chosen Wendy to be his first passenger. That ride had ended with a kiss—a first for both.

The kiss hadn't been the magical moment Tommy had expected. The moment their lips touched, Tommy's thoughts had turned to Melody, leaving Tommy in a state of confusion about girls. While it was rewarding to be seen with Wendy, Melody was the one with which he was the most at ease.

He roared to the end of the driveway before skidding to a stop and forlornly dealt with the reality that it was too late to take her for a ride. A greasy smear and the tiny speck were still stuck to his pants leg. He felt contempt for the tiny inanimate piece of carbon, and then flicked it away.

After allowing himself a few more seconds of self-pity, Tommy trudged into the house to call Melody but found his mom was using the phone. He motioned that he needed the phone, and she knowingly smiled. While waiting for her to finish, Tommy used Comet to scrub his greasy fingers, exfoliating a layer or two of skin in the process. His mom was hanging up when he stepped out of the bathroom. "Don't you need to get going?" she asked.

"I need to make a call first."

She got a perplexed, motherly look. Tommy rarely used the phone in her presence. She stood there and waited. Tommy, on the other hand, had hoped she'd find something else to do. His mother didn't particularly like for him to take girls for a ride. "They're too delicate," and "I don't want to hear it from their parents if you have a wreck," she'd repeatedly told him. He wasn't going to lie, but he wasn't making any effort to the reveal the truth. Being vague and unclear was a tactic he often found useful. "Who are you calling?" she asked.

While the phone rang on Melody's end, Tommy answered his mother, "Melody. I need to talk to her about something we discussed during band." It was a partial truth. Tommy anxiously listened while the unanswered phone continued to ring. He concluded she must be in the driveway waiting for him. His stomach began to churn.

He contemplated the perplexing behavior of girls and the differences between Melody and Wendy. Any time things didn't suit Wendy, she'd get mad and make snippy remarks. Melody, on the other hand, would merely sulk, which was much worse. The notion with which he wrestled on the way to the stone was that he wasn't good at handling either. And Uncle Cletus, his mentor on all manly subjects, had only chuckled when asked about the dilemma. Tommy decided to try calling Melody from Gooche's.

"Downtown" by Petula Clark was playing through the Houn-Dawg Drive-in's outdoor speakers; the tune boosted his spirit.

He coasted the last fifty yards before the town square. The magnificence of the fall colors competed with Melody for his thoughts. Wind swirling around the giant maples on the courthouse lawn created funnels of leaves that rose skyward, drifted a few feet, and then fluttered gently to the ground.

A sudden gust of wind caused a new batch of fluttering leaves to wiggle free from their fragile hold—several stayed aloft long enough to make their way to the street, where they swirled over and around passing cars. A few made it to the leaf devil stage and lived their last airborne moments held aloft by a miniature funnel.

Caleb, Flop, Everett, Checkers, and Booger, also known by their parents as "the band of boys," were hanging out in front of Gooche's. Flop's real name was William, and that was how his pious mother referred to him, but one look at his ears and the nickname was easy to understand.

Checkers's real name was Clyde, but he was given his nickname after his mother was overheard telling him that eating too many Moon Pies had made him chubby. Clyde was flattered to be considered a member of the band and felt a sense of pride to have a nickname that associated him with the King of Twist.

Booger was sitting on the stone whittling on a stick with his Tuff-Nut knife. Checkers and Everett were eating Moon Pies. Caleb was practicing a new skill, spitting two spitballs simultaneously. He'd seen one of the courthouse bench Codgers do it and had been developing his twin-stream spitting skill since. Flop was trying to fit in—even though he'd survived the summer, he was still considered the new kid.

Delivering the afternoon paper didn't pay well—in fact, the pay was abysmal. Counting the time spent waiting for the paper, it calculated out to about twenty-five cents per hour, at a time when carryout boys were making a dollar per hour, plus tips. In fact, except for household chores, a paper route was the worst paying job in town. And the paper had to be delivered regardless of the weather. There was no excuse for not delivering the *Colby Telegraph*.

Ironically, a paper route was the most coveted job in town, at least by pubescent boys. Putting on a paper bag elevated one to celebrity status; it was almost as good as having whiskers. A basket loaded with newspapers converted a bicycle from a toy to a tool.

When the weather was good and the days long, the band of boys kept each other company. They cruised the town and delivered papers. Tommy and Booger's friends often used "helping with the paper route" as an excuse to delay doing homework and a reason for riding their bicycles to all points of town.

Tommy looked through the massive plate glass front window and saw that Mr. Gooche was using the phone; anxiety filled his senses. He plopped down on the stone and slumped.

Booger, noticing Tommy's pained expression, asked, "What's the problem?" Tommy explained and pointed at the grease smudge on his pants.

Booger wasn't particularly impressed. "Did she let you kiss her yet?" Booger asked. Tommy shook his head no, letting Booger assume the problem was with Melody. The truth was, he'd never gotten up the nerve to try.

Booger continued to whittle, and Tommy was watching the phone when Jupiter Storm came stomping toward them. He'd been across the street at the courthouse bench talking to the Codgers. Montgomery Fulbright, Solomon Atchison, Benjamin May, and Simon James were referred to by most by their nicknames: Monkey, Fish, Bem, and Rabbit. They were known collectively as the Codgers, which had been shortened from the Old Codgers.

Before moving to the football field to watch practice, Monkey, Fish, Bem, and Rabbit would sit sentinel on the courthouse bench. Jupiter depended on them for the names of those who'd been to the courthouse each day. After getting the information, Jupiter would march into the courthouse, intrude into every office, and interrogate county officials in an effort to determine the personal business of each visitor.

Jupiter always walked with a purpose, possessed by a relentless sense of urgency. Even when he smiled, his face looked menacing. Tommy and Booger had to stay and wait for the papers. Checkers, Everett, Flop, and Caleb, not technically paperboys, saw Jupiter coming, mounted their bikes, and skedaddled.

"You know what you're sittin' on?" Jupiter asked, seeming to imply the boys had violated a sacred custom. Jupiter launched into a lengthy explanation before Booger or Tommy had a chance to answer. They'd suffered through the stepping-stone story several times since taking over the paper route. Jupiter had chosen this day to share his own version with them.

Tommy was certain that every living soul in Colby knew the history of the stepping-stone. He'd known it since forever. It's not that the stone had played any significant role in history; it's simply that it had a unique shape and had once served a specific purpose.

Jupiter was a large man, not particularly overweight, but big-boned with heavy facial features, deep-set eyes, was seldom seen without a wooden match dangling from his mouth or hanging behind his ear. An ear, by the way, that was covered with thick tufts of hair. It wasn't a feature unique to Jupiter; Tommy had noticed that other older men were similarly afflicted and had surmised that thick tufts more than likely obstructed sound waves and explained the loss of hearing in older men. Jupiter's bulbous belly, combined with the absence of a rear end, made keeping his pants in place a struggle. His constant tugging at them was almost as distracting as his garlicky breath. Jupiter liked to talk more than anything, but not about anything in particular. His enthusiasm for sharing his opinion always exceeded his knowledge of the subject or his victim's level of

interest. Tommy had heard his mother describe Jupiter as having excessive self-confidence. Adults could tell him to shove off. Kids, at least those
with manners, had to suffer through Jupiter's diatribes.

Eye contact was important to Jupiter, even though he had one eye that
was permanently squinted from years of smoking and one that wandered
on its own. The squinted eye seemed to be under Jupiter's control. He usually focused it on the person being interrogated. The wandering eye was
probably no more than that, but because of Jupiter's nature, Tommy and
Booger were convinced he was able to look at two people at once. He was
taller than most men, and he towered over Tommy and Booger. He had
a way of holding people optically captive. The unwavering squinted eye
was on Tommy. Every time Tommy moved to keep Mr. Gooche's phone
in view, Jupiter moved too. Booger and Tommy impatiently endured, in
excruciating detail, how the stepping-stone was originally a creek-bank
rock but so closely resembled a step that it had been placed in front of
the post office to be used for that purpose. Jupiter told how women, the
weaker sex, to use his term, had used the stone for getting on and off of
horses or in and out of carriages.

Since Booger and Tommy had started delivering papers, Jupiter made
more of an effort to include them in his rumor rounds. He seemed to
think the boys' status as paperboys gave them an in with the reporters for
the newspaper, or maybe it was because he was hoping to get a few morsels of hearsay from them.

Gooche's grocery and the Colby post office shared a facade of tall windows. Gooche's window box always featured a variety of displays, usually
cardboard cutouts. One window had a life-sized cardboard Aunt Jemima
hawking pancake syrup, and the other had a cardboard of Mr. Clean making a proclamation. The cutout was attached to a real toilet. Uncle Cletus
had told Tommy he thought it strange that an aging bald man could be
so happy cleaning toilets and thought Mr. Clean weird—he was probably
from California, or worse yet, France.

The post office windows were nothing more than tall transparent walls
revealing a spartan, but patriotic display of American flags.

During Jupiter's stepping-stone lecture, Tommy watched Mrs. Koch
make three attempts at her mailbox combination before successfully retrieving her mail. Mrs. Koch, sometimes considered a living fossil—which
was how Mr. Koch had been known to affectionately refer to her—had

given Booger and Tommy the stepping-stone history lesson the first day she'd seen them waiting for the paper. Her explanation was full of interesting detail and included the colors and styles of dresses worn by the ladies who had once used the stone, as well as the names of those who had originally found the stone and the ordeal it was to move it to its present location. An air of mystery shrouded her; maybe it was the way she pulled her hair tightly into a ball on the back of her head, or the layers of makeup that she caked onto her face, or the way she held her chin skyward when she marched about, the bridge of her nose parallel with the ground. Or it could have been her accent-free intonation, which didn't match that of most Colby residents. She and Mr. Koch lived in the apartment above the post office.

Tommy watched Mrs. Koch sort through her mail while Jupiter droned on about the stone. The story was fairly simple, but unlike Mrs. Koch, Jupiter didn't have a way with words, and worse yet, often got off track talking about other people's affairs and spreading rumors. "Are you listening to me?" he'd ask when Tommy's eyes began to glaze over. The thought occurred to him that when Jupiter's parents had decided to name all their children after a planet, they'd chosen the perfect planet for him. All the others, except a sister named Venus, had left Colby years earlier.

While lecturing Tommy and Booger about the stone, Jupiter managed to mention that he'd heard that Alison Tatum's daughter, Tippy, was pregnant. The evening before, Tommy had overheard Marsha, his sister, and a couple of other cheerleaders talking about Tippy. While eavesdropping, he'd learned several adjectives describing one who is pregnant, including "knocked up." The word had gotten out after Tippy's doctor's secretary had let it slip while at the Colby Curls.

So, Jupiter's mention of Tippy's condition wasn't news to Tommy. His only reaction was a small eyebrow squeeze. Tommy knew Jupiter expected a more exaggerated reaction.

Jupiter kept his good eye focused on Tommy while his wandering eye seemed to be following Booger. For a couple of seconds, both eyes focused on Tommy. Booger took advantage of the lapse to escape Jupiter's optical grip and moved to the drop-zone, the spot where the papers were delivered and staged. The *Colby Telegraph* truck rounded the corner by the Sinclair. Tommy had visions of Mackenzie's Raiders topping a hill to save a wagon train from a horde of Mexican bandits, except in this case it was a paperboy being saved from an obnoxious self-appointed town crier. The truck's arrival provided Tommy with ample excuse to walk away from Jupiter and join Booger.

Jupiter stopped midsentence, gave Tommy a stern look, tugged at his ill-fitting pants for the umpteenth time, and then headed back across the street toward the courthouse bench, mumbling under his breath.

Tommy saw that Mr. Gooche was off the phone and rushed inside. "Mind if I use the phone for a minute, Mr. Gooche?" Mr. Gooche, deep in thought, didn't immediately reply. "It'll only take a minute, promise," Tommy persisted.

Mr. Gooche noticed the stress on Tommy's face and opened the gate to his office area. "Make it quick, it's the only line."

Tommy dialed Melody again, but got no answer.

HE AND BOOGER BEGAN THE route by putting the *Colby Telegraph* into the stands at Gooche's, the Houn-Dawg, and the post office, and then they loaded their bike baskets with the remaining papers. The big news that everyone was expecting to read about was the announcement of the new hat factory manager. Supposedly he'd graduated *summa cum laude* from Chicago State University and subsequently spent ten years there as a professor before going to work for International Hat. Tommy hadn't known a *summa cum laude* from a sumo wrestler. Uncle Cletus had explained both and Tommy had shared the information with the band of boys. Tommy and his friends often felt a step ahead of others after being informed by Tommy's Uncle Cletus.

Having been occupied by Jupiter, neither boy had yet taken the time to look at the front page and had forgotten about the expected announcement. Booger looked at Tommy and frowned. "How many times you figure we'll hear 'bout that steppin' stone?"

"Long as it's here and people remember, the story will be told," Tommy replied, sounding more poetic than he'd intended. "Trouble is, most of these old people can't remember who they've told. And they all seem compelled to make sure that the stone's part in Colby's history gets passed down." The boys pushed their bikes across the street to the courthouse. "That's part of being a paperboy. People are always telling us stuff."

"I don't mind it," Booger continued. "It's just that you'd think that Jupiter could have skipped the stone story and gotten straight away to tellin' us about Tippy. That's what had him all stirred up anyway." Booger's comment reminded Tommy that listening to people was part of the job. Sometimes the messenger got credit for the message. And knowing that Booger liked feeling needed by others filled Tommy with a peaceful sense.

Each quarter, Tommy and Booger collected subscription fees from customers who didn't pay by mail. This quarter, they had to explain an increase in the subscription rate. The courthouse was their first collection stop.

The courthouse, a cavernous hundred-year-old structure built after the original had been burned, was still referred to as the new courthouse. Everything about it was massive: tall ceilings, large offices, and a wide hallway extending from front to back. The oak floor creaked with every step.

"Yes, yes. Come in, come in," Judge Grant said loud enough for everyone on the first floor of the courthouse to hear. He didn't have an indoor voice; anything he said was echoed throughout the courthouse. The boys had been told by their predecessor to collect from Judge Grant first so that everyone else in the courthouse would know it was collection day and have their money ready. It was a timesaving maneuver.

"So, Tommy boy, how was Philmont?" Judge's previous paperboy, Mickey Murphy, had gone to Philmont. Since Tommy and Booger had taken over the route, Judge Grant routinely asked the same question. After several attempts, Tommy gave up trying to explain that it wasn't him who'd gone. Judge had never fully understood, and Tommy had grown tired of trying to explain.

"Philmont's a great Boy Scout camp, Judge. Thanks for asking." It was an answer Tommy had grown comfortable with. It wasn't a lie and satisfied the Judge's annoying questions.

"Yes, yes, seven dollars and eighty cents. Got it here in the envelope," Judge blared out for all to hear.

"It's eight dollars 'n' five cents now," Booger said. He had the receipt book and timidly waited for the Judge to pay.

"Eight bucks and a buffalo nickel—my, my, my," Judge thunderously announced while giving Booger a death sentence glance, then, "My, my, my," again, clearly disturbed by the slight increase. His head continuously shook, giving most the impression that he was in the final stages of Parkinson's. His smoldering cigar rested precariously on his lower lip, defying gravity while barely hanging on. He continued to groan and dug into his pocket for more change. The more he talked, the louder he got. It would have been annoying except for the fact that his boisterous behavior served to save the boy's time.

"Inflation, yes, yes, inflation … inflation, that's what it is, Booger Boy," Judge said and handed Booger more change. Judge checked each nickel, looking for a buffalo. Booger didn't mind the extra tag on his name; the fact that Judge had remembered his name at all was gratifying. Judge patted Booger on the back with enough force to perform the Heimlich maneuver. Judge's spine-dislodging tap was no doubt a show of affection; at least Booger took it that way.

Mrs. Burk, the circuit clerk, and Mr. Bailey, the recorder of deeds, had their money ready when Tommy and Booger finally made it to their office. They had, of course, heard the judge. Booger laid their receipts on their desks. They were too preoccupied with the front page to offer an obligatory complaint about the rate increase. Before getting on his bike, Tommy stopped to take a look at the paper to see what the big fuss was all about. The hat factory announcement was front page, but that wasn't the only thing. The new manager's name was Carter Webster and the article featured a photo of him with his family. Tommy had never seen a photo of the new manager and hadn't given much thought to what he might look like. He was expecting a willowy man sporting a pocket protector and horn-rimmed glasses. He didn't need to read the article; the photo was enough to help Tommy understand why everyone had been so interested in the newspaper. Tommy looked across at Gooche's and saw a few pods of people standing and sharing a paper. The phones throughout Colby were no doubt already ringing.

Cast of Colby

A LONG STAIRWAY LEADING TO the Koch's apartment separated Gooche's and the post office. A tall, paneled door with a transom opened to a small landing. Tommy rang the doorbell. A single bulb hanging from the narrow stairway ceiling blinked on—the Koch welcome signal.

"How does she know it's us?" Booger asked.

"Don't know, some say she's omniscient." It was a word Tommy had learned in Sunday School. Using it made him feel smart. Booger frowned and looked unimpressed. Tommy waited anxiously for Booger to ask the meaning of the word. Booger, knowing that it would delight Tommy for him to do so, didn't.

A thick, pungent, unidentifiable odor hung in the air, and breathing was to be avoided in the confines of the stairway. The lungs seem to revolt when the air being breathed isn't healthy—each breath, regardless of how shallow, resulted in a dry cough.

"Place wouldn't stink so badly if they'd open the window on 'at transom," Booger whispered when they neared the top. Tommy merely nodded—talking would have required an unnecessary breath. Scout's litter box, an odd thing for a dog, was situated in the corner of the upper landing, which partially explained the odor.

Mrs. Koch opened the door. "Please come in," she said without moving her lips. Mrs. Koch's makeup was so heavy that her face was smooth and wrinkle-free.

"Mr. Koch and I were discussing the new hat factory manager." Unlike Jupiter Storm, Mrs. Koch generally liked a response to her comments. Since her statement was declarative rather than interrogative, Tommy hoped to get a pass. Tommy glanced at Booger, who seemed to be think-

ing likewise, if he was thinking at all. It was possible Booger had yet to
resume breathing. The look on Booger's face told Tommy that the apartment smell rated in the odor category on Booger's olfactory scale. Mrs.
Koch's statement and the odor lingered.

Mr. Koch was sitting in an overstuffed chair. Scout, fifteen years old
in human years and ancient in dog years, was curled up on Mr. Koch's
lap. His breathing was labored, his eyes were milky, and his facial orifices
oozed. Tommy could only imagine the condition of Scout's other end,
which was settled in his master's lap. Scout had a few redeeming qualities—he was a faithful and gentle pet, and he'd learned to use the litter
box.

Mr. Koch had moved to town shortly after WWI and opened an office
for Northwestern Mutual Insurance. Originally from Michigan, he had
no friends or family in the Colby area and had been a frequent visitor
to the library where the future Mrs. Koch, the librarian at the time, was
drawn to his northern accent. It was a refreshing departure, she'd said,
from the annoying hillbilly twang of most people in Colby. George was a
short but powerfully built bulldog of a man. His large, balding head was
snuggled between two shoulders. The courtship was brief.

Mr. Koch joined the Rotary and Optimist Clubs. With the combination of his endearing personality and the endorsement of his wife's family,
he quickly made friends. His insurance business was moderately successful but for reasons he never explained to anyone in Colby, he sold the
agency in the summer of 1937 and spent the next year working as a con-
sultant on a classified project for Lockheed Aircraft in Marietta, Georgia.

His trips home were infrequent. Most figured that he'd served Lockheed in an executive financial capacity—he never elaborated on his duties
there. During the Christmas of 1937, Mrs. Koch joined him. They returned to Colby in August 1938. The following month, after sixteen years
of marriage, Mrs. Koch gave birth to their only child, Jackson.

Jackson had been named after his father's hometown of Jackson,
Michigan, known for being the birthplace of the Republican Party and
the abolitionist movement. When growing up, Jackson was an excellent
student but extremely introverted, so he didn't have many friends. He'd
left Colby immediately after high school graduation to attend college. On
the rare occasions when he returned, such as Christmas or Thanksgiving, he was seldom seen in public. Jackson earned degrees in philosophy,

history, and other such thinking areas and he had "changed," or so it had been said. Most considered Jackson odd—Colby wasn't a haven for intellectuals. "Not sure what happened to that boy" was a typical reference to Jackson by the Codgers. The Kochs claimed that Jackson had chosen a career in law enforcement, but since they couldn't or wouldn't elaborate, their claims fell on deaf ears.

Tommy had never known Mr. Koch to be in good health. He was mostly known for his antics, his cigars, and Scout, the pug that accompanied him everywhere. Scout possessed a passive nature, unusual for a pug, and was allowed, but not necessarily welcome, almost anywhere. Even Mr. Rosolini, who had a strict no-dog policy, would let Scout sit under Mr. Koch's chair when the Kochs dined at his cafe. The moment they left, Mr. Rosolini would spray enough disinfectant around and under the chair to kill every germ within a country mile.

Mrs. Koch never revealed her actual age, but admitted that she'd been born before the turn of the century. That fact, combined with her claim to have been born in the apartment, made her age easy to figure for anyone with minimal math skills. She also claimed to have actually used the stepping-stone for its intended purpose. Her grandfather was listed on the historical marker, along with others who'd fought in the Civil War. The wording on the marker was vague and didn't make clear on which side Colby had fought, but there was nothing indecisive about Mrs. Koch: she was a Yankee.

Mr. Koch broke the silence with a question. "Ever heard of the Tuskegee Airmen?" he asked. His voice, while not particularly loud, somehow filled the room.

"No, sir," Tommy replied. Mr. Koch turned toward Booger.

"It's eight dollars and five cents," Booger abruptly announced. Mrs. Koch made a barely audible huff. Tommy wasn't sure if it was in protest of the increase or because Booger hadn't responded to her hat factory comment or had apparently ignored Mr. Koch's question. She began rummaging through her purse for the money.

"The Tuskegee Airmen," Mr. Koch continued, once he had the attention of both boys, "were an all-black fighter squadron during WWII. Their performance ranked among the highest of any squadron." He moved his gaze slowly back and forth between the two when he spoke. He paused long enough to take a small draw on his soggy cigar. "The men who became Tuskegee Airmen were bright, patriotic, and educated. Most had college degrees." Mr. Koch's voice wasn't provocative or defensive—it was authoritative, yet not intimidating. This was the boys' first meaningful conversation with the town's patriarch.

When Mr. Koch paused to take a long breath, Tommy asked, "Why'd they call 'em Tuskegee Airmen?"

"Well, because they all trained at an airbase near Tuskegee, Alabama. Over four hundred fifty pilots left Tuskegee to serve overseas." Mr. Koch took another long, deep breath. "In a way, those men fought two wars." When he spoke, it was as if he was giving a speech. His mannerisms reminded Tommy of the news clips he'd seen of Winston Churchill giving the Iron Curtain speech in Fulton, Missouri. His breathing resembled Scout's.

Booger frowned a question when Mr. Koch suggested the airmen fought two wars. "How's that?" Booger asked.

"There was the war with Nazi Germany, that's obvious. But then there was the battle with racism." Mr. Koch examined the soggy cigar then situated it in the corner of his mouth. "Guess racism is still a problem," he added.

Neither boy fully understood Mr. Koch's point. While they'd seen explicit examples of racism on TV, examples of racism in Colby were subtle.

The look on Booger's face said he wanted to hear more. "What was the racism battle like?" he asked.

Mr. Koch keyed in on Booger's interest and looked mostly at him. "Not all of them transferred overseas. One group was stationed in Indiana. Tuskegee Airmen officers were told not to go the officer's club. And when they went anyway they were arrested." Mr. Koch paused again, looked down, and shook his head. "It was all about the color of their skin."

"Were they good pilots?" Booger asked.

Mr. Koch gave Booger a skeptical look, and then he continued. "Oh, yes. And there was never a discipline problem—rare for fighter pilots. After the war, the Army Air Corps became the Air Force. A fighter pilot competition was held. The Tuskegee Airmen had by then become the 332nd Fighter Group, but they remained an all-black outfit. The 332nd were invited to compete."

Mr. Koch paused for yet another long breath, followed by a coughing fit. Scout stretched and yawned, oblivious to the jostling Mr. Koch's coughing caused. Booger's curiosity was clearly aroused. "How'd they do?" he asked.

Mr. Koch slowly nodded. He appreciated the question. He scratched the top of Scout's ears and grinned. "First place."

Tommy was surveying the room. It was the first time he'd been inside the apartment. He could see the courthouse through the balcony windows. There was a nest of books, newspapers, and magazines lying around the chair. It was apparent the old man spent most of his day in the same chair and spent most of that time reading.

On the wall behind his chair was a small dusty plaque. Engraved letters read "X608" and smaller, barely legible letters on a second line declared "Project Advisor." A display of photos caught his eye next, and he didn't give the plaque any further thought.

Mrs. Koch had put the money in an envelope. She noticed Tommy looking at the photos hanging above the radio. Tommy's scan stopped on two young pilots standing next to an old biplane. A large black prancing horse was painted on the side of the plane. "That's Mr. Koch when he flew for the Canadians." Her eyes twinkled when she spoke of him, and a smile struggled to break out from under her heavy veneer of make-up.

"Canada?" Tommy asked.

"Before the United States got into WWI, several of our men went to Canada so they could fly for France. That's much the opposite of those going to Canada today." Mrs. Koch told them.

Both Kochs continued to narrate the photos. The boys did their best to listen to both.

A photo of two men standing next to a plane with unique insignia caught Tommy's eye. He assumed one man to be Mr. Koch. Tommy pointed at the photo and asked. "Who's the other pilot?"

Mr. Koch chuckled through a grin. "Count Francesco Baracca. He was a larger-than-life Italian fighter pilot." Tommy's confusion was compounded. The photo was of an American who had become a Canadian, standing next to an Italian, both fighter pilots for France.

Booger nudged Tommy, reminding him that it was collection day. "Our bikes are loaded with newspapers. We need to go," Tommy said during one of Mr. Koch's long, deep breaths.

Mrs. Koch placed the hand holding the envelope on one hip and leaned against her kitchen counter with the other. "When I was in the post office I noticed Jupiter Storm giving you two a good what-for," she said. "Was he asking or telling about the Tatum girl?" She knew the boys couldn't leave until she handed over the envelope.

"That and the stone," Booger replied. "But mostly about the stone."

"Your version of the stone is much better," Tommy added. Mrs. Koch's eyes danced. Her facial muscles tugged at the corners of her mouth as a smile struggled to spring forth. Tommy could tell she relished the compliment.

She handed over the envelope, and the boys raced down the musty stairway. The light went out the second Tommy's foot touched the bottom landing. He and Booger squeezed through the door together, neither wanting to be second. Both took deep breaths of clean, fresh air.

"Did you know that?" Booger asked.

"Know what?" Tommy asked.

"That stuff 'bout the Tuskegee Airmen," Booger replied, somewhat perturbed at Tommy's lack of interest.

"How much of that you think is true?" Tommy asked.

Booger was taken aback. "He told it for the truth."

Tommy burst Booger's bubble. "Yeah, but you know how old people are. They get confused between what they've actually done and what they've read." Tommy contemplated the Mr. Koch he'd just spoken to and the one in the WWI photo.

THEY GRABBED THE REST OF the papers and crossed the street to Burt's Sinclair. Concern for Melody took up residence in Tommy's mind, and he forgot about the WWI photo and the stairway stench. Burt was checking the engine oil in an out-of-town car while the gasoline tank filled. Tommy waited for Burt to read and replace the dipstick before asking, "Mind if I use your phone?"

Burt gave him a curious look. "Problem?"

"No, just need to make a call."

Burt looked at Tommy, then at Booger, then back to Tommy. "Al's on a long-distance call. You can use it when she's finished."

"Thanks," Tommy said. "It will only take a second."

Booger walked through the shop area toward the water fountain.

Tommy stepped inside and paced back and forth outside Burt's cluttered office. Al was on the phone, doing more listening than talking.

Alison Tatum always dressed in men's clothes; strangers thought she was one. The locals had begun calling her Al and in most cases treated her like a man. She'd even been known to use the men's room at the Sinclair, or so it was told. Little was known about her. She'd moved to town years earlier with an infant daughter and never spoken of her past. Shortly after going to work at Burt's she'd proven herself as a reliable mechanic. Her past was rarely discussed, but assumptions had been made.

She saw Tommy pacing and held her hand over the receiver. "You need to use the john?" she asked.

"No," Tommy nodded at the phone. "I need to make a call."

"I may be a while." Then she kicked a block of wood out of the way and swung the door closed—but it hadn't been shut for so long that it had become warped and wouldn't completely shut. "Yes! He's from Chicago, the north side," Tommy heard her say into the phone when she reached to close the door. "I'm sure it's him," she continued.

A tool company calendar featuring a voluptuous model on Burt's office door caught Tommy's eye. "I once worked on his car and bowled against him in a bowling league," Tommy heard Al say into the phone.

Since Al had asked, Tommy realized he did need to use the john. His Uncle Cletus had explained the "urgency by suggestion" phenomena. He took the key from the wall, walked around the side of the building. Booger was waiting outside the door when he finished. "Last guy didn't flush," Tommy said.

Booger took the key, careful to touch only the key and not the oversized and filthy rabbits foot attached to it by a beaded chain. Burt always had some large and gross novelty item attached to keys so that people wouldn't forget to return them. Booger took a deep breath and then looked inside the restroom. "Bad aim too," he said, wasting a breath.

Tommy went back inside. Al was still on the phone. Since the door was slightly ajar, he stood outside the office, resumed his ogling of Miss October, and eavesdropped. Al was still on the phone when Booger returned with the key. Already short on time from visiting too long with the Kochs, they headed out the door.

"Still worried about Melody?" Booger asked.

"Yeah," Tommy said, sighing. But at the moment he was in fact giving more thought to what he'd heard Al say into the phone than what Melody was possibly thinking.

Burt was watching the car pull away and said, "Never seen that car before." He massaged his chin in thought. "City sticker on the windshield said St. Louis." He pulled his cap back and scratched a thick tuft of salt-and-pepper hair. "Sticker on the other side said something about the International Hat parking lot."

Burt liked to read the windshield stickers and use the information to strike up a conversation. "He said he was passing through. I saw him reading the historical marker at the courthouse about an hour ago. Then right after you two loaded the machine, he walked over to Gooche's and got a paper." Tommy continued to eye the office door while listening to Burt, but Al never came out.

"He handed me a copy of the paper and asked me if I'd seen it. I pointed at you two and told him my copy was on its way. The new factory manager is front page news, he told me." Burt's lower jaw moved back and forth and he chewed on his lower lip—he looked to be figuring out a complicated math problem. "Then he asked me what people were saying about a black family moving to town." Burt looked reflectively skyward. "If I hadn't seen the picture in the paper, I wouldn't have known what he was talking about."

Turning to Tommy, Burt changed the subject. "Make your call?" he asked.

"No, Al's still on the phone," Tommy replied.

Burt paused, wiped his hands on a shop towel, and frowned slightly. "That's interesting—Al hates to talk on the phone." The boys had to keep moving. Their next stop was Clemo's and The Chatterbox.

CLEMO KUTSINGER AND HIS SISTER Marty McCutcheon claimed to own the oldest building on the square. Their great-grandfather had built it himself, and besides patching the roof, little had been done to it for more than fifty years. It was a single-story building with an interior wall that divided the building. Clemo operated a barbershop on one side, and Marty ran a tavern on the other.

The sign under the barber pole read "Clemo's Barber Shop," but everyone knew it as Clemo's. The Norman Rockwell–style window painting, done years earlier by a traveling artist depicted a young boy smiling and sitting in a barber's chair being attended to by a barber wearing a toothy grin, a head covered with dark curly hair, and a crisply starched lab coat. Tommy looked at the window art, then at Clemo's bald scalp. He smothered a chuckle and figured Clemo had probably never seen a lab coat, let alone exhibited a sense of humor. Under the art was a hand-printed sign taped to the window that read "No Beatle Haircuts."

Clemo's half of the building was meticulous. Once inside, patrons were greeted with another show of Clemo's cordiality, a sign that read "No Cussing, Drinking, Smoking, Hustlers, Cavorting, or Loitering." Clemo made it clear what he wouldn't do and what he didn't allow. A row of has-been dining room chairs lined one wall; no two chairs matched. Conversely, three mint-condition Koken barber chairs lined the other wall. One barber chair, the one furthest from the door, was always covered. Clemo used the middle chair to cut hair, and the next-in-line customer sat in the third. Arriving customers were greeted by the smile of the next customer in line sitting high in the waiting chair, rather than Clemo's scowl. Tommy and Booger saw through the window that Clemo had a customer. They looked at each other and sighed relief. It was always better if Clemo had a customer.

Tommy and Booger had learned not to split up when delivering papers to either place. During their first delivery, Clemo didn't have anyone in the chair and had insisted that the boys listen to him tell the history of the barber pole while he viciously stroked a razor back and forth on a razor strap. Clemo bought two copies of the newspaper—one for himself and one for his customers. A Hillerich & Bradsby baseball bat was leaning in the corner. Rumor was he'd used it on a few of Marty's patrons.

The faded window art on Marty Mac's tavern depicted people with distorted faces crowded along a bar, some on stools and some standing, but all smoking cigarettes. The art was a poor attempt to emulate the style of Vincent Van Gogh. Some of the distortion was intentional, and some had been caused by time. It was eerily accurate. Large block letters across the top of Marty's half of the building read the name she'd cleverly given the establishment, "Colby Chatterbox."

A bar ran almost the full length of the Chatterbox. Behind the bar was a mirror, dulled from years of cigarette smoke. It was of little use anyway since countless dusty bottles of liquor and mixes were stacked in front of it.

The boys knew a few of the adults who went there at night to play pool, and there was always a crowd before a football game, but on weekday afternoons, when the paper was delivered, it was inhabited by a relatively chatter-free subculture. One man who was always at the bar, smoking and flicking ashes into an overflowing ashtray, was particularly strange. He was too sickly to be dangerous—his stick-thin legs protruded from what had once been work pants. He'd most likely kept the work pants after getting fired from his last job. He always spoke to the boys, but they never understood what he was saying. His voice was cryptic, low, and menacing. And he'd point at the boys with a cigarette held between two filthy fingers when he spoke. Tommy had noticed that his fingernails were longer than most of the women at Colby Curls. But they were jagged and corroded, as if he'd been using them to hull walnuts or scrape caked oil off an old motor.

Marty had a no-nonsense air about her. She seldom looked anyone directly in the eyes, constantly vigilant of other patrons. She never went anywhere without her purse, which was rumored to contain both a pair of brass knuckles and a Bowie knife. She was on the phone when the boys cautiously entered. She took a drag off her cigarette and exhaled while talking into the phone. Booger laid her paper on the end of the bar nearest the door. Marty nodded, and the boys scooted out. Clemo and Marty both paid by mail, and Tommy and Booger were glad of that.

"That place gives me the willies," Booger said.

"Yeah, stinks worse than Koch's stairway too," Tommy added.

They left the square and started down a residential street, rolling and binding papers with rubber bands while they rode along with no hands on the handlebars. They learned a little more about each customer with each collection. They knew who had carpet, who had ghost-turds clinging to the ceiling corners, who had piles of dirty dishes in their kitchen sinks, who covered their sofas with plastic, and countless other personal details that only the paperboy knows.

BOOGER AND TOMMY HAD FINISHED half the route when Tommy's Uncle Cletus, Booger's Aunt Penny, and their schoolteacher, Bridgette—Miss Anderson to the boys—pulled up on their Honda Scramblers. They were enjoying one last motorcycle ride before the cold, damp Missouri fall set in.

Aunt Penny's husband had left her for another woman several months earlier, and since the divorce papers had been signed, she'd been seeing Tommy's Uncle Cletus. So, in a way, Booger and Tommy shared an aunt and uncle. Penny was riding behind Cletus. Bridgette, or Miss Anderson, was riding single.

Tommy looked toward his Uncle Cletus. "Seen the paper?"

"No, but heard there's an article about the new hat factory manager," Cletus replied. "Carter Webster is his name, I heard someone say."

Tommy handed him a paper. Penny looked over Cletus's shoulder. Booger handed one to Bridgette. He blushed when she winked at him. Bridgette had recently started seeing Booger's dad. Her arrival in town was timely, almost providential. Her zestful disposition reminded Booger of his mom before her severe depression over losing an older son in Vietnam, which eventually ended in suicide. He knew Miss Anderson wasn't a replacement for his mom and didn't see her that way.

Cletus, Penny, and Bridgette exchanged discreet looks. Cletus's brow furrowed. Bridgett and Penny's eyebrows canted downward, expressing concern. Cletus handed back the paper. "It's not going to be easy for them."

Penny giggled. "Some around here got stirred up when a single female school teacher showed up driving a fire-engine red GTO," she said, referring to Bridgette, who months earlier had been the talk of the town when she'd taken a teaching position and moved to Colby. Her red GTO and motorcycle had awed the boys and appalled the Colby Curls crowd.

Bridgette had made the right friends, including Velma, the checkout lady at Gooche's. During a checkout counter conversation, Velma learned that Bridgette's mother had been a WWII ferry pilot and that Bridgette had learned to fly at an early age and was a flight instructor. Velma's mother had worked in a plane factory during WWII. Bridgette and Velma immediately bonded, and a friendship ensued.

Bridgette won the hearts of the local historical society when, after being asked to talk about her mother's WWII experience, she also brought to their attention a Colby native, Ira Biffle, who had taught Charles Lindbergh to fly. It was a fact she'd happened upon while reading Lindbergh's autobiography. The knowledge filled everyone in Colby with pride. Nobody from Colby had ever been famous.

"We gotta get goin'," Tommy said.

Before getting out of earshot, Tommy heard Cletus say, "Frank Fritz is the only person that comes to mind who is openly racist."

Penny winced. "He's the only one who admits it."

"Fritzie isn't a troublemaker, but he's got some Nazi stuff hanging in his shop," added Cletus.

Cletus was explaining Frank Fritz to Bridgette when a mother-daughter pair, Emma and Erma Duke, known locally as the Ducklings, marched by. They lived up the hill from the courthouse, at the base of Church Hill, and walked to town at least once each day. Emma always walked inches behind Erma. Both of their faces tilted down watching each step, their arms swinging in unison. Emma rarely spoke, and Erma only spoke when absolutely necessary, such as telling Leon Goolsby, the butcher at Gooche's, how thick to slice their braunschweiger.

Bridgette watched the Ducklings. It was the first time she'd gotten a good look at them since moving to Colby. She turned and with surprised eyes, looked at Cletus and Penny. "What's their story?"

Cletus took a deep breath; a sign the story was going to be lengthy. He explained to Bridgette how Erma, the mom, was mildly retarded and had never been married. The mental capacity of Emma, the daughter, was probably less than the mother. The father was unknown, or at least his identity had never been made public. Everybody watched out for them and left them alone. The Methodist church took them food on holidays and paid them regular visits. Bridgette watched the Ducklings walk rhythmically away.

After a slight pause, Cletus continued. "Erma has to lock Emma in at night."

Bridgette flinched. "Not in a cage!" Cletus quickly added. "Erma locks the doors to the house from the inside and then hides the key," he continued. "Supposedly, Emma sleepwalks. Sheriff Dooley found her wandering around town one night."

"All alone?" Bridgette asked, still looking off in the direction they'd marched.

"She was scared to death when he found her. She couldn't tell him where she lived, and kept repeating, 'Home, wanna go home.' He said she had a grocery bag full of something, but she wouldn't let him see what was in it. Since the Ducklings were somewhat exempted, protected, and considered harmless, Sheriff Dooley didn't press it. He never saw what was in the bag. The next day, Sheriff Dooley bought Erma some locks for her doors. Until then, Dooley assumed that the only person roaming around at night was Milton Merle."

Uncle Cletus was then obliged to explain another colorful Colby resident. Milton Merle was notorious for stealing women's underwear. Most women liked to hang their underwear out to dry at night so no one could see them. And that's when Milton was rumored to strike. Milton had more than once been hit in the head with a baseball, coal clinker, or whatever else a startled woman could quickly get her hands on. He'd had hot soapy watered poured on him from second story windows, and there were rumors of him being shot with pellet rifles. Generally considered harmless and another accepted oddity in Colby, he rarely missed a church service and was always the first to arrive at a potluck dinner.

Bridgette laughed. "Sounds like Colby has an active nightlife."

Cletus chuckled and nodded and was continuing to explain the Ducklings and Milton to Bridgette when the Codgers, on their way to watch football practice, rode by in Monkey's golf cart. Monkey had accepted the old golf cart as payment for tree trimming he'd done at the Fairview golf course. He'd replaced the bag holders with a make-shift bench. Some had thought it strange at first, but everyone eventually became accustomed seeing the four curmudgeons cruising about in the wobbly wheeled contraption.

Bridgette watched them roll by, and then asked, "So why does the town put up with this Milton Merle?"

Cletus assured her that Milton had undergone therapy and was "supposedly" no longer prowling the streets at night and stealing underwear. Besides, he now had a girlfriend who wouldn't put up with him prowling around at night.

"Who's the girlfriend?" Bridgette asked. "I mean, who would be *silly* enough to be his girlfriend?" The question evoked a giggle from Penny.

"Venus Storm," he replied.

Bridgette frowned. Since Venus worked in the school kitchen and was a sister to the town's provocateur, Jupiter, Bridgette was somewhat familiar with her.

Venus lived alone in a small house a block off the courthouse square. Her yard was packed with flowers, bushes, and ornamental trees. A meticulously maintained decorative picket fence ran along her property line.

When she wasn't working in the school kitchen, she spent her time working in her yard, snipping limbs and pulling weeds. She'd never married, and like her brother, Jupiter, possessed an enormous appetite for the affairs of others and leaped at the chance to offer an opinion.

Bridgette shook her head in amusement. "This couldn't be goofier if you made it up."

TOMMY AND BOOGER CIRCLED BACK to Gooche's for the rest of the papers and then pedaled toward Twin Oaks. Six quadraplex buildings circling a pair of giant oaks provided maintenance-free housing for senior citizens. Newt Thorpe and Ted Thompson, Tommy's dad, had led the effort to raise the seed money for the project. Newt had learned of the opportunity while at a newspaper editor's meeting. Since he was a Democrat, he'd asked Ted, a Republican, to join him in the effort. The two of them rallied the entire county to financially support the project. After raising 2 percent of the needed funding, the Farm & Home Administration made a low-interest loan for the balance.

Eugene Meisenheimer and Finis Pribble had beaten the odds and outlived their wives. They were surrounded and doted over by the widows who occupied the balance of the complex. In exchange for changing an occasional light bulb or plunging a toilet, they were constantly plied with sweets. When they weren't providing handyman services, they whiled away the days sitting on Eugene's front stoop. The men always greeted Tommy and Booger with an offer for a cookie or brownie. Always suspicious of who had prepared the delicacy, Tommy usually passed, but Booger always gobbled up anything offered.

Eugene and Finis complemented each other in many ways, even in their verb usage. Eugene never used "did" and Finis never used "done." After picking up on the anomaly, the boys began to refer to the two as Did and Done.

Tommy began to tell Eugene, the oldest Twin Oaks resident, about the rate increase. Eugene didn't let Tommy finish. "I done heard it while polishin' the door knobs on C building. Jupiter was here tellin' about the new factory manager and the newspaper rate increase. I done decided not to worry 'bout it. Jupiter's pro'bly worryin' enough for everyone."

Finis ambled over. He slapped Booger on the back. "You gonna deliver papers or talk to Eugene all day?" he asked.

Booger, knowing that one of the lady residents had asked Finis to dig up a place for a flower bed asked, "You get that flower bed worked up?"

"No, haven't did that yet," Finis replied. Mostly, the boys liked to provoke conversation with the two men. The boys were intrigued at how the two men, while speaking to each other, couldn't discern their improper use of the irregular verb. Miss Anderson wouldn't have stood for it. Anyone using that sort of grammar would have been writing sentences on the board until the cows came home.

"Finis says he's gonna drop the paper," Eugene offered.

"Well, I ain't did it yet," Finis replied.

"That's not what you said 'while ago," Eugene argued. "You said you done decided."

"Well, I ain't yet did it," Finis repeated, changing the word order as if it made a difference.

Eugene shook his head. "Don't nobody do what they say anymore."

Eugene opened the paper, squinted, and then held the front page at arm's length. "Say here, they done hired a new plant manger."

"Not from around here, I can see," Finis added after looking at his copy.

"Hope he's not some kinda post turtle," Eugene added.

Eugene noticed Tommy and Booger looking quizzical.

"Ever heard of a post turtle?" Neither boy answered, so he continued. "Ever see a turtle sitting on top of a fence post?"

"No, but I've seen hawks," Booger replied.

"Not the same thing," Eugene snapped.

"Tell 'em what a post turtle is and let 'em get goin'," Finis said.

"A fence post turtle doesn't know how he got there, doesn't know what to do once he's there, and eventually everyone begins to ask who the dummy was that put him there."

Finis made the application. "What Eugene is sayin' is, he hopes this new plant manager knows what he's doin'. Me and Eugene seen a few plant managers in our day. Most of 'em knew what they was doin' but one or two ov'em were post turtles."

"That's for sure," Eugene agreed.

Tommy noticed a telephone sitting on a small outside table near Eugene's front door. It was plugged into a phone jack mounted on the outside wall. He waited a few seconds after Finis finished before asking, "Does that phone work?"

"Finis done that for me," Eugene replied. "He's got 'lectrical 'sperience."

Finis smiled. He didn't have his lower dentures in. "I've did that for everyone what wants it," he said.

Tommy only wanted to use the phone, not hear how Finis had run phone wires for Eugene and several others so they could bring their phones outside. Finis paused for a breath and Tommy asked, "Can I use it to make a call?"

Eugene looked at him suspiciously. "Local?"

Tommy nodded and Eugene moved out of the way and pointed toward the phone. Tommy dialed Melody's number. This time she answered, and he explained what had happened. He could hear the cheerfulness in her voice when she thanked him for calling. The acid taste in his mouth subsided.

With Melody taken care of, Tommy's mind began to wonder about the new plant manager and racism. The thought had been competing with Melody for mind share since hearing it mentioned. He wasn't sure if he understood how people became racists and wondered what people would say about Carter Webster.

THE DRIVER OF THE CAR with a St. Louis city sticker drove to Fairview and found a phone booth. He made a collect call to the office of the president of International Hat. The charges were accepted and his call was put through.

"Surprised is the best way to describe most people," he told the president. "A guy at the filling station seemed more interested in Carter's son's military service."

"That's good news," the president had to admit. "Thanks for calling. We'll see what happens when he actually shows up and people see him in person." The president had been overruled by the board in the decision to give Carter a chance at running his own factory. While Carter had proven himself as a competent manager, the president wasn't sure small town America was ready for a black factory manager.

Football

THE BELL RANG, SIGNALING THE end of sixth hour. Tommy and the band of boys raced to the locker room; the first to arrive got the new lockers, the laggards had to settle for the shelf baskets. Seventh hour physical education was a prerequisite for pubescent boys who wished to eventually play high school football, and everyone in Colby lived for high school football.

Coach Heart had aspired to be a high school football coach and made his students refer to him as Coach. It was Coach Heart's first year in Colby, his self-proclaimed title as coach was a stretch. He taught PE and driver's Ed. His older brother, the klutz who had divorced Booger's Aunt Penny, had helped Coach Heart get the job. The school board had understandably given Heart the benefit of the doubt since he'd served in Vietnam, where he'd lost an eye and gained an attitude.

Seventh hour PE had once been something looked forward to, a rite of passage—now it was considered torture. The sign on the door to Coach Heart's closet-sized office read "Arnold Heart—Kinesiologist." Tommy and his friends weren't sure what the word meant, but they were pretty sure it had some satanic connotation and probably a more appropriate title.

Coach Heart had convinced the school board that it would be in the football program's best interest to adopt President Johnson's physical fitness program. Most saw his appeal for what it was: an excuse to introduce a formal PE program to elementary students. But since Stan Musial, the St. Louis Cardinal great, had been appointed by LBJ as the first chairman of the fitness program, the board had approved. And since every boy in Colby wanted to be like Stan the Man, they looked forward to qualifying and getting a certificate with Stan Musial's signature.

That wasn't enough for Heart; he'd also sold the board on the notion that the sixth grade boys, at least those hoping to play high school football, should be mixed with the junior high boys. "It'll toughen them up," Heart promised.

So, while the rest of the PE class danced to "Chicken Fat," Tommy and his gridiron aspirants were at the other end of the gym doing rigorous calisthenics with the junior high boys. They did push-ups, pull-ups, sit-ups, and ran sprints. Leg-lifts weren't part of the president's physical fitness requirement, but they were on Coach Heart's regimen of torture—a page everyone wished had been ripped from his book of kinesiology.

Tommy and Booger didn't appreciate the benefits of the workout since, for them, it was followed up with their paper route, a long ride carrying a heavy load.

Coach Heart always ended the PE hour by making the boys do the dreaded and excruciating leg lifts. It was his way of teaching the aspiring football players to endure pain, even though it was only sixth grade PE. Anyone caught letting their heels touch the ground for more than a split second was called out drill-sergeant style. Tommy and his band of boys agreed that Coach Heart literally had no heart.

Finally, heartless Heart mercifully blew his whistle. "Hit the showers, boys." The boys made their way to the locker room, all walking with a slight forward tilt, nursing stomach and lower back muscle pain.

Once inside the locker room and away from Coach Heart, Booger asked, "Ever get the feeling he doesn't like us?"

"He's only tryin' to weed out the weaklings," Caleb replied, holding his side and wincing in pain.

Checkers and Everett, both overweight and the brunt of most of Coach Heart's rants, were out of breath, collapsed on the damp floor, and leaning against their lockers. "I know one thang," Everett muttered between gasps. "It wasn't me who shot out his danged eye."

"I'm not sure it's worth it," Checkers moaned. "Three years of this?" He was referring to three years of seventh hour PE under heartless Heart only to earn the privilege to *try out* for football once they reached high school. Colby was too small to offer a junior high football program.

Caleb flipped Checkers with a towel. "Thang of it is," he began, "big as you are, you'll probably be a four-year starter." Checkers and Everett, having experienced an early puberty, were both large for their age—Checkers was already taller, thicker, and hairier than many of the high school boys.

Flop stripped and headed for the shower. "Like ah said," he started, even though he'd yet to say anything. "We better get movin' before the high school lets out." The rest of the boys rolled their eyes. Flop continued past Checkers and Everett, hairless and naked as a jaybird, whistling while his pencil-thin neck waved his tiny bulbous head about in a cheerful display. Every rib and vertebrae were clearly outlined in his thin-skinned frame. His knock-kneed march to the shower was something no one wanted to watch, but they couldn't keep themselves from looking.

Checkers watched Flop disappear into the steaming shower. "He ain't right," Checkers whispered.

"Thang of it is," Caleb repeated, "his legs are so skinny they don't weigh nothin.'"

Flop's hairless, gangly, emaciated body had miraculously done enough sit-ups and push-ups on the first day to qualify for the Presidential Fitness Award. To make matters worse, he could do leg lifts all day long. Most boys with Flop's build would have been humiliated at being forced to join more developed boys in a group shower, another first after reaching junior high. Flop was thrilled to have found something at which he was athletically superior. He considered his physique an advantage. Modesty had never been Flop's strong suit; he had a self-confidence that had surely been meant for someone else.

"Flop's right," Tommy agreed. "I don't want to be here when school lets out." Part of the accepted ritual was for high school football players to harass anyone who hadn't gotten out of the locker room by the time they arrived for practice. The football players, also called Letter Jackets, rushed from their last class to the locker room in hopes of finding a victim.

Every once in a while, Coach Bodenschatz, the real football coach, would have to step in. Like the time Cecil Becker, a mouthy but standout receiver, had gotten to the locker room before Checkers had left. Cecil—small body, tiny brain, and big mouth—had attempted to harass Checkers. The problem was, at least for Cecil, it was only the two of them in the locker room. Checkers, already aggravated from being harangued by heartless Heart, had promptly stuffed the little big mouth into a locker, slammed the door shut, and then high-tailed it for the bus. It would have

gone bad for Checkers if the coach hadn't declared him off-limits to the
rest of the team. Checkers had never seemed worried and in fact welcomed the chance to test himself against a varsity football player. Truth be
told, the Letter Jackets were probably glad Coach Bodenschatz had made
Checkers off-limits.

Coach Bodenschatz could have put a stop to all of the hazing. But he
found the tradition served a purpose. The younger boys cleared out in a
hurry to avoid the football team. The Letter Jackets rushed to the locker
room to catch their prey. The result was that no one was late for football
practice.

The final bell rang. The boys, some half dressed, raced from the locker
room. Tommy and Booger sat together on the bus, both exhausted from
the workout, but still looking forward to delivering papers on a beautiful
fall day.

MONKEY, FISH, BEM, AND RABBIT were sitting under the centennial
sycamore in Codger's Corner. The area had been aptly named for the oc-
togenarians who generally took up daily residence there during football
season. Codger's Corner was located on a small hill overlooking the football field.

Tommy and Booger used football practice as an excuse to take a short
break from delivering papers. Listening to the Codger's revere the football
team helped them understand why they would continue to endure Coach
Heart's relentless PE class. Monkey's golf cart was parked nearby. The
football field, reverently referred to as the pit, was a sacred place where
boys, in an attempt to earn their small-town rite of passage, suffered
through anything and everything coach Bodenschatz and his demented
minions could dish out, all in an effort to suit up and take the field on
Friday nights as a Fighting Indian.

The Codgers had been watching the practices for so many years that
they'd become a fixture. Coach Bodenschatz, in a rare show of compassion, had set four old desk chairs under the tree, one for each of his most
vocal critics. The Codgers hadn't requested the chairs and the coach's ploy
didn't work, they continued their vociferous criticism of the coach. Win
or lose, the coach never got it right, at least in their eyes. Fortunately for
Coach Bodenschatz, most in Colby revered him. The Codgers never did
any writing and mostly used the desktops to lean on and slap real hard

when one of the freshmen got knocked on his butt. During football season, the boys delivered the Codgers their papers at football practice.

Tommy handed Monkey his paper. He looked at the front page and declared, "Well I'll be darned." Fish tried to look at Monkey's paper. Monkey jerked his paper out of Fish's view. "Get your own," he told him. Fish sat back down, and Booger handed him his paper.

Bem chuckled. "Ole Jupiter was so worried about Al Tatum's daughter being pregnant that he missed the big story." Bem's belly bounced while he continued to find humor in Jupiter's miss.

Milton Merle, who had actually played football for the small liberal arts college that had once existed in Colby, watched from a distance. Even though he'd voluntarily sought professional therapy to treat his nocturnal affliction, he wasn't welcome in Codger's Corner. During the depression, college enrollment had fallen, and the Colby College ceased to exist. Along with its demise went Milton's college football career and a free education. Milton was said to have been very quick, but visualizing Milton in pads was more than Tommy's imagination could muster.

Several Letter Jacket dads were gathered to watch practice. A smaller number of moms were discussing recipes and football player body odor. Each mom laid claim to the stinkiest son while simultaneously feigning disgust. The dads were second-guessing the coaches, talking about themselves, and reliving their high-school games, telling of great plays that most likely never occurred except in their minds.

Down a slight incline below Codger's Corner was the "shack"—a small, single-car-garage-sized building that was meticulously cared for by the coaches. It was packed with gear, tackling dummies, an ice machine, every species of spider known to man, ghosts of players past, and just like the field, considered sacred. The shack also served as a screen between the football field and the cheerleader practice area. Coach Bodenschatz wouldn't allow the cheerleaders to practice in view of the players. One had a clear view of both from Codger's Corner, which was possibly the primary reason the location was chosen.

A couple of the coaches were setting up a homemade contraption with multiple spigots that shot water in several directions. The players affectionately referred to it as the octopus. It allowed eight players to get drinks simultaneously. The cheerleaders would sneak peeks at the players and their sweaty, wet bodies during water breaks. The players rarely noticed unless one of the girls would let loose an uncontrollable shivering giggle, which the players found more annoying than flattering.

Fish observed Monkey watching the cheerleaders stretching and told Bem and Rabbit, "Monkey's gonna need wun'na his nitroglycerine tablets if he don't get his mind back on football."

Rabbit, the only one of the four who'd had a stellar high school football career, was focused on the practice field and ignored the banter.

Monkey leaned closer to Fish, "Been watching that Tatum girl. Think she ought'r be cheerleadin'?" Fish ignored him.

Rabbit, listening more closely than it appeared, offered, "My woman never changed any of her habits till the last month." And then he spit a long double string of tobacco juice, hitting the trunk of the sycamore. Some of it splattered on Booger's foot, but that was Booger's fault—Rabbit had been spitting in that spot for nearly a decade.

Monkey leaned in close to Fish again. Tommy could barely hear him. "Who you figure the father is?"

Bem then asked a question that took the conversation to another level. "The father of who, Tippy's baby or Tippy?" Bem's provocation conjured up a couple of possible questions. The fact that Tippy's father had never been spoken of was discussed at length with ample speculation. Tippy's dark olive complexion and tightly curled hair brought into question her father's nationality. She'd grown up in Colby and had always been accepted and few had given her unique features much thought. After she'd matured into an exotic looking young lady, her striking beauty had been mentioned countless times by the Codgers, but always in a flattering context.

Rabbit spit another double string. The speed with which his saliva glands recharged was a scientific wonder. He leaned forward on his desktop and turned toward Monkey, saying, "Thought you were a deacon? Not s'posed to be gossipin' if'n you're a deacon."

Monkey flinched guiltily. "My comments are out of concern," he said self-righteously.

Bem weighed in. "If that's the case, then I'd suggest you discuss it at the deacon's meeting."

Monkey couldn't let it go. "She's a looker." He shook his head in disgust. "Seems like the good lookin' ones always 'tract the trouble."

Fish listened, but didn't participate in the prattle. There was more to the story than the others knew, or all of Colby for that matter, but it was confidential. So he kept the privileged information to himself. However, even Fish didn't know the whole of it. He and Tippy's eyes met briefly—each smiled discretely.

Fish gave Monkey a disapproving look. By then the cheerleaders had finished stretching and were standing around talking, giggling, and doing what high-school girls do. So far, Tippy Tatum had done every stretch and exercise the others had.

Monkey responded to Fish's glance. "You're quiet all of a sudden. Cat gotcher tongue?"

"Thinkin'," Fish replied.

Monkey continued the provocative questions. "How long you 'spose they'll let her keep playin' the piano at church?" he asked.

Fish, a deacon at First Baptist and getting a little put out, shot back. "What are you gettin' at, Monkey?"

Monkey made a "don't know" gesture. "You know what they say," he said, which was Monkey's way of maneuvering out of a gossip corner he painted himself into. Booger and Tommy, rested and having heard enough of the Codger's endless banter for one day, continued on their route.

Tippy had been spending most of her spare time at Burt's Sinclair, where Dwight Seabaugh had worked before leaving for Ft. Leonard Wood. Tommy began to connect the metaphorical dots. He remembered seeing Dwight and Tippy together at the movie, and how Dwight had started tucking in his shirttail and lathering himself with Jade East cologne.

TOMMY AND BOOGER APPROACHED THE Tatum's old house. Al's well-fed mongrel followed Tommy along the property line that bordered the street. A rusty, flimsy chicken wire fence was the only barrier between Tommy and a mouth full of snarling teeth. The mongrel occasionally choked from growling and snarling so aggressively.

Tommy didn't mean to and hadn't planned it, but he'd developed a curiosity for conversations taking place inside the homes he passed by. After leaving the paper on a porch, he'd sometimes linger a bit and listen to what was being said inside. Few homes had air-conditioning, so most windows were open wide.

There was never any eavesdropping around Al Tatum's. Al's mongrel dog clearly longed for the flesh of Tommy's calf. An unfamiliar car parked in front of Al's aroused his curiosity to the point that his pulse quickened. Considering Tippy's situation, Tommy found it difficult to keep from staring. He slowed his pace but kept watching. He had a good view of the living room area and was surprised to see Al home—she usually worked later and sometimes closed the Sinclair for Burt. He could see three people. Two men dressed in suits were talking to Al. One was standing next to her and had his arm around her, as if to be half-hugging. The other was holding his hat and nodding affirmatively. Tommy didn't know who they were, but figured their visit had something to do with Tippy. The barking mongrel made it impossible to hear what was being said. Tommy rode his bike slowly past the black sedan. He flinched when he saw a short-barreled shotgun vertically mounted to the dash. The men had to be police officers, Tommy figured. He was too addled to reason the purpose for their visit.

When the boys met up again at the end of the block Booger asked, "What's up with you?"

"What?" Tommy asked.

"Your eyes are all bugged out like you saw a ghost."

Tommy related to Booger what he'd seen, and while doing so, the dark sedan drove by. Neither of them knew what to make of it and, considering the peculiar nature of Al Tatum, weren't inclined to ask questions. They delivered the next several papers in silence—each was lost in thought. Tommy contemplated the bits and pieces of Al's phone conversation he'd overheard at Burt's.

Tommy stepped onto Mrs. Whitener's porch and could see her inside, polishing her dining room table. She was singing to herself—Tommy couldn't make out the song, only that she frequently repeated "come lassies and lads." Tommy had to knock extra hard on the door to get her attention. He peeked in and saw her waddling toward the door. Mrs. Whitener was short but built to last.

"It's collection time again, is it, lad?" she said. Her accent was no surprise to Tommy, but it always intrigued him. He wasn't sure if she'd asked a question or made a statement. "Step inside won'tcha?" she asked or said, Tommy wasn't sure.

"Yes, ma'am," Tommy replied and then broke the news about the increase. The inside of her house smelled like a bakery. A large painting of a whaling ship hung above her fireplace mantle; beneath the painting was a portrait of a bearded man wearing a sailor's cap. A plaque of the Rotary four-way test hung next to the front door.

She must have sensed Tommy's angst in advising her of the higher rate. "Not to worry, lad," she said. "It could always be worse." She paid in change and painstakingly counted each coin. "You've beans for yer belly and a roof o'r yer head." She gave Tommy a couple of oatmeal raisin cookies. "One fer you and one fer the other lad what comes a callin' with ya.'" She grabbed her dishrag and while scurrying away pointed a stub of a finger at Tommy. "See that he gets it."

Tommy caught up with Booger and dutifully gave him the cookie. Booger stuffed the whole thing into his mouth in a single bite. Tommy asked Booger a question the answer for which Booger couldn't have known, and if he did know, he wouldn't have been able to respond with a mouth full of nuts, raisins, and oatmeal crumbs: "You ever wonder why Mr. Whitener married an English lady?" Booger shrugged and kept chewing. Tommy answered his own question. "Guess he got her during the war."

Booger swallowed. "Did you ever know Mr. Whitener?" he asked.

Tommy had to think. "No, but there must have been one," he said. "How else would she have gotten here?"

"There's a Whitener on that plaque that lists everyone who contributed to the new school," Booger added.

"Must be him," Tommy surmised. Booger nodded. The matter was settled.

AGENT GAMBAIANA LOOKED AT THE fuel gauge and winced. Against his better judgment, he decided to a make quick stop at Burt's. The next filling station wasn't for several miles down a curvy, hilly, narrow state highway. He didn't like to linger in town after visiting the Tatums and run the risk of arousing unnecessary curiosity about a federal agent's presence in Colby.

The second man, Agent Douglas, contemplated the coincidence of a former Special Forces buddy who had recently moved to Colby and resisted the notion to give him a call. He stayed in the car. Gambaiana, short on cash, paid for fuel with the agency-issued Sinclair credit card.

———————

THE DUCKLINGS WERE SITTING ON their porch when the boys passed their house. They didn't get the paper, and neither did either of their neighbors. Tommy avoided eye contact, but he did offer a quick wave.

"Watcha wavin' at those nitwits for?" Booger whispered.

"Don't know," Tommy replied. "Just bein' nice."

"They're weird," Booger said.

"Doesn't hurt anything to wave," Tommy argued.

The Ducklings stood, ignoring the boys, and moved toward their front door. Tommy was sure that they hadn't, but he still felt a sting of guilt that the two ladies may have overheard the short conversation. He whacked Booger on the head with a rolled-up newspaper.

"What's 'at for?" Booger protested.

"Now you're even," Tommy said.

"Even with who?" he asked while rubbing his head.

"The Ducklings. You shouldn't be talkin' 'bout them like you did," Tommy said and smiled.

Booger grinned briefly, which he'd rarely done since summer. Shaking his head, he said, "You're weird, too."

"Takes one to know one," Tommy shot back. The two continued to exchange juvenile playground barbs until reaching the next house.

VELMA SEABAUGH WAS WATERING PLANTS on her front porch when Tommy got to her house. He'd talked to her about how he dreaded collection day while working at Gooche's as a carry-out boy. She was expecting him. "Please come in. I have your money ready," she said. "It's on the kitchen table; I'll go and get it." Tommy stepped inside and waited. Even though collecting took longer, Tommy enjoyed scoping the inside of people's homes.

An army photo of Dwight was sitting on top of the TV next to the tin foil-covered rabbit ears. In the photo, Dwight had short hair and a clean-shaven face. Even with the scar, the photo made Dwight look much better than when Tommy had last seen him at Burt's.

A photo book was on the end table. The cover photo was of Dwight and Tippy Tatum. Tommy studied the photo closely.

"Here you go," Velma said, after returning with the money. Given a few more seconds he would have been able to pick up the photo book and look inside.

"Thanks," Tommy said without taking his eyes off the photo. Thoughts flooded his mind. He made eye contact with Velma. "Thanks," he said again and then left.

"THAT MRS. CRAWFORD IS CREEPY," Booger said when they met on the street. "She insisted that I go inside, but she made me take off my shoes. I could have waited on the porch."

"How many cats did you count?" Tommy asked.

"Didn't. I was too busy watching to make sure one of 'em didn't jump me. Got cat hair on my socks, I'll probably have to throw 'em away." Booger shuddered at the thought.

"She always fixes scalloped potatoes for the potluck," Tommy said, referencing the monthly church social.

"Yeah," Booger nodded. "I never like scalloped potatoes and ain't about to start with hers. No telling how many cat hairs are in those potatoes."

"Anybody who likes scalloped potatoes deserves cat hairs," Tommy said. Booger nodded in agreement.

THEIR LAST COLLECTION WAS FROM Joseph Williams, also known as Joe-Bill. Joe-Bill was a local artist known mostly for his metal sculptures, but he also dabbled in woodwork and pen and ink drawings. He was tall, lanky, and possessed a flamboyant, carefree spirit. Most knew to give him a wide berth as he was extremely expressive and spoke with flying arms. From a distance, he looked to be fighting off hornets while simply engaging in a normal conversation.

His place was at the edge of town, the furthest customer from Gooche's. A long gravel driveway snaked through a heavily wooded lot adorned with an eclectic display of Joe-Bill's work. A ten-foot-tall rearing horse with a cowboy fighting to stay on was next to a busty mermaid in a Marilyn Monroe pose. Next, a man made of wire was sitting on a bench. Joe-Bill was talented—complicated, but talented.

Frank Fritz's old army truck was parked next to Joe-Bill's garage. Nearly opposite Joe-Bill in nature, Frank Fritz was short and wore a scraggly beard that naturally trailed off to a point; he somewhat resembled a leprechaun. The black slits he had for eyes looked thread-thin behind his thick, frameless, and cloudy glasses. Fritz had radically conformist notions. The two men rarely agreed on anything and argued incessantly, but somehow managed to be inseparable best friends. Usually Joe-Bill did the talking and Fritz mumbled his disagreement when Joe-Bill stopped for a breath.

Possessed with the gift of gab, Joe-Bill gave new meaning to the run-on sentence and simply had no need for a verbal pause. His diatribes had plenty of verbal semicolons, but no hard stops. It was probably years of listening to Joe-Bill that had caused Fritz to rarely do more than mutter.

Joe-Bill's arms were flailing around when Tommy and Booger rode up. Joe-Bill didn't notice the boys when they arrived. Fritz saw them, but he didn't interrupt Joe-Bill, who was ripping President Johnson for sending more troops to Vietnam. Fritz was changing the oil in a truck while Joe-Bill painted the owner's name on the door. Joe-Bill complained each time Fritz did something that made the truck move. Fritz ignored Joe-Bill's perpetual protests.

Joe-Bill turned to see what Fritz was looking at and saw the boys. He immediately changed the subject and began to harangue the boys. "Since you spent so long at the football field, I had to hear the news from Jupiter." Fritz had taken refuge under the truck, probably removing the oil plug. "Guess you're here to collect," Joe-Bill continued.

Tommy broke the news. "Yeah, and the rate's gone up."

But Joe-Bill had already heard. "Yeah, Jupiter told us that too. Bet you can't guess what the paper cost when I was your age," he challenged, but he wasn't looking for a reply. He had a declarative way of speaking that didn't invite a response. "You boys ought'r pay more attention to FFA than football." He continued offering unsolicited advice while digging into his leather apron for money.

Fritz responded to the FFA comment from under the truck. "I joined FFA when I was in school."

Joe-Bill winked at Tommy and Booger and whispered, "He probably thought it was the high school version of the KKK." Joe-Bill made an "I don't understand it" gesture with his long, wispy arms. "He's got that Aryan blood in him."

ACROSS TOWN, ERMA LED EMMA into their house and locked the dead bolt on the front door—neither of them had any reason to use the front door again until morning. She would lock the back door after the last visit to the outhouse.

Before making their daily trek to Gooche's, Erma had unplugged the

TV and used the outlet for the vacuum cleaner. She'd forgotten to plug the TV back in after finishing. While Erma fixed dinner, Emma turned on the TV and plopped down in her usual place, the same rocking chair she'd been rocked in as a baby. She waited for the TV to warm up. When the TV didn't come on, Emma lost interest and began watching Erma.

Erma, unaware that she was being studied, went about her usual evening routine, which included hanging the key to the front door behind the painting of the Last Supper. She'd been hiding it there since Sheriff Dooley had installed the locks. Emma twirled her hair around her baby finger and stared curiously at the key's hiding place.

Erma always kept the key to the back door on a rubber band and put it on her wrist each night before going to bed. That had been Sheriff Dooley's idea—that way she'd always have it in case of a fire.

Once Erma realized the TV wasn't on, she plugged it in and finished fixing supper. While watching TV, Emma frequently glanced at the painting. Erma was too busy with supper to notice Emma's fixation with the key's hiding place.

A BEAUTIFUL FALL SUNSET WAS washing over Colby when Fritz returned home. His property was surrounded by a fence overgrown with honeysuckle vines, poison ivy, and a variety of unidentified vegetation known to flourish in poor soil. He was self-sufficient, even to the point of owning a large diesel generator for his electrical needs. Except for the honeysuckle-infested fence, which provided a perimeter barrier, he kept his property trimmed, neat, and orderly—a German trait.

Fritz pulled into his driveway. "Never would do in the old country," he muttered to himself, referring to the junk piled in and around the shed that sat in Al's backyard, only a few feet from the entrance to his driveway.

The shed had been an eyesore for several years, long before Al Tatum moved into the rental house. A rusty antique hay rake and manure spreader sat on one side. Trees had sprouted and grown up through both implements and was probably the only thing that kept them standing. Old gearboxes and wagon wheels were scattered all around. Except for Fritz, few noticed the shed. It sat at the edge of town and wasn't something that most people were concerned about. It was a piece of property so nondescript that even Jupiter Storm didn't care who owned it. Fritz had to look at it every day, and he had given the shed considerable attention. The weeds and clutter exasperated him.

A couple of years earlier, while standing in his drive and contemplating burning down the shed, he had noticed a telephone repair truck pull up. An unfamiliar repairman, not the local phone-company guy, had examined a telephone wire going into the shed, and then had gone inside for several minutes. But Fritz's frustration with the weeds and junk superseded his momentary curiosity about the phone wire. He never mentioned the wire or stranger to anyone.

On top of it all, a black family was moving to town. Fritz grumbled to himself as he unlocked the door to his house. Once inside, he headed straight to the chest where he kept his WWII memorabilia. He'd recently attended a reunion of the company with which he'd served during the war. He was looking for the address of his commanding officer, who now lived somewhere in Mississippi. While Fritz had never cared for the man during the war, the two agreed on issues of race. Fritz had learned at the reunion that his former commanding officer was now a Grand Dragon for the Ku Klux Klan.

DURING DINNER, TOMMY TOLD HIS dad about the armed car. Marsha rolled her eyes. "Brother," she sighed. "Do you have to exaggerate everything, Tommy?" He kicked her under the table. Their mother's stern look said it all; Tommy fought the urge for further retaliation.

Tommy's dad swallowed and said, "I'll give Dooley a call after dinner and see what he knows."

Tommy twitched and squirmed all through dinner. His dad made the call while he and Marsha were doing dishes and cleaning up. Their mother had taken a cup of coffee and was sitting on the front porch.

"Dooley, Ted Thompson," Tommy's dad said. "Got a minute?" He turned away and began to speak in a low voice. Marsha was making too much noise washing the pans for Tommy to hear.

After hanging up, he said, "Dooley didn't know anything more than Burt having reported a car with a dash-mounted shotgun stopping for gas." Tommy gave Marsha a *na-na-na* look.

Flying Food Mystery

As soon as the school bus doors folded open it was obvious, Miss Barbara, queen of the bus drivers, was in one of her moods. Her bouts with melancholy weren't the typical monthly hormonal excursions that Tommy's Uncle Cletus had explained—Miss Barbara had those, too. Her dispositional excursions were sporadic, intense, and couldn't be tracked by any lunar or solar cycle, and they possibly explained why at the age at which gray streaks of hair had begun to appear, she was still a Miss. Until Coach Heart appeared on the scene, Tommy didn't know any men ornery enough to deal with her.

The students boarded while Miss Barbara scanned the all-seeing mirror. The scowl on her face made her look like Brutus. To be on the safe side, Tommy let Wendy and Beth board first. He avoided eye contact with Miss Barbara and took a seat across the aisle from the two girls. Marty Blanken and Wilma Bodenschatz were sitting together. The smile on Marty's face declared that all had been forgiven since last spring when Wilma had stabbed him in the leg with a pencil. Miss Barbara was looking at them; their pathetic adolescent giggles intensified her misery.

Marsha hip-checked Tommy toward the window then sat down beside him. Tommy acted like he'd scooted over, instead of getting shoved. He leaned forward, pretending to tie his shoe, and glanced at Wendy. Wendy didn't notice, but Tommy got goose bumps when Beth shot him a double-dimple smile. Even though he now liked Melody, other girls continued to stir his senses. He was sure that Beth was destined to movie-actress stardom. She was even prettier than the girls in the chewing gum commercials.

Gazing out the window, Tommy watched Mickey Murphy cruise by, well under the school-zone speed. Mickey's compensating muffler made his presence obvious. Tommy figured Mickey's slow driving was more about being seen than concern over kids crossing the road. More than that, he wanted everyone to see that he was driving to school. Tommy grinned. Mickey was in a car with a bunch of guys, and he was on the bus surrounded by girls. *So there!*

Tommy could feel his ears turning red hot while he recalled the previous evening. Mickey had come over to see Marsha and had made fun of him after watching Marsha beat him at arm wrestling. The fun for Mickey ceased when Marsha beat him, too. It's one thing for an older sister to beat her brother arm wrestling, but quite another for a girlfriend to do so. Tommy didn't have the heart to tell Mickey that Marsha had more hair on her upper lip than he did. Tommy had decided to save that morsel for the next time Mickey got horsey.

Tommy's dad had coined the term "compensating muffler." He'd explained it to Tommy. It basically meant that boys with loud mufflers were compensating for an inadequacy in another area, and his dad had been specific about what the inadequacy might be. Tommy tucked that bit of information away for future use.

Miss Barbara shot everyone a scrunch-faced frown through the mirror before turning on the radio. The radio was her control; without it, there would have been total chaos, much like on the other buses. Everyone understood that if they acted like a bunch of spineless drones, the radio would stay on. Miss Barbara was truly a tormented woman. The tunes caused one's body to want to move with the beat, but too much show of jubilance would result in no more music. Causing discomfort in others was definitely her calling.

"Summer Rain" by Johnny Rivers was playing. The drizzly fall day made it almost poetic. After Johnny Rivers stopped lamenting the rain tapping at his window, the disk jockey reported that over fifty-five thousand people had participated in a war protest march in Washington DC. Dwight Seabaugh would be going to Vietnam soon, but not before coming home one last time. The previous evening news had aired shots of several helicopters dropping off soldiers into fields of tall grass. Tommy had fallen asleep thinking about Dave Blue, a flight instructor from Fairview who had been flying helicopters in Vietnam for several months. Tommy was watching a drop of water meander down the window, lost in a thought prism, when the bus arrived at school. He contemplated Miss Anderson's story of her boyfriend's helicopter being shot down in Vietnam, Booger's brother's death and his mother's subsequent suicide. The scurry of students leaving the bus broke his trance.

MISS ANDERSON HAD TOLD THE class that Mrs. Enderle would be substituting for the day. Mrs. Enderle had retired a few years earlier, but she continued to substitute. Nobody learned anything on those days. She tapped the front of her desk with a Gooche's Grocery yardstick. One eyebrow was elevated when she skeptically scanned the class. She began class with a question, "What is the capital of Honduras?"

Melody raised her hand and said, "Tegucigalpa." Melody always knew the answers. If asked, she could probably have spelled it. The class had been studying Honduras all week. They'd read about how it was known for mosquitoes, hurricanes, earthquakes, and floods. Tommy questioned the importance of learning about such a pitiful place. He also knew they wouldn't be spending much time discussing the sultry jungle countries of Central and South America. It wasn't Mrs. Enderle's style.

"Now class," Mrs. Enderle said, pursing her lips. She assumed her legendary poem reading stance and commenced. "Today we're going to read," she said, then paused for effect, *The Rhyme of the Ancient Mariner.*"

"I knew it," Tommy said to himself. "She always does this." Booger heard him muttering and held in a laugh.

"It is the ancient Mariner, and he stoppeth one of three," she began. After listening to her for an excruciating length of time, Tommy was relieved when a long, deep breath signaled the end of the poem. Mrs. Enderle stood there, lost in her moment, eyelids quivering and closed. She enjoyed the reading much more than anyone enjoyed listening. Those who had managed to stay awake nudged the others. The reading was followed by a forced discussion in which only the pasty skinned bookworms participated.

Checkers flicked Tommy on the ear and handed him a note. Tommy held it below the desktop and opened it. The note was from Melody. It read, "Carbon check on the Mini-Trail ride?" She'd signed her name and then '831.' It took Tommy a second to decipher that Melody had substituted rain with carbon—they'd learned about carbon copies the previous day in language arts. He appreciated her attempt at humor. After making sure Mrs. Enderle wasn't looking, he glanced Melody's way; their eyes locked. She'd been waiting for his confirmation. Tommy quickly turned back so Mrs. Enderle wouldn't get suspicious.

Melody looked the other direction, and shivered a smile. Tommy faced the front of the class and hoped that Mrs. Enderle hadn't noticed the exchange. He was sure that Mrs. Enderle possessed an extraordinary sense when it came to covert events in her classes. It was a sense that one acquired in their second century of life, he'd decided. He wondered what '831' meant.

Melody was wearing lipstick with tiny sparkles. Tommy had noticed right away, and he wanted more than anything to kiss her sparkly lips. His pulse thundered through his temples and he couldn't shake the notion that everyone in the room, especially Mrs. Enderle, could read his mind. He tried thinking about bananas. That didn't help. Desperate, he focused on the miserable Ancient Mariner. That made him sleepy.

An hour before lunch, Mrs. Enderle excused Tommy and Melody for marching band practice. Tommy grabbed Melody's French horn and his coronet from the band room shelf, and the two hurried toward the football field. One of the cool things about making the marching band was getting to walk on sacred ground of the football field—the Pit.

Sometimes the turf was damp from the morning dew. Tommy usually wore his last year's Converse All-Stars; a few of the guys wore their hunting boots. He found it curious that the girls seldom wore suitable shoes and constantly complained about the wet grass, but they never did anything to help themselves. His Uncle Cletus had once explained that women preferred style to comfort. It was in the marching band that Tommy began to understand the impractical concept.

The instrument and skill level determined one's position in the formation. The best were on the edges—that's where Wendy and Beth lined up. Melody and Tommy took their places in the center. Tommy was directly behind Melody, which worked well because she was always dropping things. Mr. Tobin had chosen "Georgy Girl" by the Seekers as the feature song for the football game that week. The high school band had been practicing the song since the previous spring, when the song had made it to number one on the hit parade. Melody had practiced several hours learning the notes. Tommy chose an easier path; he simply moved his fingers randomly and didn't blow. He used his paper route as an excuse for not practicing.

Lunch followed marching band practice. On the way to the cafeteria, Tommy waited until no one was looking and then handed Melody the tube of lipstick and bottle of fingernail polish that she'd dropped during practice while digging in her pocket for a frayed tissue.

The junior high lunch bell rang. A wave of students came pouring from the junior high wing. They'd raced from their classrooms to the end of the corridor, and then before turning the corner and into view of Mrs. Cain, slowed to a fast walk.

Mrs. Cain always sat at the cafeteria entrance and made kids who'd been running report to Mr. Franklin's office. The result was a wall of undisciplined students pushing, shoving, and race-walking their way down the hall. Tommy and Melody reached Mrs. Cain a few steps ahead of the mass of frustrated and starving junior high kids. She punched their lunch tickets while keeping a close eye on the advancing wall of raging hormones. Tommy and Melody got in line behind the sixth graders. He caught himself licking his lips while watching Melody apply lipstick.

Tommy worked in the kitchen. He could have gone to the front of the line, but he chose to wait his turn. It wasn't that he was struck with a sense of fairness but because waiting gave him a chance to linger with Melody. Conversations with her about nothing in particular were getting easier and more interesting for him—a phenomenon he acknowledged, but shared with no one.

Just before starting down the serving line, Tommy turned and noticed Wendy walking into the cafeteria. She'd gone to her locker after band practice and returned with the rest of the junior high students. She and several other cheerleaders joined the end of the line. The center of conversation, he imagined, was Tippy Tatum, because they were giggling and making occasional globe-like hand gestures over their stomachs. The cheerleader with braces kept covering her mouth. Their demeanor changed when Cecil Becker and two other Letter Jackets joined the line behind them.

Once served, Tommy said good-bye to Melody and took his tray into the kitchen. She brushed the back of his shoulders with her fingertips when he walked away. He turned, and she gave him a wiggly finger wave while doing a full-body giggle. Her shoulders moved up and down and her knees oscillated unnaturally. Tommy considered her actions further proof of the odd nature of girls about which his Uncle Cletus had warned him.

The cooks treated Tommy like one of their own and offered him seconds on everything. Tommy welcomed the seconds except on the days when they were serving beets or green Jell-O mixed with shredded carrots.

Today's menu was shredded beef (affectionately known as monkey meat) with mashed potatoes and green beans. The dessert was Tommy's favorite: cherry crisp. Tommy mixed his monkey meat and mashed potatoes together and devoured them while looking forward to the cherry crisp.

Venus Storm doted over him more than any of the others. Tommy wasn't sure if the attention was because she liked him, or because she wanted to extract information. He and Booger mowed her lawn, which only amounted to a few strips of grass separating her meticulous flower beds. But she paid them well, so long as they didn't blow grass into her flowers. They'd ingeniously devised a way to keep the grass out of the flowers. While Booger pushed the mower, Tommy scooted a strip of roofing tin along the ground between the mower and the flower bed, blocking the discharge shoot. It was probably a good way to lose an eye, but worth the risk to get paid the extra money. Unlike Jupiter, Venus's disposition was charismatic.

She brought Tommy seconds on monkey meat and a bowl of cherry crisp with a large scoop of ice cream. She winked and said, "Private stash." He only had a few minutes before his shift in the wash bay began. He ate the cherry crisp first then the ice cream. The large bites of ice cream made his head throb.

Venus paused while on her way to the serving line with a pan of mashed potatoes. In a hushed tone she asked, "What are the kids saying about the Tatum girl?"

Tommy shrugged and waited for his temples to stop throbbing before taking the last bite of ice cream. "They're wonderin' if she'll get married," he said.

Venus paused and wiped her hands with a dishtowel. "Well, if you ask me," she said, and nobody had, but that didn't matter, "I'm not sure an unwed mother should be attending school." The comment made Tommy uncomfortable, and he took the last bite so as not to have to respond and looked at the clock to avoid eye contact. He wondered why Venus cared.

She took Tommy's bowl while he was still swallowing. "Guess she needs to figure out who the father is," Venus said. Tommy recalled the photos he'd seen at Velma's and was struck with the notion that, although he liked the extra food, he found Venus annoying.

He got to the wash bay about the time the high school students were starting through the serving line. The high school teachers and office help had already been served and were seated in their usual place, directly across from the tray return area.

Trays were returned through two small horizontal windows a foot tall and four feet wide. Students passed by and handed their trays through the windows onto a stainless steel counter. Waves of students returned their trays. An entire table of students would decide to leave together and arrive at the return all at once. So, throughout lunch hour there'd be a series of small squads, all trying to squeeze near the return window, then a lull, then another blitz. It was Tommy's observation that few junior high or high school students did anything on their own, it was always *en masse*.

Tommy worked one window and Booger the other. They got their lunch free in exchange for working in the washroom for a twenty-minute shift. Most thought working the window the least desirable position in the washroom. The most sought-after job was taking trays out of the washing machine and returning them to the serving line. That job didn't require hot steamy sprayers or the handling of trays half full of food.

But Tommy and Booger knew something the others didn't. The lipped edge, designed to keep water from spilling into the cafeteria, also served another purpose. An occasional misdirected spray, deflected off the lip, was known to splatter students passing by, usually upperclassmen, particularly those wearing letter jackets.

"Here comes 'at Cecil Becker," Booger said. "He's wearin' those white pants." Tommy didn't have to look to know that Booger was grinning. Cecil had been one of the first high school boys to wear jeans a color other than denim. He'd recently gotten a pair of snow-white jeans. Tommy's only thought on the subject was how impractical they were. After hearing Wendy tell Beth how cool Cecil looked in them, he'd begun to loathe the white jeans. On Booger's signal, Tommy emptied a tray full of mashed potatoes mixed with shredded beef near the lip and gave it a direct shot with the hot-water high-pressure sprayer.

"Dang!" came a voice from outside the window. Tommy quickly gave the counter another shot and filled the area with a cloud of steam, making it impossible for anyone on the outside to see in. "Idiots!" shouted the same voice.

Tommy cleaned a few more trays, then leaned over and looked out the window. Cecil was standing by the exit of the multipurpose room and rubbing on his pants with a paper towel. He was only making it worse while his friends pointed and laughed. Tommy remembered the time Checkers had stuffed Cecil into a locker and was struck with remorse for a split second.

Seed sailing was another benefit of working the window. The water retention lip also served to direct well-aimed corn or peas upward, toward unsuspecting victims. The original intention was to flip pieces of food at the students when they piled their trays onto the counter. It was clear to Tommy that, by using a minimal amount of good sense, they'd have plenty of time to return their trays without causing such a stir. But the students' haste gave Booger and Tommy a chance to find pleasure in their cafeteria job. In some respects, Tommy was grateful to the impatient high school students. They created the opportunity for amusement.

On pea or corn days, Tommy kept a few of the returned morsels, soon to be projectiles, off to the side. Since most students ate neither, there was always ample ammo, and he only needed a few. When students began piling trays one on top of the other, he'd flip a piece of corn or a pea into the crowd. What he discovered was that the water retention lip sent the food parts on a flight path that, if it missed a student, would land in the area where the teachers sat. The cluster of students provided cover, and best of all, the students usually got the blame.

"Miss!" Booger said after Tommy flipped a kernel of corn that had cleared the student pod but sailed over the teacher table.

"Face shot! Nice one," Booger whispered after a kernel glanced off the face of a Letter Jacket. The clusters of students arrived and departed very quickly, Tommy rarely got off more than one shot into each group.

"Bonus points!" Booger said, almost too loud. Tommy had landed a kernel in Mrs. Cane's hair.

Tommy giggled. "She didn't notice." A few student pods later, Tommy landed a kernel on Mr. Franklin's shoulder.

"You're dead meat," Booger whispered. Tommy kept his head down and focused on cleaning the trays. His pulse raced. He'd heard the rumors about Mr. Franklin being in the Special Forces. Mr. Franklin noticed the kernel, flipped it off, and then casually glanced around. A feeling of relief swept over Tommy. He spent the remainder of his twenty minutes simply performing the task at hand and praying the flying food remained a mystery.

A LOW, OVERCAST CLOUD COVER began moving in after lunch. The cool air was refreshing and made staying awake easier, even when Mrs. Enderle read Tennyson to the class. Tommy's Uncle Cletus had told him the medical term for his after-lunch sleepiness: postprandial crash. That's when the blood flows to the digestive track, leaving less for the brain and causing drowsiness. Miss Anderson normally covered math immediately following lunch. Her style was dynamic and invited class participation. The anticipation of being called upon kept everyone alert. But Mrs. Enderle chose to read *The Charge of the Light Brigade*. "Cannon to the right of them, cannon to the left of them, cannon in front," she droned. By the time she got to the last stanza—"When can their glory fade?"—all minds were doing just that … fading. The postprandial had crashed.

Mrs. Enderle finished and stood motionless with her eyes closed. She was holding the poetry book tight to her chest and wearing an eerie, satiated expression. A clap of thunder bolted everyone to their senses. Mrs. Enderle staggered while regaining her bearings. The temperature had fallen precipitously, and a damp fog engulfed Colby. Tommy contemplated delivering papers in the cold rain. Every paper would have to be placed inside the customer's storm doors, which would take much longer.

THERE WAS NO GLAMOUR TO being a paperboy on bad weather days. On clear, dry days, the band of boys frequently showed up to help, but when the weather turned sour, Tommy and Booger were on their own. They divided the papers and went their separate ways in the cold drizzle.

Tommy lost the coin toss and had to climb the stairs to deliver the Koch's paper. Mrs. Koch gave him a brownie for his trouble. He held his breath and chewed on the way down the stairs.

He placed ten papers in the rack inside Rosolini's, and then lingered longer than usual. Standing there in the warm vestibule, he breathed in the aroma of the baking garlic bread, and dreaded going back out into the cold drizzle. When he wiggled his toes, water oozed from the shoestring holes of his Converse All-Stars. Tommy was watching beads of water zigzag through large white letters that read "Rosolini's Café." From the inside, the letters were backwards. Mr. Rosolini was on the phone, but his baritone Italian voice carried well. Tommy did a Jupiter and eavesdropped.

Fairview was getting a new bowling alley with ten lanes and automatic pinsetting machines. Tony Rosolini had acquired the old lanes for a fraction of what they'd cost new. But the deal required he remove them from the old Fairview Lanes building before next week. Tommy heard him fretting with someone on the phone over the terms of the deal. He waited for Mr. Rosolini to finish the call, and then he impulsively offered the services of his buddies and his dad's delivery truck.

"I can get my buddies to help you move 'em," Tommy offered.

Mr. Rosolini's expression brightened. "You think so?"

"Sure, so long as you include some pizza on the deal," Tommy assured him. Having never seen a bowling alley, Tommy expected the move to be more of an adventure than work. Since working for Mr. Rosolini always included lots of free food, he was sure it would be an easy sell to Booger and the rest.

Tony Rosolini excitedly explained to Tommy how he'd recently purchased a vacant building next to the Houn-Dawg Drive-In. The building had been empty for more years than most could remember. He was in the process of converting the building to a recreation center for the church; the lanes would complete his plan.

Dinner customers began to arrive. Tommy picked up the damp paperbag and headed out to finish the route. The rain caused the town to get dark earlier than usual. Street lights, one by one, began to illuminate. Tommy looked back toward Rosolini's and saw Tony, arms waving, no doubt telling a table of customers about the bowling lanes.

Origins

THE BAND OF BOYS MET at Rosolini's early Saturday. On the promise of food, Checkers and Everett hadn't bothered to eat breakfast.

Tony pointed at Booger and Tommy. "You two ride with me." He then motioned toward his wife, Angelina. "The rest ride with her."

Tommy and Booger climbed up into the cab of the two-ton flat-bed truck. Painted on the door was "Colby John Deere" arched over an A-model tractor and the address and phone number of Colby John Deere. Tony had taken Tommy up on his offer and borrowed the truck from Tommy's dad.

The other boys raced to Mrs. Rosolini's car. "Shotgun!" Caleb shouted and plopped down in the front passenger seat. The others piled into the back. Angelina scanned the backseat through the rearview mirror. Flop was in the middle, his wispy frame getting crushed from both sides by the big-boned Checkers and Everett.

"We gonna eat somewhere?" Everett asked right away. He and Checkers anxiously awaited an answer.

She grinned. "I'm sure Tony will treat you boys to a nice lunch once the lanes are loaded." It wasn't the answer the two were looking for—the growl from Everett's stomach matched the frown on Checker's face. Flop's thin frame had nearly disappeared between the two large boys, and he was struggling to breathe.

Tommy watched Mr. Rosolini with a critical eye. Operating a two-speed axle required a little more skill than a three-on-the-tree small pick-up. Tommy knew the purpose of each lever and knob. To Tommy's surprise, Mr. Rosolini deftly handled the large truck.

Tommy was particularly impressed when Mr. Rosolini properly double-clutched at each stop and, without grinding the gears, put the truck into first gear without coming to a full stop.

"You driven this truck before?" Tommy asked, knowing full well that Mr. Rosolini had not.

Tommy's question was simple, but it was as if Mr. Rosolini had been waiting for the time and place to speak of his past. He began with, "Before moving to Colby, Angelina and I lived in New York City … Brooklyn. I drove a delivery truck." He went on to describe growing up in New York City, verbally pausing only when shifting. His mouth didn't seem to function unless his arm could be waving around to accentuate the words.

He said that he and Angelina had always dreamed of owning their own restaurant. They'd saved their money and then one day, at their wits' end, launched westward. Colby was the first town they'd driven through with space for rent on the town square. They'd rented at first, and then eventually purchased the building. Tony's eyes welled with tears when he talked of the family he'd left behind, but then a mask of anger enveloped his face when he spoke of the mob and how they'd extorted his family.

Tommy and Booger learned to view Mr. Rosolini from a different perspective. Tommy had always assumed that everyone in Colby had always lived there and always would. He'd considered Flop's family moving to Colby from Chicago somewhat an anomaly and had never given much thought to the Rosolinis, even with their accent. The Websters moving in from Chicago and Mr. Rosolini's story had started him thinking about the origin of others.

Before reaching Fairview, Tommy considered the origin of Al and Tippy Tatum. He figured they too had moved to Colby from someplace, but from where he didn't know. The curiosity circuitry of his brain kicked into full gear. He struggled to make sense of the strangers in the out-of-state car and Al's phone conversation he'd overheard.

THE OWNER OF THE FAIRVIEW Lanes, a fellow with artificially colored and curled hair, a hairy chest, a nervous facial tic, and an oversized gold necklace, was waiting for them. Nick something was his name. Nick unlocked the door and showed Tony the lanes. He lit a cigarette on the way out the door and wasn't seen again.

The day before, carpenters had removed the trim planks that covered the understructure of the alleys. Each alley consisted of thick hardwood flooring mounted onto laminated blocks of wood. Each block was bolted together by pairs of long rods. The blocks were numbered and had a series of large dowel pins sticking out one end and holes for dowel pins on the other.

Tony used a large wrench to remove the nut from each rod, and the boys carefully removed each section and loaded them onto the truck. They worked nonstop for three hours. After they'd loaded the last piece of alley flooring, Tony noticed the boys standing slouch-shouldered and staring at the large, heavy looking pinsetting machines.

He grinned. "We're not moving those," he told them.

Backs straightened and shoulders squared immediately.

"Well, I was gonna say," Everett mumbled.

The other boys rolled their eyes, each knowing full well that Everett hadn't been on the verge of saying anything. Checkers had claimed an old chair with stuffing pouring out of ragged holes. His head was tilted back and his eyes were closed, leaving himself vulnerable to a prank. It would have been a risky position if it weren't for his robust size.

"Hungry?" Tony asked. Everett's knees buckled, and he fell spread-eagled to the floor. The smile on his face let everyone know it was an act.

The other boys ignored him and looked at each other with delight. They'd continuously spoken of starvation and the Bataan death march while loading the alley.

Tony grinned. "Lunch is on me. Pig's Tail okay?"

Everett rubbed his stomach and replied. "Dang betcha!" The other boys nodded enthusiastically. Checkers's knees popped when he stood up.

The Pig's Tail was famous for its barbeque sandwiches, coleslaw, and fries. The sandwiches weren't particularly large, but they were exceptionally good. Even though the boys were mostly dehydrated from working all morning without a break, their mouths watered in anticipation of the Pig's Tail barbeque.

They were looking for a place to park when Tommy noticed his Uncle Cletus walking along the row of businesses. Tommy was about to say something when Cletus disappeared into a jewelry store. Everyone else was focused on the big sign with a picture of a curly tailed pig with a smiling face—at least as much of a smile as a pig can have. Tommy remembered his uncle saying the pig wouldn't be smiling if he knew he was about to make the ultimate sacrifice.

"Order as many as you want." Tony said after they'd been seated.

Angelina gave him a look. "I don't think you know what you just said." Tony grinned and winked. Angelina added, "You can have as many as you want, but don't order more than two at a time."

Everett ate five sandwiches. Checkers, in an effort to be polite, stopped at four. The others had three each. Tommy was quiet, his thoughts centered on his Uncle Cletus and what he was doing at the jewelry store.

The waiter handed Tony the receipt. Tony let go a gentle whistle. "Sure glad I don't have to feed you boys every day," he chuckled.

After sucking the bottom of his milkshake completely dry, Everett followed up with a shallow hiccup-burp and said, "Them bowling lanes is thickern' I thought." Checkers gave him an elbow jab.

Flop, not to be outdone added, "Like a' said, they gotta be thick if they're gonna hold up while people are doin' all 'at bowlin'. Not to mention knocking the dang pins over and such."

Caleb stood and reminded everyone. "Thing of it is, we got to get this stuff unloaded 'fore Mr. Rosolini is gonna pay us."

After paying the tab, Tony returned to the table with a toothpick dangling from his mouth. The thought crossed Tommy's mind that Mr. Rosolini probably knew better, but he felt at liberty to enjoy chewing on a toothpick since Mrs. Rosolini had already walked to her car. Except for the men at Burt's Sinclair, Jupiter Storm was the only man who walked around in public with a dangling toothpick.

RETURNING TO COLBY, TOMMY AND Booger again rode in the truck with Mr. Rosolini. "A Summer Place" by Percy Faith was playing on the radio. The soothing instrumental was hypnotic—Tommy's chin bounced off his chest and his eyelids drooped.

Mr. Rosolini turned down the volume on the radio and asked, "What are the kids sayin' about Tippy Tatum?"

Tommy had lost the battle to stay awake and had fallen asleep thinking about Melody. The question jolted him out of his trance. He glanced at Booger, who was chewing on a fingernail. Tommy answered for them both. "Whaddya mean?"

Mr. Rosolini shrugged. "Do you think she'll stay in school?"

Initially the question struck Tommy as unusual, and then he realized, for the first time, the obvious: that Tippy being pregnant meant she'd eventually give birth to a baby. It seemed natural for a grown woman but strange for a cheerleader.

Booger stopped chewing on his fingernail long enough to add. "No one's sayin' much about it." Tommy contemplated the comment that Venus Storm had made about pregnant girls and school.

"During the summer, she and Dwight used to come in for dinner fairly regular," Mr. Rosolini volunteered. "They'd usually get a carry-out order too. I always figured it was for her mother. Dwight usually paid."

An awkward silence prevailed for the next few miles. Mr. Rosolini turned up the volume when "Wendy" by the Association came on. Booger grinned and elbowed Tommy, knowing that the song reminded him of Wendy. For the next few miles Tommy's thoughts drifted back to his Uncle Cletus and what he was doing at the jewelry store.

AFTER BACKING UP TO THE newly remodeled building that was soon to be Colby Lanes, Mr. Rosolini went inside to turn on the lights. Mrs. Rosolini pulled up. The boys stretched and rubbed their eyes.

Since it was a warm Saturday afternoon, there were plenty of people milling around the courthouse square. Several were looking in Rosolini's windows and wondering why it was closed. Word about the bowling lanes had spread. Once the truck pulled into town, it didn't take long for a crowd to gather.

The Codgers were piled onto Monkey's golf cart; they were the first gawkers to show up. They kept a safe distance, getting close enough to see what the lanes looked like but not close enough to be expected to help carry anything. Of course, they'd seen a bowling alley before, just not one that had been disassembled.

Several others ambled by. No one offered to help. Most stood around, hands jammed in their pockets and thumbs pointing. Jupiter Storm elbowed his way to the front of the gawkers. "How much did you have to give for this pile of used lumber?" Jupiter indignantly asked. Tony ignored him, as did the others. "I don't see the setting machines," Jupiter continued. "How are you going to set the pins?"

The New York side of Tony appeared. "Jupiter," he said, cutting Jupiter off halfway into his next question. "If you're not going to help, then you need to move on. These young men are tired and so am I. Lend a hand or hit the road." Jupiter looked around, and then he left in a huff. The rest of the gawkers, not wanting to help, moseyed on as well.

Flop began putting on his work gloves with a got-something-to-say look. And he did. "Mrs. Rosolini said they're gonna need people to set pins." He looked to the others for encouragement but got none. "I'm gonna see if Mom will let me." The other boys rolled their eyes in disbelief. As far as anyone knew, he still hadn't learned to change a flat tire on his bike. Setting pins just wasn't in the cards.

Tommy and Booger were struggling to move a section of a lane when Al Tatum showed up. She grabbed one end and helped them lower it to the ground. "Did you get the pinsetting machines too?" she asked.

Tony answered. "Yes, but I'm having them professionally moved."

She ran her hand along the smooth surface of the section of a lane. "Are the setters Brunswick?" she asked.

Tony rubbed his chin. "I think so. Why?"

"Just curious. Manual or automatic?" she asked.

"Manual," he replied.

She smiled, reminisced briefly, and added, "Pinsetting will be a fun job for somebody."

Flop looked at the other boys, and with a know-it-all look he said, "Told ya!" The boys were too intrigued with Al Tatum to be annoyed by Flop.

"Need any help getting the lanes put back together?" she asked. It was more an offer than question.

Tony looked at Angelina for approval before answering. "We could use a little supervision," he said. "We tried to stack them into the truck in the same order that they came apart."

Al studied the end of a couple of sections. "They're marked. See here," she said, pointing at a small metal tag. "Shouldn't be too hard to get back together." She walked into the building and looked at the space allocated for the lanes. "You'll want to leave room to get the pinsetting machines in. They're heavy, probably a ton each."

Al and Tony talked strategy and agreed on the precise placement of the lanes so there'd be room to move the pinsetting machines into place.

With that settled, moving the lane sections into place commenced. Al's presence energized the boys. They weren't about to be out-worked by a woman. Angelina pitched in, too. She and Al exchanged a few glances before striking up a conversation.

"It's nice of you to help," Angelina began.

"It's a good cause," Al replied. "The kids around here need something to do. They'll enjoy bowling." She paused momentarily and smiled. "The adults will too."

Angelina had been taken aback by Al's volunteering to help and then her warm smile. It was the first time Angelina had been close enough to Al to realize she wasn't just an anomaly or freak, but merely a woman in man's clothing. Angelina realized there was nothing intimidating about Al.

"Do you bowl?" Angelina asked.

"Long ago," Al answered. That was all she offered before Tommy and Booger came through the door with a section. Al helped them put it in place. By the time they had it positioned, Caleb and Everett had another section ready. Al showed Flop how to put on the flat washer and get the nut started on the bolt that held the sections.

Angelina won the popularity contest among the band of boys when she said, "I'm not much help here. How about I go and fix some pizzas?" Smiles prevailed and mouths watered.

By the time Angelia returned with the pizza, all of the sections were assembled. Al suggested they let the sections acclimate to the temperature and moisture of the building before tightening. No one argued—not that they knew enough to agree, they were just tired. The boys stuffed themselves with Angelina's famous pizza, and then Tony paid them twice what he'd promised and walked them to the door.

While they walked away Booger nodded his head toward Mr. Rosolini and said, "I like him. He's nice."

"And the food's pretty good too," Everett added, rubbing his ample stomach.

Caleb, his mouth still stuffed with pizza, motioned toward Al and whispered. "She ain't as weird as people think." He forced a swallow. "She's actually kind of nice." The others nodded in agreement.

AL HUNG AROUND A FEW moments longer. Curious, Angelina asked her, "Where did you used to bowl?"

"Where I lived before coming here."

"Were you in a league?"

"Women's league," Al answered. "But I don't like to talk about it," she said, courteously closing the subject.

Angelina moved on. "Do you plan to play here?"

"I'd like to," Al said, taking another bite of pizza. She inhaled deeply, and said, "I don't know many women here. I mostly deal with men at the service station."

Angelina considered the things she'd heard people say about Al and wondered how many women, if any, had actually taken the time to have a conversation with her. She decided that the woman she was sharing pizza with now was nothing like the one she'd heard described at Colby Curls. She looked at Al and saw a person of substance and competence, but lonely. She knew Al and her daughter were facing tough times. She sensed that Al needed and wanted a friend, but she was hiding something that caused her to keep people at arm's length. The cold exterior had been part of her persona for too many years.

Tony took advantage of the lull in conversation. "I appreciate you helping. I'm not sure Angelina or I would have been able to get the boys to stay on task if you hadn't come along. Thanks." Tony sat down between the two women. "Why did you ask if the setting machine was a Brunswick?"

Al didn't answer right away. She looked at Angelina, then at Tony. "I've worked on Brunswicks."

"But not these particular machines?" he asked.

"No, that's not likely, but probably some just like 'em," she said. Tony got a look from Angelina and didn't press the issue.

Al stood to leave. "I need to be going. Tippy will be wondering what happened to me." Tony and Angelina walked her to the door. The night air was crisp.

When Al hesitated at the door, Tony asked, "Would you be able to help calibrate the setting machines?"

Al's face lit up—she'd obviously been hoping that he'd ask. "It has been a while since I've fiddled with one, but I'd be glad to give it a shot," she answered, grinning.

Tony returned her enthusiastic smile. "The company that's installing the new machines at Fairview agreed to move the old ones here. They're going to be delivered on Thursday."

"I can come by after work," Al said without hesitation.

"That'd be great. Seven?" he asked.

"That'll work," she said and headed for the door. Walking backwards through the door on her way out she added, "Better get a couple of those boys here, too. We'll need some help hoisting the lane section that connects to the machine."

Tony smiled. "I think with the promise of Angelina's pizza we'll have as much help as we need."

They both watched her walk away.

"I didn't realize she wasn't from around here," Angelina said.

"Me either," Tony replied. "She was already living here when we came to town. Did you get the feeling she wanted to talk?" Tony asked.

"Yeah," Angelina agreed. "I did."

Super Fan

THE FOLLOWING MONDAY, TOMMY STOPPED by Rosolini's with the paper. "Hey, Tommy," Tony said when Tommy entered. "Think you could get your friends to help put the setting machine in place?"

Tommy, sure that the others would jump at the chance to see how the setting machine worked replied, "Sure, so long as there's food." Tony's eyebrows danced and he let go an ear to ear smile.

"Can you have 'em here on Thursday night?"

"Have some pizza ready, and I'll have the gang here," Tommy replied, a bit overconfident.

Tommy called the others and was disappointed when Flop and Booger were the only ones willing to help. Even the lure of food wasn't enough get the others to miss an episode of *Batman*. The goings-on at Gotham City were more appealing than Angelina's pizza.

The three of them arrived at Rosolini's at six thirty. Angelina seated them at a table with a large pizza. They could hear Tony singing in the kitchen. After giving them less than fifteen minutes to finish their pizza, Tony came through the swinging doors, wiped his hands on a stained towel that he swung across his shoulder. "Stuff it down, boys," he said. "I told Al Tatum to meet us at seven."

They walked with Tony to the lanes where Al was waiting. Even though they'd seen a softer side of her, they still weren't sure about her, and they avoided direct eye contact. The boys watched Al while she and Tony inspected the machines and assessed the task.

It took all five of them to position the last lane section into place on each machine. Once in place, Al worked furiously, making adjustments. Her hands moved continuously, making all the complex connections and adjustments. "Put that there" or "hand me that" was about all she said until it came time to see if each machine would work.

One by one, she loaded pins into each tray, pulled the cord that started everything in motion, and watched while each machine lowered the pins to the lane. The only additional calibration needed was a tray height adjustment—she knew her stuff. Al quietly and meticulously fine-tuned each machine. After everything was in working order, she reviewed the machines' operation with Tony and the boys.

While pedaling home, Tommy mulled over his notion of Al, the strange men in the dark sedan, and Tippy.

"You stink," Marsha greeted Tommy when he got home. He tried to go straight to bed, but his mother intervened and made him take a bath.

"There's no telling what kind of creepy crawling crud you've got on you after working on those old machines," she said. He sat in the tub and let the warm water fill in around him. He couldn't remember ever being so sore. He sunk down until the only thing sticking out of the water was his face.

Tommy wasn't sure how long he'd dozed off, but he awoke to Marsha pounding on the bathroom door. "What's taking so long?" she yelled. "I need to go." Tommy toweled off, went to his room, and ignored Marsha's harping about the ring in the tub.

MORNING CAME TOO SOON. TOMMY was exhausted but still got out of bed on the first call for breakfast. He knew that to fall back asleep or act sluggish meant running the risk of being told he couldn't set pins for Mr. Rosolini. Tommy imagined pinsetting to be almost as prestigious as delivering papers. He maintained an energetic charade until heading for the bus stop.

After fighting sleep all morning, Tommy ate an extra helping of beans and corn bread for lunch, and that was a mistake. Gas pains kept him alert for most of the afternoon. He worried that if he relaxed too much he'd lose control. After recess, his head felt as if it weighed fifty pounds. He'd drift off and then wake up to a head-spinning sensation. The final school bell finally rang. In a stupor, Tommy boarded the bus, having no idea what had transpired that day.

Booger was in the same condition. That afternoon, the two buddies sat on the stone, slumped against each other, and waited for the paper van.

They were too tired to talk. Tommy watched Al Tatum servicing cars at Burt's. He wasn't sure what to think of her.

Burt's newly acquired SS 396 Chevelle was still parked in the tire change bay. Burt's customers admired the Chevelle while waiting for their car to be filled with gas and the oil checked. Even the Codgers had been curious enough about the new muscle car to walk from the courthouse bench across the street to Burt's. However, the conversation among those gathered didn't necessarily center on the car.

The *Colby Telegraph* van arrived, and Tommy and Booger began their rounds. When they'd made it to Burt's, they slipped into the tire change bay to check out the SS Chevelle. Tommy watched Booger's demeanor turn from tired to melancholy. Booger's brother Johnny had often talked of getting an SS when he returned from Vietnam.

The Codgers, one by one, slowly circled the car, hands in their pockets, and thumbs pointing while they made their inspection. Nobody noticed the paperboys. Tommy and Booger were used to being ignored.

Joe-Bill and Fritz pulled up in Fritz's army truck. Joe-Bill got out and left the door open and walked toward the Chevelle. The door on the big truck was high and difficult to operate from the outside, so Joe-Bill usually just left it open and Fritz always jumped him for it.

"You raised in a barn?" Fritz asked rhetorically while he walked back to the truck and slammed the door.

"Even a barn door is easier to close than that thing," Joe-Bill replied. "Afraid some of the dust is gonna fall out?"

Fritz made a hand gesture and mumbled, "Dumbkopf."

"You got a vacant house over by you," Rabbit said, his voice strained from bending over to examine the wheels.

Monkey looked up from the engine and replied defensively. "That ain't the only house for sale. I agree with Burt—they oughta live in Fairview." Monkey had a way of expressing his opinions as if they belonged to someone else.

Rabbit nodded casually. "I'm just sayin.'"

Tommy was sure that Burt hadn't said anything of the sort. He glanced at Booger. Both boys knew the men were talking about the Websters.

Monkey gave Rabbit a look. "You can stop 'just sayin' anytime. They can find someplace else to live."

"They couldn't be any worse than that Tatum gal, or whatever she is,"

Fritz said, making a reference both about her property and her apparent lifestyle.

"She'll clean your clock," Monkey whispered, and then he motioned toward the pump island where Al was servicing a car.

Bem, having been at the rear of the car examining the dual exhaust, had missed the comments. "Guess you heard who the father is."

Monkey and Rabbit stopped midsentence and gave Bem their attention. Fish, who had been standing at the entrance of the bay and watching the pumps for no particular reason, turned around an inch or so at a time and listened. Bem rarely spoke.

"Leon Goolsby was telling it," Bem continued. "Yep, he told it for the truth, don'cha know." Bem enjoyed everyone's attention and strung out the announcement. Tommy and Booger moved into the shadow of the front-end alignment bay and waited to hear the revelation that was about to be imparted.

"Leon said he heard Velma Seabaugh had told it," Bem continued.

Rabbit snapped. "Tell what? You ain't said nothin' yet."

"Dwight Seabaugh."

Fish raised his hand slightly and shook his finger, a sign he was about to speak. He was gathering his thoughts and taking a deep breath. "Didn't the Seabaugh boy leave for the army a month or so ago?"

Rabbit looked at Fish like he was an idiot. "It takes a month or two before you even know."

"I understand that," Fish replied. He'd offered a lame hint and was frustrated that he couldn't share what he knew.

"So you think it's Dwight?" Monkey asked in a hushed tone. Al was walking toward them, then turned and went inside to the counter.

Rabbit shrugged, "I'm just sayin.'"

Tommy and Booger desperately wanted to hear more, but they had papers to deliver. They stepped out of the shadows; the Codgers nodded a hello, but little more, demonstrating once again the transparency of the paperboy. While they made their way around the square, Tommy told Booger about the photo he'd seen at Velma's.

By the time the boys got to Clemo's, the Codgers had changed location. On game days, which meant no practice, the Codgers traditionally hung out at Clemo's. Clemo had once pointed out the homemade "No Loitering" sign, and since then, each of the Codgers made it a tradition to get a game-day haircut. Clemo liked the barbering business, but dealing with the Codgers frustrated him. They had little patience, sparse hair, and didn't tip.

Tommy peeked through the window and saw George Koch in the chair. Scout was sitting on his lap, his runny nose barely visible under the apron. The top of George's head was chrome dome slick, but the hair on his neck was thick and curly. It was as though his hair line had slid down his back. The Codgers were seated along the waiting wall.

Clemo was whipping up a bowl of warm shaving cream. Booger waited outside—there wasn't room for both of them inside Clemo's, and he didn't want to go into Marty's tavern alone.

"Yeah, Russell brought him and his wife by," Clemo was saying when Tommy stepped inside, making reference to having met the Websters.

"What d'ya think?" Rabbit asked.

Tommy laid Clemo's copy of the paper on the shelf next to the Brylcreem and Wildroot.

"What is there to think about?" George asked.

"I'm just sayin'," Rabbit replied.

"Fizzle sticks, Rabbit," Fish said. "You're always sayin' that when you ain't said nothin.'"

Tommy handed over the Clemo's customer copy and a copy for each codger to Fish, who was sitting in the next-in-line chair.

"You need to hold still," Clemo said to George. "If you or that dog flinches I'm liable to cut your jugular."

George looked at Clemo through the mirror. "I'm worth more dead than alive anyway," he replied.

"It's the blood he don't like, don't 'cha know," Bem said. "He gets squeamish at the sight of it." Clemo gave Bem a surly look; Bem wasn't intimidated. He'd been Clemo's Little League coach, and knew he couldn't hit the broad side of a barn with a baseball bat.

George chuckled. "You ought to take down that barber pole if you can't handle a little blood." This was a perpetual topic of conversation, since Clemo had fainted after nicking a customer during a shave years earlier.

Fish had stopped paying attention to the banter and was looking at a photo of the football team in the paper. "It's going to be a perfect night for the game," he said.

"Sure enough," agreed Bem.

Tommy had almost slipped out when George Koch asked him. "How's the Burger boy doing?"

Tommy looked through the window. Booger was standing on the sidewalk, looking skyward, waiting. "He's doing okay."

"Heard they're going to retire his brother's jersey tonight," George continued.

"Yeah," Tommy replied. "Some Marines are going to be there too."

Tommy was looking at a poster Clemo had recently put up above the door; it was the Optimist Creed. He read the first few lines before stepping outside.

Promise Yourself . . .

To be so strong that nothing can disturb your peace of mind.
To talk health, happiness, and prosperity to every person you meet.
To make all your friends feel that there is something worthwhile in them.
To look at the sunny side of everything and make your optimism come true.

He glanced back at Clemo; a single word came to mind—ironic.

"What were they talking about?" Booger asked.

"Nuthin' much," Tommy said. Tommy mulled over what he'd just read and felt the urge to recommend to Clemo that he make all his customers read it.

DURING THE FALL, MOST CONVERSATIONS centered on football, or at least were rich with football metaphors. It's possible that a few in Colby didn't care about the game, but they feigned interest so they wouldn't be suspected of having arrived on a UFO.

After delivering the papers, Booger and Tommy headed for the game. They met Caleb and Flop at the Houn-Dawg. Flop was energetic as usual, running his mouth. A standing-room-only pregame crowd had already gathered. Mrs. Pope was standing over the grill, flipping burger patties and moving sizzling shaved onions around. Booger and Tommy didn't have to pay for their burgers and sodas since they were her paperboys.

"Like a' said," Flop started before he'd said anything. "Mom said I could set pins at the bowling alley.

Booger and Tommy glanced at each other; Caleb's cheeks, stuffed with fries, looked like a chipmunk. He'd probably blocked off his ear canals and hadn't heard Flop's announcement. Tommy was sure that Flop's mom had no clue what setting pins amounted to. Cletus had once set pins and told Tommy about someone getting their nose broken by a flyaway. Mrs. Westwood had probably visualized an indoor job running a machine with every safety shield and switch known to man.

"That's great," Tommy lied, and he immediately began to worry about Flop.

"Your mom seen the Colby bowling alley?" Booger asked.

"Like a' said, no, but she's been to some in Chicago, before we moved."

After swallowing, Caleb caught on. "This ain't Chicago," he said, stating the obvious. "Guess you heard that Dwight Seabaugh dang near got his arm ripped off by one of them settin' machines." Caleb looked at Tommy and Booger for effect and confirmation.

The "nearly ripped off" arm was in reality a broken finger Dwight had suffered while working at Fairview Lanes, and he'd done that changing syrup tanks at the soda fountain counter. After Dwight lost his license from a DWI, he'd had to go to work at Burt's so he could walk to work, and he had embellished the finger injury so as to disguise the real reason he no longer drove to Fairview.

THE FOOTBALL FIELD HAD GOTTEN lights fifteen years before the town had voted to install a sewage treatment system. Most felt outhouses and septic tanks more than adequate. The Colby football field was dedicated to football—it was not a multipurpose field, no track, strictly football. Getting between a Colby resident and Friday night football was akin to standing between a one-ton bull and a cow in estrus; it wasn't a good place to be. The bleachers on both sides were only a few feet behind the player's benches. This was intentional. It made it easier for the crowd to be heard by the players—good for the home team, bad for the visitors.

On Friday nights, otherwise normal people took on a Neanderthal persona. Chants hurled at the visitor's bench had reduced visiting players to tears and, in a couple of instances, to wet their pants. Visiting coaches long ago realized it a waste of time to complain. An ejected Colby Fighting Indian fan would be instantly replaced by an equally insane Indian booster. Legions of backups waited, each eager to vengefully pour it on while the one or two volunteer sheriff deputies available for the game were occupied in escorting a face-painted banker by day and lunatic by night to the gate. There was no shame in getting ejected, which generally resulted in a free meal at Rosolini's and the Houn-Dawg.

Burt had given Al Tatum the honor of delivering the effigy car to the pregame festivities. The first time she'd done so, Jupiter had once made a few remarks about her, or "him" as he'd called her. All disparaging remarks about Al ceased after Burt backed Jupiter into a corner at the filling station and challenged him about what he'd been saying. Rumor has it that Burt had threatened to knock Jupiter's goggle eyes normal. Al wasn't at the station at the time and unaware of the confrontation.

Burt's influence throughout Colby was understated but certain. His endorsements always carried considerable weight.

Everything about football included some sort of tradition mixed with superstition. The crowd waited impatiently while Al unhooked the wrecker from a three-hole Buick. Several fans had already paid to get their four hits for a dollar. It was important to be one of the first in order to get a chance at knocking off a rearview mirror, doorknob, or something chrome.

The car looked to be in fair condition. The top and sides were slightly caved in and scratched, indicating it had rolled. The seats, windshield, transmission, and engine had been removed. Every side window remained; some were cracked but not broken out—a bonus. Cletus, chairman of the booster club, jumped up onto the hood of the car and conducted a quick auction. He stopped the auction when the bid on each window reached a dollar.

"Last Kiss" by CC Rider began playing on the public address system while the one-dollar people knocked out each window; it was fitting, almost poetic. The four-for-a-dollar people followed, methodically reducing one of Detroit's finest to a heap of scrap metal.

"Light My Fire" by The Doors played over the PA system while the football team warmed up. The giant maple tree on the west end of the field still had most of its coppery red fall leaves—a few naked branches were visible. The flagpole was situated between the tree and the scoreboard. The flag waved rhythmically in the southerly breeze. A thin, high overcast cloud cover radiated the red glow of a clear fall sunset, a perfect backdrop for the national anthem.

Melody and Tommy sat together in the marching band section. Two Melodys could have fit inside the jacket she was wearing.

"Mom found a spider's nest in my pants." Tommy offered the informa-tion mostly to make her think he'd had trouble with his uniform, too. Tommy barely got the words out before Melody jumped up like she'd been shot out of a cannon and ran toward the restroom. Suffering from momentary paralysis and unable to speak, he watched her tugging at her pants while she made her way through the crowd.

A few minutes later, she returned, squeezed through the upper class-men, and sat down next to Tommy. "Loose thread," she said. Her sudden sensitivity to fraying threads was clearly a case for the power of suggestion.

Mr. Tobin signaled that it was time for the band to take the field. Line-up for the first game was simple; find the assigned yard line and march out. Tommy had written his assigned yard line on his sheet music. Be-ing buried in the middle of the band reduced the chance for marching mistakes: just watch the person next to you and stop when they do. Only parents watched the marching band anyway.

It was unusually warm, and sweat trickled down Tommy's legs. He felt sorry for the fat guy playing the tuba, whose temples shined with perspi-ration.

Bobby Jackson raced up and down the sideline, waving his hands in the air when the team ran onto the field. The players howled like a bunch of jackals, and that only made Bobby more animated. Bobby had graduated a few years earlier, but he had received a "special" diploma. Occasionally, after a bad call by the officials, he'd need to be physically restrained.

The band played the alma mater. A U.S. Marine color guard marched onto the field and presented the flag, a job normally done by a member of the pep squad. The band then played the national anthem. Brother Baker prayed for good sportsmanship and, typical of a Baptist preacher, included several other petitions not related to the game. He thanked the Lord for the football equipment, the grounds maintenance, the crew who had painted the bleachers the previous summer, the mothers of the coaches, the parents of the players; it went on for nearly ten minutes. Tommy's neck cramped before Brother Baker finished. Brother Baker's voice crackled when he mentioned the boys in Vietnam. No doubt several were praying that the other team would have a chance to be gracious los-ers.

Booger, his dad, Coach Bodenschatz, and Mr. Thorpe assembled at the center of the field. Mr. Thorpe, the president of the school board, held a framed number forty-five jersey, Johnny's number. Johnny had been a star football player and had received scholarship offers from several colleges. After graduation, instead of playing college football, he'd patriotically enlisted in the Marines. He'd been killed in action only a month before his tour in Vietnam would have ended.

Bobby Jackson paced nervously and anxiously nearby. He had been Johnny's biggest fan. Bobby suffered an undisclosed mental disorder and behaved much like an idiot savant and was known to rattle off the statistics for every starter in every sport. He could quote the scores of games going back several years, but he couldn't manage to pick out matching shoes. Conversations were difficult for him—he'd shift and sway, using minimal eye contact, and usually looking at your ear, unless you were a girl. Sometimes his eyes seemed to roll back and his eyelids fluttered out of control. Cletus had told Tommy that the excessive saliva that manifested itself as foam on the edges of Bobby's mouth was due to his medication. His attention span was too short to be measured. Bobby liked to help and made every attempt to do so, but his assistance oftentimes resulted in more work for others. Due to his enthusiasm for every sport, some had begun referring to Bobby as Super Fan.

Mr. Thorpe, himself a WWII veteran of the Battle of the Bulge, stepped to the microphone. "In honor of his service to our country, his ultimate sacrifice on our behalf, and his performance as an athlete, and in recognition that he embodies the spirit of the Fighting Indian—proud, brave, and willing to die for his cause. Johnny Burger's number forty-five will be forever retired. Mr. Burger, on behalf of the Colby Fighting Indians and the community of Colby, I present to you and Randy number forty-five."

Mr. Burger accepted the framed jersey. He and Booger held it between them for one photo. Super Fan stood back and wrung his hands for a full twenty seconds, possibly a record for him, then jumped in between Booger and his dad. When Booger and Mr. Burger made room for Super Fan, the crowd returned a thunderous applause.

The band had practiced the "Marine Corps Hymn," but to everyone's surprise, the Marine Color Guard sang a cappella. Those who didn't break into tears broke into song.

From the Halls of Montezuma
To the shores of Tripoli

We fight our country's battles
In the air, on land and sea.
First to fight for right and freedom
And to keep our honor clean;
We are proud to claim the title
of United States Marine.

It was a very sobering moment, and even more so when the Color Guard fired a seven-gun salute. At the report of the rifles, tears dried, adrenaline gushed, and every man, woman, and child steeled into a warrior frame of mind. During the fusillade, Super Fan held his ears and spun around a couple of times, then sprinted for the sideline, holding his arms straight down at his sides. For one night, the football team transformed from Indians into fighting Marines. The opponents weren't kids from another school. They'd become the enemy, an effigy of the North Vietnamese, the very same people who'd taken Johnny Burger from them.

Before climbing to the top of the bleachers, Tommy adjusted his suspenders for the umpteenth time. "My danged pants are so big I can barely keep 'em from fallin' off," he complained. He and Melody were surrounded by upperclassmen who ignored them.

Melody nodded in agreement, and then she registered a wardrobe problem of her own. "My spats keep coming undone. And I keep tripping on them."

Tommy glanced down and noticed that she had them on the wrong feet. He helped her switch them, moving the snapped seam to the outside of each ankle. Her spat problem was fixed, but there was no easy solution to his Humpty Dumpty-sized pants.

HALFTIME WAS LESS THAN A minute away, so the Codgers began their trek to Codger's Corner. While they were walking, a field judge missed a blatant clipping call. Rabbit raced to the nearest line judge and began to rant and rave. The line judge, in an attempt to pay attention to the game, ignored Rabbit. Rabbit, infuriated by the judge's lack of attention, spit on the judge's shoes. This set in motion a cascade of events typical of Colby football. Sheriff Dooley, who always stood near the visitors' bench, immediately started toward Rabbit. The line judge turned toward Rabbit and in doing so missed an offsides call.

"The quarterback is being helped up by the tight end that missed the block, eh, looks like he's okay," announced Dale Purdy with the pronounced accent he had since moving to Colby from Canada. Everyone clapped, including the visitors, when the quarterback did a shoulder roll, shook his arms, and did a few ankle hops, indicating that he was fine. The defensive end who had jumped offsides and sacked Colby's QB was taken out of the game. No one knew for sure, but many suspected the coach wanted to send a signal to the charged Colby crowd that he'd seen the missed call and was self-imposing a penalty.

"Looks like the young man who jumped offsides is being taken out of the game, eh," Dale continued. "And Simon James, or Rabbit, as he's affectionately referred to here in Colby, is getting pats on the back while he's escorted out of the stadium by Sheriff Dooley. Those two were a pair in their day, eh."

Those listening to their radios at the game looked for Rabbit and Sheriff Dooley. Dale Purdy chuckled. "It's my guess that Rabbit distracted the line judge and caused the missed call. But the fans here tonight will never be convinced of that."

While Sheriff Dooley and Rabbit were in the parking lot having a laugh and talking about their football days, Super Fan was being restrained by four Colby football players.

Coach Bodenschatz called a running play, which kept the clock running. At the buzzer, the referees ran to the safety of two highway patrolmen, and the players headed for the locker rooms. Halftime provided a needed break as much for fans as it did for the players. And most personalities returned to normal: deacons became reverent, insurance agents became charming, and bankers became charismatic. Of course, a comfortable lead provided the most influence on calming the crowd.

Mr. Tobin, the band director, gave the signal; the drum major led the band onto the field. The notion of competition turned to jubilation when the marching band, replete with their military-style uniforms, took the field. The majority of fans remained in the bleachers and listened to the band perform. After each song, the band moved in what seemed a chaotic march that eventually resulted in the formation of a symbol or string of letters. They performed the Marine anthem after shaping USMC, one letter at a time. One by one, the fans, or at least the parents who knew what the band was supposed to be spelling, stood when the letters began to take shape. The rest stood when the anthem began. Eventually, everyone joined in chorus, even the visitors.

After the band left the field, Tommy and Melody huddled and confided. "I had no idea where to go," Tommy chuckled.

Melody looked around to make sure no one could hear. "Me either," she confessed. "I'm glad it's over. I'm not sure the marching band is that much fun."

"It's supposed to be an honor," Tommy reminded her. He stood there in his itchy wool pants looking at Melody in her oversized coat. Their eyes met for an uncomfortable moment. "We'd better sit down," he said. "We'll have to play again when the team comes out of the locker room." Tommy could feel Melody's light grasp on his elbow while they stumbled through the upperclassmen to their assigned bleacher spots.

After they'd sat down, Tommy feigned a yawn, scratched the back of his head, and then put his arm around Melody. She leaned into him. The top of her head smelled like the inside of a marching band cap.

Saturday

TOMMY WASN'T SURE HOW LONG he'd been lying there, but he knew he was awake and not likely to fall back asleep. Melody was on his mind. She'd written '831' on his sheet music the night before. He'd been too bashful to ask her what it meant.

It was still dark outside. He looked at the luminous dial on the Timex he'd gotten the previous Christmas: 5:45. He wondered why getting up on Saturdays was so much easier than school days.

His mom heard him stirring, got up, and fixed him eggs, kissed him on the forehead, and then returned to bed. She'd fried enough eggs for Tommy and his dad, but Tommy ate them all. He'd hear about that later.

Booger's internal clock was similar to Tommy's. He was waiting at the end of his driveway when Tommy arrived. They'd planned to ride their Mini-Trails to Chester Bird's farm. The sky was crystal clear—several morning stars were still twinkling.

The lack of cloud cover had allowed the temperature to dip near freezing. A thick fog roped through the valley. The change in temperature from the ridge top to the valley floor was dramatic. They stopped on the bridge to let their fingers warm and listened to morning forest sounds. A brilliant burst of sun peeked over the ridge. The dark overhead sky slowly became a mixed band of purple, blue, and then orange with ridge-top trees forming wiry silhouettes.

The sunrise was too sensational for words; the boys sat there in silence. After a few minutes, Booger started his bike and continued toward Bird's farm. Tommy followed. Mr. Bird was standing at the barnyard gate with an empty corn bucket watching the chickens when Tommy and Booger rolled up.

He walked toward the fence. His heavy eyebrows moved in unison
with his thick lips, which were waving a long straw stalk. One eye was
squinted, the other moving back and forth between the two boys. Tommy
expected him to launch into one of his spontaneous political diatribes, but
he didn't. Mr. Byrd gave Booger a thoughtful look. "That was nice what
they done fer yer brother," he said.

Mrs. Bird yelled from the porch. "You boys want to join us for breakfast?"

Tommy's mouth immediately began to flood. He'd just learned in science about Pavlov's dog and now understood the principle firsthand.
"Thanks, Mrs. Bird, but we shouldn't," he yelled back, after swallowing.

Booger gave Tommy a "speak for yourself" and started unbuckling his
helmet. "Yes, ma'am," he answered enthusiastically. Tommy felt a tinge of
remorse for turning down the offer so quickly, especially when he remembered that Booger didn't have a mom to fix him breakfast.

Mrs. Bird read their minds. "We have plenty. Chester has to go to town
right away; he won't make you do any chores." That made all the difference—the boys had learned that there was no such thing as a free meal at
the Birds. Mr. Bird gave the boys liberty to ride around on his farm and
camp in a giant cave on his property, but he wasn't shy about asking for
help with whatever it was he happened to be doing when they came by.

"Actually, I have to be at Gooche's before long," Booger added while at
the same time putting down his Mini-Trail's kickstand and removing his
gloves. Tommy tucked Booger's comment away as insurance for a reason
to leave, should Mr. Bird decide to dish out chores.

Booger and Tommy filled their plates with scrambled eggs, biscuits,
and freezer jam, but there was a trade-off. To the Birds, the boys represented two sets of fresh ears. Mr. and Mrs. Bird both talked continuously
and not necessarily about the same subject. Mrs. Bird carried on about
the beautiful fall colors and shared her memories of past years. Mr. Bird
complained about the government, taxes, and the war in Vietnam. While
the Birds talked, Tommy and Booger gorged themselves and listened politely—it was the least they could do.

There was a short lull in the talking when both Birds took a couple
large bites. Mrs. Bird swallowed and said, "Last week's paper had an article
and picture of the new hat factory manager." It was a declarative statement

meant to provoke a comment. Mr. Bird didn't respond, kept chewing, and gave Booger and Tommy a "tell us what you know" look.

Tommy and Booger glanced at each other. Each chewed his food to shreds, hoping the other would swallow first and have to respond. As paperboys, they'd heard more than they were supposed to and certainly more than they cared to share.

Booger swallowed, and then went first. "They're looking for a house," he said, then stuffed his mouth with a biscuit heavily loaded with sorghum-molasses and butter.

The Birds looked at Tommy, expecting him to pick up the conversation from that point. A small plane had flown over while Booger was talking, and Tommy was struck with a thought. "You ever heard of the Tuskegee Airmen?"

Mr. Bird tilted his head up slightly and furrowed his brow. "Is that Webster fellow a Tuskegee Airman?"

"Don't think so," Tommy said. "But when Mr. Koch saw the paper he started tellin' me'n Booger about the Tuskegee Airmen."

Mrs. Bird stared into space, and then said, "I'da thought him too old for WWII, Chester."

Tommy broke the silence. "Mr. Koch said that he flew fighter planes in WWI."

Mr. Bird gave a surprised look. "You shore 'bout that?"

Booger piped up. "He's got a picture of himself standing beside an old airplane."

Mr. Bird looked to Mrs. Bird. "Can't say I knew that, but I suppose anybody can have their picture made next to an airplane." His comment cast doubt on Tommy's assertion.

Mrs. Bird added her two cents. "Still doesn't explain the Tuskegee Airmen."

Mr. Bird jabbed his butter knife into the air—he was word searching. Eventually, he began speaking while still chewing and crumbs tumbled from the corners of his mouth. "I remember when he came to town. He was selling insurance." Mr. Bird tilted his head in thought and then swallowed. "Then he left town for a while and worked somewhere else—can't remember what that was all about. Guess that didn't work out, 'cause he come back and went to work at the bank."

Mrs. Bird shook her head. "Yeah, the bank he married into," she said sarcastically, making reference to Mrs. Koch's family owning the bank.

"I'll be dog," Mr. Bird said between bites. "That's right." He shook his head doubtfully. "Fighter pilot. George tell you that?" He took another bite and with a mouth full of food continued, saying, "Just because he had his picture taken next to an airplane doesn't make him a fighter pilot. He may have been pulling your leg."

Tommy wasn't sure what to think. Mr. Koch's story had seemed believable, but Mr. Bird's skepticism cast doubt on the validity. Tommy visualized Mr. Koch laboring to breathe with that old dog on his lap and began to question the story.

A few minutes of silence prevailed, rare at the Bird kitchen table. The only sound was that of smacking lips and um-ums. Mrs. Bird started clearing dishes from the table. "Guess you two need to head back to town," she said. "You don't want to be late." Both boys got the message, thanked her for breakfast, and headed for the door, both anxious to leave before Mr. Bird pressed them into service.

LEON AND IRVIN WERE STANDING on the loading dock smoking cigarettes when Tommy and Booger got to Gooche's. Irvin had a fresh haircut, long on the sides, slicked back to a ducktail, and a short butch waxed flattop. Leon's melon head was evenly cropped—he'd probably done it himself.

The engines of the Mini-Trails made ticking sounds as they cooled. Leon pointed at the Mini-Trails. "Engines sound hot."

Tommy shrugged nonchalantly and said, "No more'n usual." The fact was, the return trip had turned into a race. Both mini bikes had been ridden at full throttle almost the entire way.

Irvin, Gooche's manager, took one last drag, flicked his cigarette butt across the parking lot, blew out a long plume of smoke, and then pointed at the pile of boxes in the back of the truck. "Those need to go to the incinerator. Don't burn the place down." He was referring to an incident the previous summer when Booger and Tommy had nearly caught the grocery store on fire. It had occurred during one of their first trips to the incinerator, a trip of less than a hundred yards. Tommy and Booger had learned that a burning box easily becomes airborne, and the gentlest of breezes will carry one a long way, and in their case, to the very dry and flammable weeds growing along the wall of Gooche's.

Since Booger had won the race to town, he got to drive the old truck, filled with flattened boxes, down the alley to the incinerator. Among carry-out boys, the truck was legendary. Once bright red, the paint had faded and had turned a chalky pink. "Gooche's Grocery" was faint but legible on both doors. Since most Colby families had cars, Gooche's no longer delivered. An expired license plate hung by one twisted strand of wire. Stuffing spilled from the cracks in the upholstery on the bench seat. A bent antenna provided a signal to a radio that was weak, but worked after a lengthy warm-up. Somebody had tuned it to KXOK, 630 AM, and broken off the tuning knob. Tommy and Booger were oblivious to the truck's age spots. It was something they could drive. Taking boxes to the incinerator had been the highlight for most carry-out boys for countless years since the days of delivery had ended.

Returning from the incinerator, Booger shifted the truck into second gear and got going fast enough to nearly bounce both of them off the seat, almost 15 mph. He got his foot on the clutch and the truck slowed down just before Russell Gooche stuck his head around the corner of the dock. Booger still hadn't mastered the clutch, but managed to slip-clutch the truck back into place while Mr. Gooche and Irvin watched. The stench of Irvin's Lucky Strike masked the smell of burning clutch plates.

Mr. Gooche stood on the dock waiting for them. "Was wondering if you were going to show up this morning," he said.

Booger climbed up on the dock. "Irvin said to empty the truck," he told him.

Mr. Gooche gave Booger's neck an affectionate squeeze. "No problem," he said. "I just didn't see you come in."

Booger looked back at Tommy and waved. "See ya this afternoon."

LATER THAT DAY, AFTER CLOCKING in at Gooche's, Tommy was bagging on Velma's lane. Booger was stocking shelves. Shelf stocking required more training and experience than bagging and carried more prestige, and customer interaction was interesting. When a new recipe was being circulated, probably at Colby Curls, women would ask for rarely sold spices, such as ground turmeric or coriander seed. Men rarely asked for help and generally stumbled around until they forgot what they'd been sent for and settled for a gallon of milk.

Tippy Tatum stepped behind the check-out counter and began whispering to Velma. Tippy had no groceries—Tommy heard Jupiter's name mentioned. He walked over and read the public announcements on the bulletin-board and gave them some space. Tommy's heart sank when he saw Tippy's tears. He figured the Codgers had been right about Dwight being the father. Tippy and Velma moved outside to finish their conversation. Tommy visualized the photo of Tippy and Dwight he'd seen at Velma's.

The Ducklings began emptying their cart onto the counter. Emma had shadowed Erma throughout the store, always standing behind or beside her. Milk, bread, pork and beans, braunschweiger, a one-pound block of American cheese, a jar of pickles, and Oreo cookies—the same thing each week. They had a garden for vegetables and chickens for eggs. Tommy shuddered after catching himself wondering if the Ducklings split the Oreo and licked off the creamy filling.

When Tippy left, Velma began checking them out. "It's a pretty fall," Velma said. Her voice was strained and weak.

Erma nodded a confirmation and, just above a whisper, said, "Uh huh."

Emma turned away and looked down. Tommy had learned to act as if their behavior was normal. More and more, he'd learned that grownups often did that, just as Velma was acting like all was normal in her life. He'd surmised that part of being an adult was not talking about certain things, and sometimes pretending they didn't exist.

Tommy double-bagged their groceries since he knew they were walking. Each Duckling tucked a bag under her left arm and started home, Emma right behind Erma and both swinging their right arms in unison.

Wendy's mom was the next in line. Tommy acted like he didn't notice the box of feminine products she'd covered with a box of laundry detergent. Velma kept a supply of small paper bags under the cash register and placed the box of sanitary napkins in the bag before placing them on the counter along with the other items. Tommy went along with the charade and acted oblivious. Who did they think had stocked the shelves in the first place?

He remembered the time Checkers had snuck into the locker room during an away football game and stuck a package of sanitary napkins in Cecil Becker's letter jacket. Visiting teams always dressed in the girls' locker room. Checkers had observed provisions in the girls' locker room that he'd never seen in the boys'. Cecil hadn't noticed the addition to his wardrobe until one of the cheerleaders pointed it out.

After Wendy's mom left there was a lull. Velma made small talk. "Heard Penny was showing the new hat factory manager some houses yesterday."

Tommy told her what he'd heard from his paper route customers. "They're just looking at the yards and the outside of the houses. Supposedly, Mr. Webster says it would be a waste of time for him to look inside without his wife." Tommy paused a second, and then said, "They'll both be here on Tuesday. I heard the Codgers sayin' it."

Actually, Booger's Aunt Penny had told him, but he'd also heard the Codgers say so while discussing the Websters. Tommy didn't think it a good idea for Velma to think that Penny was telling things about her customers. At any rate, the Websters were coming to town to look for a house, and pretty much everyone in Colby knew and was fretful. The Websters would be Colby's first black family.

Frump Queen

DURING THE FALL, BROTHER BAKER was always punctual—in fact, his sermons were noticeably shorter that time of year. His attentiveness to the clock had less to do with the lack of chlorophyll reaching a tree's leaf as it did with grown men taking the field and wrestling with an oblong-shaped pigskin. Most, particularly the men, welcomed the brevity, but a few of the traditionalist, mostly frumpy women, didn't appreciate his motive: televised football.

Mrs. Enderle, queen of the frumps, was on to Brother Baker's motive for being punctual. She stepped to the podium to lead the singing. "Please turn to hymn number 318, 'Are You Washed in the Blood?' and a-like-a-that." She always ended her sentences with "and a-like-a-that." She waited for the sound of flipping hymnal pages to stop, then straightened stoically, cleared her throat, raised one arm conductor-like, and pointed toward Tippy with the other. Since Jupiter had made sure that every living soul in Colby knew about Tippy's condition, including and-a-like-a-that herself, she'd stopped making eye contact with Tippy. Tippy didn't let the snobbery affect her worship service performance. Fish had picked up on Mrs. Enderle's snooty indiscretion and resisted the urge to breach the confidence he had with Tippy, and set Mrs. Enderle straight. Tippy played the first stanza on Mrs. Enderle's exaggerated hand movement, and the congregation came alive in song.

If it had been spring and Mrs. Enderle had gardening to tend to, she would have eliminated at least one verse, usually the third. But it wasn't spring—it was fall and that meant football. The bulletin listed two songs to be sung—they'd already sung every verse in both. But before Brother

Baker could get to the pulpit, Mrs. Enderle asked everyone to turn to hymn number 235, "There is Power in the Blood." Brother Baker approached, or more accurately commandeered, the pulpit during the last verse, and with a smile, gently hip-checked Mrs. Enderle from behind the pulpit before she called for a fourth song. Mrs. Enderle knew exactly what she'd done, smirked, and pompously returned to her seat.

Tippy smirked and quietly closed the piano key cover, then made her way down the side aisle. She could sense people looking at her differently. A feeling of grace swept over her when Fish gave her a warm, understanding smile. She took a seat toward the rear, saved a place next to her, and then bowed her head in silent prayer.

Brother Baker didn't waste any time getting started. He'd prepared a sermon and was anxious to deliver it. His anxiousness was driven by both the content of the sermon and the need to get home in time for the pregame show. He didn't disappoint on either. Knowing that most of the men would be thinking about the game, he titled his sermon "Play to Win." Green Bay, the defending champions of Super Bowl I, were set to square off with their biggest rivals, the Minnesota Vikings. Half the boys in town had a Bart Star football, one with his autograph imprinted on the side. The other half wanted one. Nobody cared about the Vikings—Vince Lombardi was America's coach and the Packers were America's team.

Brother Baker quoted Coach Lombardi when he said, "Perfection is not attainable. But if we chase perfection, we can catch excellence." He was of course referring to how each person needs to strive to be more Christ-like. Even though his thought bridges were football related and Lombardi-speak, even the women understood the metaphors, and a few may have been converted to Packers fans. Of course, none of them admitted it, and football wasn't a likely topic for discussion at Colby Curls.

"Determination," Brother Baker shouted. "I Corinthians 9:24 says 'All run; only one gets the prize.'" His sermon could have been a Lombardi pep talk. "Discipline, verse 25, 'Everyone who competes must go into strict training.'"

Everyone heard the Lombardi parts, and the scripture reference for the reason for training "to get a crown." All of the men, and most of the women, were engaged in the sermon, and Brother Baker sensed the focus. He expected to have the attention of the men, but he seemed to feed on the unexpected attentiveness of the women. His volume reached multiple crescendos. Occasionally, he'd chirp a few syllables in high soprano before taking a sip of water.

All heads swiveled to see the late-comer. Tippy's silent prayer had been answered. Al sat next to her in the spot Tippy had saved for countless Sundays. Al was wearing a new pair of pressed bib overalls and a pink blouse. Her hair was fixed in an up-do, a modified Pentecostal, piled on top of her head in a loose bun, with bangs hanging to one side of her face. Without the engineer's hat, some had to do a double take to recognize her. A very light application of make-up, a first for her since moving to Colby, made her look more like Tippy's sister than her mother. She was showered with countless genuine, approving smiles. Al had expected the stares, but the warm expressions were a surprise and nearly brought her to tears.

Brother Baker, wearing his reading glasses to see his sermon, didn't recognize Al. He didn't give her much thought and had probably figured she was a friend of Tippy's. He jabbed his finger skyward and shrieked, "Desire!" And after taking a deep breath, he continued, saying, "Do not run like a man running aimlessly. Do not fight like a man beating the air." He paused for effect, looked around, and savored the moment. He closed his Bible and his eyes and softly said, "Determination, discipline, desire." He bowed his head and said, "Lord Jesus, let us run to win. Amen."

By the sermon's end, everyone felt like they'd had a workout. In the final moments, the men were all engaged and saw in Brother Baker the embodiment of Vince Lombardi. Male minds were spiritually focused. The women had enjoyed the message, but their thoughts quickly turned to pot roast or whatever it was they'd planned for Sunday dinner.

Brother Baker made his way to the foyer while the choir and the congregation sang the doxology. Al, not wanting to field questions, moved out just after "Praise Him, All Creatures Here Below." Since they were sitting near the rear, Al and Tippy were two of the first to leave. Brother Baker gently shook Tippy's hand then stuttered and choked on inhaled saliva when he finally recognized Al, just before she nearly crushed his soft pink hands with her callused, vise-like grip.

One by one, the rest of the congregation filed from the church. The women were gentle, but the men gave Brother Baker crushing, enthusiastic handshakes—their gusto was enriched by the spirit of the message. During lunch, he had to use his left hand to eat his fried chicken. He later soaked his right hand in Epsom salt while watching the Packers game and contemplating changes to his evening sermon, perhaps something on gentleness.

Milton Merle lingered, hoping to get a chance to speak to Venus Storm, but instead got a threatening stare from Jupiter. He ambled off, slump-shouldered, without getting to say good-bye to her.

Incongruous

MONDAY'S EDITION OF THE *TELEGRAPH* included an article about the new bowling lane. The article described the move, but to the disappointment of Tommy and Booger, had no mention of the boys who helped. They loaded their bikes with papers and split the business district. People who worked on the square usually got their *Telegraph* at work. In some cases, Tommy or Booger would put the paper in their cars. A few businesses paid for extra copies to be left inside. The ladies at Colby Curls preferred their papers brought to their individual stations.

Tommy eased open the door and his olfactory senses revolted at the rich mixture of damp heat, ammonia, hair spray, dye, fingernail polish, and cigarette smoke. He announced his arrival with a sneeze. He'd never been successful at slipping in unseen. Faye, the owner, was never any help in his stealth efforts. "Hello, Tommy Thompson," she said, tilting her head flirtatiously and throwing her hip to one side when she faced him. Tommy surmised she liked saying his name more than she actually appreciated the delivery of the paper. He didn't read anything untoward in her body language—he viewed her in the same sense as he would an aunt. Her voice had the raspy tone caused by years of cigarette smoking. She had just finished getting a snaggle-toothed woman with a large bulbous tipped nose situated under a hair dryer.

"Hi, Faye," Tommy replied. Faye was one of the few adults he called by their first name. But she'd always insisted that he do so. She winked and gave him a big red lipstick smile. Tommy made his way through the maze of women with puffy faces sticking out from under large noisy dryers, some with their heads tilted uncomfortably into a sink, and others

smoking cigarettes while getting their fingernails repaired. He was no longer embarrassed to enter the parlor, but he was still anxious to leave. He
eventually realized that few of the women even noticed him. His primary
goal was to get in and get out before the stench of Colby Curls salon permeated his clothes.

"Guess you heard about the Tatum girl," Snaggletooth announced out
of the blue. She'd been aptly named by Tommy and Booger for her extra
large and crooked teeth and an unusually small mouth. Since her head
and ears were covered by the space helmet-sized hair dryer, she was talking loud enough that listening to her wasn't optional. She had her face in
a magazine and was broadcast talking to no one in particular. The magazine cover featured a model who most likely weighed less than one of
Snaggletooth's thighs. Another lady, who was getting her mustache waxed
and unable to speak with the wax-wrap applied, nodded enthusiastically
in agreement.

Mable Sappington, also known as Chubby Cheeks to Tommy and
Booger, was getting a manicure. She had to add her two cents. "Oh,
brother me," she said loud enough for Snaggletooth to hear under the
dryer. "But that's not the worst of it."

Snaggletooth dropped the magazine to her lap. "You talking about
Dwight Seabaugh being the father?" she asked.

"No, I was talking about that squalor her mother calls a home," Chubby
Cheeks replied.

Linda Heart, coach Heart's neurotic trophy wife—young, thin, new
in town—had her hair wrapped in strips of tinfoil. She tried to join the
conversation. "Kinda feel sorry for them," she said. Tommy could tell the
others despised her—probably her good looks and svelte figure were
the problem.

"Think she got pregnant on purpose?" Chubby Cheeks asked.

"How long you think they'll let her continue playing the piano at
church?" Linda asked. The others ignored her comment. Tommy felt
sorry for Linda. First she had coach Heart for a husband, and then the
Colby Curls ladies were giving her the cold shoulder.

"Can't expect the girl to do much better than her mother," added a lady
new to the exchange. Her head was tilted backward deep into a shampoo
sink. Tommy could see her uvula when she spoke. "You'd think the state

would do something about …" She noticed Tommy after sitting up and stopped midsentence. Her comment caused Tommy to wonder if the two men in the sedan had been from the state.

"I wrote a letter to the school," Chubby Cheeks announced proudly. After making the declaration, she pompously pointed her nose skyward and exhaled several cubic feet of cigarette smoke.

Foil Pigtails, sensing she was being ignored, feigned disinterest, picked up a magazine with Twiggy on the cover, and brooded while chewing her fingernails to the quick. The last comment Tommy heard on his way out was, "I'll bet she's not even sure Dwight Seabaugh is the father."

Tommy closed the door behind him, sniffed his shirt, and replayed the exchange. By the time he met up with Booger, he'd concluded that most of Colby Curls's patrons weren't ladies. In many respects, they were no better than Jupiter Storm, just easier to ignore. He'd noticed how Faye hadn't participated in the banter—he held the visual of her smiling pose in his mind. Oftentimes, he'd wanted to say something to them, but he had remembered what Uncle Cletus had said: "Trying to correct a group of salon women is like trying to make friends with a rattlesnake. Nothing good can come of it, and it's a dangerous waste of time."

TOMMY WAS TELLING BOOGER WHAT he'd heard at Colby Curls when Al Tatum whistled to get their attention. Tommy was surprised to see her home. He and Booger cautiously approached her gate. Every inch of the exterior of the house was weathered and in need of paint or repair. The porch posts were rotten at the tops and bottoms and looked as though a strong gust of wind would send them tumbling. Tommy wondered why someone so mechanically inclined would let her house go in such disrepair.

Her backyard was overflowing with a collection of rusted, worn-out farm implements, bicycle parts, pick-up truck hoods, wooden window frames, and countless pieces of lumber of every width and length. Frank Fritz, her neighbor, perpetually perturbed by the unkempt mess, had tried to get the city to force Al to clean it up, but the property was technically out of the city limit. Al didn't own the property and couldn't see the shed from inside the house. She claimed the mess was there when she moved in, so she wasn't inclined to make any effort on Fritz's behalf.

"How much is the paper?" she asked. Having worked with her on the setting machines, Tommy was no longer afraid to make brief eye contact. Close up, he realized that she had probably, at one time, been an attractive lady. Her features seemed to fit that magic ratio that defines beauty. He contemplated how different she'd looked in church.

"Eight dollars and a nickel every three months," Booger finally replied after realizing that Tommy had developed lockjaw.

Al kicked at the ground with her Redwing boots, gave the notion some thought, and then smiled. "I sometimes get a chance to read Burt's while at the station. I've decided that I'd like to start getting a copy delivered here." Tommy was scarcely paying attention, still moved by her subtle beauty, her perfect teeth. Something about her grammar and inflection caught Tommy's attention. He'd always been mystified by her, mostly because she'd always dressed man-like. And he had always been somewhat intimidated by her, but he now realized a kind and gentle spirit resided under her rough exterior. After listening to her at the bowling alley, and then again now, her accent finally dawned on him. Many of her words sounded like those of Flop and his family. He became angered by the Colby Curls comments of her being some sort of a sex change experiment gone badly.

She opened the gate and invited them in. "Let me introduce you to Max." The box-jawed mongrel that had always growled at them when they passed by was now shaking its stub of a tail and submissively wiggling its dust-caked body. Since the bundle of muscle and teeth was a female, Max was probably short for Maxine. Tommy wasn't fooled by the wagging tail and considered it a sign that Max was anxious to dig into his flesh.

"Let her lick the back of your hand," Al told the boys, and then she showed them how to hold their hand for the dog to sniff and lick. "Don't try to pet her until she asks you to." Tommy walked through the gate, taking very short steps. Booger waited.

"Give me your hand," Al said, grabbing Tommy's wrist with her heavily calloused hand. She held his hand in front of the dog's face.

Tommy's mind raced. His choices were to bolt and make it appear to the dog that he was struggling with its master, or he could let Al feed his hand to the dog. Either way, he was going to get bitten. And judging by the grip that Al had on his wrist, Tommy didn't think it possible to get free. While he prepared for the inevitable, he found small comfort in the fact that Al had chosen his left hand and not his right. Tommy closed his eyes, steeled himself, and prepared for the clinching jaws. However, the bite he'd anticipated didn't occur.

Instead of jaws crushing his wrist, a warm, raspy tongue gently licked the back of his hand and then aggressively cleaned between his fingers. Al turned Tommy's hand over, and Max licked Tommy's palm clean.

"I'm going to release your hand," Al said.

Tommy hadn't been looking at Max. He'd been too interested in noticing how Al's long, thick hair was tucked up under her ratty old engineer's hat. Both of her ears were pierced and had tiny, barely noticeable posts in each. The entire lick-down had taken less than a minute.

Almost immediately after Al released Tommy's hand, Max stopped licking and yawned. After the yawn, the snapping jaws sounded more like an alligator than a dog named Max. The next few seconds may have taken a day or two off of Tommy's life. Max took a half step forward, lowered her head, and moved toward Tommy's other hand. Tommy, in a paralysis of sorts, didn't move a muscle. But instead of removing a finger, Max nudged Tommy's hand. When Tommy didn't move Max repeated the nudge—a little more forcefully.

"She's asking to be petted," Al informed him. "But don't stoop down just yet. A dog needs to know you before you get in their face." Tommy wasn't particularly assured by Al's coaxing. Max let Tommy stroke her head a few times, then began licking his hand again.

"I think she likes whatever you have on your hands," Al said.

"Mostly newsprint," Booger said. He'd been quiet through the Max introduction but had slowly eased through the gate and was standing beside Al. Max spun around to see who had spoken. Max's tail quivered rhythmically and she let go a faint growl.

"Same thing for you, Booger," Al said.

Booger hesitantly held out the back of his hand. Max sniffed his hand, then his ankles, and then spent a few seconds nudging around Booger's crotch before returning to his hand for more newsprint ecstasy.

Al smiled. "I think you two have just made a friend."

Tommy slowly reached into his paper bag, pulled out a *Colby Telegraph*, and handed it to Al. "I always have a couple of extra."

"When can I start getting it?" she asked.

Tommy shrugged. "Soon as you start payin."

"So I can pay you now?"

"Sure," Tommy said.

"Come on in, I'll write you a check," she said. "Be careful stepping through all the junk."

Tommy and Booger chose their steps carefully and made their way through the maze of engine blocks, transmissions, and rear differentials that was Al's yard. Al held open the front door to her house, and Tommy prepared himself to see clutter, filth, and stench. Booger followed.

Tommy expected the filth he'd heard described at Colby Curls, but he found the opposite to be the case. The living room was spotless. Rather than experiencing any unpleasant stench, as was the case in many of his route customer's homes, his nostrils were filled with a pleasant fragrance. Al slipped off her boots at the door and placed them under a bench alongside several other pairs of shoes and house slippers. She looked at Tommy and Booger's shoes and said, "You two wait here."

An artist's easel was set up in one corner, and a thin sheet covered the canvas being worked on. The room was appointed with several paintings, all mountain scenes, some with streams and some with cabins draped in heavy snow. Tommy noticed the calligraphic signature on the one nearest: "AT."

The couch had a wool blanket with 101st Airborne logo and an eagle's face embroidered on it. Above the couch was a wall shelf with several framed photos. One was of a soldier who looked to be black, but not exactly. After looking closer, Tommy realized the man in the photo looked something like those he'd seen of Ira Hayes, the Pima Indian famous for his heroic efforts on Mt. Suribachi. There was another photo of the same soldier standing next to a girl that looked something like Tippy. Situated in a prominent spot was a photo of Dwight and Tippy—a duplicate to the one Tommy had seen at Velma's.

Al stuck her head around the corner. "To whom do I make the check payable?"

"Colby Telegraph," Tommy said. Tommy tried to make sense of it all. Incongruous, a word he'd recently learned came to mind.

She returned with the check and had removed the engineer's hat. Her long, thick hair was pulled into a ponytail that bounced when she walked.

Tommy's perception of Al was completely disrupted. After leaving, he and Booger didn't speak for a few minutes, both boys wandering deep in thought.

Puzzled, Tommy mentally collected all of the pieces: the photos of Dwight and Tippy, the two strangers, Al's meticulous home, her recent behavioral change, and the phone conversation. But he wasn't able to draw any conclusions. He mentally chuckled and whimsically wished for the assistance of Maxwell Smart. His temples began to throb.

FEDERAL AGENT GAMBAIANA SAT IN his Chicago office and reviewed a teletype he'd received moments earlier. He'd been assigned to the case since the beginning and had been expecting the new set of orders. The last defendant convicted in the United States of America versus Giordano Luigi and a long list of other characters, all with Italian names, had died in prison ten years earlier.

Agent Gambaiana had participated in the case review and agreed that the witness should no longer be considered at risk. He clasped his hands behind his head, leaned back, and mentally reviewed the particulars. Only a few months from retirement, he'd begun handing over cases to his replacement, Danny Douglas. The Tatum case was special to him, and he'd made that clear to Agent Douglas—Alison was an innocent victim, not one who testified to avoid prison time. And Alison's testimony helped the government prosecute a huge Chicago crime family. Meanwhile, Gino Luigi, who was an overlooked threat, bode his time.

To Another Day

WHILE WAITING FOR THE WEBSTERS, Penny Heart sat at her desk and admired her engagement ring. Cletus had given it to her as soon as the divorce was final—there'd been no courtship; that had occurred fifteen years earlier.

Norman, her now ex-husband, had initiated the divorce proceedings. And since there was another woman involved, Penny didn't fight it. She'd spoken to Brother Baker and Solomon Atchison, head of deacons. They'd assured her that since Norman had admitted committing adultery, the divorce was not forbidden by Scripture. She kissed the ring and shook her head, wondering why she hadn't waited for him when he'd served in Korea. The Websters pulled up, so she took a deep breath and made an effort to stop punishing herself for wasting fifteen years of her life married to a loser.

During an earlier visit to Colby, Carter Webster and Penny had narrowed the search to two houses for Gloria Webster to see. Carter was fairly certain she wouldn't like either. So Penny had decided the visit was primarily a tour of the town and didn't expect to make a sale.

She stepped outside the real estate office to greet them. The fresh air helped with her attitude. Carter opened the car door for his wife, and she gracefully stepped out of the car. The Websters greeted Penny with warm smiles. Penny reached out and gently grasped the smooth, delicate, ebony hand. "It's so nice to meet you, Mrs. Webster," she said.

Mrs. Webster returned the greeting. "The pleasure is all mine. Please call me Gloria."

Penny realized that no matter how much she refused to admit it, skin color did influence how she viewed people. She caught herself staring at Gloria Webster's fine facial features and had a guilty thought: "She must have some white ancestry." Penny was ashamed of the need to hide her surprise each time Gloria spoke completely accent free.

Gloria sensed Penny's pensive behavior. "Are you all right?" she asked.

Penny made an excuse. "Oh, please excuse me. I'm just a little preoccupied. It's nothing." Penny needed a few seconds to work through deepseated racial notions. Her mind continued to flood with thoughts and emotions surrounding the challenges that the Websters had surely encountered in other places as she contemplated Colby's reception. She continued to work at convincing herself that race wasn't an issue, but the ugly truth was so danged persistent.

"If you aren't well, we can do this on another day," Gloria offered.

Penny put her hand on Gloria's wrist. "No, I'm just fine. There's nothing more that I'd rather do than show you around Colby. Plus, we get to have lunch with the Kochs."

Gloria and Carter looked at each other.

Penny fumbled through her purse for her car keys. "Oh, the Kochs. I didn't tell you. They've offered to have you for lunch. I hope you don't mind. They're a great couple. Mrs. Koch's family has been in Colby for several generations."

"Gloria and I have been looking forward to meeting them," Carter said.

Carter's comment momentarily struck Penny as odd, but she kept looking for her keys. "Here they are," Penny said, holding up and twiggling the keys. "The Kochs have been anxious to meet you since the moment they heard you were coming." The Kochs's enthusiasm for meeting the Websters dawned on Penny—she became curious. Then Carter's previous comment registered. "You've heard of the Kochs?" she asked.

"My older brother and Mr. Koch knew each other while in the service," Carter replied. "They haven't spoken for years, but I've been given orders from big brother to say hello to the famous Mr. Koch."

"Famous?" Penny asked herself.

"Why don't we have a cup of coffee and visit first?" Gloria suggested.

Penny again caught herself staring at Gloria, who was standing on the curb looking more like the wife of a president than that of a hat factory manager. Penny envied Gloria's perfect complexion and the perfect symmetry of her facial features. "Great idea. We have plenty of time," she finally said.

"The Houn-Dawg is open," Penny suggested.

Gloria looked perplexed. "The what?" Penny instantly realized how corny the suggestion must have sounded to Gloria.

Carter let out a chuckle. "You'll love this place, Gloria. It's a little diner with a neon sign in the shape of a hound dog. The blinking light makes it look like it's running. If you look close, you can see a little rabbit painted on the sign in front of the dog."

GLORIA GRINNED WHEN SHE SAW the neon hound dog running and running and never gaining on the faded, painted-on rabbit. Penny was relieved when she saw Gloria's reaction. Mrs. Pope, a petite, nervous bundle of energy, was wiping down tables and emptying ashtrays when they stepped inside.

Mrs. Pope looked up, quickly folded the dishtowel, smiled, and extended her hand. "What an honor," she said.

Carter extended his hand. "I'm Carter Webster the new—"

Mrs. Pope interrupted him—he was talking too slow for her rabbit-fast mind. "I know, I know, I'm Patty Pope." She turned to Gloria and winked. "This must be your daughter." She vigorously shook Gloria's hand.

Gloria was visibly flattered and, in fact, she was nearly ten years younger than Carter and truly could have passed for his daughter. Carter grinned. "I've heard that before."

"Here for breakfast?"

"No, Patty, we'd just like some coffee," Penny answered.

The morning coffee crowd had cleared out, and the lunch crowd was more than an hour away, so they had the place to themselves. Mrs. Pope seated them and brought a fresh pot of coffee and set it in the middle of the table. "These are new mugs; you're the first to use 'em." Each mug was adorned with the school mascot, a fierce looking Indian chief. "'Course, everyone knows you're lookin' at houses today," Mrs. Pope volunteered while she poured coffee.

Gloria and Carter glanced at each other over their coffee mugs. "How's that?" Penny asked. She knew there were no secrets in Colby but feigned surprise anyway.

"Jupiter," Mrs. Pope replied in a tone suggesting that Penny should have known, which she did. "Guess he saw the Websters at your office, put two and two together. He was here just before the coffee crowd left and was tellin' everyone."

Carter looked at Penny. "Who's Jupiter?"

Mrs. Pope rolled her eyes. "You'll get to know him soon enough," she said. "I suppose every town has a Jupiter." She smiled. "He's got his good points."

"Speak of the devil," Mrs. Pope said, then rushed to put up the "Closed" sign and let the blinds down. On the way back to the kitchen, she said, "Jupiter just pulled up. I'll make him go to the window."

Jupiter tried the knob, and then knocked on the door.

"The dining room is closed," Mrs. Pope shouted from the carryout window.

"What do you mean you're closed? You were open earlier." Jupiter's baritone voice poured through the take-out window and filled the café.

"Window's open—dining room is closed," Mrs. Pope said.

"Why?" Jupiter asked. His persistence wasn't new to Mrs. Pope.

"Just is. Can I get you anything, Jupiter? I've work to do," Mrs. Pope replied. Her voice was delicate but firm. Several years at the Houn-Dawg had conditioned her for about any kind of customer, particularly those standing on the other side of the carryout window. Jupiter craned his neck to see past her with no luck. The window was situated so the dining room wasn't visible from the carry-out window.

"I can hear people talking," he said.

"People do that," Mrs. Pope replied, then slammed the window shut and resumed scrubbing the grill.

Jupiter huffed and turned to leave and nearly bumped into Tommy. "Closed," he said and showered Tommy with saliva in the process, another thing Jupiter was known for.

Tommy stood there bewildered, watching Jupiter stomp back to his car. He heard the door bolt slide. "Come on in. Hurry," Mrs. Pope said just above a whisper.

On his way through the door, Tommy turned and glanced at Jupiter, who was standing by his car wearing a scowl. Tommy followed Mrs. Pope to the cash register, set down the frozen ground beef, and handed her the receipt.

Assuming the place to be legitimately closed, Tommy hadn't noticed anyone sitting across the room. Penny startled him when she spoke. "Hello, Tommy." He turned and right away recognized Mr. and Mrs. Webster from the photograph he'd seen in the paper. Mrs. Webster was prettier in person—actually beautiful. Penny quickly stood up and walked toward Tommy. "Tommy's the paperboy," she told the Websters. She put her arm around his shoulder and walked him their way. "Why aren't you in school?" she whispered.

"Teacher's meeting," he whispered back.

"Tommy, this is Mr. and Mrs. Webster."

Carter stood and shook Tommy's hand.

"Nice to meet you, sir," Tommy said, remembering to use his good manners. "So you're the new hat factory manager?" Tommy couldn't help but notice the contrast between the dark color on the back of Mr. Webster's hand when compared to his palm and cuticles.

"Yes, that's right. And this is my wife, Mrs. Webster."

Gloria stood and shook Tommy's hand. Tommy was taken by her pearl white teeth and her striking resemblance to Marilyn McCoo of The Fifth Dimension—he'd recently seen them on the Ed Sullivan Show. Mrs. Webster's skin color was considerably lighter than that of Mr. Webster. Tommy thought that odd. In fact, he thought, Mrs. Webster's skin color was nearly the same as Tippy Tatum.

"So you're the paperboy?" Carter said, making conversation, and causing Tommy to jump. He'd been so momentarily enthralled with Mrs. Webster that Mr. Carter's stentorian voice nearly caused him to wet his pants. He felt like he'd been caught, but at what he wasn't sure.

"Yes sir," Tommy replied. He couldn't get "Up-Up and Away," a Fifth Dimension tune, out of his mind.

Mrs. Pope handed Tommy an envelope with the money for the ground beef. "Here's a little extra for you," she said, handing him two quarters.

"Thanks, Mrs. Pope," Tommy said. He was still in his extra polite mode. There was an awkward lull in the conversation, Tommy took the hint and headed for the door.

"Nice to meet you, Tommy," The Websters both said. Tommy turned and smiled. Mrs. Webster's beauty had nearly caused him to swallow his tongue. He sang the song to himself on his way back to Gooche's, careful to make sure that no one heard him mimicking Marilyn McCoo.

> Would you like to ride in my beautiful balloon
> Would you like to ride in my beautiful balloon
> We could float among the stars together, you and I
> For we can fly we can fly
> Up, up and away

The lyrics lingered in Tommy's mind the rest of the day.

DURING THEIR TOUR OF COLBY, people didn't stare as much as Penny had expected. Jupiter had spread the word, so no one was shocked when they saw a black couple driving around. Penny directed the Websters down every paved street; the tour took less than fifteen minutes. They passed through the courthouse square twice—the second time getting waves from the Codgers. The only houses that were for sale didn't interest the Websters. One had been occupied by smokers and would need a lot of work to get the odor out, and the other had a damp basement, which would have been a problem for Gloria's allergies.

Carter had been right about his wife's lack of enthusiasm for the available houses. Before meeting Gloria, Penny had decided it best that the Websters located in Fairview. But after meeting her and getting better acquainted with Carter, Penny decided they'd be an asset to Colby and that people would warm up to them.

The Kochs were expecting them. Penny parked the car in front of her office and they walked. She was explaining to them the history of the stone when Al and Tippy Tatum walked out of the post office together. Tippy was sorting through the mail, no doubt looking for a letter from Dwight, and almost bumped into Gloria.

She caught herself just in time. "Oh, I'm sorry," she said.

Gloria, who had dodged Tippy, smiled and replied, "No problem."

Tippy and Gloria made eye contact for an awkward length of time. Since Tippy was showing, she was used to people making double takes. But the eye lock she and Gloria experienced reached beyond her pregnancy. Penny noticed Tippy and Gloria's exchange, but Carter's observation of Al went unnoticed. Tippy and Gloria both had very striking features, with similar characteristics. The curl in Tippy's hair wasn't as tight as that of Gloria's, but the color and texture were similar. Gloria's complexion was a shade darker than Tippy's, but in a crowd the two could have been mistaken for mother and daughter, or possibly sisters.

Tippy smiled politely and continued on her way. Penny finished telling them the history of the stone, but Gloria was distracted. After Tippy had crossed the street, Gloria pointed discretely at her and asked Penny, "Is she from Colby?"

"Sort of," Penny replied. "That's her mother walking with her."

"Oh, okay." Gloria frowned slightly—she was visibly confused. "But ..." she said, and then she didn't finish. Al's overalls and engineer's hat would have confused anyone.

"Tippy and her mother moved here when Tippy was very small. I'm not sure that anyone has seen the father," Penny said. The question had now aroused Penny's curiosity regarding the identity and the heritage of Tippy's father.

Gloria paused in thought, and then whispered. "The daughter looked like she might be pregnant?"

Penny's face made a pained expression. "Afraid so."

Gloria winced. "She seems so young to be married."

"She's a senior in high school," Penny said and then tried to think of where to begin.

The door leading to the Koch's apartment creaked open—perfect timing. Penny wouldn't need to explain Tippy's complicated situation.

A diminutive, albeit confident Mrs. Koch stood there smiling. "You must be the Websters."

Gloria smiled and took Mrs. Koch's hand. She introduced herself. "I'm Gloria, and this is Carter."

Mrs. Koch shook both of their hands and bowed slightly with each shake. "Please come in, and please call me Marie."

The apartment had been cleaned. Tommy and Booger wouldn't have recognized it. The sheet covering Mr. Koch's chair was new. The double doors to the balcony were open.

Scout sniffed their ankles and made a few cursory licks of their shoes before being called back to the chair by Mr. Koch.

Mr. Koch began the arduous process of getting up out of his chair.

After finally getting stabilized on both feet, he introduced himself. His massive knuckles were evidence of the larger man he once was. He looked Gloria Webster directly in the eyes during their gentle handshake and bowed slightly just as Marie had, then he turned to Carter.

Tears welled up in Mr. Koch's eyes. "I certainly see the resemblance," he remarked.

"Washington says to say hello, Mr. Koch," Carter reverently replied.

Mr. Koch continued to shake Carter's hand. "I haven't spoken to him in years," he said, then slowly released Carter's hand. The two men looked deep into each other's eyes—a soldier's exchange of sorts. "And please call me George."

Marie kept the conversation moving. "The day turned out so nice that I had the table and chairs moved out onto the balcony," she said. After a few more pleasantries, they headed in that direction.

Marie helped George walk to the porch and get seated while Scout curled up under his chair.

She pointed toward the street. "There's the Rosolini van. Perfect timing."

"Rosolini?" Penny asked.

"Of course! I'm not much of a cook anymore. Can't smell, so it's almost impossible to cook anything … good, that is."

George smiled to himself.

Her loss of her sense of smell explained a few things.

Marie leaned over the balcony railing. "Come on up."

She sat back down and exhaled. "About two trips a day up and down those stairs is all I'm good for."

The entire courthouse square was in view from the balcony. The fall colors were peaking, and every tree was heavy with quaking leaves. An occasional gentle breeze continuously refreshed the air.

"Find a house?" George asked.

"We plan to keep looking," Gloria politely replied.

She sank back into her chair and took a deep breath. She gestured with both hands toward the apartment and said, "This place is incredible." She looked at Penny. "Are there any more places like this in Colby?"

George chuckled. "This is the only one. But I'm not sure how much longer we're going to be able to stay here. Scout and I can hardly make it up and down the stairs." Scout perked up momentarily when he heard his name. George reached down again and scratched his head.

"Where would you move?" Gloria asked.

"Russell Gooche recently finished building a duplex. Everything is ground level and we'd even have a yard," George answered.

"Not that we'd know what to do with a yard," Marie added.

George grinned. "Scout would."

"We saw the duplex," Gloria said. "Aren't they for senior citizens?"

"That's right," George replied. "Russell got some government subsidy to build them. He can only rent them to old coots like Marie and me." He looked at Marie and winked.

Angelina Rosolini peeked in. "Hello." Nearly as wide as she was tall, she burst in carrying lunch. It's doubtful she'd be described as thin, but it's almost impossible to describe someone with Angelina's stamina as being fat. Her body was made up of ample proportions in all areas, but she moved around with the energy of a cheerleader.

Penny half-trotted to the door, and Carter followed. Gloria and the Kochs kept their seat. It was clear to Penny why Carter was good at management—he had a knack for pitching in and making people feel at ease. After a quick introduction, the three of them started the final preparations.

Gloria turned from the view of the courthouse square and surveyed the apartment. "What will happen to this place when you move?" she asked.

"Probably just collect dust," Marie replied. Her eyes drooped and her chin quivered when she spoke.

Gloria, sensitive to the moment, paused before going on. She touched one cheek with an index finger as if to be deep in thought. "If it had a second bedroom, I'd insist that you rent it to us while our house is being built." Before Marie could respond, Gloria continued. "Shoot, if it had more room I'd just as soon live here as in a house. It's so charming."

Marie looked pleasantly surprised. "We'd never considered anyone else wanting to live here," she replied, her eyes once again reflected a gleeful glint. "All we hear from others is how we need to move to ground level."

"I love it. Too bad there's not another bedroom," Gloria said dismissively. Marie was about to respond when Angelina Rosolini stepped onto the porch with a pan of steaming lasagna. She placed it in the center of the table.

"Hi, I'm Angelina." She gave Gloria a double-handed shake.

"And I'm Gloria."

"Marie basically ordered me to stay here on the porch, or I would have helped you serve," Gloria said.

Angelina looked back and forth between Marie and Gloria. "Looks like you've already learned who's the boss around here." Carter, a dishtowel draped over his forearm, started around the table with bowls of salad.

"Sit down," Marie ordered. "You're the guest."

Carter took a seat. "I always do as I'm told," he said.

"Especially by your elders," George said, which earned him a kick from Marie.

Penny set a basket of bread next to the lasagna and took a seat.

Angelina Rosolini stood next to the table with her fists resting on her ample hips. "Unless you need something more, I'll head back to the restaurant. Tony's alone and the lunch crowd is probably already there."

Marie tapped her on the forearm and smiled. "You're such a dear."

Angelina gave Marie a wink. "I'll let myself out."

Carter breathed deep and closed his eyes. "Everything smells delicious."

George cleared his throat—his signal that he was going to say the blessing. Marie extended her hands each way. The Websters picked up on the tradition and did the same. They all held hands while George prayed.

Immediately following the blessing, George and Marie tapped their tea glasses together. "To one more day," George said.

Marie smiled and returned the toast. "To one more day."

Curious, Gloria asked. "To one more day?"

Marie put her hand on George's. "Yes, to one more day of being happily married," she said.

With that, Carter raised his glass and looked at Gloria. "To one more day," he said.

"To one more day," she replied then turned to Marie. "That's an interesting toast."

A few minutes into the meal, George looked at Gloria, then at Carter, and asked. "Who's your favorite American hero—dead or alive?" It was his favorite dinner game. "Here's the deal," he continued. "You're allowed to change your mind. Who's the first person that comes to mind?" The question initiated a lively exchange that continued until the First Baptist Church bells played the first stanza to "Für Elise," then gonged twelve times.

The chiming bells interrupted their discussion. Gloria smiled. "That's a beautiful sound," she said.

"They were a gift from Jupiter Storm," George added.

"Isn't he the man who was at the Houn-Dawg this morning?" Gloria asked.

"He's into everybody's business," Marie added. "But he means well."

George looked at Carter. "He's a decorated WWII veteran." Carter met George's eye. "Europe," George added. "Sniper."

There was a lull in the conversation while everyone considered George's comment. During lunch, the two couples, separated by a generation, discovered that they had a great deal in common. They never got back to the favorite American hero discussion.

Marie began clearing the table. Gloria stood. "Let me help you."

"I'll just let you," Marie said. "Once we clear the table, I'll put a batch of cookies in the oven, and while they're cooking I'll show you the rest of the apartment."

Marie slipped the pan of cookies into the oven, and then motioned for Gloria to follow her. What had appeared at first to be a paneled wall turned out to be pocket library doors. Marie removed a painting on one door and slid it open. It creaked from lack of use. "Nothing a little 3-in-1 oil won't cure," she said.

Marie flipped a switch, turning on a dusty crystal chandelier hanging above a covered dining room table and chairs. She removed the sheet, revealing a large, antique dining room table and pressed back chairs.

Gloria ran her finger along the table's fine finish. "It's beautiful," she whispered.

Marie explained the rich history of the dining room set. "The table, hutch, and chairs were made from the wood of a giant oak. It stood on the courthouse lawn until it had to be taken down after being struck by lightning.

"The tree was over a hundred years old," continued Marie. "And fifty inches wide at the base. Several things were made from its wood and sold at a benefit auction."

"What a splendid idea," Gloria said.

"Oh yes," Marie said. "The money raised at the auction was used to build the shoe factory building. Brown Shoe had agreed to put a factory here if the town would provide a building."

"They wanted a free building?" Gloria asked.

"Just for three years," Marie said. "They eventually bought the building."

"Did the town get back all of its money?" Gloria asked.

"And more," Marie replied. "The timing of the lightning strike was providential."

"That's a great story," Gloria said.

"There's more," Marie said. "When Brown Shoe bought the building, the city used that money to pave several streets and build a water treatment plant."

"It sounds like Brown Shoe and the citizens of Colby had a very good relationship," Gloria said.

"Very much so," Marie confirmed.

Marie continued removing covers and eventually revealed a room full of beautiful furniture. Gloria followed her through each room, remarking on the beauty of each piece. One bedroom had a mahogany canopy bed and matching dresser. The other had a pair of twin beds made from walnut.

Over cookies, Marie and Gloria told their husbands of the plan. Penny wasn't as enthusiastic about the Websters moving into the apartment. It wasn't that she'd lose a chance to make a sale; she was concerned about how the move would be received by Colby.

Penny reminded the Websters that Russell Gooche had planned to introduce them to a few chamber members. There were hugs all around before they headed down the stairs.

As PRESIDENT OF THE CHAMBER of Commerce, Russell Gooche had the responsibility to introduce the Websters to the Colby business community. Like most in Colby, he'd known of the Webster's plans to have lunch with the Kochs and had decided to make the introductions after that. His responsibilities as president were primarily to schedule, start, and end meetings, and he was anxious about making the introductions.

Penny introduced the Websters to Russell Gooche and then walked back to her office. She'd had such a pleasant morning that she caught herself breaking into a skip and self-consciously looked around to see if anyone had noticed. She replayed Gloria Webster saying "the apartment was perfect" and smiled. But she was worried about what people would think about the Websters moving into the Koch loft.

RUSSELL BEGAN THE INTRODUCTORY TOUR with a walk around the square at the courthouse. Judge Grant was standing in the hallway—he'd been watching and waiting, but he acted like they'd coincidentally caught him out of his chambers. "Yes, yes," he said. "Nice to meet you, yes, fine, nice to meet you." He shook Carter's hand and gave Gloria a hug, then held the embrace a little longer than was considered appropriate. To Russell's relief, the rest of the courthouse heard the commotion and came out of their offices and introduced themselves.

Mr. Bailey, the recorder of deeds, was the first to speak up. That was unusual for him, for he was normally a crotchety introvert. "Let me show you what we do." Mrs. Burk, the circuit clerk, rolled her eyes. She knew that had Gloria not been so attractive, Mr. Bailey wouldn't have given her the time of day.

Everyone was competing for the Websters' attention when Judge Grant spoke above them all. "Yes, yes, well, well," he said. "Once you see how the records are kept, come to my chambers and I'll show you where people are sentenced to hang." The judge's remarks were meant to make his duties sound the most important. But the fact of the matter was, the judge was famous for his lenient sentences. Rumor had it that years ago, as a young prosecutor in Kansas City, he'd helped get a man sentenced to death. Evidence proving the man's innocence surfaced after the execution. Since then, he rarely issued a sentence more severe than five dollars and cost.

The Websters listened patiently while each county officer explained their jobs. Neither was familiar with county government. The attention they were getting from the county officers was unheard of in places like Chicago. Their genuine curiosity was getting them off to a good start in Colby.

"There's much more to what goes on in the courthouse than initially meets the eye," Carter offered. They finished their visit and continued around the square.

At Rosolini's they met Angelina's counterpart, Tony. Tony was powerfully built and looked so much like Angelina that they could have been brother and sister. He, too, had the gift of gab. He and Angelina oftentimes spoke at the same time and competed with each other for Carter and Gloria's attention.

"Listen to me," Tony's baritone voice boomed. He gently touched both

Websters on their forearms. "It's my turn to talk." He wanted to show them his brick oven.

Carter breathed in the aroma of the baking bread, closed his eyes momentarily, and then said, "Gloria tells me it's hard to cook for two. With a place like this, there's no need to cook." The Rosolinis smiled and returned a low bow.

"I understand you're responsible for bringing the bowling alley to town." Carter said.

Tony's eyes lit up. "That's right. You bowl?"

"We used to, years ago," Carter said.

Tony looked perplexed. "Why'd you stop?"

Carter shrugged. "A son, school, career." Carter and Gloria exchanged glances. "This might be the perfect time to pick it up again," he said.

The walls at Rosolini's were covered with photos and posters. Each poster featured an exotic Italian destination and was enthusiastically explained by both Tony and Angelina. Sometimes they spoke separately, but mostly the explanations occurred simultaneously. The photos were a mixture of current family photos taken both in Italy and America. Gloria and Carter balanced their attention between Tony and Angelina. Once finished with the poster tour of Italy, Angelina grabbed a couple of menus from the counter and handed them to the Websters.

"Oh look," Gloria said. "The menus are titled 'Ini Stuff.' That's cute."

Angelina explained. "Well, when we first opened, everyone kept talking about how all the dishes end with ini. So I figured why not just go with the flow." Gloria started to put the menu back, but Angelina protested. "No, you take," she said. "That way you make up your mind before you get here."

Gloria smiled. "Grazie," she said. Angelina's smile stretched the corners of her mouth from one oversized earring to the other.

At the *Colby Telegraph*, Newt Thorpe showed them the Linotype machine and how the type was set using tiny blocks of lead. Carter was impressed with the giant rolls of paper that fed into the offset machine. Newt didn't have time to visit, but he apologized for his brevity. "We're in a dead run until the press starts to roll."

On the way back toward Gooche's, Carter noticed a group of men gathered at Burt's. He asked Russell to introduce him. Russell had hoped to avoid the Codgers, but Carter had seen them standing in the wheel alignment bay looking at Burt's Chevelle.

The Codgers had noticed Russell and the Websters making the rounds, but they didn't expect to be included in the tour. Probably driven by Gloria's striking good looks, shirt tails began to get stuffed into waistlines artificially reduced by the holding of one's breath.

Russell introduced each by their given name: Solomon, Montgomery, Simon, and Benjamin. Hearing their real names as opposed to their nicknames, Fish, Monkey, Rabbit, and Bem were caught somewhat off guard. Each hesitated momentarily when he was introduced, as if he didn't know his own name. Russell made a stab at explaining their nicknames, and then finally stated that it was a small-town thing. The Websters were entertained. And the Codgers, ogling Gloria, weren't paying attention anyway and couldn't have cared less. Gloria's striking beauty conflicted with their prejudiced notions.

Al was in the other bay working on a car. She'd replaced the points and plugs and was pointing a timing light at the fan-belt pulley. Because the engine was running, she hadn't heard the exchange with the Codgers. After twisting around on the distributor cap several times, she seemed to be satisfied with the strobe light results, shut off the engine, and slammed the hood shut.

Gloria left the group of men and introduced herself to Al. The conversation among the Codgers slowly trailed to silence while they watched the exchange.

Al was still wiping her hands with a shop towel when Gloria extended hers. "Gloria Webster," she said. "That's my husband there with Mr. Gooche."

Al grinned, pulled the bill of her engineer's hat down, and partially shielded her face by rubbing her eyebrows with her forearm. "Yeah, the two of you kind of stand out around here." Al's remark eased the tension; they both laughed.

Gloria continued. "We're just making the rounds and introducing ourselves. I'm happy to meet you, and now I know where we can bring our cars when they need repairs."

"It's very nice to meet you too, I'm Alison Tatum," Al replied, avoiding direct contact with Gloria. Al, surprised, realized she'd introduced herself as Alison rather than Al. Cutting their conversation short, she continued with, "I'm sorry but I'm the only one here and need to wait on that customer." With that, she trotted to the fuel pumps toward a car that had just run across the bell hose, and thus she avoided Carter altogether.

On their way back to Gooche's, Gloria noticed Carter deep in thought. "Is there a problem?" she whispered. She stopped and pretended to dig for something in her purse, allowing them some distance from Russell Gooche.

"I'm not sure," he struggled to say. "I just have this sense that I've met that Al Tatum before."

Gloria chuckled. "I know what you mean, but it's highly unlikely. She dresses so oddly that I think you'd remember her."

"You're probably right."

"I spoke to her. Regardless of how she looks, she seems pretty normal."

Russell was waiting for them at the stone. He thought it clever to finish their introduction to Colby with the obligatory history lesson of the stone.

LATER THAT AFTERNOON, TOMMY AND Booger were delivering papers to the courthouse. Jupiter was telling the Codgers what he knew about the Webster's visit, which wasn't any more than anyone else knew. "She's a looker," he said. And having seen her, they all enthusiastically agreed.

"Where you suppose he got her at?" Fish asked.

"Pro'bly Chicago—he went to college there," Rabbit offered.

"He's from Mississippi, don'cha know," Bem said.

"I'm just sayin'—she don't have no accent," Rabbit replied.

Tommy and Booger had almost made it to the courthouse door before Jupiter positioned himself between Tommy and the door. Looking down at Tommy, he asked, "What kind of secret meeting were they havin' at the Houn-Dawg?"

"They were just havin' coffee," Tommy replied. Jupiter kept repositioning himself between Tommy and the door.

Jupiter asked, "Why'd they let you in and not me?"

"I had a delivery from Gooche's," Tommy replied.

"Why weren't you in school?" Jupiter asked.

"Teacher's meeting," Tommy replied.

Booger opened the door and held it open for Tommy. Tommy faked one way, then darted the other around Jupiter and into the courthouse before Jupiter could fire off another barrage of questions.

THE INTERNATIONAL HAT SPY WAS more discreet during his second visit to Colby. He borrowed a pick-up from a friend and wore the clothes he used when his wife made him do yard work. While the Websters had lunch at the Kochs, he dined in at the Houn-Dawg. He fielded a few stares while sitting alone at the counter and pretended to browse a regional farm equipment classified ad newspaper while listening to the table conversations. He left town without having a single conversation, except to order his cheeseburger. Upon reaching Fairview, he called from the same phone booth he'd used the previous visit.

"Nothin' unusual," he reported. "They seem to be more interested in Friday night's football game." The president asked if he'd heard any talk of the Websters. "One kid mentioned that Mrs. Webster looked like the lead singer in the Fifth Dimension. And another had to have the Fifth Dimension explained to him."

"I see," the president said.

"So far, I don't anticipate a problem," the caller reported.

"The next step will be when they choose a neighborhood and a house," the president said. "That will be the real test." The tone of his voice implied hope for a problem.

"There aren't many choices," the spy replied. "There just doesn't seem to be many people moving in or out," he said. "It's difficult to explain—that town seems to be frozen in time." He paused a moment. "It's like being on the set of one of those sappy TV shows." He continued to describe Colby.

The president of the hat company cut him off. "I get the picture—it's a regular Mayberry RFD or something."

"Yeah, exactly."

"Sounds like you've spent enough time there. Better head back before you're tempted to buy a pair of bib tuck overalls and start eating Moon Pies."

The caller chuckled to himself after getting back into his car and enjoying a recent purchase, a Moon Pie.

The board president had a chuckle too. He thought about his Mayberry RFD comment and grinned after concluding that there were no blacks in Mayberry.

Gossip Queens

MISS ANDERSON CALLED TOMMY to her desk. The lyrics to "Up, Up And Away" had popped into his head while Miss Anderson was lecturing on the history of Thanksgiving; he was afraid she'd noticed him daydreaming. Instead, she asked him to go to the office and get some colored paper for art class.

Mrs. Cain was sorting the mail when Tommy walked into the school office. "I'll have to get it from the supply closet," she said as if it was going to be a lot of trouble. While she was gone, Tommy scanned the items on her desk. He noticed a letter addressed to the school board with Mable Sappington as the return address.

He heard Mrs. Cain coming down the hall and stopped snooping. "Here you go," she said, handing him the ream of paper. Tommy returned to class thinking about the consequence of the letter, the song lyrics completely forgotten.

Lucille Cain resumed mail sorting and, like Tommy, wondered about the letter. She'd been eyeing it, moved it to the top of the pile, and fought off the urge to open it. Noting the return address, she was certain of its contents.

Mable had written the letter confidentially, but Lucille and every other customer or friend of a customer at Colby Curls already knew precisely what it contained. The tell-a-woman communication network went something like this: manicure lady hears it from Mable Sappington, she shares the morsel with Chubby Cheeks during a pedicure, Chubby Cheeks in turn shares it with the mustached lady while her head is tilted back, almost upside down, getting a shampoo. It was an excellent kick-off for a juicy rumor.

Lucille had been the school secretary since the death of her husband nearly twenty years earlier. They'd originally moved to Colby as part of the shoe factory management team. She'd been trained as an executive assistant, and she was known to be stoic and professional. After her husband died, her aloofness and lack of people skills eventually led to her dismissal. Management's official position was that her husband's benefit package provided for her, and they were therefore doing her a favor by dismissing her. With no kids to care for, no garden, and no hobbies, she needed something to do; the school board, made up of her husband's former friends, had sympathetically hired her.

To the board's surprise, her office experience and ornery disposition had combined to be a perfect fit for the school's head office. She'd single-handedly increased the efficiency of the office and helped the superintendent negotiate savings in a variety of areas, such as insurance, office supplies, and other services. Her unique personality also turned out to be an asset in working with manipulative, uncooperative students and their contrary parents.

The content of the letter and the pregnancy issue it raised weren't the only reasons for the rapid spread of the rumor. People used the letter as an excuse to discuss the Tatums in general and maliciously speculate on the identity of Tippy's father, as well as the father of her own baby.

An interesting phenomenon occurs in a small town: people rush to defend each other from outsiders, but they can be cruel and vicious to each other. It's also known as the bear pack mentality—defend the pack against outsiders, but occasionally eat one of your own.

BEN FRANKLIN, THE NEW COLBY High School principal, had been expecting the letter. Because of his position, his wife was seldom included in the first wave of gossip calls. But this piece of gossip was so juicy and had so much potential that it made it well past the first wave. Some women called as many as five others, ostensibly out of concern, but in reality spreading the gossip like wildfire. It was late that first evening when Mrs. Franklin eventually got a call. New in town, she wasn't on the top of anyone's list. She shared the news with her husband while watching an episode of *Rat Patrol*.

The next morning, Ben held the envelope to the light, tapped his thigh with it, tossed it on his desk, and looked at a photo of him with members of his Navy SEAL team. A week earlier, he'd spoken to Danny Douglas, who after leaving the SEALs had joined the U.S. Marshal's office. Ben was given a piece of highly confidential information. He treated the information as such and repeated it to no one, not even his wife. As part of his top secret clearance, he'd been trained to compartmentalize information that was to be known but not shared. The information had to do with the Tatums. He realized that a teenage pregnancy was serious, but he assumed the town had dealt with it before. But he was sure that Colby had never dealt with what they were soon to learn about the Tatums.

Ben called Lucille into his office. She strutted in wearing a dress of particularly thick material; it looked to be bulletproof. It was one of those magic dresses that help ladies look thin in areas in which they're too thick while augmenting deficient areas. The darts were double stitched, apparently in an effort to make something out of nothing. Worst of all, the hem line was a couple of inches above her aged knees. "What do you know about this letter?" he asked.

"Just who it's from," she replied. "I didn't open it." Ben tilted his head slightly, looked away, then squinted one eye and looked back at her. "People are talking," she confessed after an uncomfortable pause.

"Close the door," he told her. "Sit down." Ben knew he was making her nervous, but he didn't care. In fact, he relished the notion that he could intimidate the woman that everyone else in the school system tiptoed around and dared not cross. She sat and crossed her legs, showing more thigh than Ben cared to see.

All of Colby, including Lucille, had no idea who they were dealing with in either Ben Franklin or Al Tatum. Colby was soon to learn more about Al Tatum, but Ben would forever keep much of his past to himself. But that didn't keep him from intimidating people when it served his purpose. The high school boys had told rumors of how he slipped through the jungles of Southeast Asia, hunting down enemy officers and slitting their throats. He made no effort to stop the rumors, which for the most part weren't true. They worked to his advantage. His training had been rigorous, both physically and mentally, but the fact was he'd never encountered a single instance of hand-to-hand combat. Since his arrival, disciplinary problems at the school had significantly decreased. Smoking in the restrooms had ceased. He knew the boys' imaginations had gone wild.

Ben had attended college on a football scholarship, earned a teaching degree, and intended to be a football coach. Knowing that coaching didn't pay that well, he'd earned his administrative credentials along the way. During his second year of teaching, his first wife had been killed in a car accident and his therapist advised him to change his routine as a way to cope with his loss. Taking the advice to the extreme, he joined the Navy.

He'd served most of his time in the SEALs program training sea lions to attack enemy divers. It wasn't much different than training guard dogs, except in this case the sea lions would kill and sometimes devour their target rather than mangle a wrist or forearm. The biggest difference between a dog and a sea lion was that the sea lions could not discern friendlies from the enemy, so the training had to be done very carefully.

Ben hadn't given much thought to his SEAL days until Danny had called the evening before. Danny had waited until returning to Chicago to let Ben know he'd been to Colby. Since the call, the memories had flooded Ben's mind. Danny had trained dolphins to attach charges to bridge works. He had been given the nickname Flipper.

Ben's nickname had been Lion. Once the program was terminated, he was known by his team members as Kitten—another part of his past that he kept to himself.

At the U.S. Marshal's witness protection unit, Flipper had been assigned to Vincent Gambaiana, who planned to retire within the year. Since being briefed on the Tatum file, Danny had quickly connected the town to Ben. Flipper had told Ben about the Tatums and said there was a local contact, but nothing more.

Ben pushed that to the back of his mind and gave Lucille a look intended to intimidate. "Why did you put the letter in my inbox?" he asked her. "It's addressed to the school board."

"I knew it would eventually make its way back to you, so I—"

Ben interrupted her. "But you don't know what's in the letter?"

Lucille wasn't as intimidated as Ben first thought, and she didn't mince words. She was nonplussed by his reputation. Her late husband had been an Army Ranger in WWII—the real war, she'd oft said.

"Don't be a jackass," she said. "I have other things to do if you don't need anything."

It was a defining moment in the relationship between the two. Just like him, she had a reputation that most likely exceeded reality. He considered her remark, but rather than being angered he was amused. Besides, he'd been called much worse. He grinned, and then asked, "What's the school policy on pregnant students?"

"There's no published policy," she said. "We haven't needed one. The few girls that have gotten pregnant have dropped out before they began to show."

"Do you think she knows who the father is?" Ben asked.

She nodded affirmatively. "Yes, except for the gossip queens, most don't think there's any question. She's not a tramp."

"The school board will look to me for a suggestion on how to handle this." He was clearly looking for her advice, but he didn't think it appropriate to ask.

Lucille nodded. She thought she'd sized up Ben, but she wasn't sure she could read him. "What are you thinking?" she asked.

"I don't have any experience in this area," he said.

Lucille didn't respond immediately. "Have you met Tippy's mother?" she finally asked.

Ben thought the question curious.

"I know who she is," he replied.

"She's a little different, you know," Lucille warned him.

Ben thought back on the conversation he'd had with Flipper and replied, "I'm familiar with her background."

"You're the only one then," Lucille retorted. Ben thought maybe he'd said too much. Lucille was most likely referring to Al's persona. The two sat there in stressed silence.

After a few moments of thought, he made his decision. "Get in touch with Al Tatum and see if there's a time that I can meet with her."

Lucille made a note and replied. "She works at the filling station. Would you want to meet with her after hours?" After hours would mean Lucille would have to stick around. School policy prohibited the principal meeting with single women without a witness.

"Whatever works best for her," he said, then paused in thought. "I'd prefer to meet at her home." This elicited a frown from Lucille. "Strange," he said. "I haven't opened this letter, but both of us know what's in it." He grinned, somewhat disgusted. "Small town."

Lucille's frown deepened. "I'm not sure I follow you."

"Isn't there something in this letter about the condition of the Tatum home, as well as the pregnancy?" he asked.

She shook her head. "Maybe you should stop playing games, open the letter, and read it."

Ben grinned. "The moment I open this letter, the information becomes confidential, and I can no longer discuss it with you or anyone else except the superintendent and the school board."

Lucille stomped out of his office in a huff. Ben waited until he got home to call Flipper.

"Go," answered the voice on the other end. Flipper didn't mince words. Ben began to explain the situation, but Flipper cut him short and assured him that his office was on top of it. Flipper said that he couldn't give him any further details, but he urged Ben to convince the school board to delay any decision for at least a month and that all of their concerns should be alleviated with forthcoming information.

Ben had always found dealing with partial information difficult, but he had complete confidence in Flipper. He was determined to convince the school board to delay a decision regarding the Tatums. He wished Flipper could have been more specific.

Out of spite, he left the unopened envelope on his desk the rest of the week. The board's next meeting wasn't scheduled for two weeks. It wasn't that he didn't want to deal with the issue, but he was curious as to how fast word would circulate. He wanted the rumors to circulate before opening the letter so he couldn't be held responsible. More specifically, he knew that the unopened envelope would drive Lucille batty. Ben enjoyed bringing Lucille out of her stoic cover. Anyway, Tippy Tatum wasn't going to get unpregnant, so the longer he waited, the more likely another distracting development would emerge.

By Friday afternoon, Lucille had chewed her fingernails to the quick; one fingertip was covered with a Band-Aid. Like all good rumors, the receipt of the letter had been repeated "confidentially" to every breathing soul in Colby. Members of the school board were beginning to receive calls. And some of the board members had phoned Ben, who acknowledged the existence of the *unopened* envelope.

The Webster's decision to move into the Koch's loft was received with mixed emotions. Those with homes for sale on their street were relieved they wouldn't be getting a black family for neighbors. Others were appalled that the Kochs were allowing a new family, let alone a black one, to take up residence in their perch.

Frank Fritz had gotten a letter, too. He pulled the envelope from his roadside mailbox. After seeing that the return address was Mississippi, he looked around to see if anybody was watching.

Starting Over

ALISON'S GRANDPARENTS ON BOTH SIDES had immigrated to America from Italy. They'd joined other family members in Montclare, an Italian community on the north side of Chicago. Alison's father owned a corner filling station. Instead of playing with dolls, Alison preferred to tinker with cars. When she wasn't attending Our Lady of the Angels school, or Assumption Catholic Church, she was watching her father work on cars. It was during confirmation classes that a young man with exotic looks caught her fancy.

Reginald Tyson's father was a full blood Seminole Indian and his mother had emigrated from Cuba. His parents, looking for work, had migrated from Miami to the Chicago garment district. He'd noticed Alison first at the filling station and then at Church. Their union, while not culturally acceptable, was inevitable.

The world was at war. Reginald enlisted in the army on his eighteenth birthday. He and Alison were deeply in love, and they announced their engagement. Alison's mother had grown fond of Reginald, and she convinced her husband to bless the mixed-cultural union. The two were married at a small ceremony, attended only by family. While the Giordano family didn't consider the marriage a disgrace, they didn't consider it a cause for celebration. They wanted to be proud of both Alison and Reginald, but they struggled with the notion that a cultural boundary had been crossed.

During the war, women's bowling leagues became popular throughout the country. In most cases, the league rosters were made up of wives of men serving in the armed forces. Most of the women didn't take the competition seriously and considered the weekly conclave more of a social event.

Alison was naturally athletic. Working at the filling station had strengthened her arms well beyond what was considered normal for a lady. Her physical strength and competitive spirit combined to make her a champion bowler. By war's end, she'd reached near-celebrity status among women bowlers in the Chicago area. She'd recorded multiple perfect games before Reginald's return, at which time the bowling ball and shoes were stored away.

Like all the other war veterans returning from war and anxious to catch up on the years lost serving their country, Reginald went to work as soon as he could find a job. He began working in construction. He enjoyed the physical demands of the job and the gratification of seeing the finished building projects. His broad shoulders and distinctive Seminole features easily set him apart from the Italians with whom he worked. More interested in functionality than fashion, he'd begun wearing bib overalls. After first making considerable fun of him, many of his workmates soon followed suit. They'd noticed the handy pockets. But they never wore the engineer style hat that became one of Reginald's trademarks.

ONE ELEMENT OF ORGANIZED CRIME in North Chicago at that time was job procurement. Those looking for work were forced to pay an extortion fee in order find and then keep their job. Likewise, employers would be forced to hire Italian-Americans and also pay extortion fees in order to keep their work sites from being vandalized.

Reginald's military training and his stout demeanor made him a prime candidate as an enforcer. Once approached by a member of organized crime, the option was to join them or instantly become their enemy. Sadly, Reginald was approached. There was no middle ground. Since Alison had recently learned they were expecting their first child, Reginald agreed to provide muscle for the local crime family. He didn't want harm to come to Alison or their unborn baby. They discussed their options. The two of them began looking forward to the day they'd leave Chicago and the Mob.

Each evening after dinner, Reginald and Allison sat on their front porch and discussed their day. It was difficult for Reginald to tell Alison about his day and what he'd learned about her relatives and the lengths to which they'd gone to extort money from business owners. He was likewise surprised to hear what Alison had learned from the other wives. Apparently, the wives knew more than the husbands realized. The more they learned, the more they longed to move. They didn't want to raise a child in a crime family environment.

The FBI had done their homework. They recognized Reginald for his true character and recruited him. He and Alison agreed to cooperate. It was their only ticket out. While at the church, Alison masked her knowledge well and went about her daily routine as if ignorant of the truth, as did all the other women. One peaceful afternoon while she was waiting on the porch for Reginald to come home, a mysterious fear suddenly gripped her. She passed it off as a kick by her unborn baby. Reginald didn't come home that day, or the next. Her worst fear had been realized.

One week, two weeks, and finally a month went by without a word from Reginald. Alison became an emotional wreck. Each day without Reginald sent her further into depression. She felt like there was no one she could trust, including her parents. She sat home alone, too fearful to contact the police. She wasn't supposed to know of his "other" job.

It was painful for Alison to look into the eyes of uncles she'd learned were capable of sadistic acts. She suspected them of Reginald's disappearance.

Jokes about the runaway Indian began to circulate.

A month and a day after Reginald had gone missing Alison gave birth to a baby girl, whom she named Tippy. She'd liked the name since reading the slogan "Tippecanoe and Tyler too" while studying American history. Tippy's nose and mouth resembled Reginald's. Seeing the resemblance eventually drove Alison to get revenge for Reginald's disappearance. She called the number on the card.

An FBI agent disguised as a priest, known to Alison as Father Phillip, began to meet with her at a local park. Locals suspected nothing when they'd see her sitting on a park bench talking to a priest. After all, she was obviously in need of special counseling. Over the course of five weeks, she provided the FBI all the leads and evidence they needed to charge two of Chicago's most notorious mobsters. However, the FBI's case depended largely on her testimony. That dangerous situation would necessitate that she enter the Witness Protection Program.

In an effort to help with her grieving, the family hosted a large baby shower for Alison. All the family attended the shower, bringing gifts and food. The celebration of Tippy's birth soon turned into a memorial service for Reginald. Congratulations were followed by disingenuous condolences regarding Reginald. Alison knew who the guilty among the family were, making it easy to detect who was truly grieving and who was happy to finally be rid of the Cuban-Indian.

Father Phillip contacted Alison a few days after the party and convinced her that it was time. She'd already begun to feel like an alien in a foreign land, and she trusted no one. She agreed to an immediate extraction. Her parents were the only ones she'd regret leaving behind.

Without Reginald, the house was no longer a home. Tears flooded her eyes when she recalled the hours and days she and Reginald had spent making endless repairs to their modest home. Now she was going away, to where she didn't know. She clenched her teeth in anger, thinking of bringing to justice those responsible for the death of her daughter's father. Tears streamed down her face. It was the first time she'd allowed herself to think of Reginald as being dead. She broke down. It was impossible to contain the sobs and keep the neighbors and passersby from seeing and hearing her pain. All of the pent-up grief poured forth in a flood of tears. The tears were mentally cleansing. She found strength through prayer. It was a turning point. She steeled herself to build a new life for Tippy. It's what Reginald would have wanted.

SHE'D EXPECTED FATHER PHILLIP to pull up in a government sedan, but instead he came strolling, half skipping, down the sidewalk. When he got nearer, Alison could hear him whistling "Take Me Out to the Ballgame." It reminded her of the movie by the same name starring Gene Kelly. The thought struck her how the Mob in the movie had dealt with Gene Kelly's character. She was processing all this when Father Phillip reached her house and did a little two-step at the front stoop.

While appearing light-hearted to the neighbors, his voice was sobering. "Our car is two blocks away." He pointed at a passing patrol car. "That car is our signal. We have five minutes to get all of your things moved to just inside the front door. When our car pulls up, we'll hear a siren. The siren will be blaring from two blocks away, it's a distraction. An agency car with heavily armed FBI agents will be standing by a half block away in case we run into problems."

The words "heavily armed" reverberated in Alison's mind. She felt the full weight of the Mob on her already slumping shoulders. Anyone watching would have guessed all was well at the Tyson home. In fact, some may have suspected the priest to be flirting with Alison, rather than giving her specific extraction instructions.

The quick string of instructions snapped Alison out of her moment of sorrow; she focused. "I'm ready," she said. She caught herself squeezing Tippy a little too hard and relaxed her embrace.

He put his right foot on the first step, adjusted his ankle holster, and said, "From now on it's just Phillip."

At that, Alison became concerned. "Who will take me to my new home?"

"Don't worry. I'll be with you for the entire trip. I'll fill you in once we're clear of the city and sure we're not being followed."

Alison could hear the patrol car's siren from a distance. Phillip glanced up and down the street, his eyes stopping momentarily at each house, looking for anything out of the ordinary. He saw nothing.

A dark sedan approached Alison's house. Two patrol cars, sirens blasting, went racing through the intersection a half block north. Neighbors working in their yards or sitting on their front porch looked toward the patrol cars and several headed that way. Phillip, satisfied with the diversion, stepped inside the house, scooped up Alison's belongings, and walked quickly to the curb. He helped Alison and Tippy into the back seat, and they were on their way.

The driver constantly scanned left and right while Phillip, half-turned, watched for cars that might be following. Alison thought of her family, and particularly her father, each time they passed a service station. Her emotions hurtled from tearful sentiment for her parents to raging anger against the others.

She felt as though Phillip could read her mind—there were moments when she thought of him as a real priest. Their eyes met. "Just remember, it's about the safety of the baby and you." The look on Alison's face was one of uncertainty. "You'll begin to feel as if you're safe. And then you'll begin to think that the others will forgive you for what you've done." He paused a few moments as he continued his visual sweep. "But that never happens. And in the minds of most of the community, your baby is a half-breed." Alison braced at his words. "If something were to happen to you, she'd be turned over for adoption and probably end up in an orphanage."

Alison was so upset that simple breathing became laborious. She closed her eyes and asked, "What do you know about where I'm being taken?"

Phillip glanced at the driver. "We'll have plenty of time to discuss that later, or even tomorrow."

Exhausted, she fell asleep. When she awoke, picket fenced neighborhoods had been replaced by corn fields. The sun was directly ahead, she knew they were headed west, possibly to Iowa.

They were pulling into a roadside park when she awoke. Phillip explained that they were going to change cars, and it was vital that the driver not know the description of their next car. The driver helped them unload everything then drove away. The length to which the agency was going in order to keep her location secret began to unnerve her.

A 1946 Chevy Fleetmaster pulled up a few minutes later. Phillip and the driver of the new car loaded Alison's belongings into the spacious trunk of the luxurious car, and they were on their way. Alison made a soft mat for Tippy on the floor, and then she stretched out on the long back seat.

When she awoke, the rising sun was to her left, so Alison knew they were headed south. "When do I find out where I'm going?" she asked.

"Colby, Missouri," Phillip told her. Alison shifted slightly and turned questioningly toward Phillip. "It's a small town in southern Missouri," he explained.

Phillip explained to Alison in detail how the program would work. All of her expenses would be covered, but she'd need to integrate into the community and avoid any discussion about her past.

"You'd mentioned that the agency would have a contact in the community," she reminded him.

"Yes, we have a contact, but unless there's an emergency you won't know who it is. Their primary role is to let us know what people are saying about you." Alison understood but remained anxious about living in a small town without knowing a single person.

"The house looks rough on the outside, but the inside is clean. A retired banker owns the house."

"What does he know about me?" Alison asked.

"He thinks you're being relocated by the welfare office." It was a necessary half-lie. In fact, the owner of the house knew precisely why Alison and her baby were moving to Colby.

"Will I meet him?"

"Yes, he and his wife will help you get settled and be available, but they won't ask any probing questions."

A few minutes later, she asked, "How soon do you think I should wait before I get a job?"

"Let's see how it goes," he replied. "It's a small town, and people will be asking questions. By keeping a low profile, you won't have to explain your past." Alison gave an understanding nod. "Give people a chance to get used to someone new in town," he continued. "Have you thought about a new name? This is your chance to give yourself the name you always wanted."

"No," she replied, "there have been too many other things to think about." She'd been told that going into the program would require a name change. But now that the moment was at hand, the thought brought on feelings of anxiety and guilt. She stared at Tippy. The realization that she had left everything behind, including her name, fully dawned on her. Then she looked at her baby and realized that everything of value to her was wrapped in a blanket and resting in her arms. She glanced at Phillip. "Any suggestions?"

"Yes," he replied. "We've done some research and think Tatum would be a good choice, Alison Tatum." The agent had done this before. He'd learned that it was best to provide a name, rather than ask the witness to conjure up something clever. But he always asked, just to make them part of the process. "Your initials will be the same, and there are no Tatums in the Colby area." They made eye contact through the rearview mirror. "It's always best to take a name that's unfamiliar. That way, people won't be asking you if you're related to so and so."

"One more thing," Phillip said. "My real name is Vince Gambaiana."

She flinched. "That's Italian," she said. He'd expected the response. Alison thought about it for a few moments, her mind in a state of flux. She'd trusted him with her life, and now it was too late to go back.

VINCE HAD PLANNED THEIR ARRIVAL to be after dark so as to draw less attention. A Sinclair filling station was the only establishment still open for business. It looked like a new building. A nice-looking man about Reginald's age was standing near a pump island, looking at the building as if to be admiring it. When Alison saw the two service bays, she made up her mind where she'd find work.

They pulled into the drive of a house with a large yard, almost a field, on the edge of town. The lights were on inside. Vince turned and smiled. "This is it—home sweet home." A late middle-aged couple and a young boy who looked to be about ten or so came out to meet them. The man opened the door for Alison, took her hand, and introduced himself. "Welcome to Colby. I'm George Koch, this is my wife, Marie, and this is our son Jackson. We call him Jack."

Mrs. Koch looked inside the car at Tippy, who was still bundled up on the floor and just beginning to wake. "And this must be Tippy." Alison held her for the Kochs to see. Jack wasn't too interested, but both Mr. and Mrs. Koch admired her and made the cutesy noises that adults make when fussing over a baby.

Vince carried Alison's belongings into the house, then motioned for them to go inside. "Why don't we go inside where we won't draw so much attention?"

George chuckled. "It's too late for that, Agent Gambaiana. I'm sure everyone in town knows that someone new is moving in.

"Just the same, let's move inside."

A shiver shot up Alison's spine when she saw the inside of the house. After getting a description from Agent Gambaiana, the Kochs had appointed the Colby house much like the home Alison had left behind. It wasn't exact, but the colors and wallpaper were eerily similar. She liked what she saw, but was unnerved that strangers knew so much about her. An easel and several blank canvases were sitting in the living room. The furniture was used, but better than what she'd had in Chicago.

Marie watched Alison's expression for a response. "So, you like it?" Marie asked. Alison began to weep, and Marie gave her a motherly embrace.

Agent Gambaiana let them have their moment, then he said, "There's one more thing I need to show you, and it's best I show you while it's dark." Carrying Tippy, and being careful where she stepped, Alison followed him out the back door, through the yard, to a shed. "This is in case of emergency," he said, aiming a small flashlight at the shed's door. He opened the door to a small room within the shed. The room looked newly built and definitely out of place. She followed Agent Gambaiana into the small room. "This phone is a direct line to my office. It's only to be used for an emergency." He lifted the receiver and identified himself to the person on the other end, then handed the receiver to Alison.

"Hello?" she said timidly.

"Hello," a male voice replied. "The connection is working."

"Thank you," Alison replied, not knowing what else to say. She handed the receiver back; Agent Gambaiana hung up after a short conversation.

"Should something happen, and you need help, run to this room and call." He pointed at the phone. "You don't even need to dial." Alison saw that the phone didn't have a dial. "It's a direct line," he repeated. "Chances are you'll never need it," he assured her, "but it's here just in case you do."

Alison was overwhelmed. She was in a strange town; being shown an old shed to run to for cover, and her baby was restless. Her emotions were pinging out of control, and she was mentally exhausted.

Mrs. Koch was waiting at the door when they returned to the house. She touched Alison on the wrist. "Let me show you the rest of the house." The pantry and refrigerator were stocked. Just off the kitchen was a small laundry room with a Maytag wringer washer. "There's a clothesline just outside the back door. You'll be able to see it in daylight." Alison had never had a washing machine of her own. She closed her eyes and smiled.

There were two bedrooms, one with a crib for Tippy. A small bag sat on the bed in the other room. "I'm prepared to spend the night," Marie said. "If you wish. If not, I'll leave with George and Jack."

A feeling of relief swept over her. "I'd appreciate that."

Agent Gambaiana's good-bye was difficult. Tears streamed down Alison's face, his eyes welled, and they hugged. "You have my card," he said, his voice breaking. "The Kochs are here to help you as well."

She looked at the Kochs and remembered that they'd been told she was escaping an abusive situation—at least that's what Alison thought they'd been told. For the sake of Reginald's memory, she longed to tell them the truth, but knew she couldn't. Keeping that secret would be the most difficult part of her new life. She steeled herself. I'll be fine, she told herself. She lied, but it didn't matter.

Agent Gambaiana touched Alison on the shoulder. "The quicker I get out of town the less chance people will be asking questions," he said. "I'll call on a regular basis to see how you're doing, and to let you know how the trial is progressing." She understood and walked him to the door of her new home.

———

ALISON AWOKE TO TIPPY'S MURMURING and the smell of frying bacon. She stumbled half-asleep into the kitchen. Jack was sitting on the floor flying a model airplane with each hand. In one hand, he held a plane adorned with American colors, and in the other, one decorated with Japanese insignia. "My dad was a fighter pilot in World War One," he announced proudly. His comment surprised both his mother and Alison. Mrs. Koch rarely heard little Jackson brag in such a way.

"Jackson," Mrs. Koch said, "you should begin by saying good morning."

Jack landed the two airplanes in his lap and smiled up at Alison. Alison felt the smile was forced. "Good morning," he said dutifully. Jackson looked up at her and whispered, "He weely was." Alison tousled the top of his head and gave Jack's comment little thought.

Marie had been up a while. She'd already applied a ton of make-up and was dressed as if going to church. Alison would soon learn that was Marie's way. The two of them visited while Alison fed Tippy. She let Marie hold Tippy; she was the first person other than Alison to hold her since Reginald's death.

"That's certainly different," Marie said after Alison shared her plan to adopt a masculine persona. "But I understand your reasons. You're a very pretty lady." Alison blushed.

While they were talking, Jackson moved into the living room and continued to mock dogfight the two airplanes. A discerning eye would have noticed that the American model was a P-38. Jack was aware of the significance. Like all young boys, he wanted his dad to be the hero of heroes. He occasionally bragged of his father being a WWI hero. His friends' fathers were mostly WWII veterans. Jack would brag that his dad also served in WWII. His friends refused to believe his dad had served in WWI, let alone WWII. His parents never confirmed Jackson's claims.

Word about Alison had spread. People were courteous but avoided direct eye contact when Alison shopped for groceries. Once she began wearing bib overalls and the engineer's hat, people began to avoid her. That was fine with Alison.

She began to appreciate bib overalls and understood why Reginald preferred them, except when using the toilet. Wearing a hat made taking care of her thick bundle of hair easier. She put out a garden and got along with all of her neighbors except Fritz.

The agency provided her with a car. She became familiar with the hilly surroundings during frequent drives with Tippy. She introduced herself to Burt at the Sinclair station during her first stop for gasoline. He was the only person in Colby, other than the Kochs, whom she spoke to on a regular basis. Most of those conversations were her trying to convince Burt that she knew something about cars. She began to suspect Burt of being the local contact.

Less than a year after relocating to Colby, Alison had been summoned back to Chicago to appear in court for her testimony. Vince had warned her that she'd begin to have regrets and second-guess her decision. He told her that during low times she'd need to focus on the loss of Reginald, remembering that only the bad people were going to jail. Throughout the trial, Vince never left her side.

Alison was waiting outside the courtroom in a crowded corridor. Caring for her small daughter occupied her mind. She'd been provided a dress and wide-brimmed hat for the trial and had to avoid showing her face. While sitting in the corridor, she peeked out from under the hat and noticed a young, curly haired boy staring at her. He looked to be about eight or ten. Alison found him cute.

Just before she was ushered into the courtroom, the small Italian lad gave Alison a hard look. He was being tended to by a large grandmotherly woman. The Italian matriarch stared at Alison, looking her up and down with piercing dark eyes. She snapped her head around, and then positioned herself between Alison and the small boy. His name, she learned later, was Gino Luigi.

Vince noticed the exchange and explained. "That's Domenici Luigi's wife and grandson." Luigi was one of the top crime bosses that Alison would be testifying against. If he was found guilty, Domenici Luigi would spend the remainder of his life in prison. While Vince explained, the grandson looked around his grandmother's ample hips and continued to stare. Vince failed to mention that Gino's parents had both been killed in an automobile accident. He was being raised by his grandparents. Alison's testimony would leave Gino with only his grandmother.

Her testimony lasted all afternoon. She broke down several times as she relived conversations with Reginald and recalled specifics. The defense began its cross examination by trying to discredit Reginald, which only served to steel Alison's resolve. The maneuver was disastrous for the defense. The jury quickly returned a "guilty on all counts" verdict.

ONCE BACK IN COLBY, AND after getting Tippy settled for the night, she browsed the *Colby Telegraphs* that Mrs. Koch had left for her. It was Alison's understanding that Mrs. Koch thought she had gone away to finalize her separation from a violent and estranged husband. The charade disturbed her. She longed for the day when she could set the record straight. The FBI perpetrated the pretense to reduce the chance that Alison would be tempted to discuss the trial.

There was nothing in the *Colby Telegraph* about the trial. For most in Colby, organized crime was another world, something fictionalized and glamorized by Hollywood. Alison envied the naiveté of the people she'd met since moving to Colby. She neatly folded the dress she'd worn at the trial—Reginald would have liked it. She doubted she'd wear it again.

For the next few years, she kept to herself, developed her masculine persona, and shortened her name from Alison to Al. She made few friends and purposely remained aloof. A parade of preachers invited her to church. She visited a few, but having been raised Catholic, didn't understand the evangelistic nature of Protestants and felt the socializing too difficult to handle. She didn't understand the forward friendliness of rural America. She gradually grew independent of the Kochs.

Soon after Tippy started school, Al got the job at Burt's and quickly earned a reputation for competence with all things having to do with cars. Men didn't know what to think of her, and women thought of her as if she were a man. Her metamorphosis complete, Al became comfortable and safe while cocooned in her private world.

Meandering

WHEN IT CAME TO ODD characters, Al wasn't alone. Small towns have a way of assimilating those with peculiar traits; they're accepted, almost embraced. Their behavior, while anything but normal, is eventually accepted. Emma and Erma were prime examples of acceptance of those with differences.

The inseparable pair had returned to their house after using the outhouse. Erma, the mom, locked the dead bolt and slipped the rubber band holding the key onto her wrist—she always kept one key on her wrist and the other hanging on the nail. She then helped Emma, the simple daughter, unfold the sleeper sofa and make her bed. After reading to Emma from the book of Psalms, Erma moved into the only bedroom and fell fast asleep. A light rain sprinkled on the tin roof and muffled all other sounds. It made for perfect sleeping, at least for Erma.

Colby's emergency siren sat atop a tall light pole beside the sheriff's office. The sound of it meant a tornado warning or a call for the volunteer fire department. Erma woke briefly to the sound but chose to ignore it—a flue fire, she surmised. The cloudy night sky was pitch black except for the occasional flash of lightning. Erma quickly fell back to sleep. Emma had taken advantage of her new find and was already on the move.

TOMMY ONLY HAD TO BE shaken once before springing out of bed to the sound. For firemen, the town's siren is a call to duty, no matter the hour. Tommy wasn't a fireman, but his dad was fire chief.

The Thompson's house was less than a block from the firehouse, so Tommy and his dad were the first to arrive. Tommy stood aside while his dad began his routine.

Booger and his dad were second to arrive. Jack Burger saw Ted on the phone and proceeded to open the giant overhead door.

After hanging up the phone, Ted trotted toward the truck. On the way he yelled to Tommy, "It's the shed in Al Tatum's backyard."

Tommy considered that and wondered how a vacant shed could catch fire on a night when it was pouring down rain? He and Booger listened to their fathers' discussion.

"Lightning?" Jack asked.

"Didn't say," Ted replied.

Tommy and Booger took the middle of the bench seat, and the two fathers squeezed in on each side—the boys were only recently allowed to ride along on fire runs. The truck rolled out of the fire station door less than fifteen minutes after the fire alarm siren had sounded. That's considered lightning speed by volunteer fire department standards, but sadly fires don't distinguish between paid and volunteer. By the time the fire truck pulled out of the station, two other volunteers were in position on the rear platform, and several more cars, driven by testosterone-filled volunteer firemen with blinking blue lights, were following.

Bill Westwood had recently joined the volunteer force. He and Flop joined the trail of cars with honking horns and flashing blue lights. Some, having seen the flames, drove directly to the fire. Every car in Colby, except one, was headed for the shed.

The most dangerous part of volunteer firefighting is the drive to the fire. Normal rules of driving are abandoned. Men jacked up on adrenaline race through otherwise calm streets, fly through intersections, and use the emergency as an excuse to flip on their blue flashing lights and sirens and exorcize their demon of speed.

The charged firefighters arrived at the shed to find it completely engulfed in flames—the fifteen minutes that it took to get the truck rolling were ample time for the fire to spread to every part of the shed. Mixed thoughts abounded—relief that nobody's home was burning, disappointment that they couldn't save the building, but exhilaration because a real fire needed to be extinguished. Everyone scrambled about, putting into action all they'd practiced.

"This is great," Ted told Jack.

"Yeah," Jack agreed. "Just an old shed, but the guys get some good practice at putting out an actual fire."

Ted made a mental note to log the night as an exercise. The shed was slightly outside the city limits, so technically, they couldn't respond unless called upon by the county. That would have required an official request by one of the county commissioners, which would require waking one of them, and that was never good. The delay would have to be explained to the adrenaline-engorged men, who were already dragging water hoses toward the flaming shed. Ted kept the dilemma to himself.

The last car to arrive failed to slow down before pulling off the road and slid down the wet embankment and into Fritz's hedges. "Not bad," thought Ted. A one-car mishap on a rainy night was acceptable, all things considered. A fire call during working hours generally resulted in a couple of fender benders, and the paperwork dealing with them was usually more time-consuming than the actual firefighting.

After extinguishing the fire, everyone pitched in to fold the hoses and put them back onto the truck. Once the truck returned to the firehouse, a crew would have to unload the hoses and hang them to dry. There was much more to fighting fire than driving fast and squirting giant water guns, and the Colby volunteer force reveled in their training and applying their skills.

RATHER THAN STAND AROUND AT the fire, Sheriff Dooley patrolled the nearby area. He'd learned at a law enforcement seminar that arsonists like to watch their work. While most fires are accidental, particularly in towns such as Colby, the proper protocol was for law enforcement to look for people near the fire who have no business being there.

Sheriff Dooley had never encountered such a suspect, but with the weather, he readily followed protocol and cruised Colby in the comfort of his warm and dry patrol car. He'd gone to Fritz's house, but he hadn't gotten an answer after knocking repeatedly on the door. He'd looked around and noticed Fritz's VW was missing, and he thought that strange. Fritz would have some questions to answer.

Sheriff Dooley made a pass through town. His pulse quickened when the headlights on his car shone on someone walking hunched over less than half a block away. When he got closer he recognized the gait—it was one of the Ducklings, most likely Emma. He stopped the car at the end of the block and waited. She walked around his car and kept going. Finding this too strange to ignore, Sheriff Dooley called dispatch to advise them of what was going on, then he got out of the car and approached her. She was sopping wet, quivering uncontrollably, and wore a terrified look. Dooley approached cautiously; she turned submissively toward him, just as she had always done when he used to find her prowling around before installing the locks for Erma. He walked her back to his car and helped her into the back seat.

While Dooley was helping Emma into the car she noticed a car with no lights going down a side street and pointed. She was so cold her teeth were chattering and Dooley couldn't understand what she was trying to say. By the time Dooley looked the VW was out of sight.

Ted and a few of the crew were within earshot of the scanner and heard Sheriff Dooley's call to dispatch. Dooley had reported picking up Emma. Knowing Dooley to be kind and gracious but somewhat of a klutz around women, Al offered to go help Dooley with her.

THE KNOCK ON THE DOOR startled Erma—frightened her in fact. She peeked through the window to see who was at the door in the middle of the night. Somebody with car trouble, she first thought. She sensed something amiss when the crumpled pile of blankets she thought was Emma didn't stir. And her heart sank when she reached for the key and her finger found only a bare finish nail. She slumped to the floor after seeing Emma standing on the porch with Sheriff Dooley and Al Tatum. Sheriff Dooley tried the door—it was unlocked.

Al Tatum was standing over Erma when she came to. "What's going on?" Erma asked.

"Everybody's okay," Al assured her.

"Emma?" Erma asked.

"She was walking along the street," Sheriff Dooley told her. Erma's mind was still foggy.

"She's right here," Al assured her and helped the two of them join hands.

Al held a cold cloth to Erma's forehead and explained what had occurred. Sheriff Dooley continued with details of the fire.

Dooley stopped midsentence and asked, "Where's the key?"

Erma answered, "It's gone."

Dooley sighed. "Figured as much."

Erma glanced back and forth from Al to Sheriff Dooley. "Guess Emma found it."

They looked at Emma, who by then had curled up on her sofa bed and was sound asleep. Her still wet hair clung to her small, delicate skull.

"Think she set the fire?" Erma asked.

"I can't imagine that she did," Al replied. "But it's a strange coincidence that she'd be out and my shed caught on fire." Al never considered the possibility that Emma frequently prowled the streets at night.

"It doesn't make sense," added Sheriff Dooley. He was sure Emma being out had to be coincidental. He kept her previous meanderings to himself. "I think I'll ask the fire marshal to take a look. More than likely it was lightning."

"Would you like for me to stay and help you with her?" Al asked.

"No, I'll cover her up and let her sleep," Erma replied. Al could sense that Erma just wanted everyone to leave.

After everyone left, Erma dried Emma's hair and removed her wet clothes. She noticed that Emma was wearing several pairs of brightly colored panties and had stuffed a couple of bras under her dress.

Erma immediately thought of Milton Merle, looked through Emma's nightstand, and found several women's items that didn't belong to her. She looked down at Emma, who was exhausted and in a deep but fitful sleep. Her body was rigid, and her right hand was balled into a tight fist. She felt bad that Milton was being blamed for something Emma had been doing, but not bad enough to tell anyone.

The next morning, Erma found the missing key lying next to a then-relaxed hand. Emma slept until noon. Erma contemplated how to speak to her about the undergarments.

Won't Be Al Forever

THE CODGERS WERE HEADED TOWARD the football field when the fire marshal's car got their attention.

"Must be the fire marshal," Rabbit said. The black sedan had "Fire Marshal" emblazoned in giant neon letters on both sides and trunk.

The others elbowed each other. "You sure?" Simon replied sarcastically.

"I'm just sayin'," Rabbit rebutted.

No sooner had the car gotten out of sight then the conversation returned to football.

TOMMY, BOOGER, AND THE BAND of boys had already begun delivering papers and were anxious to see the shed. Tommy made his daily stop at Colby Curls. Chubby Cheeks was there again, this time getting a shampoo. Tommy wondered if she did anything for herself. Faye had Chubby Cheeks's head tilted back deep into the hair-wash sink and looked to be either trying to drown her or break her neck. "Hey, Tommy," she said and motioned toward her station. "Lay the paper there."

Chubby Cheeks flinched. "Ouch!" she said. "That's hot."

"Sorry," Faye said and winked at Tommy. "I'll cool it down a bit." The thought crossed Tommy's mind that Faye enjoyed inflicting a little pain on the queen of gossip.

Even with her head partially submerged, the gossip queen managed to participate in the salon prattle. "Heard Mr. Franklin has the letter lying on his desk," she broadcast for all to hear. "He's meeting with the Tatums this afternoon." Lucille had called Chubby Cheeks before Mr. Franklin had made it to the school parking lot.

Tommy made his way along the row of stations and delivered the rest of the papers. A rare moment of silence fell upon the gossip nest while the provocative comments were being processed. Most of the ladies were probably anxious to call someone and begin speculation about Mr. Franklin's visit.

Snaggletooth was back too, this time getting a manicure. The notion struck Tommy that she should spend less time at the salon and more at the orthodontist. "Who do you think set the shed on fire?" she asked no one in particular.

A lady Tommy had seen at Twin Oaks Senior Citizens had her feet soaking in a murky solution. "Think they're calling it lightning," she commented.

Another resident from Twin Oaks, Finis Pribble's neighbor, sat next to the lady soaking her wrinkled feet. The two had probably come together. She'd always struck Tommy as having a mouth much too small for her swollen face. But that didn't keep her from offering her two cents. "Sheriff Dooley is callin' it that because he don't want to mess with 'at man-woman, Tatum."

Faye motioned for Tommy as he headed for the door. She reached into her purse and dug out a quarter. "Here, don't say I never tip." She handed it to him and tussled his hair.

"Thanks, Faye," Tommy said. Once outside, he pocketed the quarter and sniffed his sleeves to make sure he'd gotten out before the stench set in. He caught up with the others just before going to the shed.

UNBEKNOWNST TO ALISON, MR. KOCH was the local contact. He'd been up since receiving an earlier call from the U.S. Marshal's office and was sitting on his balcony. Alison's shed fire had disconnected the line, and the Marshall's office had immediately followed up with Mr. Koch, who, after a call to the sheriff's office, let the marshals know what was going on. After watching the fire marshal's car, he rolled his wheelchair to the phone and made a call to Chicago. Since he was unable to get up and down the stairs without assistance, he couldn't help with the necessary next steps.

Agent Gambaiana was out of office. His replacement, Agent Douglas took the call and without official approval, solicited the help of another Colby resident, his buddy, Ben Franklin. This type of resourceful thinking was typical of a Navy SEAL but verbotten by U.S. Marshals.

Lucille Cain stuck her head into Ben Franklin's office. "You have a call on two."

Ben looked up. "And?"

"He won't say," she said, knowing that "And?" meant "Who is it?"

"A parent?" he asked.

"I don't think so. I don't recognize the voice, and he's got an accent." She squinted her face in thought. "Sounds like a gangster."

Ben hoped that his face didn't give it away, but with that information he was almost certain who was on the line—Flipper. "I'll take it."

He pushed the blinking button on his phone. "This is Mr. Franklin. How may I help you?" Ben noticed that Lucille was taking her time moving away from his doorway and was rearranging items on the top of the filing cabinet that stood just outside his door.

"There's a problem, and we need your help," Flipper said.

"I'm not sure how old our lockers are," Ben replied. He was speaking for effect.

"Can you leave your office immediately?" Flipper asked.

"I can probably get that information for you fairly quickly. In fact, I'm sure that I can," Ben replied. Lucille moved away from the door and began typing; she'd lost interest or just wanted to avoid being given the task of researching the age of the lockers.

"Are you listening?" Flipper asked.

"Yes. What's up?" Ben asked. Flipper sensed that he finally had Ben's full attention and filled him in regarding the Tatum phone line, but nothing more.

"I'm supposed to meet her this evening," Ben told Flipper.

"About the pregnancy?"

"Uh huh," Ben said.

The phone was silent for several seconds. "That works. Just show up early," Flipper advised.

"The daughter won't be there, but I'll just act like I expected her there," Ben said. Then he asked, "How'd you know about the fire marshal?"

"We have a local contact," Flipper told him.

"Why can't he go?"

"He's not able," Flipper responded. "That's all I can tell you at this point."

Their entire exchange took less than a minute. The men had perfected the art of fragmented conversation.

Ben stepped out of his office and told Lucille that he was on his way to meet with Al Tatum.

"Who was on the phone?" she asked.

Ben shook his head as if in disgust. "Locker salesman," he said, and then he gave Lucille a raised eyebrow look. "You're usually better at filtering solicitors."

"She's not expecting you until after five. Why don't you call her?" Lucille asked, changing the subject.

Ben ignored Lucille's comment about being early. "I'll just drop by her house on the way home." He moved toward the door. "I'll see you tomorrow." It was all he could do to sound casual and not break into a run. On the way to Al's house, he found it difficult to focus on the mission as he wondered about the identity of the local contact and why he or she couldn't respond. He put that train of thought out of his mind. It wasn't necessary. He had his orders, so to speak. He needed to focus.

Al and the fire marshal were standing in the middle of the charred remains of the shed when Ben arrived. His military training taught him that everyone was either an enemy or an ally. He struggled with that notion and knew that it didn't apply in this case, but he nonetheless caught himself regarding the fire marshal as the enemy.

Ben walked their way, hands in his pockets, and doing his best to act casual and appear uninterested in the burned shed. "Looks like that lightning sort of did you a favor," he said to Al.

Al eyed Ben suspiciously. "You're early," she said.

The fire marshal pulled out a notebook. "What makes you say the lightning did Mrs. Tatum a favor?" he asked.

"No specific reason," Ben replied. "It was just an old shed full of junk. I'm sure Mrs. Tatum is glad to see it gone." He turned to Al. "I know I'm early. I was on my way home and stopped on the chance you'd be here." Already knowing the answer, he asked. "Is Tippy home?" Al gave him a suspicious look.

Ben noticed the phone wire. The insulation was burned off and the purpose of the wire wouldn't be obvious to the average person. It stuck out of a piece of conduit that was barely noticeable in the gravel and ran to the closet that Flipper had described. The fire marshal was nearby.

The fire marshal scribbled a few notes, then asked, "What time do you think the fire began?"

"Probably right before the sheriff's office got the call," Ben replied.

The fire marshal gave Ben an annoyed look. "The question was for Mrs. Tatum."

Ben shrugged. "Answer's the same," he replied. "Must be a slow fire day if all you've got to do is investigate old sheds that have been struck by lightning."

The fire marshal stopped poking around the ashes for a moment. "We know it was probably lightning. But we also know that your neighbor has made a few idle threats about burning down the shed. He was apparently out of town when this happened." The fire marshal turned toward Ben. "And what's your purpose here?"

"I'm the school principal."

"Since when do school principals investigate fires?" the fire marshal asked, getting back at Ben for his previous snide remark.

Ben turned to Al Tatum. "I need to speak to you about—"

Al cut him off. "I know why you're here."

Ben kept eye contact with Al, winked, picked up a rusty disc blade, and rhetorically asked, "Wonder what this was used for?"

The fire marshal, still smoldering from Ben's remark, answered, "That's a disc blade. It's used for farming, something anyone, even a school teacher, should know something about."

"I'll be darned," Ben replied, and then he plopped the disc down on top of the exposed conduit. With the conduit covered, the bare wire running through the gravel appeared insignificant.

He saw a change in Al's expression and thought that maybe she realized that his visit involved something more than Tippy's pregnancy. He noticed the charred telephone, with the wires still connected. He nonchalantly inched that way.

"Our appointment isn't until five thirty," she whispered to Ben.

"Five thirty?" Ben said. "Dang! I had it written down as three thirty." Al squinted while she contemplated Ben and why he had shown up early, and, especially, why he was so interested in the charred remains.

Ben was concerned that even though he wasn't supposed to know anything about her case, she'd eventually realize that he'd been tipped off by the marshal's office. He wondered if she knew the identity of the local contact.

Al turned toward the fire marshal and answered his original question. "The power was off, and I couldn't see the time," she told him.

While the marshal was making a note, Ben knelt down, pulled the wires from the phone, and stood up with the burned remains. He took several steps and announced, "Well, look here. Isn't this an old phone?"

"Mr. Franklin," the fire marshal admonished. "You're disturbing a crime scene."

"Crime scene?" Ben asked. "An old shed got struck by lightning." He started walking away carrying the phone.

"You need to leave that here," the fire marshal ordered.

Ben tossed the phone several feet away from where he'd found it. "Sure." He looked Al's way. "I'll come back later. It looks like you've got your hands full, what with the crime scene and all."

After reaching his car, Ben began to sense a bit of remorse for giving the fire marshal a hard time. In reality, he had a great deal of respect for firefighters and understood the difficult position investigators faced. He made a note of the fire marshal's number that was emblazoned on the car and intended to call, apologize, and explain. But for now, he'd sufficiently taken care of the line.

Before pulling away, he glanced back, Al still looked puzzled. He took a second look in his rearview mirror toward Fritz's hedgerow. He wondered about a possible connection between Fritz and the fire.

Since Booger and Tommy had told Flop, Caleb, Checkers, and Everett about going on the fire call, the boys were anxious to see the charred remains. In spite of being exhausted from no sleep, they had delivered the papers in record time and gathered at the corner looking toward the shed. Ben pulled up and rolled down his window.

"Hi, Mr. Franklin," Tommy said.

"Is that a police car?" Booger asked, pointing at the fire marshal's car.

"Fire marshal," Ben explained. "He's investigating the fire."

"What's there to 'vestigate?" Booger asked.

"Anytime there's a suspicious fire, and the fire department is called, then the cause of the fire must be determined," Ben told them.

"Thing of it is," began Caleb, "everyone knows it was lightnin.'"

"Apparently not everybody," replied Mr. Franklin.

"Like-a-said," began Flop, "let's ride on down and poke around."

Checkers and Everett just listened—they were eating Moon Pies they'd picked up at Burt's.

Ben couldn't help himself. "That fire marshal's a nice guy. I'm sure he'd be happy to tell you what a fire marshal does," he told the boys. "Go on down and ask him."

Booger looked at Tommy. "May as well."

Through his rearview mirror, Ben watched the band of boys descend upon the shed and the unsuspecting fire marshal. He giggled for two blocks, thinking about the relentless barrage of questions they'd ask.

Al had watched Ben begin talking to the boys. The fire marshal had started down his list of questions for Al just as the curious minds rolled up on their bikes.

Booger asked, "What's a fire marshal do?" The fire marshal ignored him.

"Guess ol' Fritzie will be happy," Tommy offered.

"Why's that?" the marshal, now interested, asked.

"He's always complainin' 'bout th' shed, and he's always seein' skunks and ground hogs goin' in 'n out," Tommy replied.

"Dang! Look at th' hole in 'at piece a tin," Tommy said. "You think 'at's where the lightnin struck?" he asked. Before the marshal could stop him, Tommy picked up the piece of tin and turned it over to look at the other side.

"You 'vestigate all fires or just lightning strikes?" Booger asked.

"Hey look, an old phone," Booger said.

"Don't touch that, it's—" the marshal said, but he was too late. Booger had already begun to examine the charred phone before the marshal's warning. Booger tossed it back where he'd first found it.

"Dju 'vestigate the fire that burnt down my house?" Checkers asked.

"What's your name?" the fire marshal asked.

"Checkers," he answered.

"The Goodpasture's house," Booger clarified. "It was a couple of miles east of town." Checkers rolled his eyes.

The exasperated marshal stroked his chin. "No, that one was reported as a flue fire. There was no cause for an investigation."

"That's crazy," Booger replied.

The fire marshal stopped. "Why's that?'

"A whole house burns and nobody 'vestigates. A worthless ol' shed burns in the middle of a lightnin' storm and somebody calls the fire marshal," Booger replied.

The fire marshal removed his police officer–style hat and wiped his forearm across his forehead. He put his notebook away and looked at Al. "I don't guess it matters how this fire started. As far as I know it wasn't insured. I'll just write it up as a lightning strike." He kicked over a charred piece of lumber. "Looks to me like it's good riddance to an eyesore." He turned toward the boys. "You boys need to stay away from this mess— there's broken glass, rusty nails, and probably a snake or two." The word snake got Tommy's attention and squelched his curiosity.

AL WAITED FOR THE FIRE marshal to drive out of sight before dashing to the house and placing a collect call to the U.S. Marshal's office. Al gave the switchboard operator her case number, and her call was transferred to Vince.

"Hello, Alison," he said, knowing from the case number who the call was from.

She skipped the salutations and got right to the point. "You know about the fire?" Before Vince could respond, she fired off another question. "Is Ben the local contact?"

"Think about it," Vince told her calmly. He wasn't trying to be condescending—rather, he was making an effort to calm her. "Ben Franklin has been in the community for less than a year. The local contact has lived in Colby way longer than you have. Beside," he continued, "this will all be over in a few months."

"So if he's not the local contact, then what's up?" she asked.

"You remember the agent who came with me on our last visit?"

"Sure, Marine-looking guy," she said.

"Right. He and Ben Franklin served in the military together, Navy actually, sort of." Vince didn't want to take the time to get into any details.

"And so just because they know each other it's okay to breach the confidence?" Al asked incredulously.

"It's complicated," Vince replied. "Agent Douglas should not have breached the confidence, but as it turns out, Ben Franklin still has an active top-secret clearance." It took a few seconds for Al to assimilate this.

"He's coming over in less than an hour to discuss Tippy," she replied. "And—"

Vince interrupted her. "Yeah, I know. We know all about the letter."

"The letter?" she asked.

"You don't know about the letter?" Vince asked.

"No. Remember, I'm not exactly one of the girls here. I don't get my hair done, and I don't go to the Laundromat," she said. Vince explained about the letter and how it hadn't been opened, but that Ben Franklin was sure of its contents.

"What does Ben know?" she asked. "Does he know about the marriage?"

"No. You should explain during the visit."

The line was silent for an uncomfortable length of time. "What about the school policy?" she asked.

"Agent Douglas talked to Ben about school policy," he replied. "There's no policy addressing student pregnancy, but there is one for marriage. According to Ben, nobody can recall anyone getting kicked out of school for getting married."

"So you think we should call their bluff?"

"Yes," Vince replied. "But get Ben's read. Remember, the visit this afternoon is off school property, off the record, and he's not required to report the conversation. Be candid with him and ask his advice."

Al thought for a moment then replied, "Okay. The little I've heard about him leads me to believe that he's logical and thinks for himself. I've spoken to him a few times at the filling station. He's hard to figure—seems more like a sophisticated motorcycle gang member than a high school principal."

Vince laughed. "You don't know the half of it. I think you two will get along fine."

AL SHOWERED AND SLIPPED INTO a pair of snug jeans that she liked to wear when at home. She grabbed her favorite top, an oversized Northwestern University sweatshirt that was clean but splattered with oil stains. The sweatshirt had been Reggie's, and she always thought of him when she wore it. It gave her courage. It also made her look very different from the bib-tuck overalls character she portrayed in public.

While brushing her hair, she noticed Tippy's make-up bag and for a split second was tempted. She felt guilty about wanting to look nice for Ben Franklin, so she held the sweatshirt to her nose and inhaled deeply.

For over a year after moving to Colby, she'd been able to immerse herself in Reggie's scent by doing so. Years had crept by, and Reggie's scent had been replaced with that of detergent, but her memories of him remained. After hearing a knock on the door, she dared one last look at herself, then patted her cheeks and admired her slim figure. Hard physical labor at the filling station had its advantages.

Tippy was taking a nap, which had become a daily after-school routine. Al tapped on her bedroom door. "Mr. Franklin's here," she said.

A sleepy voice replied, "Okay, I'll be out in a minute." Al, looking more like an Alison, tied her long, thick hair into a ponytail on the way to the door.

BEN FRANKLIN WAS TAKEN ABACK when Al, looking more like an Alison, answered the door. He processed what he'd heard about the lady in the blue jeans and sweatshirt standing in front of him and quickly concluded there was more to the story. More than anything, he felt that dealing with this parent was going to be different than the others, whom he found to be generally petty and closed-minded.

Alison offered her hand. "Please, come in," she said. "And thanks for helping with the fire marshal." Ben shook her strong, callused hand.

Ben, unsure if Alison was aware of what he knew about her situation, said, "He seemed like a nice enough guy, but he was making more of the fire than he needed to. I probably should have driven on by when I saw that you were busy talking to him."

Alison gave him a look. "I spoke to the U.S. Marshal's office after you left."

"I see," Ben said. While he was processing the implication of Alison's statement, Tippy staggered in. Alison and Tippy had agreed that Tippy would tell him.

When Alison turned to Tippy, Ben scanned the portion of the house he could see from the living room. It wasn't at all what he'd expected. The yard and outside of the house were certainly no indication of the interior. Tippy slumped onto the couch next to her mother.

Alison pointed to a comfortable recliner. "Please, sit down." Ben sat.

In the short time since Ben Franklin arrived at her door, Alison had sized him up. His build and demeanor reminded her of Reginald's. She guessed him to be at least fifteen years younger, so she wasn't particularly attracted to him—or at least wasn't willing to admit to it. Although she did find him intriguing. He aroused feelings within her that she'd repressed for too many years. She pushed those thoughts aside, focusing her attention on the purpose of the visit. In an effort to keep the conversation professional, she chose to call him Mr. Franklin.

Alison looked first at Ben and then to Tippy. What she was about to say would surprise both of them. "Mr. Franklin, I understand that you're aware of our situation."

"I know your witness protection situation is complicated," replied Ben, "but I'm not here to discuss that."

"I know why you think you're here," Alison said. She paused momentarily to let her comment register. "Actually, my contact at the agency has advised me to tell you the rest of the story." Ben was wondering what he could possibly not already know concerning their extremely complicated situation.

Tippy, squirming nervously, didn't mince words. She looked directly at Mr. Franklin and said, "I'm married." Ben was visibly moved by the news.

Al spoke up. "I actually encouraged it." Mr. Franklin's expression said he didn't understand. Al explained. "They're in love. Dwight was leaving for the Army, probably going to Vietnam." Al glanced at Tippy and grinned, "I guess I should have explained the birds and the bees to them."

She went on to point out that the pregnancy wasn't planned, gave Ben the due date, and let him do the math himself. By the time she finished, both hers and Tippy's eyes were flooded with tears; Ben was massaging his temples.

Ben collected his thoughts, and then said, "You're right. This is complicated." He first looked at Tippy and then at Alison. What he saw in Alison's appearance was inconsistent with the man-lady who worked at Burt's Sinclair. Focusing on the situation without getting sidetracked by Alison's obvious charade as a masculine female was proving difficult. He mentally reeled himself in. "Besides Dwight, who knows about the marriage?"

Alison answered, "Velma Seabaugh, Solomon Atchison, and my contact at the agency." She paused. "I think that's all."

"Solomon Atchison?" Ben asked in surprise. "Isn't he one of those old coots they call the Codgers? Isn't he the one they call Fish?"

Alison said, "Mr. Atchison is a deacon at First Baptist, where Tippy plays the piano." Ben was nonplussed. Alison continued, "Mr. Atchison is also an ordained minister and served as a chaplain in WWI." Mr. Franklin sat back and began to listen more attentively. Alison continued. "He served with Alvin York."

Ben sat up straight and swallowed hard. "Did you say Alvin York ... Sergeant York?"

Alison smiled. She appreciated Ben's enthusiastic response. "Yes, one and the same. He was awarded the Distinguished Service Cross on the same day as Sergeant York." Ben rubbed his chin, shook his head, and listened. "He was a conscientious objector and a sharp shooter—they met at a shooting competition." Alison shrugged. "I guess the Army put them together, thinking they deserved each other." She let Ben absorb that fact. "He was recommended to us by the agency. While serving in WWI, Mr. Atchison had a top-secret clearance."

Ben's expression was one of amazement "Does he know about the witness protection program?" Ben asked.

"He doesn't have a clue," Alison replied.

Getting back to the situation at hand, Ben asked. "Why keep the marriage a secret?"

"It's against school policy to allow students to be married," Alison reminded him.

Ben replied. "Actually, I didn't know that was a policy until I looked for a student pregnancy policy, which I never found. Nobody can remember why the marriage policy was established, or anyone getting kicked out of school for being married."

"All of this is off the record, right?" Alison asked.

"Of course," he answered. "I didn't know what to expect on the way here. And certainly the marriage is a surprise. I intend to ask the board to take a position and allow pregnant students to remain in school, providing they have a good record and keep their grades up. I've already spoken to a few of the board members, off the record, hypothetically and probably illegally. They agree." Ben's penchant for bending the rules and getting to the point impressed Alison.

"What about being married?" Tippy asked.

Ben smiled. "One bridge at a time. For now, let's just let sleeping dogs lie."

"Is that why you came?" she asked. "To tell us that there isn't a rule, but that you're going to ask that one be created?"

Ben hesitated before answering. "Truthfully, before going to the board, I felt that I needed to see your home." He paused, and then continued, saying, "There are rumors." Al flinched. Ben continued. "And, frankly, I didn't know what I might find. But now that I've seen the inside of your home, I'd bet it's one of the cleanest in the district." He looked at Tippy. "And Tippy, your school record speaks for itself." He looked at Alison. He wanted to tell her how wrong the people in town were about her, but he couldn't think of an appropriate way to express his thoughts.

It was as if Alison was reading his mind, and her eyes filled with tears. "Thanks, Ben."

"I think I understand the situation now," Ben said. He stood. "I probably need to be going. I'm glad we had this conversation. You both have my total support."

Tippy stood and said. "Thank you, Mr. Franklin. Most everyone in this town respects you," she said, then smiled before continuing, "and the rest fear you."

Ben grinned. "That's by design."

Alison walked him to the door. She asked. "So, do people think I'm …" she hesitated.

He finished her sentence. "Sexually confused?" He grinned. "As I said, you've done an excellent job hiding your true identity."

Alison smiled back. "I can assure you I'm not."

"Mother!" Tippy protested. "Mr. Franklin's married."

Alison turned to Tippy and winked. "Yes, but he has friends. And I'm not going to be Al for the rest of my life."

Code Green

Vince Gambaiana and his wife honeymooned in the Rocky Mountain National Park and had since vacationed there several times. Looking forward to retiring there, they'd purchased a two-acre lot that bordered the park. The previous night, they'd celebrated paying off the note on the lot. Vince was taking his lunch hour at the office; building permits, plans, and cost estimates for a small mountain home were spread across his desk. When the rest of the staff returned from lunch, he meticulously rolled and folded his retirement dreams and put them away.

Each day was one day closer to retirement. Vince had mixed emotions. He had complete confidence in Danny Douglas, but his inner voice told him that he needed to stay involved in the Tatum's case. He was unable to hand it off.

He reviewed the Tatum file, then called home and let his wife know that he'd be working late. Updates pertaining to each client arrived on a regular basis with the names and locations coded, thus reducing the need for cloak-and-dagger technique.

Lying on his desk were documents dealing with two additional issues. The first was the official notice that the agency felt the need to move the Tatum case to code green. The document essentially outlined, in legal jargon, what the witness had agreed to years earlier when entering the program. Vince chuckled to himself as he mentally rewound the case.

Alison Tyson, now Tatum, had gone about the witness protection program in a very unorthodox fashion. Rather than depend upon the government for living expenses, as other witnesses had, she'd made her own way. She'd taken a job, chosen a very modest home, saved, and was financially independent. Granted, much of her reclusive nature was due to the loss of her husband and the shock of finding out the truth about her extended family.

Through the years, Alison had been able to stay in touch with her parents by exchanging letters, which were passed through the marshal's office, closely screened, and appropriately edited for anything that might reveal her location or alias name.

Al treasured each piece of correspondence from them. They had forgiven her for turning state's evidence, and she'd been able to vaguely share with them about the granddaughter that they would never know.

It was painful for Al when she learned, in a letter from her father, of her mother's terminal illness. Vince had taken pictures at the funeral and shared them with her. In the photos, she saw people with whom she'd grown up; they'd aged.

During Vince's last visit, he'd had the unfortunate chore of delivering the news of her father. He'd lasted only a few months after the death of Alison's mother. After a massive heart attack, he'd keeled over at the filling station.

Alison was consoled knowing that her father had died while doing what he loved—working on a car. Alison recalled the helpless feeling she'd endured during her mother's illness. That period had been the hardest part of being in the witness protection program. She didn't consider herself a very religious person, but was nonetheless moved to offer a prayer of thanks that her father hadn't suffered a prolonged illness.

The second issue, and the one that perplexed him, had to do with the trust. A few years earlier, Al's mother and father had established a trust for Tippy into which all of their personal assets would flow at the time of their death. A real estate company had listed the filling station and expected a quick sale. Tippy's trust was about to become worth a good deal of money.

NEARLY EIGHTEEN YEARS HAD PASSED since the trial. The cute little Italian boy had kept his record impeccable, graduated from law school, and landed a job as an assistant at the U.S. Attorney's office in Chicago. He'd listed no family on his application, and in fact they were all deceased. No one suspected him; Vince had forgotten Gino existed.

Italians normally don't hold grudges, they simply get even—they "take care of business," as they say. And most in the family had felt vindicated when Reggie Tyson was taken out. In fact, Reginald's execution had become divisive; many thought it too drastic a measure and that those who'd been jailed deserved it. They didn't care what had happened to the wife. The fact that she'd disappeared was fine with them.

Gino had watched his grandmother, a once robust lady, lose her passion for cooking, then her appetite, and then slowly wilt away. Alison's testimony had sent her husband, Gino's grandfather, to prison for life. Gino had made a vow to get even, and he'd decided he'd hurt someone she loved—the baby that Alison was clutching during the trial.

He'd kept a constant vigil on Alison's parents, hoping for a lead. He'd seen the trust documents—they'd been drafted by a colleague in an adjacent office. He bided his time. Alison's father's death occurred a month prior to Tippy's eighteenth birthday. Gino patiently waited for the sale of the filling station and the subsequent disbursement to the trust. The funds disbursement and subsequent filings would lead him to Tippy. His anger and need for revenge strengthened his patience.

Vince had every nuance of the Tyson case memorized; he'd seen the case unfold from day one and allowed it to become personal. Alison Tatum was the only witness protection case in his purview in which the protected witness was totally innocent. Danny, the replacement, had only met Alison Tatum once and had commented to Vince that he found Alison a little strange. Danny's comment had nearly brought them to blows.

Several issues had to be addressed. The first was Danny's divulging information to Ben Franklin. Fortunately for Danny, what had at first been considered a breach of confidence and an action that could have resulted in Danny's dismissal had resulted in a positive outcome. It was Ben's action that possibly kept Alison Tatum's cover from being blown. Danny and Vince agreed they should brief Ben on the entire file and enlist his service as a local contact. George Koch had served the agency well, but he was getting long in the tooth, and as they'd learned at an inopportune time, he was unable to quickly respond if needed. His balcony view had allowed him to keep an eye on Burt's Sinclair and Alison. When he moved, he would no longer be able to do even that task.

Vince reviewed with Danny the technical and legal aspects of code green. A witness protection case isn't officially closed until the death of the protected witness. But going code green is tantamount to a case closed

and a signal that it's clear to return to normal. There's no fanfare or celebration, and the time elapsed is such that those being protected experience very little change.

The Tyson case had been textbook perfect. It had been one of Vince's
first WP cases, and he was filled with a sense of pride to see it going flaw-
lessly to code green.

Even though Vince and Danny had recently been to Colby to deliver
the news of Alison's father, and the two paperboys had exhibited a little
too much curiosity, the agents agreed that since the file was going green,
there was no need to be concerned or for further cloak and dagger. Danny
was looking forward to a face-to-face visit with Ben. Vince looked forward to finally getting a pizza at the little restaurant on the square. Being
from Chicago, he felt it was his personal mission to audit small mom-and-
pop pizza parlors, particularly those with Italian names.

GINO'S PATIENCE HAD FINALLY PAID off. Two fast food franchises, Mc-
Donald's and Kentucky Fried Chicken, had been eyeing the corner lot
occupied by Alison's father's filling station. The publicity over the bidding
war made monitoring the transaction simple. Gino watched the case file
for activity.

Gino made his daily check and noticed that the Tyson case folder had
been removed from the cabinet. He casually made his way through the
office, scanning the desks of every assistant. He'd moved the name tab on
the folder from the back flap of the folder to the front; imperceptible to
most, but it was enough to allow him to spot the folder from a distance.

He located the folder on another assistant's desk, and as luck would
have it, he could see the assistant's cubicle from his office. He returned to
his office and kept an eye on the folder. He checked his pulse and focused
on calming his nerves. The next steps were crucial if he was to fulfill his
life's purpose and exact revenge on Alison Tyson.

Sitting at his desk, he thumbed through the pages of a legal brief while
keeping an eye on the legal assistant's out box. The assistant hadn't been
assigned to any particular attorney; her job was to help manage the files
in that particular office and disburse files that had been ordered by other
agents.

The assistant finished the memo that would accompany the file documents, placed it in the secure courier service bag, moved the bag to her out

box, and then left the office to smoke a cigarette. Gino took his first big risk since beginning his pursuit of Alison Tyson: he went into the empty cubicle, reached into the courier bag, and removed the package. The envelope was sealed—Gino didn't risk opening it. He memorized the address, and then returned to his office. His pulse was racing, and he'd only walked a few steps.

Needing an excuse for not having finished the brief on his desk, he stuck his head into his supervisor's office, and let him know he was going home with a fever. His racing pulse had caused his temples to glisten with sweat, and the red face completed the charade. He left the office without a plan but with a definite sense of direction.

That night, Gino studied the Bureau directory. Rather than trying to find the Tysons through the trust, he'd track them down through their U.S. Marshal contact. He made a list of the agents at the location to which the couriered package was addressed, then looked at the agency profile directory, and was able to narrow the possibilities to one likely agent: Vince Gambaiana. He was the only agent at the listed address who was old enough to have been around when Alison Tyson had been placed into the WP program. It was a long shot.

FOR THIS MOMENT, HE'D CULTIVATED a friendship with a bean counter in the treasury office. The next day he made a call and was able to gain access to the record of travel expenses for Agent Gambaiana.

Gambaiana, near retirement, made few out-of-town trips. In fact, his only trip appeared to have been to Missouri, where he'd used a credit card to make a fuel purchase. "Sloppy," Gino thought while he located the town on a Rand McNally. It was a giant break for Gino. He pondered the chance that the witness would be located in the same town.

During his drive home, his mind raced while the traffic crept. For once, he didn't mind the congestion; the delay gave him time to think. Halloween was little more than a week away. He decided that would be a good time to scope out the little, obscure Missouri town.

THE TEMPERATURE WAS FOLLOWING THE sun and slowly dropping in Colby. Tommy and Booger were delivering papers in a cold drizzle and were near the end of the route. It was one of those days when a paper route wasn't the most coveted job in town. Even The Temptations' "My

Girl" blaring from the Houn-Dawg speakers failed to add a spring to their step. Every part of Tommy's body was cold; Booger's lips had turned purple.

Seeing Sheriff Dooley and the fire marshal's car pull out of Fritz's driveway provided the freezing paperboys with a spurt of adrenaline and faux warmth. Their lips were chattering too much to discuss Dooley's business at Fritz's.

Cletus pulled up beside them in his pickup. "Want a ride?" he asked. Penny was with him. They were both wearing "I'm guilty" grins. Tommy and Booger crowded up next to the window and let the air from the cab warm their faces and thaw their lips.

"Where you been?" Booger asked. Tommy had been curious too, but he had the good manners to not ask.

"The bridge," Penny replied, and then she giggled.

"Why?" Booger plied. Penny had her arm draped across Cletus's shoulders—Tommy had already noticed the ring.

Tommy remembered having seen Cletus going into Fairview Jewelry. A kaleidoscope of thoughts flooded Tommy's mind, including the things said by the customers at Colby Curls about Penny. He couldn't imagine his uncle getting married. He'd always just been Uncle Cletus. Booger appeared to be lost in thought or just cold.

Fifteen years earlier, before serving in Korea, Cletus had put a ring on layaway. His plan was to pay for the ring while in the service, and then ask Penny to marry him upon his return. As had happened to many soldiers, she hadn't waited for him. She'd married someone else, but the marriage had been a mistake from the start.

Cletus had paid for the ring, but he never picked it up. At his request, the jewelry store had kept it in layaway. Because the ring had been custom-made, they wouldn't give him a cash refund, but he could return it for a full credit against something else in the store. Since they didn't sell fishing lures or hunting boots, there was nothing else in the store that interested him—besides, anything that replaced the ring would have been a constant reminder of Penny, so the ring remained there for fifteen years. They told him that it was the longest layaway in store history.

Penny held up her hand. The diamond sparkled almost as much as her eyes. The two boys were at a loss for words. "We're getting married," she announced with a molar exposing grin. Cletus motioned toward the passenger door. "Get in before you freeze to death," he ordered. "We're on our way to tell your mother."

The news, along with the cold, had frozen Tommy in place. An elbow from Booger got him moving. They loaded their bikes into the bed of the pickup. "Nair thought 'bout old peeble getting married," he whispered with frozen lips before getting into the cab.

"Does seem kind of weird," Booger agreed.

Cletus turned the heater fan on high. Both boys shivered and listened to the story of Cletus's proposal on the Craggy Creek Bridge. Penny and Cletus frequently interrupted each other in the telling of how Cletus had talked Penny into walking across the bridge on a cold, windy, drizzly afternoon and then popped the question. They passed the sheriff's office. Sheriff Dooley was sitting in his patrol car rubbing his temples.

Cletus stopped in front of Booger's house. "See ya tomorrow," Tommy said after helping Booger unload his bike. Tommy could tell by the smile on Booger's face that the notion of Cletus and Penny getting married set well. Tommy figured Booger was wondering if his dad and Miss Anderson might do the same.

After letting Booger out, Tommy thought of something that needed explaining. He turned to his uncle and asked. "What's racism?"

Penny gave him a look. "Wow, where did that come from?"

"I've been trying to figure it out since the Websters moved to town."

Penny nodded toward Cletus. "Good luck explaining that one."

Tommy's uncle didn't disappoint. "Tommy, racism is when someone judges another based on their race rather than their character, and it's usually not for the better."

"I know that, but how does it work? Why do people keep talking about the Websters even after meeting them?" Tommy asked.

"Good question," Penny said.

Cletus continued. "Their preconceived notions cause them to be blinded to the Webster's genuine qualities."

"How long does it take for people to stop being racist?" Tommy asked.

"I don't know."

"If enough people treat the Websters with respect, others will follow suit," Penny assured Tommy. Cletus nodded in agreement.

———

SINCE FRITZ HADN'T BEEN HOME on the night of the fire, Sheriff Dooley felt it necessary for Fritz to verify his whereabouts. He had no reason to question Fritz's story except he'd known him for years and Fritz had never mentioned an Army buddy or any connection in Mississippi. Fritz was able to produce receipts from a Jackson, Mississippi, restaurant where he'd eaten dinner the night of the shed fire and breakfast the morning after. During the visit, Dooley had noticed an application to the Invisible Empire of the White Knights, the Ku Klux Klan of Mississippi, lying on Fritz's cluttered kitchen table.

Dooley realized that Fritz was different, but he'd never been a problem for the law. After several minutes of racking his brain, Dooley concluded that Fritz hadn't set the fire but was up to something else, something possibly worse. He shook his head in frustration and contemplated the burden of keeping an eye on him.

Church

A LOW, OVERCAST SKY, HEAVY drizzle, and temperatures hovering in the low thirties had lingered for two days. Small, slushy mud puddles dotted the church parking lot. Tommy thought it made more sense to wear his boots, but his mother had insisted that he wear his church shoes. He picked his way through the maze of puddles to the basement door at the rear of the church. The mischievous side of him was contemplating getting his shoes muddy on purpose just to prove his mother wrong. He was about to do it when he saw Melody.

Science has never fully explained the drop in a boy's IQ when he is drawn to a girl. Tommy was so enamored with Melody at that moment that the sight of her caused him to temporarily assume a new identity, one of overconfidence and invulnerability. He even began to whistle the tune to "Penny Lane." He felt the dampness when his right foot entered a shallow, soft-bottomed puddle, but except for a short pause in his whistle, he didn't let on. His rarely worn Sunday dress shoe emerged from the puddle soaked and covered with a thin layer of liquid clay. Thin parallel muddy stripes formed on his other pants leg with each step. It wasn't until after Melody smiled, sent a wiggly fingers wave, and turned to go into the church that Tommy looked down and took stock of the mess. He blamed his mother.

Before Sunday school, the youth group met for an assembly where they'd sing a few songs and hear announcements. Mostly the opening provided an organized buffer for everyone to gather and visit, rather than run around like a bunch of monkeys until class began.

Not blessed with a voice for singing, Tommy slipped into the boy's restroom and worked on his shoe. He heard Mrs. Crawford clear her throat.

She had stepped to the lectern holding the Christmas program binder tight to her fleshy chest. She was on the prowl for volunteers.

Tommy hoped to get a part playing the coronet. It was a small, non-speaking role and only required a few notes be sounded to announce the approach of Roman soldiers.

Mrs. Crawford spoke in short phrases and ended each phrase with a forced smile. Her smiles were short in duration and looked painful. "Class, I'm here to talk to you about the Christmas program." Then a pause, a forced smile, a double lip smack, and then her tongue swept the corners of her mouth. "The program will be performed the first Sunday in December." It always was. This proclamation was followed by another round of painful smiling and double lip smacking and tongue sweeping.

Tommy could see and hear from the boys' room. After taking off his shoe and dumping out the muddy water, he used a paper towel to wipe off the sticky clay. He wrung the water out of his socks. Fortunately, they were the thin, worthless dress socks that he hated and they didn't hold much water. Best-case scenario was that both the sock and shoe would be ruined. The thought instantly filled him with guilt. His mother had been so proud when she came home with them. She'd made him put them on and parade around the house. He found some relief from his guilt by clinging to the notion that he hadn't actually intended to step into the puddle. The problem was going to be explaining how he'd managed to center-punch a mud puddle in broad daylight. The truth would be too embarrassing to tell without ample embellishment.

Tommy took a seat next to Melody—she'd saved it for him. "Gonna be an angel this year?" he whispered.

She nodded yes, smiled, and squirmed. The angel part was near the end of the program. The angels sat backstage with the coronet players. Tommy's desire to get the coronet part grew exponentially when he considered the chance to sit backstage with Melody during all the practices.

Tommy noticed Melody looking at his pants leg. He'd cleaned all of the clay off of his shoe, but he hadn't noticed the clay colored stripes that were now dry and clinging to his pants leg. He didn't care; contemplating the Christmas program trumped the mud.

Mrs. Crawford continued her sequence of talking, smiling, double lip smacking, and tongue sweeping for what seemed like an eternity. The lip smacking became distracting. The end result, as everyone knew, would be for each person to let the Sunday school teacher know his or her first and second choice for pageant parts. The boys without parts served as parking attendants. Tommy looked at his muddy pants and wiggled his toes in his wet shoe and decided he'd had enough of the parking lot.

When Tommy walked normally, the wet shoe trapped air along the sides, and with each step, he made a sound as though he was passing gas—so he kept the shoe rigid, which made it look as though he had a limp. After reaching the top of the stairs, he limped toward the sanctuary.

Brother Baker noticed and inquired. "Hurt your foot?"

"No, just wet," Tommy replied.

"Whad'ja do to your foot?" Cletus asked. It seemed to Tommy that the entire congregation had taken an interest in the condition of his feet.

"Stepped in a mud puddle," Tommy replied.

"Looks like it hurts."

Tommy sat down in the front-row pew and waited a few minutes for the crowd to clear. He didn't want to explain the foot again.

The Websters, visiting Colby First Baptist for the first time, had arrived early and unintentionally chosen Cletus Thornton's usual seat. Cletus had started to sit across the aisle next to Mrs. Whitener, but he got a look from her and chose another spot.

There was plenty of room on both sides of Mrs. Whitener, but she'd already made a nest and was taking up enough space for three people. She'd left enough room between her and the end of the pew for another person, but anyone who started to sit there got a look. On the other side she'd place her latest knitting project and her purse of many colors. The purse had been the subject of countless conversations over the years, with much speculation surrounding the contents. There was an unwritten rule regarding the empty space next to the end. It's doubtful that Mrs. Whitener wouldn't have welcomed anyone less than Jesus Christ himself to take that space next to her, not even the great Reverend Billy Graham.

Cletus had been watching for Penny. When she stepped through the vestibule door, they made teenage eye contact and moved in unison to sit next to Booger's dad. In the process, they took the Birds's usual place— when the Birds arrived they took Milton Merle's spot.

A pew displacement cascade is an interesting thing to watch unfold in a small church. Few realized the Websters had started it and simply gave the person sitting in their seat a scowl before going in search of an empty space. Late comers were forced to the left front, usually left vacant for those responding to an altar call.

After each row of knitting knots, Mrs. Whitener paused and gave the Websters a curious eye. Her frown gained new folds when Deacon Baumgartner enthusiastically introduced himself to them. She'd always been suspicious of Deacon Baumgartner, seeing that he was both a Republican and an undertaker. And the look on her face suggested she suspected the Websters of being Republicans. With furrowed brow, squinted eyes, and pursed lips, she kept a close eye on them throughout the entire service. The Websters didn't notice.

The Websters' displacement cascade resulted in everyone sitting next to the most unlikely people. In some cases, Democrats were sitting next to Republicans. Milton Merle took advantage of the disruption and sat next to Venus Storm. Seeing them together confirmed the rumor. Both had always been viewed as strange, but in different ways. And no one would have guessed them as a match.

The rumor of their dalliance was probably the first bit of gossip that Jupiter hadn't repeated. Jupiter was in his regular place, the back pew, on the aisle, nearest the door. It was probably the sight of Milton sitting with Venus that had him fidgeting more than usual.

Fritz, a member but not a regular attendee, took Emma's usual place. He'd cleaned his thick glasses, which made his quintessential German blue eyes look beadier and more menacing than usual. Most were too interested in the Websters to notice Fritz in attendance, which was fine with him. He began thumbing through a hymnal, probably mistaking it for a Bible.

Jupiter began doing what he regularly did, staring at the ceiling and counting the stained ceiling tiles. Once the ceiling tile count was completed, he glared at the back of Milton's balding head. Jupiter's contempt for Milton would have been considerably less if he'd known of the recent nocturnal adventures of Emma Duke, which would have explained the continued disappearance of women's apparel and vindicated Milton.

Milton and Venus had gotten to know each other while making trips to Fairview. Because Milton Merle was a WWII veteran, he received free treatment at the Fairview VA hospital. He never discussed his disability, but his treatments occurred in the psychiatric ward. Venus had a car and volunteered to take people who couldn't drive to Fairview. Milton had never owned a car.

It was said that his propensity to steal women's underwear from clotheslines had to do with his WWII experience. He'd spent two years as a Marine, fighting island to island in the South Pacific. It's unlikely that his war experience had anything to do with his odd behavior, but war veterans rightly got the benefit of the doubt. And so it was with Milton— his service to the country excused a malady that most likely predated his military experience.

Shortly after starting his treatments, he'd begun to iron his clothes and comb his thinning hair. He vehemently denied responsibility for the missing women's underwear that continued to go missing. Because Erma wasn't part of the social network, she wasn't sensitive to the gravity of the issue, so she saw no reason to share what she'd discovered about Emma. Milton mistakenly remained on the hook for the missing underwear.

Fritz, the fastidious German, would have appreciated the unstated orderly way the congregation sat in the same place each Sunday, but he didn't attend frequently enough to know. So he had no way of knowing that he'd inadvertently uprooted the Ducklings from their normal pew place. Erma glared at Fritz when she slipped past him. Emma just puckered her lip and followed Erma. Emma noticed Fritz holding her favorite hymnal; someone had drawn a butterfly on the page ends. She gave Fritz a pitiful look, stomped on his foot, and snatched the butterfly hymnal. Fritz winced, pulled his feet under the pew, and let her pass. He sat there wearing a clueless frown.

Just before the announcements, Mrs. Crawford, oblivious to the tension caused by the seating fiasco, made her Christmas pageant appeal to the congregation. Most members had heard the annual appeal many times and either covered or fought off yawns. Mrs. Crawford was gifted at organization, picking the right people for each role, assigning jobs to members of the church, and following up. Her speaking skills were archaic. She sounded as if she was auditioning for a spot in an old English courtroom drama; sort of a pompous staccato.

Following Mrs. Crawford, Monkey, or Brother Fulbright as Brother Baker preferred to call him, made the church announcements. His excitement for the missionary who would be speaking at Fairview Baptist caused him to take rapid breaths while making the announcement. Missionaries who drew a big crowd never came to Colby. Billy Sunday had come to Fairview forty-some years earlier, during Prohibition, and people still talked about it as if it was yesterday.

Monkey continued to hyperventilate while describing Jacob DeShazer, who had been a bombardier in WWII and had been captured during Doolittle's famed raid over Tokyo. He'd later returned to Japan as a missionary. Appearing at Fairview with Mr. DeShazer would be Mitsuo Fuchida, who had led the Japanese during the attack on Pearl Harbor. Mr. Fuchida had become a Christian as a result of Mr. DeShazer's missionary work. The two of them would tell about their separate journeys, especially during WWII, and then how God had brought them together. It sounded to Tommy like an event that might rival Billy Sunday.

Unable to get his breathing under control, Monkey became faint and eventually keeled over. Everyone would have gotten more excited than they did, but it wasn't the first time Monkey had gotten excited and passed out in public. In fact, Mrs. Fulbright and a couple of deacons had started to the pulpit before Monkey keeled over. Mrs. Fulbright stuck a nitroglycerine tablet under his tongue. Since he'd crumpled slowly to the floor, no one felt the need to have him checked for broken bones. And besides, he'd never broken any bones in previous episodes.

"He's made of good stock," Mrs. Fulbright said while stroking Monkey's sweaty forehead.

Rabbit raced to the foyer and got the rusty old wheelchair left there for visitors. Monkey came to, looked around all glassy-eyed, and waved to the congregation while Mrs. Fulbright wheeled him to the rear. The wheelchair had an annoying squeak.

"Needs oilin', don't cha know," Bem said unsympathetically when they passed his aisle.

Mrs. Fulbright and Monkey argued while she rolled him down the aisle. Since both were hard of hearing, they spoke loud enough for all to hear. The result of the argument was that they would stick around for the sermon, which Monkey slept through. But even in sleep, his erratic sleep apnea-disrupted breathing was a distraction.

Brother Baker's cheeks were flushed when he finally took the pulpit. All the commotion with Monkey had taken nearly twenty minutes.

Cletus had already begun to glance at his watch before Brother Baker cleared his throat the first time.

There'd been some talk about canceling the church Halloween party. Brother Baker had prepared a sermon dealing with Halloween's Celtic roots. He assured everyone that Halloween was nothing to fear. It was simply an opportunity for kids and adults to act like kids and eat too much candy. He mentioned something about the Catholics confusing people by calling it All Saints Eve, which had been an effort to diffuse the original Celtic celebration to ward off evil spirits. Most had already made their Halloween plans, and his sermon changed very few, but Monkey's announcement had stirred the interest of all, particularly the WWII veterans.

If looks were needles, the Websters would have become pincushions by the end of the service. Several women gave them a corner-eyed glance before rushing out the door to a waiting pot roast. Cletus walked the Websters to their car.

The Codgers helped Mrs. Fulbright get Monkey to their car and helped her settle the argument about who was going to drive home. The look on Monkey's face made it clear that he didn't like sitting on the passenger side. In order to reach the pedals, Mrs. Fulbright had to scoot the bench seat up so far that Monkey's knees were mashed against the dash.

Jupiter Storm gave Milton Merle a furrowed brow scowl and spun his tires as he left the parking lot, splashing Mrs. Crawford with muddy water in the process. Had it been anyone else, there would have been cause for concern, but because it was Jupiter, few seemed to give the reckless driving much concern.

Emma gave Erma's arm a fierce tug when they passed Fritz's VW in the parking lot. Using a vernacular that only Erma could decipher, Emma explained how she'd seen Fritz's car drive through Colby on the night of the fire. Erma probably didn't put much stock in Emma's claim, but she reported it to Sheriff Dooley anyway, mostly likely because Fritz had taken their pew place. Dooley thanked her for the information, considered the source, and did nothing with it. After all, the fire marshal had declared the fire a lightning strike, and Fritz had shown him the receipts proving he was out of town on the night of the fire.

Queen of Quebec

THE GOOLSBY TWINS DIDN'T RAKE leaves. They only took jobs that could be accomplished with their riding lawnmower. They'd usually mow a yard once or twice, and after skinning every tree and making an errant pass or two through the flowers, would be told their services were no longer needed. The mower, similar to the twins, wasn't all there. It was missing a hood and half the muffler. The parents had thought the rider would be safer than a push mower, and it was—at least for the twins. But they hadn't considered the damage that a rider, in the hands of the incompetent, could do to a lawn.

Mrs. Whitener had sympathetically hired them to mow her lawn, or what she considered a lawn. Since she was half deaf, she hadn't noticed the broken muffler, as had her neighbors. And now she'd hired them to rake the leaves that covered her scalped lawn. The twins had made a futile effort at collecting the leaves by dragging a couple of rakes behind the riding mower. Mrs. Whitener got her fill and sent them on their way after they refused to get off the rider and rake the yard by hand.

Tommy and Booger came by with the paper only moments after Mrs. Whitener had gotten her fill of the Goolsbys. Tommy could still hear their mower in the distance while she explained the job. They agreed to return on Saturday.

BOOGER AND TOMMY HAD BEEN raking the leaves toward the street. Mrs. Whitener tapped Tommy on the shoulder and with her thick English accent said, "You can burn 'em in the yard, wouldn't you know." She'd lived in Colby since before Tommy or Booger were born, so her accent had never seemed unusual to them. They'd grown up with it. Tommy had always figured her to be a war bride.

Tommy looked at Booger and then Mrs. Whitener. "What about the grass?"

She whistled a flat tone. "What grass would you be talking about, lad?" Tommy looked around. She continued, "What grass that did peek its head up last spring got shaved off by the Goolsby twins, wouldn't you know." She shook her head and whistled an "Oh boy."

Tommy and Booger searched the yard for a spot with no visible roots. While they were looking for a safe place to burn the leaves, Mrs. Whitener lit the row they'd already accumulated.

Tommy knew that several roots were beneath the burning leaves. Worried, he asked Mrs. Whitener. "What about the trees?"

"What about 'em, lad?" she asked.

"Won't the fire hurt the roots?" Tommy asked.

"So what if it does, lad? The trees are the problem, don't you know." Tommy and Booger both gave her a perplexed look. "Wouldn't give you two cents for the trees, they hog the water, kill the grass, and then reward me each fall with the bloody leaves."

Once the leaves had been reduced to several piles of smoldering ashes, she invited them to sit on the porch. While the embers cooled, she offered them sassafras tea. "It's supposed to be good for everything, wouldn't you know," she alleged.

Booger took a sip and winced at the bitter taste. "Seriously?" he asked. Tommy couldn't tell if Booger was being polite or believing the herbal malarkey.

"Mr. Whitener's family all drank it, so did Mr. Whitener." She paused in contemplative thought. "It was his family who planted those bloody maple trees. I never liked them, but he wouldn't cut 'em down, wouldn't you know."

Booger made a slurping sound and asked. "What happened to Mr. Whitener?"

"Consumption."

"Guess sassafras tea can't help prevent consumption?" Booger asked and immediately wished he hadn't.

"Consumption is something that you catch. Sassafras helps prevent things that come on with age, wouldn't you know." She stood and stretched her cube-like five-foot frame. "Things like arthritis and wrinkled skin." After stretching, she removed her sunbonnet to reveal a deeply furrowed face. Pulled tight, there was probably enough skin to cover three faces.

"See what you mean," Booger said, winking at Tommy.

In an effort to hold in a laugh, Tommy snorted and a string of snot shot to the bottom of his chin. Mrs. Whitener reached into her skirt pocket and retrieved her Barlow knife. She walked with a purpose toward Tommy. He braced himself and was relieved when she kept going past him, oblivious to the gooey mess that strung from his nostril to his Adam's apple.

"It's time to carve a pumpkin." She leaned over and rolled a pumpkin from out of the corner of her porch. "Carry this into the yard, lad." Tommy, much relieved that he wasn't the objective of the Barlow, wiped his face with his sleeve and jumped to help her.

While artistically carving the jack-o-lantern, she told them her story, which explained the accent. Her mother had died when she was born. At the time, her father was on a whaling ship and couldn't return to England for nearly a year. She and her eight brothers and sisters had been split up to live with various members of their congregation. Her father never returned. Less than two years later, her adopted parents moved. She was so young that she never knew her brothers and sisters—she only knew of them. At twelve, she and her family moved again, this time across the ocean to Canada.

Cooking had always come naturally to Mrs. Whitener. She eventually landed a job at a prestigious restaurant in Montreal, Quebec.

It was during an International Rotary convention in Montreal that she met Mr. Whitener. He had been on the banquet committee, met with the kitchen staff, and had been taken with her accent. They'd kept in touch through letters and the rare long-distance call. Eventually, Mr. Whitener proposed. "He wasn't exactly a feast for the eyes," she said. She suspected he wasn't able to find anyone locally, so she'd gotten the nod. Her eyes welled with tears. "He always called me the Queen of Quebec."

After sharing her memories, a life's journey that seemed incredible to Tommy, she asked, "Ever eat the seeds?"

Tommy was still processing her story and didn't respond. He was visualizing her journey from an orphanage in England to Canada and then to

Colby. He wondered if the painting of the whaling ship hanging above her mantle and if the portrait of the sailor was her father, the one she never knew. It was more than his imagination could handle.

"No," Booger answered for both of them.

"Wait here," she said, and then she darted inside.

Tommy and Booger, still at a loss for words, admired the work of art that had once been a pumpkin.

"Did you know that?" Booger finally asked.

"Think she wonders about her brothers and sisters?" Tommy asked.

Booger introspectively ran his finger along the contour of the pumpkin. "She doesn't talk much, but when she does, she gets going."

The two of them sat there, neither one talking, thinking about Mrs. Whitener's journey. The sun had begun to set, and they were about to slip away when the aroma of baking pumpkin seeds filled their nostrils. Mrs. Whitener came through the door with a platter of baked seeds and had returned to her normal quiet self.

Tommy mustered the nerve to ask. "Is that portrait on your mantle your father?"

She gave Tommy a wild-eyed look. "Lands no, lad," she said. "It came with the painting. I got 'em both at a flea market in Fairview." For Tommy, learning the origin of the wall hangings was anticlimactic.

After gorging on the salty pods, the boys headed home, humbled by what they'd learned. Booger told Tommy that he had gotten ash dust on his face. Tommy wiped his faced again, using the same sleeve as before.

"Is that better?" Tommy asked.

"Not really," Booger replied. "Looks like you got side-swiped by a coal car," he added, and then laughed at his own cleverness.

Tommy gave him a shoulder shove. "I don't care," he said. It was dark by then, and both boys were exhausted. Gorged on seeds, they conjured up a variety of excuses for a lack of appetite at dinner and eventually settled on telling the truth.

Stranger

A few days later, Tommy was leaving his house to go trick or treating, or so he'd told his mom. She knew there'd be more tricking than treating and followed him out the door. "You just remember what I told you," she said while making threatening gestures with her weapon of choice, a wooden spoon. She'd told him to be a good example for others. He met Booger and they discussed "the plan" on the way to meet the others. He tucked away his mother's words.

By the time Tommy and Booger got to the stone, Caleb and Everett had already torn apart several bottle rockets and Black Cat firecrackers. They both hovered over a small pile of gunpowder. The ends of their fingers were stained dark silver from the powder. Checkers had brought a bag of potatoes and was using a pencil to punch small holes into the sides of each one.

Flop strolled up a few minutes later. Caleb looked up. "Got the hair spray?" Flop held up the bag and tried to look sinister, but it didn't work.

"In here," he said. Then he leaned in close and whispered to Caleb and Everett, "Did you know the Chinese use human crap to make gunpowder?" Caleb and Everett stopped momentarily and examined their fingers.

"Actually it's made from sulfur and saltpeter," Tommy said.

Everett frowned. "Never heard of saltpeter," he said.

Flop held up the label from one of the packages. "Look on the package. Says made in China."

Booger chimed in. "Says made in China—doesn't say anything about made with crap in China."

Flop countered, "Doesn't say anything about sulfur or 'at salt whatever. Those Chinese are sneaky."

Everett shook his head and handed out potatoes. "Here. Stuff some of that powder into each hole."

Flop protested. "I'm not touching that stuff!" The others exchanged frowns.

After the last potato was packed with gunpowder, they were divided, and each boy carried an equal number in his trick-or-treat bag. The plan was to collect treats until dark. So focused were they on their plans for the night that none of the boys noticed the spectacular fall sunset. The enormous harvest moon rise went unnoticed, too. Legend had it that a full moon caused erratic behavior.

Caleb sniffed his fingers and frowned. "Wonder if I can use Gooche's john to wash my hands?"

Flop snickered. "Thinking about that Chinese crap?"

Caleb braced. "No, just don't want to get gunpowder on everything." It was clear that Caleb had given Flop's comments considerable thought.

Tommy chimed in. "There's an employee john next to the loading dock. I'll go through the store and make sure it's okay to use it."

Mr. Gooche didn't mind the boys using the toilet, but told Tommy, "Your friends didn't pick a very good spot to collect their gunpowder." Tommy failed miserably at acting like he didn't know what Mr. Gooche was talking about. "And the potatoes?" Mr. Gooche asked. Tommy explained what they'd planned and then asked about using the employee john. Mr. Gooche grinned. He gently squeezed the back of Tommy's neck. "Make sure you stick with the plan." Tommy trotted through the store, blending Mr. Gooche's admonition with his mom's warning.

USING AN AAA MAP TO find Colby, Gino arrived just before dusk, cruised through town, and parked in the lot shared by a grocery store, dumpy looking theater, and a hamburger joint with a ridiculous neon sign of a hound dog. On his way through St. Louis he'd stolen a set of Missouri plates from a car parked in the long-term parking at Lambert Airport. He'd had the good sense to realize that a car with Illinois plates would be quickly recognized in a small Missouri town.

He drove by the Colby high school that Alison Tyson's daughter most likely attended. School had already let out for the day and the football team was practicing. Gino circled the school twice, and on the second sweep spotted the cheerleaders practicing near the field. They were all wearing identical warm-ups, similar hairstyles, and were too far away to see if any of them resembled the girl he was looking for.

Although everyone was speaking English, their accent and the culture that permeated Colby gave Gino the sense that he was in a foreign country. He didn't see a deli, but he had heard that in small towns it was typical to order fresh sandwiches from the grocery store meat counter. While everything seemed foreign to him, he was, in fact, the foreigner. Heads swiveled as he made his way through Gooche's to the meat counter. Gooche's regulars made no bones about staring.

Leon Goolsby, a cousin to the twins, was packaging ground beef when Gino swaggered down the aisle toward the meat case. Leon noticed him looking around as if searching for something. "Can I help you, bub?" Leon asked.

Gino looked around, saw no else standing at the meat case, and realized the butcher was talking to him. "What was it he called me?" Gino thought. "Bub?"

"Got a menu?" Gino asked.

Leon looked perplexed. He stopped momentarily. His hands were buried in a mound of greasy ground beef. Leon knew what a menu was, but since the question was so out of place, he seemed to misunderstand. "A what?" he asked.

"A menu," repeated Gino, adding unnecessary emphasis with his arms and hands. Leon stepped to the meat case and looked across and down at Gino. Gino led with his hands, "A sandwich. Can I order a sandwich?"

Leon wiped his hands with a blood-stained towel. "Sure, whatcha' want on it?"

Gino didn't see a menu and didn't recognize any of the cuts of meat in the case. "Surprise me," he replied. "Meat, cheese, lettuce, tomato, the works."

Irvin Enderle, the store manager, was standing in the aisle listening. Leon and Irvin looked at each other and grinned. Velma was watching from the checkout counter. She too had noticed Gino and was curious as to his business in the grocery store. Gino, not savvy to small town culture, had no idea he was being analyzed.

Leon handed Gino a thick sandwich neatly wrapped in butcher's paper with the price hand-marked on the side. "Pay at the counter," he said with no show of appreciation for Gino's business.

After choosing a bag of chips, Gino noticed a display of Moon Pies. He'd heard about Moon Pies and had seen people in movies that depict life in rural America eating them, but he'd never had one. Velma, who pretended to be filing her nails, watched Gino grab a bag of chips, several Moon Pies, and a Reese's peanut butter cup.

Gino's Italian looks were somewhat exotic for Colby. Velma became flirtatious. She looked first at the Moon Pies and Reese's cup and jokingly said, "Guess you're not planning to get much candy tonight?"

Gino, not used to casual conversations with a checkout lady, was taken aback. But he'd rehearsed a line to be used when questioned. "Just passing through," he replied. Velma, infatuated, wasn't listening.

While Gino was checking out, Jupiter Storm invaded the counter area with a cart full of Halloween candy. He'd waited until the last day in hopes that the candy would go on sale. Mr. Gooche, to spite Jupiter, traditionally waited for Jupiter to do his last-minute shopping before marking the candy down. To Mr. Gooche's delight, Jupiter had never caught on.

Looking down at Gino with his squinted eye, Jupiter asked. "Salesman?"

There was no escaping Jupiter's interrogation. Gino repeated, "Just passing through."

"Heard that the first time," Jupiter said, tugging up his ill-fitting pants. "From where to where?" he persisted. "What are you peddling?" When Gino didn't immediately respond, Jupiter tilted his head slightly, focused his good eye on Gino, and continued his questioning. "Callin' on someone here in Colby?"

Mr. Gooche stuck his head over the half wall of his office. "Jupiter, give the guy a break." Mr. Gooche then looked at Gino. "Sorry, sir. It's just obvious that you're not from around here, and everyone is curious. Please enjoy your visit in Colby for whatever reason you're here." Mr. Gooche then shot Jupiter a look before sitting down and resuming his work.

Jupiter, likewise, gave Gino a suspicious glare.

Gino smiled disingenuously, nodded appreciatively toward Mr. Gooche, and left. On the way out he picked up a copy of the *Colby Telegraph*. He got in his car and circled the block before parking under the neon hound dog. He ordered a chocolate milkshake from the walk-up window and returned to his car. The aroma of grilling burgers caused his mouth to water.

He opened the glove compartment and sat the milkshake on one of the shallow and practically worthless cup rings. He opened his sandwich and got a surprise but not one he'd visualized. He'd visited numerous deli shops and had enjoyed countless gourmet deli sandwiches. What lay before him on wax butcher's paper were several pieces of thickly sliced mystery meat enveloped by two pieces of plain white bread. Furthermore, the bread was slightly crusty, a sure sign that it was most likely day-old. Instead of spicy mustard, the bread was coated with a white, sweet, creamy substance that Gino could not identify.

Gino remembered the fly-strip he'd seen hanging above the meat case and the dirty hands that had handed him the sandwich—and he lost his appetite. While fuming, he noticed the people in the car next to him eating burgers and fries and got another whiff of the exhaust being blown from the Houn-Dawg kitchen. He returned to the window and ordered the burger basket, which came with fries, a fried pickle, and a small fountain soda.

MOST MEN CARRY A PHOTO of their wife and kids in their wallet, a comforting visual. But for a much different reason, Gino's wallet included a twenty-year-old photo of Alison and Reggie Tyson. It was wrinkled and faded. A daughter of Alison and Reginald Tyson wouldn't be difficult to spot in a sea of what looked to be people of mostly northern European descent.

THE ONION-SMOTHERED BURGER, FRIES, AND fountain soda had hit the spot. He'd seen others order from the window and return to their cars, so he'd done the same. He drained the milkshake so quickly that his temples throbbed. Everyone had their radios tuned to the same station and the volume ridiculously loud. Small town thing, he decided.

The setting sun cast an orange under glow on the western overcast sky. The darker the sky got, the more the neon Houn-Dawg's strobe-like effect annoyed him. He felt the first signs of a headache; the throbbing was in sync with the pace of the running neon dog.

A mild carbonated burp turned into a major gastric eruption when he saw her. A girl in a cheerleader's warm-up who looked as though she could be the daughter of Sophia Loren got out of the passenger side of a wrecker truck. She and the driver of the wrecker went inside. Gino, so enthralled with the young girl and her striking beauty, didn't get a good look at the driver. After they'd gone inside, he eye-twitched through several mental images of both people. He studied the wallet photo.

There was little doubt in his mind that the cheerleader was the Tyson girl, but he had to be certain. He continued his observations throughout the night. The driver of the wrecker—was it a man or a woman? He couldn't tell. He, or she, wore garage overalls and an odd looking hat that struck Gino as both strange and familiar.

Gino sat there motionless and suddenly, the epiphany stormed his memory. The driver wore the same kind of hat that Reggie Tyson was wearing in the wallet-photo. He looked around to see if anyone could tell what he was thinking. The thought struck him that his parking under the illumination of the neon dog wasn't the best plan.

He circled through the grocery store parking lot, keeping his eye on the wrecker. Several minutes passed before the two returned to the truck. From a safe distance, he followed the truck through Colby. It stopped momentarily in front of an old house where the passenger jumped out and ran inside. The wrecker continued. Gino followed it to a Sinclair filling station, where the driver parked and went inside.

Gino drove to the edge of town and waited for dark. When he returned to town every neighborhood was lined with cars, some parked and some moving slowly down the street. Kids, some dressed in costumes but most wearing homemade disguises, were carrying trick-or-treat bags and darting from house to house. A few residents, in an effort to keep marauding hordes from trampling their shrubbery and covering their porch windows with sugar-laden fingerprints, had set up tables street-side. He noticed a long line had formed where a lady was making something homemade.

Gino parked the car at the end of one street, grabbed his plastic pumpkin, and hopped out. He headed toward the house where the Tyson girl had been dropped off. On the way, he made mental notes of the neighborhoods and which streets led directly to the highway leading out of town. A getaway in a town with only a few roads leaving town would be a problem, he realized. He was nearing the house where the line had formed and the smell of something being deep-fried filled his senses. "Do people in the south fry everything?" he wondered. And then, "What smells so good?" He headed in the direction of a diminutive lady who had clearly won the popularity contest to see what she was serving. Several balls of dough were on the table where the lady was seated. She was working each ball with a rolling pin until it was flat, and then using a cookie cutter to make small discs. She tossed a batch of dough discs into the boiling oil, and then she went to work rolling another sheet of dough. When the boiling discs surfaced, she'd scoop them up with what looked like a guppy net, spread them on a sheet of wax paper, and dust them with powdered sugar. She shook the rolling pin at anyone who attempted to take more than one.

Mrs. Whitener noticed Gino standing nearby. And being Mrs. Whitener, asked, "Who are you?" The question and her accent caught him off guard. He wasn't sure what to do but knew running would draw too much attention. "Just 'a wait'n on my kids," he replied, trying to use the local vernacular, then turned and walked away.

"Wunna 'ose Fairview squirrels," Checkers snickered as Gino disappeared into the crowd.

"He wasn't from Fairview," Mrs. Whitener said. "Chicago," she continued.

She now had the attention of all the boys. "Chicago?" Checkers asked. He'd assumed the adult to be a parent from Fairview.

"Yep," she said.

"What makes you say Chicago?" Tommy asked.

"Accent," she replied. Tommy and Booger glanced at each other. The others paid little attention and had already gotten back in line for seconds.

After his second serving of fried cookie dough, Flop held his sack of treats up and said, "I'm tired of carrying all this stuff. Let's shoot the potato gun. It's dark enough."

Everett looked at Caleb. "Did you stash the gun?"

"Yep," replied Caleb. "It's under the bleachers by the football shed."

The band of boys headed for the football shed. Caleb found the gun and met the others at the end of the football field. The plan was to see what would happen if the potatoes were laden with gunpowder. Realizing the threat of fire, they had chosen the football field since the grass was almost nonexistent after the last two games had been played in the rain.

While they were laying out the potatoes, a few people could be seen milling around the dark side of the football shed. The boys quietly moved around the end of the bleachers so they wouldn't be easily noticed. Checkers and Everett slipped through the bleachers to see who it was. A few minutes later they returned.

"Just a couple of those cheerleaders and Letter Jackets," reported Checkers.

"What're they doin'?" Flop asked.

"Whadaya think?" Everett joked, and then he lightly swatted Flop's bulbous head. "Smokin' and smoochin'," he continued.

Caleb grinned. Tommy had seen the look before. "What're you thinkin'?" Tommy asked.

"We can reach 'em easy enough," Caleb replied.

"Do we have any potatoes that don't have gunpowder in 'em?" Tommy asked. The admonitions from both his mother and Mr. Gooche nagged him.

Caleb spoke as though he was an expert in potato-launching, "Even if the powder ignites, it'll burn out before reaching the football shed."

"What if the potato catches on fire?" Flop asked.

"Potatoes don't burn, stupid," Checkers chided. The rest of the boys rolled their eyes.

The ground was damp in the low areas. Tommy walked around, putting all of his weight on his toes, causing water to ooze out of the damp ground. He was satisfied the risk of fire was minimal.

"Stop your lollygagging and help us aim," Caleb told Tommy. The previous summer, the boys had practiced lobbing potatoes at targets. Tommy was the best at guessing the right angle to hold the barrel of the potato gun.

"I'm going to aim for this side of the shed," Tommy said.

"Why's that?" Caleb asked.

"The ground should be wet in that area," he replied, then aimed toward the area where the coaches normally set up the water octopus.

Checkers chuckled. "You ain't that good," he said. "You'll be lucky to get within twenty yards of the building."

Booger came to Tommy's defense. "Betcha!" he said.

"Betcha what?" Checkers asked.

"I don't know, just betcha," Booger replied, folding his arms. Checkers didn't press the matter; the boys were still sensitive to Booger's fragile disposition.

Tommy held the gun at what he thought was the perfect angle.

"Those cheerleaders are gonna scream like a bunch of monkeys," Caleb said.

"Heck with those cheerleaders, I'll bet the Letter Jackets crap their pants," Checkers added.

"Somebody gonna twist the igniter or ya' just gonna yap all night?" Tommy asked. Caleb got the honor since it was his gun.

None of the boys could have anticipated the result of using a flammable propellant to launch a potato stuffed with gunpowder. The flames exploding from the powder-filled holes made the potato glow in the night sky. The report echoed off the bleachers and startled the smokers hiding behind the football shed. By the time the flaming potato reached the apex of its trajectory, it had the full attention of everyone within a block of the pit.

The cheerleaders and Letter Jackets scattered as the flaming projectile fell toward the area that, just seconds earlier, they'd believed to be private and remote. When the fiery potato hit the ground, several feet from the shed, it exploded into tiny pieces that scattered across the damp ground and were immediately extinguished.

The cheerleaders and Letter Jackets flicked their cigarettes into the shadow of the shed and nonchalantly moved toward the bleachers. The cigarette butts landed on the dry leaves and instantly ignited.

Cheerleaders screamed and football players ripped of their letter jackets and used their prized possessions to beat down the spreading fire. The Letter Jackets were successful in putting out the fire before it did any significant damage to the sacred shed, but the gallant firefighting ruined their jackets.

Within minutes, a crowd gathered. Several heard the report, and more had seen the flaming object arc through the sky. Some had only seen it fall and thought it possibly a meteorite. The entire town was running toward the football shed while Tommy and the band of boys ran in the opposite direction. The boys reached the stone and were catching their breath when Caleb realized he'd left the potato gun behind.

GINO FOLLOWED THE CROWD. HE got near enough to see that a couple of high school boys were being heralded as heroes for having kept the fire from spreading. A couple of older men were standing nearby. "Good thing it didn't burn down the shed," Gino heard one of them say. "Yep, hate to lose that shed," another said. Gino contemplated the significance of the shed. He had already decided the residents of the small town were peculiar.

The fire department arrived shortly after the fire had been safely extinguished. Several men were hanging onto the back of the small fire truck while more arrived by car and truck. Everyone had coordinated on the style of blinking blue lights for the car dashboards, but a variety of sirens could be heard. Some sounded traditional, while others sounded more like those used in Europe—all were annoying.

The firemen sprayed the smoldering leaves and then opened the shed to make sure no embers had gotten inside. Gino eased closer to see what was inside the shed that made everyone revere it so. The shed held nothing but football gear. He didn't understand the mystique of small-town high school football.

On his way out of town, Gino stopped by a phone booth and ripped a map of Colby out of the phone book. After crossing the Mississippi River Bridge at Fairview, he stopped in the parking lot of one of the many strip joints, popular on the Illinois side, and replaced the stolen plates with the originals. He continued several miles into Illinois before stopping and paying cash for a motel room. He sat on the worn-out mattress of a fleabag hotel, used mostly by goose hunters, and read the *Colby Telegraph*. He was looking for anything that might help accomplish his mission. Reading about Colby community events made him seethe. "Regular little Mayberry," he said to himself. He grew to resent the town that had harbored the mother who'd sent his grandfather to prison. He stood, tossed the paper across the room. "I'll show them," he shouted into the mirror.

After a long shower he picked up the paper again. An article about a Veterans' Day parade caught his attention. "Parade Promises To Stop Traffic In All Directions" blared the headline. The accompanying article went on to describe the number of entries in the parade and its start and stop point. Pictures and names from last year's parade were included. And there she was, the girl he'd seen at the Houn-Dawg, Tippy Tatum. Clever, he thought, Tyson was now Tatum.

The primary photo was of the veterans leading the parade. It looked like most of the same old men he had seen watching football practice. He turned to the sports page and saw that Colby had a rival football game scheduled for the Friday after Veterans Day. He was sure they'd practice all week, even on Veterans Day. And, more than likely, where there were football players, there'd be cheerleaders. A plan began taking shape.

SHERIFF DOOLEY, TED THOMPSON, AND several volunteer firemen scoured the area around the shed in an effort to determine the cause of the fire. Even though the high school students thought it a well-kept secret, nearly every adult knew that the smokers used the shed to hide behind and smoke. The perpetual pile of fresh cigarette butts was a tell-tale sign.

The Letter Jackets knew the butts had started the fire. The potato had landed too far away and on wet ground. They wouldn't have been willing to use their coveted jackets to beat down the burning leaves had they not felt responsible. But everyone had heard the report of the potato gun and had seen the flaming potato arc through the sky before splattering near the shed. A compromising situation for the Letter Jackets had instantly turned into a heroic event.

AFTER BUILDING A FIRE IN his wood stove, Fritz reviewed the notes he'd made of the things his former commanding officer, and now the most notorious grand dragon in Mississippi, had told him about the KKK. He'd said there's a bond that exists between those who have served together in heavy combat. After a few beers, the former CO had told Fritz all about his involvement in the KKK, more than he should have. Fritz, the fastidious German, had later made written notes of the entire conversation.

Jackass

Tommy and Booger were sitting on the stone, moping and waiting for the paper. They were discussing the subjects of the essays they'd been assigned as part of the punishment for the potato gun incident. Tommy noticed Mrs. Koch fumbling with the lock on her mailbox. It usually took her a couple of attempts with the combination. He always felt the urge to go help, but he didn't want to embarrass her.

He and Booger had both been grounded and would remain so until they finished their public service requirements, the other part of their potato gun punishment. They had strict orders to go straight home after delivering the paper. The band of boys and their parents had met with Mr. Franklin. The adults had agreed that a few hours of public service and an essay would be sufficient punishment for nearly burning down the football shed.

Mr. Franklin wasn't upset with the boys, and there was a reason. Wendy, torn between her affinity for Tommy and her allegiance to the football team, had favored Tommy and told Mr. Franklin how the fire had actually begun—she'd asked him to keep the information confidential.

Tommy was contemplating talking to his Uncle Cletus about the matter when Jupiter came stomping up to deliver his daily dose of rumor. He tugged at his pants, confrontationally faced the boys, and announced for all to hear, "So the Kochs are moving. Guess old lady Koch is tired of helping the old man up and down those steps."

Tommy looked past Jupiter and noticed that Mrs. Koch had gotten her mail and worked her way through the crowded post office. She was just passing through the doorway when Jupiter made his insolent remark. Tommy could see her eyes and watched them begin to well up with tears.

His emotions overcame him—his next move was reflex. He looked Jupiter squarely in the eyes and before thinking, said, "You're a jackass."

Jupiter pushed his thick glasses up higher on his nose, squinted his good eye, and stepped closer. "What did you say?"

Tommy's mouth had gotten way ahead of his courage. Unable to face Jupiter, he looked to Mrs. Koch for solace. To his surprise, she was pushing people out of her way and making a beeline for Jupiter. Her hurt expression had turned to one of rage.

"I heard him plain as day, Jupiter, and I was inside the post office," she said. Jupiter turned to face a lady nearly twice his age and half his height. She squared off with Jupiter, held her mail with one hand, and reached up with the other and jabbed her tiny finger into his fleshy chest. "Is it that you didn't hear him, or is it that you need it explained?" Jupiter ignored her and turned to leave, but Mrs. Koch whacked him in the back of the legs with her cane. He spun around. "There's more where that came from, jackass." Jupiter knew better than to argue so he walked away, holding his leg. Mrs. Koch turned to the boys. "Jupiter the Jackass—has a nice ring to it," she said. Tommy was shocked.

Mrs. Koch's smile was fleeting. She got uncomfortably close to Tommy. "Tommy, you know better than to use that kind of language. And I'm sure that your mother would be most interested to know." She'd instantly converted from a club wielding feline warrior to a brittle old lady. "Tell you what," she said, moving her face inches from Tommy's—she'd had garlic for lunch. "Get some of your friends to help me and that *old man* move, and I'll make sure your mom never knows of your new name for Jupiter."

Tommy still wasn't thinking clearly, but he was coherent enough to be disappointed in Mrs. Koch's apparent lack of gratitude. He thought his challenge to Jupiter somewhat heroic. At the same time, he was relieved that his mom wouldn't find out about his outburst. Mrs. Koch squinted her eyes and tried to look angry, but she couldn't suppress a mischievous smile. "Plus, I'll see to it that it counts toward your hours of public service for nearly burning the town down."

She turned and disappeared up the stairway. She'd been gone several minutes before Booger said, "Dang! Can you believe that?" Tommy, still reeling mentally, didn't answer. Booger gave him a quizzical look. "You okay?"

Tommy finally spoke. "It's weird. It actually felt good."

Booger grinned. "You didn't say anything that everyone else doesn't already think but is just too chicken to say." Tommy was already thinking that his stunt would someday be legendary. He hoped that Booger would tell the others.

The *Colby Telegraph* truck arrived, and their attention returned to papers. Tommy waited for Jupiter to leave the courthouse before delivering the paper to each office. He was glad that no one in the courthouse said anything about the incident or acted differently toward him. Booger tried to convince Tommy that Jupiter wouldn't be telling people about a grade-school kid calling him a jackass, especially since it involved getting whacked by an old lady.

Tommy was relieved that the football shed fire wasn't the headline, but it had made the front page, below the crease. The football players were being heralded as heroes for extinguishing the fire. According to the story, the origin of the fire was still under investigation. Tommy knew differently. Sheriff Dooley had been to his house the previous night. The band of boys were being blamed; Sheriff Dooley had found the potato gun.

THE PREVIOUS DAY, THERE'D BEEN an article about the upcoming Veterans Day parade. Each year, the paper listed the names of the veterans who would be marching in the parade. A basic paragraph or two on each veteran who'd volunteered to march was included. The information provided for each veteran listed a summary profile, their area of military expertise, and in what theaters they'd served.

Miss Anderson, disappointed in the brevity of each veteran's description, got an idea for essay topics. She felt the boys would benefit from learning more about those who had served America and assigned each boy a veteran on whom to base their essay. She assigned Burt to Booger and Mr. Koch to Tommy.

COLBY CURLS WAS PACKED. "HEY, Tommy," Faye said.

Tommy nodded. "So much for not being seen or heard," he thought. Tommy, deep in thought and already regretting the jackass performance, handed each beautician their paper. His thoughts were interrupted when Chubby Cheeks announced, "Didn't take Cletus Thornton long to corral Penny Lane."

Every last drop of moisture in Tommy's mouth suddenly evaporated. His tongue seemed to swell and stuck to the roof of his mouth. Hearing the Colby Curls crowd talk about others was entertaining, but hearing family being discussed was a different matter. The mention of his uncle's name at the salon jolted him. Walking without stumbling required concentration; he vaguely remembered hearing that Penny's maiden name was Lane. The notion that her name was also a Beatles song replaced the Jupiter encounter.

"Not talking today?" Faye asked him.

Tommy snapped out of his mental excursion and unstuck his tongue from the roof of his mouth. "Oh! Hi, Faye."

The fuzzy faced lady sitting under a space helmet-looking hair dryer added her two cents. "It was common knowledge that he never married because he never got over Penny marrying that Norman Heart clown." When Tommy wasn't looking, Faye whacked the lady on her fleshy thigh, nodded toward Tommy, and made a zip up the mouth motion.

Tommy had heard enough and didn't linger—he was nearly two blocks away before his pulse and saliva glands returned to normal. He decided to discuss the cause of the shed fire with his Uncle Cletus.

WHILE MAKING THE DELIVERY AT Codger's Corner, Tommy noticed that the Koch's move had displaced football as the primary topic.

"Everybody always thought the old man would die up there," Monkey said.

"How long they been living up there?" Fish asked.

"Guess they been there since they got married," Rabbit answered.

The cheerleaders weren't practicing, so the boys didn't linger. It was the first time Tommy could remember the Codgers talking about anything other than football, cheerleaders, or calls at the recent football game.

THAT EVENING, TOMMY'S MOM WAS at the PTA meeting. He and his dad were watching *Gunsmoke* when the phone rang. Tommy was half watching the program and half thinking about his upcoming interview with Mr. Koch. The ringing phone reminded him that he needed to talk to his Uncle Cletus. Neither Tommy nor his dad moved a muscle in an effort to answer; they knew call was most likely for Marsha. It rang several times before Marsha came stomping out of her room, where she'd been studying. "Can't anyone answer the phone?" she asked rhetorically. Of course, the call was for her.

"No!" Marsha said into the phone. "That's hilarious." She continued. *Gunsmoke* was reaching the climax, and Marsha's exclamations were distracting. Chester and Kitty were pleading with Marshal Dillon, trying to talk him out of facing down a notorious gunslinger. Tommy gave Marsha a quiet-down look and got a grin and wink in return. "Tell me about it," she continued, agreeing with the caller. "He's creepy."

The fragments of Marsha's conversation began to take shape in Tommy's mind. He lost track of Marshal Dillon's impending doom and began to consider his own—and how he'd explain his spontaneous outburst. While he was sure that all would agree with his assessment, he'd been taught to show respect for adults, even unbearable ones like Jupiter. Not only had he been disrespectful, but there was the language issue, not to mention name-calling. He'd only been home two hours and already Marsha was talking about it on the phone with one of her friends. Tommy considered the marvel of the telephone and the grid of wires stretching from house to house. His stomach began to churn. He wondered if Booger had spilled the beans, then remembered he'd hoped that he would. He didn't know what he wanted.

Marsha finally hung up. "Who was that?" Tommy's dad asked.

"Nobody," Marsha replied.

"You sure got excited for a minute—must have been somebody," he continued. About that time Marshal Dillon squared off with the man in the black hat. The line of questioning ceased and Marshal Dillon saved the town. He and Kitty never kissed.

Marsha winked at Tommy. "I have more homework to do." Then she sashayed down the hall to her bedroom.

Tommy's mother returned from the PTA meeting and told his dad she had something she needed to discuss with him, but that it could wait until Tommy went to bed. Throbbing temples competed with Tommy's churning stomach in a contest to keep him awake. He lay in bed and watched the shadows cast by the streetlight through the maple tree dance on his wall and thought about the day he'd had and considered the morrow with trepidation.

THE NEXT DAY BEGAN WITH the normal family chaos. Marsha, consumed with putting on her face and hogging the bathroom, acted as if nothing had happened. Tommy's mom had breakfast fixed and asked the usual questions about school. His dad read the morning paper and feigned interest. She didn't mention anything about PTA. Tommy was perplexed but decided to let dead dogs lie.

The dead dog came alive with a roar at the bus stop. Tommy felt as if he slew the dragon. By a single slip of the tongue, he'd become an elementary school phenomena and potential legend. Mickey Murphy idled slowly by, his car loaded with football players—Tommy got a thumbs up from everyone in the car. He was reminded of a scripture he'd had to memorize for Sunday school—1 Timothy 4:12: "Don't let anyone look down on you because you are young, but set an example for the believers in speech." He contemplated the verse and was emotionally conflicted. The adulation felt both good and wrong.

Tommy continued to be conflicted throughout the day. He'd told his Uncle Cletus that he needed to talk to him about something. While sitting on the stone and waiting for the paper, he told Booger what he was going to tell his Uncle Cletus. Booger wasn't sure it was a good idea.

The truck arrived, they gathered the papers, and began the route. It was a cold, breezy, overcast day. Few people were out, and the boys were making good time since they weren't being stopped by people wanting to chitchat.

Shots being fired from the behind the Legion hall suddenly got their attention. They were curious to see what was going on. Shooting matches weren't held during the daytime, and besides, they could tell the shots weren't from shotguns. Tommy and Booger recognized the cars in the parking lot. Since they were making good time, the boys took time to creep to the edge of the Legion building and watch.

Burt Brown and several other Colby veterans traditionally gathered prior to Veterans Day and "let loose a few rounds," as they called it. Burt, Sheriff Dooley, Joe-Bill, Eugene Meisenheimer, Carter Webster, Finis Pribble, and Jupiter were gathered around a picnic table. George Koch, with Scout on his lap, was seated on one end in his wheelchair. Mrs. Koch was nowhere in sight. Frank Fritz hadn't shown up. He claimed to have a virus, but everyone, including Carter Webster, suspected otherwise. The table was covered with a variety of weapons. Sheriff Dooley saw the boys watching and waved them over.

Tommy wasn't sure if Sheriff Dooley was inviting them or ordering them—it didn't make any difference, they'd been seen. He looked at Tommy and asked, "Think you can shoot a rifle as good as you can aim a potato gun?"

Tommy was feeling anxious until his Uncle Cletus pulled up. "You're late," Burt said.

"Didn't know we'd set a specific time," Cletus answered.

"Penny for your thoughts," Dooley said. Everyone laughed. Cletus was late because instead of coming straight to the range after school, he'd stopped by to see Penny. Cletus smiled.

Cletus looked in Tommy's direction. "Thought you were grounded?"

Tommy held up a folded *Telegraph*. "Delivering papers." Being a paperboy did have its advantages. Cletus nodded approvingly.

Jupiter Storm started their way. Tommy noticed Jupiter's walk was more a swagger than a stomp. Tommy wasn't sure what to expect next, but he knew he was safe with so many adults nearby. Surprisingly, Jupiter patted him on the shoulder, gently squeezed the back of his neck, and said, "He's a spunky little runt. I'll give 'im that." The others laughed. A special camaraderie existed between the men that Tommy had never seen—and it included Jupiter.

Tommy looked at the rifles and boxes of ammo lying on the table. He'd been at Burt's when deer hunters had shown off their rifles, but these rifles were different—they were bulky and looked heavy. Tommy realized they were the same rifles he'd seen the veterans carrying in parades. Up close, they looked more menacing. Their stocks, rather than being replete with intricate engravings, were rugged and scarred. Tommy was momentarily overwhelmed, but snapped to after realizing that his mouth had been hanging open and his tongue half out. If Marsha had been there, she would have bopped him on the head. Eugene Meisenheimer pointed at Jupiter and said to Tommy. "Jackass there was a sniper. He's done outshot all of us today." The others laughed. Tommy looked at Booger for assurance and got none. After noticing his tongue hanging out, he pulled it in and swallowed.

Jupiter grinned, picked up a rifle, and pointed to a spot at the end of the picnic table. "Take a seat." Tommy sat down—still unsure of the world he'd just stepped into. Jupiter helped him situate the rifle using a small sandbag for support. Tommy cautiously gripped the rifle and peeked through the scope. "We'll do a couple of dry fires first," Jupiter said. He explained, "After I show you how to aim, you'll squeeze the trigger a couple of times without actually firing off a shot." He grinned. "That's so you'll get used to the pull of the trigger. It's a little different than a Red Ryder."

Jupiter's comment caused Tommy's adrenaline to surge even more. Tommy resisted the urge to tell Jupiter that he'd graduated from the Red Ryder to a Benjamin pellet rifle, not to mention that only a few weeks earlier he'd shot his Uncle Cletus's .410 shotgun. Inexplicably, he wasn't intimidated by Jupiter, but he was certainly overwhelmed by the situation and particularly the feel of the heavy rifle.

"Look through a scope before?" Jupiter asked.

Tommy was familiar with scopes, just not ones attached to sniper rifles. "I have a scope on my Benjamin," Tommy answered proudly. He referred to his pellet rifle as a Benjamin in a dismal effort to sound experienced with guns.

"You'll want to hold your face back from the scope a little more than you do on your pellet rifle," Jupiter advised. The advice stung a little, even though Jupiter's tone wasn't condescending. Tommy was feeling sorely inadequate. He concentrated on keeping his lips closed and his tongue in his mouth.

"Yes, sir," Tommy replied, his voice an octave or two higher than normal.

Jupiter instructed him on how to aim with a scope. "Now aim at that target and squeeze the trigger." To Tommy's surprise the pull of the trigger was very light. "Perfect," Jupiter said. He worked the bolt action. "Do it again." Tommy took careful aim and squeezed the trigger once more. Jupiter picked up the rifle, loaded a round into the chamber, and said, "You're ready!"

This time the trigger squeeze resulted in an explosion that made Tommy's ears ring. Jupiter looked at Tommy's eye while the others checked the target. Although he'd been warned, Tommy had not been prepared for the recoil. He'd held his face too close to the scope. He concentrated on doing just as he'd done before, but when the rifle fired, it reared back and the scope hit his eye socket. Tommy's eyebrow stung and his right jaw throbbed. He'd learned firsthand what he'd heard deer hunters at Burt's Sinclair refer to as a scope-bite. City slickers were usually highly susceptible to scope bites.

The veterans grinned among themselves. Jupiter towered over Tommy with his arms crossed. He smiled. "I can still remember my first one."

"Everyone's done it a least once," Finis added.

Burt handed Tommy a set of binoculars. "Here, see if you hit the target." Tommy studied the target through the binoculars, being extra careful not to touch them to his sore eye. "The holes we shot are marked with an X. See any holes with no X?" Burt asked.

"Looks like there's one on the right side," Tommy said.

Burt tussled Tommy's hair, and then handed him a neatly folded handkerchief. "Here, hold this on your eyebrow a minute," he said. Tommy dabbed his eyebrow, realized he was bleeding, and visualized the city slickers he'd seen with the tell-tale ringed wound.

While Tommy was dabbing his eye, Jupiter took the binoculars. "Let me see." It took him a second to evaluate the shot. "You're vertically on line—that's good, but you pulled to the right. That's easy to fix." Jupiter sat down and explained how to overcome pulling to the right. Booger, standing there stiff as a statue, listened too.

Tommy shot once more, this time without further injury, and then it was Booger's turn. Jupiter took a seat next to Booger and patiently helped him make a couple of shots. Booger had learned from watching Tommy and didn't let the scope get too close.

Eugene sat down beside Tommy, put his arm on his shoulder, and tried to comfort him. "I done that just last year," he said. "It ain't no big deal." Tommy, still rubbing his eye, was filled with mixed emotions, both embarrassment and a strange sense of pride at being a new member of the scope-bite club.

After the two boys had each made a shot near the bull's-eye, Cletus said, "Jupe, why don't you show 'em how it's done."

Tommy was looking through the binoculars. "It doesn't look like anyone has hit the bull's-eye yet."

Jupiter chuckled, twisted a knob on the side of the scope—it clicked twice—and then he chambered a round. It wasn't until then that Tommy noticed that Jupiter's scope was also a range finder. Jupiter took aim and while slowly exhaling, squeezed the trigger.

The men were standing, arms crossed across their chests and wearing smirks and grins. Burt asked, "Did he hit the bull's-eye?" Tommy studied the target, didn't see a new hole, and said it appeared that Jupiter had completely missed.

Cletus chuckled, "Could be that you're looking at the wrong target." Tommy lowered the binoculars and saw the men grinning. "There's another target on further down. Look to the right."

Tommy could barely make out what looked to be another target further away, nearly twice the distance. Looking through the binoculars, he could easily see the target, but he didn't see any new holes.

"Here," Burt said, taking the binoculars. He twisted the zoom knob, making the binoculars stronger. "That'll bring it in a little closer." The down-range target now clearly visible, Tommy could see that the bull's-eye area was completely destroyed, and only one hole was outside of the center. "You can probably see one hole, that's mine," Burt said. "The cluster in the middle is Jupe's."

Tommy handed the binoculars to Booger. They exchanged the binoculars back and forth a few times and continued to stare in disbelief. "Wow," Booger finally said. Tommy had seen the veterans with their rifles in several Veterans Day parades, but he had never given any thought to them actually using them. He put his hands on the stock of Jupiter's rifle. "Can I look through it again?" he asked.

Jupiter made sure the rifle was unloaded and carefully handed it to him. "Sure."

"Is that the actual rifle you carried during the war?" Tommy asked.

"The very one," Jupiter said. Tommy looked through the scope at the farthest target—it appeared in the scope much smaller than the target he'd shot. He rubbed his hands along the stock and let his fingertips glide along each scar. Booger took his turn doing the same. He wondered how many Germans Jupiter had shot. He was sure that Booger was thinking the same thing.

Booger stared at Burt several seconds before saying, "I'm supposed to write a paper about your war experience."

The jovial spirit that had prevailed among the veterans evaporated. They exchanged solemn, eye-twitching glances. Burt gave Tommy a curious glance, "Ya don't say?"

Booger continued, "Tommy's supposed to do the same about Mr. Koch."

"It's part of our punishment for getting blamed for the football shed fire," Tommy added.

"Why me'n' George?" Burt asked.

"Miss Anderson assigned each of us a veteran," Booger answered. "She thinks the article in the paper didn't do any of you justice."

"Wonder if she stopped to think that it's not something we want to talk about?" Jupiter asked.

"So what kind of questions are you supposed to ask?" Burt asked.

"When and where you served ... what was your most memorable experience ... and anything else you'd like to add," Booger said.

The veterans exchanged more nervous glances. Burt finally said, "I'll have to think about it." After a long pause, he continued, "Stop by the station sometime—we'll talk." Mr. Koch remained silent. His elbows were resting on the arms of his wheelchair; his chin was resting on his clasped hands. Nobody spoke for nearly a minute.

"We better get going," Booger said, breaking the silence. "It's gonna be dark soon." The boys thanked the men and shook their hands before leaving. Tommy remembered what his dad had told him about shaking hands, and he squeezed hard and shook vigorously.

"I'll stop by tonight," Cletus told Tommy. Tommy nodded.

DURING THE LAST STRETCH OF the paper route, the sun and temperature had dropped. Tommy could hear "The Ballad of the Green Berets" coming from the Houn-Dawg. He'd heard Staff Sgt. Barry Sadler, a real Green Beret, sing the song many times and had always visualized the glory of being a soldier. He'd always liked the song, but since Booger's brother had been killed in Vietnam, the words had new meaning.

He contemplated the difference between how war was glamorized on TV and the actual consequences, which were death and sacrifice. At some point, it dawned on him that he'd discovered respect for Jupiter.

The boys went their separate ways at the corner. Tommy removed his boots before going in, ran to the heater grate, and was letting the warm air run up his damp pants legs when his mom came from the kitchen.

"What happened to your eye?" she asked. The combination of chilly air and discussions of war with Booger had taken his mind of the throbbing wound.

"Nothing," he answered, and then began piecing together an opaque explanation.

His dad overheard the exchange and came out of the bathroom with half his face covered with shaving cream. "How'd you get the scope bite?" he asked.

Tommy's mom then turned to her husband for an explanation. While the term "scope bite" was being explained, Tommy sorted through a number of possible scenarios and settled on the truth—at least the shooting part.

Marsha, curious, examined his eye and took the opportunity to play nurse. She dabbed his eyebrow with hydrogen peroxide as his mom fried chicken. Tommy, now the center of attention—the good kind—began telling of shooting rifles with the veterans. Marsha's eyes squinted suspiciously each time Tommy mentioned Jupiter in a favorable sense. They optically communicated as only siblings can—the jackass episode was never mentioned. When Tommy said Jupiter wasn't so annoying once you got to know him, she huffed and left the room. She recovered from her fit in time to help her mom set the table for dinner.

Cletus stopped by after dinner. He came through the door with his rifle. "Mind if I teach Tommy how to clean a rifle?" he asked. Tommy's Dad looked to his Mom for her reaction—she nodded approval. Tommy and Cletus went to the basement.

They were alone. "So what's on your mind?" Cletus asked Tommy.

Tommy was running a cleaning brush through the rifle barrel and waited several seconds before responding. "It's about the shed fire."

"Uh-huh," Cletus said, handing Tommy a small piece of oiled fabric with which to clean the rifle barrel.

"You see," Tommy began, "we didn't actually start the fire." Cletus gave him a curious look, so Tommy explained.

When Tommy finished, Cletus grinned. "I see," he said. "It's something you'll just have to live with."

Tommy wiped down the bolt and handed it to Cletus. "I know," he said. "I just wanted you to know that we had better sense than to shoot that potato into the dry leaves." Cletus gave Tommy an affectionate pat on the shoulder and they walked upstairs.

After Cletus left, Tommy's mother asked. "What were you two talking about?"

"Nothing," Tommy replied, and then he went into the bathroom to wash his oily hands and escape further questions.

CLETUS ENTERTAINED HIMSELF ON THE way home giving thought to the various ways he could make life difficult for the cigarette smoking football players.

Colby Lanes

Tony Rosolini slumped against the wall with his arms crossed—he was exhausted, but extremely satisfied. He shook his head and breathed a silent prayer of thanksgiving: "Lord, thank you for this blessing. Thank you for this town, these good people, for bringing my wife and me here ..."

He watched the three lanes of bowlers laughing, eating, and shouting out friendly taunts at each other. Colby Lanes had been open four short weeks, and business was booming. It was open five nights a week—and it could have been more, but Angelina had put her foot down. The snack bar and pizza made enough profit to pay the help. He cleverly billed his bowling lanes as a place for "Fun, Family, Fellowship, and Food." It became an instant hit with the local churches, and even a few from surrounding small towns. Fairview's monopoly on bowling was over. No problem getting people to come in to bowl or eat his steaming hot pizzas—but staffing, now that was another story. He hired mostly high school kids, along with an adult to supervise on the nights he and Angela stayed at the restaurant. It was hard work. But the Lord rewards hard work, doesn't he?

And then there was Al. "Now if that wasn't the Lord's doing," he thought. She seemed like she had been waiting for something like this. He couldn't recall whether she had any hobbies or interests other than work, or even friends, until Colby Lanes opened. She came over almost daily for the first couple weeks to tinker with the machines and would never accept pay. So she got to eat free at Rosolini's from then on. He'd even had to insist on that. "Boy, can that woman bowl," he thought. He decided to ask her if she would consider offering bowling lessons after the Christmas holidays. It would help business, and she could make some money to boot.

Colby Baptist Church had reserved the evening. Patrons could get a fifty-cent discount if they brought in their church bulletin from Sunday. He noticed Monkey Fulbright handing them out at the door but let it go. The place was packed anyway, and most didn't have any intention of bowling. Tony's observation from the alley and the restaurant was that he was right: Protestants loved to eat. Never was there a gathering of two or more without food. Being Catholic, he had always assumed that Protestants, especially the Baptists, had overcompensated for not drinking alcohol by overeating, which was fine with him. Because he served no alcohol, he rightly noticed that his fellow Catholics spent more "fellowship" time at the Knights of Columbus Hall than at his alley. They had horseshoes and washers and booze. He had great food and wholesome fun, and that's what most of the town seemed to want.

A twinge of guilt began to stab at his heart. Should he offer a better discount to church groups? Or let them bowl for free since they ate like there was no tomorrow? He quickly took the thought captive and buried it under the fact that he *always* gave his tithe—10 percent plus, right off the top, no matter what. And now that he made more money, his tithe had grown equally. Even at that level of commitment, he never felt that he was doing enough even if he was always a cheerful giver.

"Mr. Rosolini! Mr. Rosolini!" He looked up to the pin pit and saw Checkers, wide-eyed and anxious. No doubt he wanted a snack break. A steadfast rule of "no food or drink in the pin pit" had been modified as the bowling interest increased. The boys were allowed free soda, but they had to keep their drinks on a small table away from the machines. But no food—not even gum—was allowed after Al spent a good half hour cleaning a wad of Super Bubble out of one of the machines.

"You need a break?"

Checkers didn't answer. He just scurried in a beeline to the snack bar. Tony had the good fortune of having the band of boys available to work the pit that night. Still working off the potato gun fiasco and wanting to get back into the good graces of the town (with their parents prodding, of course) they agreed to work. The high school had a dance of some sort, and he couldn't get his regular crew. Things were going smoothly, but he recalled the first night the boys worked in the pin pit. It was First Baptist night, and not only were the pinsetters newbies, but few patrons knew a strike from a spare. What a night!

The boys now had a routine, and the pinsetting operation was finally running smoothly. "Hey! Caleb! Pay attention. Somebody's gonna get hurt if you don't listen to me." The boys rolled their eyes and sauntered over to Flop. Self-appointed as the chief pinsetter, since he had more experience than the others, Flop was barking orders and assigning lanes. "Checkers, you're with me here on lane two—that-a-way I can keep an eye on everybody. Caleb, you and Everett on three, Tommy, Booger—you're on one."

People began to stroll in, Tommy looked through the pinsetter to see Cletus and Penny sitting down at lane one. He smiled and elbowed Booger, pointing at them. Flop was still chattering instructions and acting important when Booger's dad and Miss Anderson sat down to make a foursome. "This will be interesting," Tommy thought. He knew his Uncle Cletus and Miss Anderson were good; the pinsetters would earn their keep.

As the boys took their positions, Booger snickered.

"Whatcha laughin' at?" Tommy asked, and then looked around to see what was so funny.

"Nuthin,'" Booger said, his eyes clearly fixed on Tommy's scope bite while unsuccessfully attempting to keep a straight face. Tommy hip-checked him against the wall of the pin pit, causing them both to giggle. Flop thought the joke was on him—which it usually was, since he was still considered the new kid in town and not quite used to small town life.

"Hey, you guys! Pay attention. Like-a-said, they're almost ready to start." All eyes rolled again. Tommy felt a small sense of pride for Flop. This was good for him. Booger made a suggestion that Flop wished he'd thought of. "Okay," he said nonchalantly, "I guess you guys are ready for that." He once again barked instructions. "On three. One … two …" and making an unnecessarily long pause for effect, he said, "Three!" All three pin trays descended simultaneously, earning a healthy applause from the bowlers.

"Well done!" Al cheered from lane three. She winked at Burt and said "These boys are somethin.'" She smiled with obvious pride for the boys. Burt had invited Al to bowl that night. He tried to convince himself it would be good for her to get to know some of the church crowd. She had been to church a few times now but hadn't taken the time to visit with anyone. In truth, the church crowd needed to get to know her too. Al's choice of clothing, her manly profession, and her pregnant daughter made people uncomfortable around her. But Burt had invited her for another reason—he liked being around her. Was she changing? He'd known her for nearly eighteen years, but he couldn't remember having noticed how pretty her eyes were.

"Ladies first," Cletus said. It wasn't so much a show of manners as it was a fear of being the first to throw a gutter ball.

Flop got a wild look in his eyes, "Here we go, boys! Get ready for pins to fly!" All three women rolled their balls directly into the gutter. Brother Baker's wife, Dorothy, rolled her ball. It came to a complete stop halfway down the lane. Flop had to jump down from the platform and retrieve it.

Placing the ball in the return ramp, Flop looked up to see Caleb smiling. "Nuthin' to this," Caleb said, looking at Flop.

Flop gave him an "I know something that you don't know" look. "Just you wait. You'll change your tune in a minute." He had seen Al Tatum bowl. No one was better—not even the men. Caleb would be sweating soon enough. But as luck would have it, Caleb and Everett had the easiest job that night. Al and her team got mostly strikes, meaning fewer trays to set—something Flop had not counted on. He and Checkers, however, were hopping up and down working the pins, retrieving gutter balls, and working twice as hard.

To make matters worse, at least for Flop, Checkers placed an extra pin into the pit when Flop wasn't looking. When it was Flop's turn to place the pins, he jumped down off the platform to put them in the tray. The extra pin confounded him. He looked at the others, but they went along with the mystery and busied themselves with their work. Flop's bossiness gradually subsided. He was getting worn out, confused by the extra pin, and tormented by the fact that Caleb was getting off easy.

George Koch had wheeled himself to the pin pit area. He was more interested in the pinsetting than the bowlers. With Scout on his lap, he watched the boys and was amused by their antics. At first, having an audience had added to Flop's nervousness, which led to a heightened air of authority. Tommy and Booger were the closest to Mr. Koch, but they were comfortable with his presence. They were his paperboys and had been in his apartment, which was something few townsfolk had done.

Tommy's thoughts occasionally drifted to the picture of Mr. Koch in uniform standing next to the old airplane. Mr. Koch had flown airplanes when they were practically first invented! He was a pilot in a war and had returned home to live a long life—he'd beaten the odds. He looked at Booger, who was busy and enjoying himself, even laughing. Tommy thought, "I wish Booger's brother, Randy, had come home too."

Tommy jumped and bit his tongue when the pins came crashing into the pin-pit. Uncle Cletus got another strike and snapped Tommy from his thoughts. Mr. Koch's chuckle stirred up a hacking cough from deep in his throat. Tommy, somewhat embarrassed, grinned. He was glad to see Mr. Koch getting out and enjoying himself. He'd told Tommy how he looked forward to attending more community functions after moving to the duplex.

At break, the boys walked past Mr. Koch, Checkers leading the way, wide-eyed and drooling from hunger. He had been talking about Twinkies for the past half hour. Mr. Koch reached out and took Flop by the wrist. "Good show, young man. You run a tight ship."

"Like-a-said," Flop replied, "everything went pretty good except for that danged extra pin."

"Things like that sometimes happen," Mr. Koch said, and Flop nodded in agreement. He had no way of knowing that Mr. Koch was referring to the prank. Mr. Koch was envious of the boys. He recalled his days in the service when pranks, as a way of escaping the tragedy of war, were an everyday occurrence.

All in all, a record number of gutter balls were thrown, a record amount of pizza was eaten by Brother Baker, and only a couple of pinched fingers and broken fingernails were suffered by eager bowlers reaching for returning balls. During the second round of bowlers, a rather plump woman who was more concerned with her ill-fitting bowling shoes than her technique got her finger stuck in a bowling ball and caused quite a commotion. The finger came free after her partners held the ball over her head for a minute.

Watching the lady stagger around holding the ball over her head was too much for the pinsetters. The giggling in the pin pit was contagious, and Booger collapsed against the wall, holding his stomach with one hand and covering his mouth with the other. Tommy looked at the giggling band of boys, his buddies, and surprisingly one of the scriptures he had memorized years ago came to mind: "A merry heart doeth good like a medicine."

By the end of the night, the boys were worn out and drenched with sweat. They'd worked hard and laughed continuously.

Pearl of Wisdom

THE KOCHS' MOVE WAS ONLY a day away. Gloria, Angelina, and a couple of ladies from First Baptist were helping Marie Koch clean. Although seeing her collection of fine furniture uncovered after so many years emotionally stirred Marie, she wasn't having second thoughts about moving—she knew it was the right thing to do. The ladies observed her pausing over certain items that were obviously dear to her. Sometimes she'd stop and share a sweet memory; she savored the memories more than the "stuff."

Marie stood motionless in front of the shadow box that held her spoon collection. She gently touched each spoon with her fingertip and then carefully removed one for closer inspection. She held it up for Gloria and Angelina: "Dawson Creek, B.C." was etched on the stem. She and George had bought it during their last trip to Alaska. They'd spent two weeks in Denali before starting south on the Alaskan Highway, and they had stopped in the little Canadian town for lunch. Reports about the great Alaskan earthquake had been broadcast over the radio while she was paying for lunch and the spoon. They were saddened to learn that the earthquake had damaged several places they'd visited only days earlier.

Gloria and Angelina stayed behind after the rest of the First Baptist ladies left. They'd planned to make dinner for the Kochs in their last night in the apartment. Neither George nor Marie could remember the last time they'd sat at their dining room table. Emulating a fine restaurant, Gloria and Angelina prepared the plates in the kitchen and served them with fanfare.

Carter had bought a bottle of champagne for the event and sent it with Gloria. She'd kept it tucked away until the others had left. It took both Angelina and Gloria to open the bottle. They found their struggle with the cork amusing, especially when the cork went flying through the open doors and over the balcony.

While cleaning, Gloria had found a pair of champagne flutes and situated them on the ornate table. The Kochs had bought them as a souvenir during a tour of Normandy. Angelina poured a half flute each for George and Marie. After doing so, she and Gloria stood back and watched the Koch's toast. Everyone knew about the Koch toast, and a few had privately adopted the same practice—just one of the many examples the Kochs had set.

"One more day," George said, looking deeply into Marie's eyes.

"One more day," she replied, matching his gaze.

Angelina gave Gloria a wink, and the two of them discreetly touched the juice glasses they'd used to pour a bit of champagne for themselves.

Marie insisted on helping to clean up. While doing so she said to Gloria. "Before you know it you'll be moved, know everyone, and it will seem like home." Gloria smiled, but sensed that without Marie and Angelina around, Colby could be a cold place.

THE NEXT DAY, TOMMY ARRIVED before the rest of the movers. Mr. Koch had agreed to the interview. Tommy opened his Big Chief note pad and got out the questions Miss Anderson had provided, just in case he couldn't think of any on his own. Scout sat drooling on Mr. Koch's lap; they both looked aged but comfortable. Tommy had just worked up the nerve to ask his first question when he realized he'd lost his pencil. It had been tucked safely behind his ear when he'd left the house. Mrs. Koch watched him searching and handed him a mechanical pencil. She showed him how to use it when she saw that he needed help figuring out how to advance the lead.

Tommy's first question wasn't on Miss Anderson's list; it was about the X608 program. He'd been intrigued by it since noticing the plaque.

"First of all, that was a top secret program, and second, that wasn't WWI," Mr. Koch said, and then he sat deep in thought. For a moment, Tommy thought Mr. Koch was about to fall asleep. "Okay," Mr. Koch said. "I'll tell you about it, but you have to promise one thing." He closed his eyes and gathered his thoughts.

"Sure," Tommy replied, anxious to learn about the project.

"Don't make any mention of the X608 project in your essay."

Perplexed, Tommy asked, "Why?"

"The project was once top secret. It's something I've never spoken to anyone about." He looked at Tommy pensively. "That plaque has sat there for over twenty years. You're the first to notice it." He looked deep into Tommy's eyes. "Can you keep a secret?"

Tommy didn't answer immediately. He knew Mr. Koch was serious. "Yes, sir," he finally answered.

Mr. Koch cleared his throat. "Because of my experience as a WWI fighter pilot, I was asked to work with Kelly Johnson." He paused for a breath.

"Fighter pilot? Really?" Tommy nearly choked getting the rhetorical question out. He imagined Mr. Koch flying an F4 Phantom Jet. Mr. Koch grinned; he knew what Tommy was thinking. "WWI," he replied. "That was long before X608. And I flew airplanes like the one in that photo." Mr. Koch pointed to a pencil drawing of a bi-plane, put his hand on Tommy's shoulder and continued. "One thing at a time." He settled and took a long breath. "Kelly Johnson was a hotshot engineer for Lockheed. They'd just landed a contract to build a new fighter plane. Keep in mind; this was after WWI, but before the United States got involved in WWII." He looked at Tommy to make sure he was paying attention. "Kelly was a Swede from Ishpeming, Michigan—that's in the Upper Peninsula of Michigan." Mr. Koch chuckled. "Clarence was his real given name, but we all called him Kelly, I can't remember why. He went on to design the SR-71 Blackbird reconnaissance plane." Tommy realized right away that he would finish the interview with more questions than answers. "X608," Mr. Koch said, getting himself back on track, "was the code name of the P-38 fighter program."

A box of books sat next to Mr. Koch's chair. He reached down, pulled out a dusty photo album, and handed it to Tommy. "That's a collection of photos of the various stages of the P-38 during its development." Tommy carefully paged through the collection of delicate photos—the book was brittle and smelled old. Mr. Koch saw Tommy pause on a photo of a heap of rubble. "It had extremely powerful engines. It cost a few lives before pilots learned what to do if they lost an engine on take-off." Mr. Koch paused in thought. "Take-off, that's the most dangerous part of the flight for a twin." Tommy nodded, even though he had no idea with what he was in agreement. "How to handle asymmetry power had to be worked out," Mr. Koch continued. Tommy nodded again as if he understood. He had no clue, but he knew it sounded important.

Tommy turned a few more pages and looked at Mr. Koch with an expression of amazement. "So you were an air force fighter pilot in WWI?"

"I was a fighter pilot in WWI," Mr. Koch said, then coughed. "But it's not what you might be thinking." Tommy listened. "Initially, I didn't fly for the U.S."

Tommy flinched. "You flew for the Germans?"

Mr. Koch patiently shook his head, smiled, and patted Tommy on the shoulder. "The French, the Lafayette Escadrille."

Tommy looked perplexed. "Americans flew fighter planes for the French?"

Mr. Koch took a deep breath and held up a pausing hand. "Canada. Let me finish." He went on to explain how before the U.S. had gotten into WWI, thousands of Americans had crossed the border into Canada, gotten Canadian citizenship, and went to Europe to fight the Germans.

Tommy squinted as if to have caught Mr. Koch in a lie. "But the paper said you flew for the U.S."

"Eventually, I became an instructor for the U.S., but that was later. By the time US fighter squadrons made it to Europe, the Lafayette Escadrille had several former U.S. citizens in the ranks. We were assigned to instruct the Americans on the art of aerial combat."

"Did you have to get your U.S. citizenship back before being an instructor in the air force?"

"Actually, the air force wasn't established until 1947. Fighter pilots in WWI and WWII were technically part of the army."

Mr. Koch didn't answer Tommy's question, so Tommy asked again, "When did you get your U.S. citizenship back?"

Mr. Koch grinned. "Never did. But of course I consider myself an American—I'm certainly a patriot." Mr. Koch could tell Tommy was processing the newspaper article. "You don't have to be a citizen to be in the U.S. Army." Tommy made a perplexed squint, one of many for the morning.

"Anyway," he continued. "One of my first students was a fellow farm boy from Wisconsin, who, by the way, could speak French." Mr. Koch paused in thought. "His name was Billy Mitchell." He looked at Tommy, whose face remained blank. "You might want to look him up in the encyclopedia."

Tommy had taken several pages of notes in his Big Chief notepad. Mr. Koch went on to explain a little history of Billy Mitchell, the famous fighter pilot.

"Did the things you taught him help him become the famous fighter pilot?"

"I helped him with his flying," Mr. Koch thoughtfully replied. "But mostly it was his stick and rudder skills and eyesight—eyesight and reflexes." Now it was Tommy's turn to look puzzled. "In those days, the airplanes were very crude. Being able to see the enemy first was a huge advantage. But if you were superior at handling the airplane, then it was possible to get the advantage even after being seen first." Tommy still didn't understand. Mr. Koch explained how a basketball coach could teach the proper form for shooting a basketball and they could diagram plays, but it took an athlete to execute. "It's the same with fighter pilots." Tommy thought about Coach Heart, and the concept of a student excelling beyond the skills of the coach seemed to register.

Mr. Koch finished the story. "Before the army canned Billy for being so insolent, he'd made a name for himself and been a part of several development programs. He orchestrated the first large-scale air-ground offensive in the history of the world. Not long before Billy died, he attended a fighter pilot reunion and while there introduced me to Kelly Johnson."

Tommy's mind was abuzz—he'd heard more than he could possibly include in a written interview, yet he hadn't asked a question that had been nagging at him since the first time he'd been in the apartment. He pointed at the photo of Mr. Koch standing beside an old airplane with another pilot. "Who is the other pilot?" Tommy asked.

"Count Francesco Baracca," Mr. Koch replied.

"Yeah, I remember now," Tommy said. "He's Italian."

Mr. Koch was silent for several seconds. Tommy had learned that this meant he was thinking, not sleeping. "Count Francesco Baracca," Mr. Koch began, "was a member of the most elite fighter club, the Squadron of the Aces. And he was thought to be the best of that group." Mr. Koch paused while his eyes welled with tears.

Tommy, pretty sure of the answer to his next question, asked, "Is he still alive?" Mr. Koch didn't speak—he just shook his head no.

"Did he get shot down?"

Mr. Koch nodded, his voice breaking. Tommy waited patiently for him to continue. "In those days, pilots carried a revolver. The primary purpose of the revolver was to shoot yourself if your plane caught on fire. You see, oftentimes, after being shot, the plane's fuel tank would erupt in flames. Rather than die a horrible death by flames and fumes, a pilot had the option of taking his own life." Tommy didn't move; he knew there was much more.

Mr. Koch continued. "Francesco didn't return after a strafing mission—his wrecked plane and body were found a few days later. He'd taken his own life." The information rocked Tommy's emotions. To him, it was incomprehensible that a fierce warrior would take his own life.

Mr. Koch clapped his hands once and said, "Let me tell you about the horse that's on the side of his plane." Tommy saw an expression of joy spread across Mr. Koch's face. "Francesco's mother knew Enzo Ferrari, the car maker. The little horse that's on Ferrari cars is the same as what you see in that photo. It was done in Francesco's honor." Tommy had only seen Ferraris on TV, but knew they were expensive, Italian, and driven mostly by movie stars. He now wanted badly to see a Ferrari and tell someone the significance of the insignia.

Tommy and Mr. Koch spent the next few minutes going through the rest of the scrapbook. People who'd promised to help move began to show up. Mrs. Koch started pointing out which items to move first. Mr. Koch was closing the album when a photo of him standing in front of a WWI fighter plane with a black pilot caught Tommy's eye. "That's Eugene Bullard," Mr. Koch said, anticipating his question. "He was the very first black fighter pilot." Mr. Koch stared at the photo as though transported to another place and time. "Tommy," he said. "We'll have to continue this conversation when it's not so noisy." Tommy noticed Mr. Koch's eyes welling with tears.

Tommy asked his last question. "Mr. Koch, I don't think anyone in Colby knows any of this." Mr. Koch shrugged. "Why?" Tommy asked.

"There's no benefit to anyone for me to go telling my life's story," he humbly replied. Tommy didn't understand. "Knowledge puffs up," Mr. Koch said. "But love builds up. I've continued to serve the community.

What one does is more important than what one has done." As the apartment filled with helpers, Tommy knew he'd just been given a giant pearl of wisdom.

Mr. Koch touched Tommy on the shoulder. "I have a question for you." Tommy was all ears. "Who's your favorite American hero?" Mr. Koch asked.

Tommy answered with the first name that came to mind. "Stan Musial."

"Why?" Mr. Koch asked.

Tommy had seen Stan Musial interviewed on TV. "Because he seems so humble," Tommy replied, and then followed up with a question for Mr. Koch. "So, who's your favorite?"

Mr. Koch couldn't remember the last time he answered the question. He usually asked it, but he didn't have to give it much thought. "George Washington," he replied.

"Why?" Tommy asked.

Mr. Koch grinned. He appreciated the question. "For many reasons," he said. "For starters, Washington's famous quote, 'deeds not words.'" George continued with a short lesson on the life of George Washington.

Tommy felt as if his feet weren't touching the ground. The urge to tell someone all that Mr. Koch had said was almost overwhelming. He valued the lesson on America's first president, but treasured Mr. Koch's secret, and kept it for another day.

SEVERAL MEN FROM COLBY FIRST Baptist showed up for the Koch's move. Some actually did more than talk and lifted a hand to help. The Codgers watched from the courthouse bench. Tommy and Booger were securing a load of furniture when Rabbit crossed the street to make sure the boys knew how to tie a knot.

Jupiter Storm made an investigative appearance and posed a few rhetorical questions regarding Tippy Tatum. When no one responded, he mentioned the letter. The boys had heard about the letter but lacked any particular notion regarding its consequence and didn't respond. After several unsuccessful attempts at getting anyone to listen, Jupiter winked at Booger and Tommy.

Jupiter moved closer to Tommy, leaned over, and whispered. "It's not the Kochs moving out that has everyone in an uproar—it's who's moving in." Tommy suffered through Jupiter's garlic breath and contemplated the comment. Jupiter gave the others one of his bushy eyebrow, predatory looks and stomped off mumbling to himself.

The Koch's moving from the residence they'd occupied for over fifty years marked the end of an era. Colby residents shared the news with each other as if they were discussing the results of a natural disaster.

"It just ain't right, and that's all there is to it," a regular at Colby Curls had said while the move was taking place, summing up the attitude of many.

"It's one thing for the Kochs to move out, but another for that new family to move in," Fritz said to anyone who'd listen while having a beer at the Chatterbox.

MRS. KOCH'S SUPPOSED RULE WAS that anytime something new was brought in, something old had to go out. Of course, this rule didn't apply to her tasteless collection of blown glass. The small space, combined with the long stairway, limited their capacity to accumulate things, compared to people who lived in houses with basements. The duplex to which they were moving was smaller and wouldn't hold all of their antique furniture. Mrs. Webster had expressed an interest in several pieces, so Mrs. Koch had marked them with masking tape. The most time-consuming items to pack and move were the pictures, photos, and small mementos. Tommy had packed the plaque commemorating Mr. Koch's participation in the X608 program. He'd held it for nearly a minute before wrapping it carefully in newspaper. None of the other helpers realized the significance of the plaque.

After everybody else had ignored it for several minutes, Tommy finally carried Scout's litter box to the truck. Then there was the piano. Booger had marked it with masking tape like the other pieces that weren't being moved. Mrs. Koch found that amusing, removed the tape, and put it over Booger's mouth. He gagged and spat air until almost turning blue.

Mrs. Koch loved her piano, although in recent years she rarely played it. Several years earlier, maybe decades, Mr. Koch had purchased her the upright player piano. The piano was still in perfect condition, and she dearly wanted it moved. However, an amateur moving a piano is a daunting undertaking. Moving it down a narrow, musty stairway was a hernia waiting to happen, bringing new meaning to the phrase "bust a gut."

During the last pick-up load of small items, the crowd of volunteers began to thin out. It wasn't so much that they knew their help was no longer needed, but more likely it was the fear of moving the piano that prompted their premature departure. As the apartment was cleared, the piano seemed to grow in size. No one had yet attempted to move it—everyone had simply removed things that were sitting on it, while mentally assessing its weight. Only the dedicated, hearty, and stupid remained to help move the dreaded piano.

The band of boys gathered around it and stared. They'd never moved a piano and stood there, droop-shouldered, ignorantly willing to help but unsure what to do. They were leaning on the piano as if to will it down the stairway when several dads came marching in. As if they'd moved pianos all their lives, the men wrapped it in moving blankets, attached ropes, and carefully edged it toward the stairway. Two of them got below while two held onto ropes from above. One riser at a time, they gently walked the piano down the stairs and loaded it into the Gooche's Grocery Chevy pickup. For the boys it was a Godsend.

After strapping down several loads of boxes and tying knots under the close inspection of the Codgers, particularly Rabbit, the boys confidently secured the piano. Their knot tying skills evoked words of praise from the dads and restored the self-confidence they'd lost while watching the men move the piano down the stairway. Rabbit, who was by then sitting on the stone, winked.

Everyone was admiring the piano perched in the bed of the pickup when Wendy, Beth, and their mom stopped by with a batch of warm brownies and several cartons of cold milk. Even the Codgers helped themselves to the treats, though they hadn't lifted a finger.

The dads and Wendy's mom congregated and let Wendy, Beth, and the boys have their space.

Flop started it when he looked at Tommy and said. "Like-a-said, you 'n Wendy ought'r jump up in 'at truck 'n play 'at duet you learned last summer."

Before Tommy could swallow his brownie and begin a defense, Checkers made matters worse. "Yeah! And maybe your Uncle Cletus will drive through town while you're play'n." The boys looked at Cletus for approval and got a broad grin and an affirmative nod.

Almost as if the spontaneous encounter had been planned, Booger hopped into the bed of the truck and began rearranging boxes, making room for the piano bench. He looked at Tommy, then Wendy, and said, "Here ya go."

Cletus made for the driver's side and said, "Let's go."

Rabbit held out his hand to steady Wendy as she climbed onto the tailgate. "I don't know if I remember," she verbally protested, but her body language said she was eager to do it.

"Don't matter," replied Everett.

Tommy swallowed an extra-large portion of brownie. "I'm not doin' it," he announced.

Checkers towered over him. "You're gettin' in th' truck," he said. Unlike a previous year's playground encounter, before Tommy and Checkers had become friends, Everett wasn't coming to the rescue. Once again, Tommy was looking up Checkers's flaring nostrils, except this time, everyone was on Checkers's side.

"That's right," added Everett. "You can climb on or we'll throw you on." Tommy realized the situation was hopeless. Wendy was sitting on the bench, waiting.

Tommy reluctantly took a seat next to Wendy. He was sure that after working all day, he smelled like the guy who ran the Ferris wheel while Wendy smelled like a bouquet of roses. When looking at his fingers to make sure they were on the correct keys, he realized that every fingernail was packed with grime.

The previous summer, Tommy had thought it a gift from heaven when he lucked into the chance to play a duet with Wendy. It wasn't the duet or the piano playing that had enthralled him, but the chance to sit next to Wendy during each practice. Time has a way of changing things, and so it was with Tommy. Strangely, every time he was near Wendy, his thoughts turned to Melody. He began to worry what Melody would think if she saw him playing the piano with Wendy. And he figured it would set the longed-for kiss back at least a month.

Two of the dads got into the cab; Booger, Checkers, Flop, and Everett hopped in the pickup bed and crowded around the piano. Beth and her mom followed in the car. Tommy and Wendy played. They missed several notes the first time through, but got better with each rendition. To Tommy's dismay, Cletus circled the courthouse twice then drove through a couple of neighborhoods.

Melody was sitting on her front porch when the entertainment cruised by. Tommy was too busy watching his fingers and trying to keep up with Wendy to notice. Melody waved, then went inside, ran to her bedroom, locked the door, fell face first onto her bed, and sobbed.

Milton Merle and Venus were taking a stroll when the mobile vaudeville act passed. Milton had completed his treatment, but he still had an eye for women's undergarments. Even after ending his nocturnal excursions, women's undergarments continued to disappear, and he continued to get harassed each time something went missing. The boys' waves to them were noticeably less enthusiastic than the full-body gyrations they'd given up for Melody. Milton knew the discrimination was harmless, but it reminded him of his frustration about continuing to be blamed for something he no longer did.

Watching the truck start down the next street brought Milton's line of vision to the Duckling's clothesline and he noticed something peculiar. Brand-new, colorful, lacy panties and brassieres hung next to large, yellowed, aged, cotton underwear. He shared the discovery with Venus.

Wedding

SOUND TRAVELS AT APPROXIMATELY SEVEN hundred miles per hour—so it's no exaggeration when one says that word gets around fast, and it had. Booger and Tommy had heard about the Letter Jackets and were sitting on the stone laughing. Unknown to the boys, Cletus had met with Principal Ben Franklin earlier that day, and he was surprised to learn that Ben also knew who had started the football shed fire. Ben conspired with Cletus to pull the prank. They'd enlisted the help of the football coach who, after learning that without his cooperation the football players would be suspended, was all ears.

HEET, an analgesic liniment when used properly, is a good remedy for sore muscles. Used improperly, such as a heavy application to a jock strap, it can result in severe discomfort. The Letter Jackets had only run a few wind sprints before collapsing on the field, curling into the fetal position, holding themselves, and writhing in pain.

"Coach," Cecil Becker squealed. "I'm on fire." He had his shorts pulled down and was clawing away at himself.

"Thar's far-ants are somethin' in my jock," another Letter Jacket yelled.

Coach unsympathetically told them, "You can go to the locker room, but for every minute you're there, it's a minute you're running wind sprints after the regular practice."

Writhing in pain, the boys didn't care; they ran to the locker room. On each of their lockers was a note. "Hot like a shed fire," it read.

After returning to the field, they'd told the coach about the notes and that their jocks smelled like HEET. He feigned shock and disgust and promised to get to the bottom of it. The cheerleaders had seen the boys

collapse and had gotten the scoop from other players during the first water break. Minutes later, the entire town knew.

After getting his laughter under control, Tommy told Booger about
his conversation with Cletus. "I'm sure he had something to do with it,"
Tommy said.

"After all, he's a science teacher," Booger agreed, then he added, "Hope
they don't think we did it."

They'd finished the paper route, worrying about being connected with
the prank and were headed home when they noticed Al Tatum, Tippy,
and Velma Seabaugh standing in front of Gooche's. Tippy was sitting on
the stone. Velma was still wearing her Gooche's Grocery apron. Tommy
and Booger were curious and took their time crossing through the square.
"They must be waiting on the bus," Tommy said.

"Wouldn't want to be in their shoes," Booger said.

"Whole town's talkin' 'bout 'em," Tommy agreed.

The boys had crossed the square unnoticed when the bus pulled up,
and a very fit-looking Dwight Seabaugh hopped off wearing his army
dress uniform. All suspicions were confirmed when Dwight and Tippy
embraced. Tommy thought it odd that Tippy's mother wasn't upset
with Dwight. It was surely the first time she'd seen him after learning
that Tippy was pregnant. For Tommy, the puzzle was still missing a few
pieces. He considered the chance that what he assumed was a prom dress
in the photo he'd seen could have been a wedding gown. But he wondered
why anyone would keep that a secret. He and Booger kept walking, frequently glancing back and trying to act nonchalant as the three women
and Dwight hugged.

THE SCHOOL BOARD WAS SCHEDULED to meet later that week. Ben
Franklin had finally opened the letter from Maple Sappington. As he'd
suspected, it challenged Tippy Tatum's ability to attend school while pregnant. He'd met with the Tatums, researched the school's options, and prepared a short report for the board.

He knew he'd nearly driven Lucille Cain over the edge by letting the
letter lay on his desk all week, plus not giving her any details of the Tatum visit. For him, it was sport. But he was sorry that he'd caused her to
resume smoking and chewing her fingernails.

Some enjoy telling all they know and hoping they'll be held in high esteem due to the fact that they are "in the know." Usually, the information is embellished so as to increase its level of importance. All too often, the subject is people rather than events. Ben, either by nature or from his training, was different. It was that feature which probably helped him earn his position as principal without first serving several years as a teacher. He always handled confidentiality with a twist. He'd made sure that Lucille knew he was withholding information, knowing full well that she'd make every effort to extract it. He enjoyed letting her believe that she was the one doing the manipulation.

She'd try being coy—and he found that awkward, almost disgusting. Next came Lucille the servant. She'd ply him with coffee, offer to get him something from the kitchen, and even dust his office. Ben acted oblivious, even when she unbuttoned her top button and kept finding reasons to lean down in front of him. This only added to Lucille's mental duress. Eventually, the information she was seeking was made public and the charade ended.

Ben was so consumed with the Tatum issue that he wasn't able to enjoy the game. He knew his car had been seen at the Tatum's house, and it didn't take long before everyone in town knew there had been a meeting. Rumors of every nature had circulated. Few believed any of the rumors in their totality, but that didn't stop the velocity with which they were spread. "You never know," was the oft-repeated qualifier.

Ben thought about a much more important secret meeting that had occurred a month earlier at the federal courthouse in Fairview. That meeting had included the Tatums, Dwight, the U.S. Marshal, and a lawyer provided to the Tatums by the U.S. Marshal's office. The pregnancy and the fire had initially complicated matters, but all of that was soon to be of no consequence. Ben wondered how the sleepy little town would handle the real Tatum story.

THE NEXT DAY, TOMMY PLACED Mr. Gooche's *Colby Telegraph* under his office door and Velma immediately grabbed it. She carried the paper back to her register, turned to a page midway through the paper, and began reading. The scene was out of character for Velma and drew the attention of several, particularly the customers waiting in her line to be checked out.

But just as people in Colby didn't honk at slow drivers, they also had ample patience for a slow checkout. In this case, everyone's curiosity weighed heavier than a few extra minutes spent getting groceries. She folded the paper, placed it back under Mr. Gooche's office door, and returned to her register. She tried to act as if nothing had occurred, and out of politeness, those who had waited in line, although somewhat frustrated, played along. It was a good thing that Jupiter Storm hadn't been in line or he'd have caused a commotion and put her through the third degree.

Knowing there was something significant in the paper, each one bought a copy from Gooche's stand; in fact, it was emptied before Tommy and Booger left on their delivery route. Tommy and Booger paged through the paper and saw the announcement. Several questions were answered. Word got around, and consequently people were waiting at each paper rack.

By the time Tommy got to Colby Curls, a copy had already been passed around. "Oh, honey, everybody has already read the paper," Faye told Tommy as soon as he stuck his head in the door. Tommy went ahead and placed a copy on each hairdresser's stand.

"I'm not sure I believe it," Chubby Cheeks said to no one in particular.

Foil Pigtails was back for another treatment, the first one had turned her highlights more orange than blonde. "Tells in the article who performed the ceremony and why they didn't make an announcement," she said. The rest of the patrons, greater than Pigtails in both age and girth, ignored her.

Chubby Cheeks was the first of the lumpy legion to speak. "But still," she replied, which made no sense except to serve as getting in the last word.

"You're just sore because your letter to the board no longer matters," Faye said to Chubby Cheeks, but for the benefit of the group. Chubby Cheeks crossed her fleshy arms, put on a pouty face, and drew her chin in so far that it nearly disappeared into her ample neck.

Tommy and Booger met up before passing the Tatums' house. "Never seen so many people interested in a wedding announcement," Booger said.

"Anything to do with the Tatums just seems complicated," Tommy replied.

Several cars were parked at the Tatum's house. And the boys could tell by looking at the cars who was there. Taking paperboy liberties, Tommy opened the gate, patted the dog, and stepped onto the porch. Booger followed. Max whined and nipped at Booger's rear end when he didn't pet him long enough. Al Tatum heard the commotion and came to the door.

Al was all smiles when she opened the door and reached for the paper. "Takes two of you to deliver one paper?" she asked.

"No ... yes," the boys stammered in unison.

Al raised her eyebrows and looked back and forth between the conflicted two. "Want a piece of wedding cake?"

Tommy and Booger agreed enthusiastically on the cake. "Yes."

It took a couple of seconds before "wedding cake" registered. Booger looked at Tommy. "Did she say wedding cake?" he asked. Tommy shrugged a yes.

The house was already crowded, so Tommy and Booger didn't go any farther than the front door. A small celebration was taking place. Burt, Fish and his wife, Velma Seabaugh, the Kochs, Mr. and Mrs. Franklin, and Dwight and Tippy were scattered throughout the living room and kitchen.

Al returned with the cake, and Tommy noticed that she was wearing jeans and her paint-speckled artist's smock. The thought crossed Tommy's mind that she could almost pass for another person when dressed in her overalls and engineer's hat. She handed Tommy his piece of cake, and he saw the heavily calloused hands, which matched the filling station mechanic but not the striking lady standing in front of him.

On their way back to the street, they both let Max lick the cake crumbs from their fingers. "I can see why Burt would be invited to their celebration," Booger said. "Why the others?"

Before Tommy could answer, Jupiter Storm, who was conveniently passing by, stopped and rolled down his window. Tommy and Booger, no longer intimidated by him, approached his car. "What's going on in there?" Jupiter asked.

"Eatin' cake," Booger told him. Booger looked around for Tommy and saw that he'd continued walking ahead. Tommy hadn't wanted to deal with Jupiter while still processing what he'd just seen. "Hey, wait for me," Booger yelled and ran after Tommy.

JUPITER SAT THERE, TRYING TO get a look inside the house. Unable to see well enough to tell who was there, he settled on identifying the cars. While doing so, he noticed an International Harvester Scout cruise by and saw that the driver looked a lot like the man he'd seen at Gooche's on Halloween. He'd never seen him before or since. To most, the double sighting would have been a nonevent. Jupiter's inquisitive mind began piecing together a variety of scenarios. He watched the vehicle turn the corner and wanted to follow, but he was due at the church for a parade meeting. Unable to make any sense of the second sighting, he let it go.

Gino noticed the strange looking man make a double take and head out of town. He took a room in Fairview and hoped he hadn't aroused too much suspicion. He'd seen what he needed to see.

Shots Fired

THE NEXT DAY, GINO PULLED into Colby shortly after noon; the school buses were already running. School must have let out early, he figured, after stopping behind a bus for the third time. He drove past the football field; the football players were on the field, but nobody was watching practice. Everyone in Colby was either participating in the parade or looking for a good spot to watch. He swung by the parade's designated starting spot and saw several cars and a parking lot full of comical homemade floats. A group of older men, decked out in a variety of military uniforms, looked to be preparing to march in the parade. Gino chuckled when he noticed them showing each other their rifles. Both the old men and their rifles were rusty relics.

He slowly cruised along the parade route. Once the parade reached the courthouse square, it would stretch all the way back and across the only bridge crossing Craggy Creek, blocking all roads coming in or going out of town. He checked out an abandoned creek crossing he'd found the day before. The crossing was still accessible and looked to have been used recently by motorcycles.

He checked his copy of the *Colby Telegraph*; the parade was scheduled to begin at 4 PM, giving elementary students enough time to ride the bus home and then return to the parade route with their parents. A photograph from the previous year's parade showed the football team and cheerleaders lining the street adjacent to the stadium as the parade passed by. Gino assumed it was a tradition, which meant that the cheerleaders, including Tippy Tatum, would have to meet prior to the parade's passing. He found the cheerleaders at their usual practice location by the football stadium parking lot.

Gino felt his pulse begin to race as he contemplated the plan and the consequences of its execution. "This will be great," he thought. "I'll take her in broad daylight. That'll show these hicks that Mayberry ain't so safe after all."

The newspaper had become damp and wrinkled from his sweaty palms. He scanned Tippy and Dwight's wedding announcement for the third time, looking at the photo intently. The soldier husband added a new dimension to his plan.

As if summoned, Tippy and Dwight turned the corner and walked toward the gathered cheerleaders. Gino gripped his agency-issued revolver. He had never had an official revolver, but he had been able to purchase one from a retired agent. He hoped that the revolver wouldn't be necessary. He steeled himself to do whatever was necessary to carry out his plan, even if it meant taking out the young soldier. He was relieved when the soldier kissed Tippy and headed back toward the town square.

He planned to let the parade get near the square before making his move. He hoped this would put the sheriff across the bridge, making it difficult for him to return and give chase should anything go wrong.

JACK BURGER AND BRIDGETTE ANDERSON had organized a team to hand out memorial candles. Following the parade, a candle vigil was to be held in the park, paying tribute to all those who'd paid the ultimate price for our freedom. A candle vigil hadn't been done since the Korean War. Following Johnny Burger's death in Vietnam, the parade organizers had thought it appropriate to bring it back. Everyone had agreed and solemnly took their candle.

Burt, Jupiter, and Carter lifted George Koch into the bed of Frank Fritz's WWII era deuce and a half, a three-axle, oversized truck once used by the army for transporting troops. Fritz had acquired the vehicle at an army surplus sale following the Korean War. He had begrudgingly agreed to follow tradition and drive his vintage truck. But he'd made it clear to his friends that he didn't like the idea of a Negro riding in it. A star and the faded words "U.S. Army" were still visible on each door. Flags representing each military branch draped both sides of the bed. George's wheelchair was secured to a stack of pallets that elevated him so he'd be eye-level with the other veterans who planned to stand in the bed. He'd aged noticeably since the previous year—his uniform hung on his shrunken frame.

The veterans had agreed they'd ask Dwight to ride with them. Dwight was infinitely humbled, particularly considering his life's journey. After barely graduating high school, Dwight had worked odd jobs in Fairview and waited to get his draft notice. He'd reached a low point in his life a year earlier, after getting a DWI and losing his driver's license. It was a humbling experience to be relegated to a Mini-Trail at a time when one's identity was too much dependent upon the car they drove.

While working at Burt's, Al Tatum had taken Dwight under her wing and taught him the basics of auto mechanics. Soon after that, he began dating Tippy.

Dwight respectfully climbed into the bed of the truck; Burt gave him a half-hug and a fatherly look. Dwight knew that Burt had taken a chance by hiring him. He looked around at the others and found it interesting that he was the only active-duty soldier on the truck, yet the only one without a weapon. Dwight studied the vintage rifles carried by the veterans. He wondered if they had the good sense to make sure the weapons were unloaded.

IT'S POSSIBLE THAT TIPPY AND Dwight's marriage had been the longest-kept secret in the history of Colby. When word finally got out, all of Tippy's friends were thrilled. That morning, the cheerleaders gathered to congratulate her. Tippy didn't have a diamond ring to show, but the girls seemed to relish her wedding band as if it was the Hope diamond. They giggled and squirmed while Tippy filled them in on the details of Dwight's proposal, their wedding, and why it had been kept secret. She spared them the details of their wedding night, even though they pressed her for more.

Tippy's mind was reeling. In addition to being free to go public with the wedding, which turned her pregnancy from cause for shame to reason for celebration, she'd learned, for the first time, many details about her mother and father and was looking forward to telling her friends. She'd never been ashamed of her mother, but after reaching her teens she had often wished her mother's choice of vocation and attire to be more lady-like. Now expecting a child of her own, she'd begun to understand her mother's sacrificial love. She understood her mother's selfless motive.

Gino watched the girls circle and embrace Tippy. The parade was approaching, the sheriff's car in the lead, followed by the marching band and the big army truck loaded with the old men and their clunky rifles. His narrow window of opportunity was upon him. Gino looked in the rearview mirror and straightened his tie. Then he hopped out of his Scout and crossed the street.

The football team and cheerleaders were standing street-side when the parade approached. Behind the army truck loaded with veterans were the scouts: Boy Scouts, Girl Scouts, Cub Scouts, and Brownies. After the band and veterans passed by, the coach motioned and the football players sprinted toward the field—the cheerleaders followed.

Tippy lagged behind the other girls a few feet. That worked to Gino's advantage. He approached her and flashed his federal identification. "Excuse me," he said. "Are you Tippy Tatum?"

Tippy glanced at the official looking ID. Her still joyful spirit fogged her judgment; she'd let down her guard. She paid little attention to the ID, assuming it to be proper. Having been raised in a small town, she'd developed a trusting nature. Innocently, she replied. "Yes, I'm Tippy."

"Great," Gino said and returned a toothy Italian smile. He explained authoritatively. "You need to come with me. We're meeting your mother at your house."

"Is this about the trust?" she asked.

Gino had anticipated a number of questions she might ask. "There are a number of items that need to be covered. It's probably best to explain it all at the house." Tippy wasn't convinced, but a brilliant notion struck Gino. "There's recent information about your father." He had her full attention. "It's good news," he assured her.

Tippy grabbed Gino's arm. "What information?" she asked. All of the news that day had been good, her marriage was public, and the people she most loved and respected now rejoiced in her pregnancy. "Where are you parked?" she asked.

Gino mentally celebrated her agreeable disposition and thought the abduction was going to go fairly easily. He pointed toward the Scout. "Across the street."

"Oh," Tippy said. "I guess we'll have to wait for the parade to pass." She then turned toward Gino and said, "I thought only two agents knew of our identity."

Gino ignored the comment and fought the urge to shove her into the street, but instead he gently touched her elbow. "I think we can cross now, there's room between the floats," he said. They hustled across the street between a boy in an FFA jacket leading a Hereford bull and a man on a single-harness surrey being pulled by a mule.

Beth thought it strange that Tippy would leave practice without saying a word, especially with an unfamiliar man who appeared to be steering her. She decided to follow. She snaked through the floats and crossed the street. Dwight had kept his eye on Tippy after waving at her from the truck. He saw her with the cheerleaders and noticed the stranger approach her. He wasn't seriously concerned until he saw the two of them cross the street. He brought it to Burt's attention, then jumped down out of the truck and started toward his wife.

Gino opened the door for her to get in, but Tippy hesitated. She began struggling. Gino had anticipated the chance that she might resist. He withdrew a chloroform-laden handkerchief from his pocket and held it over her nose and mouth. Tippy crumpled into the passenger seat. Beth saw all of this from a distance and screamed. Dwight was already in full stride and closing on the Scout fast.

Mere seconds before Dwight could reach the driver side door, the Scout roared away. Still in top shape from basic training, Dwight was winded but far from exhausted. Adrenaline flooded his system. He raced down the hill and gained a little ground when the Scout started across the abandoned creek crossing. But once across, his lungs were no match for the internal combustion engine. He slumped to his knees and cried out.

Word of the abduction and pandemonium spread quickly. Mothers grabbed their confused children while float drivers were diverted up and down adjacent streets. Upset horses were purging themselves. Sheriff Dooley had to wait for the bridge to clear before he could get back across and begin the chase.

Gino sped across a recently harvested cornfield. Until then, his escape was working according to plan. Ignorant of why farmers leave areas of a field fallow, he made no attempt to avoid an area thick with sage grass that concealed a deep gulley. The Scout had enough energy to carry the front wheels across, but the back ones sunk to the axle and spun uselessly—the Scout's movement stopped. Gino realized that he'd forgotten to flip the front hubs, so the four-wheel drive feature was useless.

Fritz's deuce-and-a-half hadn't reached the bridge. Burt motioned for him to stop when Dwight jumped out and ran toward Tippy. Fritz turned the truck toward the creek, where they had a view of the field and the Scout. By then, some of the other men had gathered. The Scout had crossed the creek, but was only a couple of hundred yards away.

"Is this a prank?" Cletus yelled to anyone within earshot.

"No," George replied. He desperately wanted to tell the men about the Tatums and why they'd moved to Colby, but there wasn't time. George's body may have been frail, but his mind was clear. He had known something like this could happen.

Burt peered through a pair of binoculars he'd carried as an Army Ranger. "Looks like he's stuck," he hollered.

"Anyone know who it is?" Carter asked.

"I saw him drive by the Tatums' house," Jupiter answered, all business. "He looked like a man I saw at Gooche's on Halloween. He was driving a car then. He's a little guy, dark, maybe Italian." Jupiter's nosiness was paying off.

Jupiter's description confirmed George Koch's suspicion. "Think you can hit the tires?" George asked. "Remember, Tippy is inside the vehicle."

"You're suggesting we shoot?" Burt asked incredulously.

"This is no prank! Tippy is in real danger, I'll explain later," George said urgently. "Shoot the tires," he ordered. The men, all junior to George Koch, took orders as though on a battlefield and under his command.

Jupiter removed a small clip of ammo from his jacket pocket and slammed it into the gun's receiver. "Distance?" he asked.

"I'd say a little more than two hundred yards," Burt advised him.

Jupiter twisted a knob on the side of the scope. Click. Click.

"Wait!" Burt yelled. "Dwight's catching up to them." Dwight had caught his second wind and was sprinting across the field toward the stalled Scout.

Gino was flipping the front hubs when he saw Dwight. He pulled his revolver and fired in Dwight's direction … pop pop pop.

"Dwight's down," Burt shouted, and then he swallowed. He kept calm, but his jaw muscles flexed rapidly. "He's moving but he's been hit." Burt looked back toward the others with a shocked expression. He couldn't believe what he was seeing. Everyone was focused on Gino and the Scout.

Hearing shots being fired sent the already chaotic town into a full-blown frenzy. Girls began to cry and run away. Mothers, already frantic, made double sure their children were accounted for.

Gino's blood pressure soared, and his head buzzed. He leaped back into the Scout and ground the gears, forcing the Scout into four-wheel drive.

Burt turned to Jupiter. "Shoot!"

The report from Jupiter's rifle intensified the already panicked crowd.

"Good shot, Jupe," Burt said, confirming the left front tire had been hit.

"He's moving too much to get a head shot," Jupiter said.

"No! No!" George screamed. "Don't shoot inside the vehicle … just the tires!" Jupiter chambered another round and put it through the back tire, rendering the Scout useless.

Gino jumped out, ran around, and opened the passenger door. Tippy didn't make any effort to help him. She let her body go limp. He gave her a hard shove, cursed, and took off on foot.

From the truck, Burt saw Gino run up the gulley and take cover next to a utility pole that was surrounded by weeds and brush. Tippy, more conscious than she'd let on, raised her head slightly and watched Gino run away. She looked toward town and saw Fritz's truck about to ford the creek.

Dwight, intent on reaching Tippy, didn't allow the wound to stop him. He removed his belt and wrapped it around his thigh just above the wound. He hadn't seen that much blood since the previous year's deer season. Fueled by pure adrenaline, he inched his way toward the Scout. He'd seen the stranger run away.

Sheriff Dooley's car skidded to a stop, siren blasting and lights blinking. He'd heard the shots. "Since when did you guys start carrying live rounds in the parade?" he yelled. No one answered. Realizing he wasn't going to get an answer, he pointed across the creek and asked. "Who's in the Scout?"

"A mobster," George replied. Nobody took him literally. "We need to get to that Scout, now!"

"Jupe, you stay here and provide cover," George said. He paused. "Burt, Cletus, Carter … you need to get to the Scout." The men didn't question George's authority; they looked at each other, nodded in agreement, then moved out.

The veterans clambered out of the truck. "I'm going too!" Dooley said.

The men were inching their way toward the Scout. "So does everybody have ammo?" Dooley asked, getting back to his original question.

"Pretty much," Burt replied. "We have deer tags." That made the carrying of loaded rifles legal.

Dwight had reached the Scout a few seconds before them, but collapsed alongside it, slipping in and out of consciousness. Carter bent to examine Dwight's wound.

Burt eased open the driver's side door and found Tippy. She crawled to him, out the driver's side. "I'm okay," she mumbled, still feeling the effects of the chloroform.

Dwight groaned and tried to crawl toward the door, but he didn't have the strength. "She okay?" he asked. Burt nodded. Tippy saw Dwight, burst into tears, and scrambled to him. The two embraced.

Dwight caught his breath and said, "He's holed up in that brush." He winced with each word.

Carter looked at Burt and nodded toward Dwight and Tippy, and then he said, "We need to get them out of here."

Dwight gave Burt a look. "I'm not going anywhere." He clenched his teeth in anger and pain. Burt returned an understanding nod.

Burt moved closer to Dwight. "Look," he said, pointing to the disappearing sun. "It'll be dark soon. With that wound, you're no good to us." He paused a moment, then put his arm on Tippy's shoulder. "And we don't know what that idiot used to sedate Tippy. Both of you need to get to the hospital."

Dwight looked at Tippy's droopy eyes. He felt his adrenaline rush subside, and the throbbing in his leg grew nearly unbearable. Reason prevailed. "Okay," he agreed.

By now, both of Sheriff Dooley's deputies had reached the Scout. Dooley had been telling them how they'd needed to stay behind and make sure the panicked crowd stayed under control. "Everyone pretty much went home and locked their doors," one of the deputies reported. Sheriff Dooley rolled his eyes and shook his head in disappointment.

"You two help Dwight and Tippy to the ambulance," Dooley barked. He'd radioed and told the dispatcher to call for an ambulance.

"I'll go with them," Carter volunteered.

Dooley had observed Carter tending to Dwight's wound. "That's probably a good idea," he agreed. The two deputies and Carter helped Dwight and Tippy leave, keeping the Scout between them and where Gino had hidden.

Dooley turned his attention to the kidnapper. "We need to force him out of the brush," he declared.

Burt nodded in agreement. "Easier said than done," he said.

"We'll smoke him out," Dooley decided.

"Got any smoke bombs on you?" Burt asked, bringing a bit of levity to the moment.

"No," Dooley replied. "But I've got that potato gun and a bag of potatoes packed with gunpowder that I confiscated after the football shed fire."

"Know how to shoot it?" Cletus asked.

"Everybody knows how to shoot a potato gun," Dooley replied.

Cletus and Burt looked at each with an "it could work" expression. "Where is it?" Cletus asked.

"Patrol car," Dooley replied. The deputies had reached the ambulance by then. He radioed them and told them the plan.

THE BAND OF BOYS—TOMMY, BOOGER, Checkers, Flop, Caleb, and Everett—were standing by the patrol car with Tommy's dad. They were being glared at by the Letter Jackets, who were now famous for their crotch dance. The band of boys would normally be delivering papers following the parade, but for the first time in the history of the *Telegraph*, there was going to be an extra edition. All the paper needed was for Gino to be caught and the presses would roll.

The deputy told the boys the plan and opened the car trunk, where the potato gun and the potatoes had been stashed since Halloween. After one whiff of the stench, the deputies weren't so enthusiastic about carrying the unorthodox contraption and fermented munitions back to the Scout.

"I'll carry it," Tommy volunteered, stepping forward.

"No you won't, little man," his dad intervened, grabbing Tommy's arm.

"Why not?" Booger asked. Tommy's dad shot him a look. The two unwilling deputies finally flipped a coin to see who would carry the potatoes. The boys were sore they wouldn't be the ones to shoot the gun, but they were excited about their potato gun being chosen. They were thinking that some redemption might be in order.

After receiving instructions from the boys, the deputies trudged back to the Scout. It took a couple of tries, but the second flaming potato smacked into the utility pole and exploded into several pieces, which worked for the better. Jupiter, looking through his scope, could see several small embers flicker into flames. Gino was slapping at them furiously. The third potato landed a few feet from Gino and instantly ignited a large clump of dry sage. The smoke and flames forced him out from the brush. Once away from the flames, Jupiter lost sight of him. The *Telegraph* extra would have to wait.

Several people had left their locked homes and gathered at the square. This was a first for Colby, but they knew what needed to be done. What had originally been planned as a candlelight vigil for Johnny Burger had turned into a prayer service for Dwight, Tippy, and for the capture of the perpetrator.

Secret Revealed

Mr. Baumgartner drove the ambulance while Mrs. B, or Rita, as everyone called her, tended to the wounded. She'd trained to be an LPN, and then ironically married into a family of morticians. At first, her family couldn't see the need for a nurse at the funeral home, but she explained that she'd be helping with the ambulance side of the business. At their wedding, she'd joked that her training might keep her clients from needing the rest of the family's services.

Tippy was still woozy but otherwise feeling okay. Rita checked Tippy's vitals and decided it safe for her to ride in the passenger seat. She gave Tippy some water and adjusted the head rest for her.

Rita had never tended to a gunshot wound. Most of her bleeders had been car accidents, and while those wounds looked worse, the ominous circumstances surrounding Dwight's gunshot wound unnerved her. "Those kind of things happen in other places, not Colby," she thought.

"What are the numbers?" Carter asked.

"Not good," Rita reported. "Blood pressure is low, pulse is weak, and breathing is shallow."

"Does the hospital know that he'll need blood?" Carter asked.

Rita shrugged. "I hope so," she said. "They know he's been shot."

"Think they know his blood type?" Carter asked.

"Probably," Rita replied. "He was in a car wreck a few years ago. That's how he got that." She pointed at a thin scar that ran between his eyes and then trailed off on one side of his nose. Carter noticed Dwight's dog tag and checked for blood type—O negative. He instantly realized the potential problem—he held the tag for Rita to see. Rita winced.

Carter squeezed Dwight's arm and said, "You'll be okay."

Rita wasn't so sure.

An ER team was waiting when they arrived at Fairview General. Dwight was rushed to surgery. Tippy was seated in a wheelchair and taken to an examining room. Gloria, Velma, and Al arrived right behind the ambulance. Gloria let them off at the entrance and they raced inside.

Al came barging into the ER, saying, "Where's my daughter?" she demanded.

Velma was close behind. "Where's my son?"

The ER nurses were used to dealing with distraught family members and sprang into action. A nurse with ample proportions but a calming demeanor invited Velma and Al into a consultation room; Velma asked for Carter to join them. Al insisted on seeing Tippy right away and was taken directly to her.

Velma was crying and wringing her hands when a balding man entered the room. His nametag read "Dr. Levi." His presence immediately had a calming effect on Velma. Expecting to see the mother and father, Dr. Levi gave Carter a curious look, and then told them that he was certain the bullet hadn't done any major damage. Velma was flooded with relief until Dr. Levi said, "But …" He then went on to explain about the loss of blood and of Dwight's rare blood type. "We're making calls to try and find some O negative."

Carter gently touched Velma's hand and said, "I'm O negative."

A fresh flow of tears streamed down Velma's cheeks, but this time they were tears of joy. She placed her pale white hand on Carter's dark forearm. "That's nothing short of a miracle," she said.

An ER nurse stuck her head into the room. "We've got a problem."

Dr. Levi stood and faced Carter. "I'll send in a nurse for you." He then hustled to Tippy's examining room.

Velma looked closer at the man who would give life to her son and noticed that his shirt and pants were stained with Dwight's blood. She gasped and almost fainted. Carter held her. "He'll be fine." She desperately wanted to believe him. She lowered her head into her hands and began to pray. When her weeping was such that she couldn't say the words, Carter prayed for her.

The nurse handed Dr. Levi Tippy's chart just outside the exam room. "Doctor, she's four months pregnant." He scanned the chart.

"Any sign of being mistreated? Bruising?" he asked.

"Her arms are bruised, that's all."

"Uh huh," Dr. Levi replied and continued to review the chart.

"The patient says the assailant covered her mouth with a rag that smelled like medicine," the nurse continued. "It made her pass out."

Dr. Levi stopped reading and looked at the nurse. "With *what?*"

The nurse shook her head. "We don't know."

"Where's the rag?" he asked. The nurse shrugged.

"We need more blood tests, stat," he ordered.

Dr. Levi then proceeded into the room as though there was no cause for alarm. After listening to Tippy's heart and lungs, and that of the baby's, he asked about the rag. For the baby's sake, he told them they needed to determine what was used to sedate Tippy. The nurse drew blood, and Dr. Levi explained that they needed to identify what was used and the level of it in her bloodstream. Tippy sensed their concern about the baby and fainted.

HOURS LATER, DR. LEVI SPOKE briefly to those crowded into the waiting room. The test results reflected the answer to countless intercessory prayers—mother and baby would be fine. The transfusion was going well. Al, Velma, Gloria, and a waiting room of people were huddled in prayer, including the Kochs. Tippy and Dwight had been admitted for further observation, but both were clear of immediate danger.

"Oh, and another thing," the doctor said. "Dwight's wound is one that, at his age, is considered a perfect wound." He got perplexed looks. "It wasn't bad enough to be life threatening, at least since the bleeding was stopped in time, but it's serious enough to most likely result in a medical discharge from the Army." A fresh stream of joyful tears rolled down Velma's face.

The waiting room phone rang, and Carter answered. Holding his hand over the mouthpiece, he said, "It's Sheriff Dooley." He spoke with Dooley a few moments. After hanging up, he explained that the license plates on the Scout had been stolen, but another plate was found inside a duffel bag, along with a bottle of chloroform. The plates were registered to Gino Luigi from Chicago.

George and Marie were sitting beside Al. George noticed Al flinch when Carter said the name. He leaned close and whispered to her, "Once he's caught, it should all be over." Al looked at him suspiciously—she wasn't sure what he'd meant by "it."

"I'm the local contact," George confessed.

He gently patted her on her knee. She slowly massaged her face and took a deep breath. Burt joined Alison on the couch and put his arm around her. She leaned against him, but never lost her grateful eye contact with George.

Until recently, it had been a long time since Alison had thought about there being a local contact. At one time, she'd suspected Mr. Koch, then Burt, then others, and had eventually pushed it out of her mind.

Years of suppressed emotion poured forth. The tough veneer was replaced with a sobbing, sensitive mother. She turned toward Mr. Koch. "Tell them," she said, her voice little more than a whisper.

Burt took her hand in his. "Tell us what?" he asked. She pointed at George.

While Al alternated between crying and smiling, George told Alison Tatum's story as only George could—slowly, methodically, and chronologically. He paused once for nearly a minute after realizing that Alison's beautiful ponytail, rather than being tucked up under an engineer's hat, was lying against a blouse, not her usual denim work shirt. He saw Tippy's youthful beauty in Alison's face.

While he spoke, Alison rewound the years. She recalled George introducing her to Burt Brown, and the comment he'd made about Burt giving her a chance. It was clear to her now that Mr. Koch had known of her mechanical abilities. Then there were the times when he and Mrs. Koch had appeared at her door, sometimes minutes after she'd spoken to Vince Gambaiana about a struggle. They were always clever about disguising the reason for their visit—checking on the house, their turn to deliver a meal from the church, always just distracting enough to keep her from suspecting them.

Alison began to tremble when George told about Reggie, his war record, and how the information he'd provided helped put criminals behind bars. She was relieved that the truth was out and people knew that Tippy had a legitimate father and that she hadn't been forced to leave an abusive situation.

Thirty minutes later, George ended the story by telling everyone about the celebration at Alison's the previous day. He sighed, patted Alison's leg, and said, "What a day this has been."

THROUGHOUT MR. KOCH'S TELLING OF the story, Carter had maintained a pained expression. Then a look of understanding swept across his face, and he grinned, slapped his knee, and pointed at Alison. "I knew I recognized you!"

Alison smiled through a tear-smeared face. "I was afraid you had."

"Giordano's Garage!" Carter boomed, pointing at her and slapping his thigh. He looked at Gloria and said, "I told you there was something familiar about her!"

Alison confirmed with a nod. "My father owned the station—I was a Giordano." She giggled. "You were our best AAA customer." A wave of memories flooded her mind. She wiped her eyes.

He continued looking at her, shaking his head in astonishment. "I remember the trial now," he added. "That was you," he said, his voice trailing off.

Carter got an elbow from Gloria. "AAA is still losing money on him," she said, bringing a welcome bit of levity to the conversation.

Carter looked at Burt. "By the way, do you take AAA?" he asked.

"Yes, but something tells me I need to stop," Burt groaned, and the rest of the waiting room, still numbed by all that had transpired and what they'd just learned, enjoyed the much-needed laugh.

Everyone stood to the sound of an approaching siren. The Baumgartner's ambulance squealed to a stop at the emergency room entrance. The Colby crowd rushed to see who it was and what had happened.

Unlikely Hero

EVERY PHONE LINE IN COLBY was hot, and everyone on party lines quickly forgot who had called whom. There was a killer on the loose, or that's what was being said. Gino was on the loose—that part was true—but he'd yet to kill anyone.

Sheriff Dooley did his best to control the revenge-seeking mob that stood on the courthouse lawn. They had armed themselves with a variety of weapons, everything from .410 shotguns to high-powered deer rifles. He shook his head—they'd seen too many westerns. Sheriff Dooley had to deliver the disappointing news that unless they were deputized, they couldn't go man-hunting while armed.

"We're allowed to protect ourselves," one man said.

"You can protect your home, but you can't go running through the countryside taking pot shots at everything that moves," Dooley responded.

"Whose side are you on?" another shouted.

Sheriff Dooley explained how they knew the identity of the abductor and that roadblocks had been established. The best thing they could do was to return to their homes. The suspect couldn't have gone far, was on foot, and probably looking for shelter. He was however, to be considered armed and dangerous.

"We'll catch him," Dooley said. "A deputy from Fairview is on the way with a pair of bloodhounds. For now, you need to protect your homes." Most men came to their senses and returned to their homes, disappointed. The rest went to Marty Mac's Chatterbox.

———

GINO RAN ALONG THE DITCH to the creek; he stopped to catch his breath and watch the ambulance cross the bridge while trying to steel his nerves. His shoes were caked with mud. He stuck his foot into the creek but couldn't find the bottom. The water was frigid. He crept along the steep creek bank from root wad to root wad, keeping low and staying in the shadows, until he found a wide spot with ripples and crossed.

He watched the patrol cars heading out of town along the highway, his intended escape route. He knew that checkpoints would be set up soon, if not already. He scanned the horizon, letting his eyes adjust to the darkness. The crowd at the bridge had slowly dispersed after the ambulance left, and he could see several vehicles near the courthouse square.

He remembered seeing delivery trucks come and go from the alley behind the grocery store. He decided his best chance to get through the road blocks was to stow away on a delivery truck. He climbed the steep bank behind a row of houses whose dark backyards bordered the creek and crept along the edge of the yards, staying in the shadows until he came to a loaded clothesline. He carefully took what he needed, crawled over the edge of the bank, and changed into warm, dry clothes.

He made his way to the street that led to the square; it looked like everyone in town was there. He passed by the Legion Hall shooting range and hid in a hedgerow that bordered the alley behind Gooche's. He crouched there watching as people slowly left the square, some on foot, while others drove. It looked like every one of them was armed. "What is it with these hillbillies?" he thought. Two simpletons were standing on the loading dock of Gooche's smoking cigarettes. Gino could barely make out what they said, but he heard his name mentioned. Chills ran down his spine. They flicked their cigarettes into the night air and left.

"They know my name!" He cursed to himself as he pounded his forehead with his fist. "They know my name!" he repeated. He took a deep breath and closed his eyes. He was freezing, exhausted, and exasperated.

An old pickup truck loaded with trash was sitting next to the dock. He crept to it and quietly let himself in; it was still warm inside. He wasn't sure how long he'd dozed off when he heard the dogs. At first, their barks were distant and sporadic, but they were getting closer and the barking more intense. By then his plan had fallen apart, he was running out of options. But then he smiled, "Not only do these hicks not lock their doors, they leave keys in the ignition," he said to himself. He peeked over the windows and saw no one in the alley.

SHERIFF DOOLEY, CLETUS, BURT, AND others had moved in after the fire had burned away the brush, but Gino had already slipped away. They'd waited by the Scout until the bloodhounds from Fairview arrived.

Dooley's office had been given instructions by the U.S. Marshal's office that he wasn't to disturb anything until they arrived. He'd never before dealt with them and wasn't sure if they even had jurisdiction. He was curious as to how they'd found out about the abduction. But since it was late, cold, and a dangerous suspect was at large, he gave the U.S. Marshal's orders little thought.

The dog handler kept the dogs on a short leash as he led them to the driver's seat. They sniffed for a few moments, and then one of them let out a piercing yelp. They both strained against the leash. The handler smiled and proclaimed, "They're ready." The chase was on.

When the dogs headed toward town, Dooley decided their noses weren't any better than his. "Why would the guy head back to town?" he wondered. But when they led the group to the bridge and dropped down the creek bank, where they found fresh shoe prints, he began to worry. He got on his walkie-talkie and alerted his dispatcher. She, in turn, made a couple of calls, each of which resulted in several more, and in less than five minutes, all of Colby knew. Women made sure their doors were locked, and the men made sure their guns were loaded.

Ben Franklin, somewhat disgusted with the mob, was walking toward his car. He'd decided he didn't want anything to do with the vigilante crowd. He could tell the dogs were headed toward town, rather than away. Thinking that odd, he stopped to listen. He thought he spotted movement behind Gooche's. He ducked into a doorway and waited, listening. "Nothing," he figured. Just as he was about to give up listening and go on home, he heard the old truck start. Ben broke into a sprint when he saw the pickup begin to move, but it turned the corner and headed toward Church Hill before he could reach it.

———

MILTON HAD WALKED VENUS HOME. When they passed the Duck-ling's house, he glanced at their clothesline. He and Venus had continued keeping an eye on the Ducklings since first noticing the brightly colored women's articles suspended on their clothesline. Jupiter had likewise been watching Milton and Venus, suspicious that they were spending so much time together, especially when he'd call Venus late at night and she didn't answer. Jupiter didn't trust Milton, and Milton had been avoiding Jupiter. He hoped that proving he wasn't the clothesline culprit would be an end to Jupiter's physical threats and verbal abuse.

They were standing on the porch when they noticed Gooche's Gro-cery truck speed by with empty boxes spilling from the bed. The last time Milton had seen the truck at night was when Tommy Thompson and the band of boys had taken it for a middle-of-the-night excursion. Venus asked, "Was that Gooche's old truck?"

"I think so," Milton answered, still picturing Tommy at the wheel. Snap-ping out of his memory, he realized the person driving wasn't Tommy, but someone he didn't recognize. They raced toward Venus's house so they could call and report the stolen truck.

JUPITER, ON HIS WAY HOME to grab a bite before joining the manhunt, didn't know the dogs had headed toward town. He was passing Venus's house when he saw Venus and Milton dash through the door. He pulled into her driveway and stomped toward the house. He could hear Venus's elevated voice but couldn't understand what she was saying. He barged in without knocking.

Hoping to find Milton making inappropriate advances toward Venus so he'd have good cause to put a few knots on his head, Jupiter entered the room with fists clenched. He found Venus on the phone and heard her frantically explaining the direction the truck was headed. Milton turned to Jupiter, wild-eyed, and as if glad to see him, asked, "Did you drive here?" And before Jupiter could answer, Venus asked, "Got your rifle?"

Milton's urgency caught Jupiter off guard and diffused his temper. "Yeah! Of course! What the heck is going on here?" Jupiter yelled.

Venus slammed the phone down and rushed past both of them. "I'll drive," she told them. "I'll explain on the way—let's go." Venus looked in Jupiter's car and asked, "Where's your rifle?"

"I'm not movin' till you tell me what's going on," he protested.

"Get in," she ordered. Jupiter got his rifle out of the trunk and got into the back seat. Venus was the one person with which Jupiter seldom argued. She explained as they roared up Church Hill in pursuit of Gooche's truck.

As soon as Gino got out of town and onto the dark road, he slowed to a crawl. The headlight switch had come completely out of the dash when he'd pulled it, but no lights turned on. He sped up slightly after glancing in the rearview mirror and noticing a pair of functional headlights gaining on him.

After Gino passed the Bird's house, the road deteriorated. He continued until the truck tires sunk to the axles in the soft creek-gravel. The headlights behind him stopped several yards back. He saw the silhouettes of people getting out of the car and heading toward him. The soft gravel made running difficult.

Milton wasn't as fast as he'd been when playing football in the small college that once existed in Colby, but his speed was still considerably above average. He gave no thought to the possibility that Gino could be armed, so when Gino made a run for it, Milton didn't hesitate. Milton had the advantage; he'd fished this creek since he was a kid and didn't have to look where he was going. Gino, on the other hand, was groping in the dark and dodging low-hanging limbs. Milton quickly caught up and tackled Gino, taking them both to the ground.

Milton may have been faster, but Gino was younger and stronger. He broke away, but before he could take a step, he was tackled by 250 pounds of Jupiter Storm. Jupiter mashed Gino's face into the sandy gravel and held him until he stopped squirming.

Jupiter, winded from running across the sandbar, slightly released his grip. It was all Gino needed. He seized the opportunity, broke one hand free, swept a throwing knife from an ankle holder, and plunged the blade into Jupiter's thigh. Jupiter screamed in agony and pushed Gino free. Too tired to run, Gino stood there waving the bloody knife and faced off with the two men and Venus. Jupiter was too furious to notice the blood gushing from his wound.

After seeing which direction Gooche's truck had gone, Ben bolted to his car and followed. He hadn't bothered to notify the authorities for fear the courthouse square mob would follow. He soon found Jupiter's car and Gooche's truck blocking the road. After shutting down his engine, he heard voices and headed in that direction. The moon was his only light.

He caught up to see Milton reaching for Gino, but Venus stopped him. "He's got a knife, Milton."

"That's right," confirmed Gino, waving the weapon. He sliced it through the air in a serpentine motion. "I won't stop at the leg next time."

"Put down the knife," Ben said, catching them all by surprise. "You're not going anywhere." Ben confidently stepped out of the shadows.

"He's got a knife," Venus warned.

"I know," Ben told her. "Put down the knife," he ordered in a commanding tone as he continued walking purposely toward Gino.

"Get back or I'll slice you wide open," Gino threatened, waving the knife menacingly.

"I don't think so," Ben said, and then with a swift motion, he kicked sand into Gino's eyes and threw a grapefruit size rock, making a direct hit on Gino's face. Gino dropped the knife, grabbed his face, and collapsed backward. Ben put one foot on Gino's throat and the other on his wrist and picked up the knife.

"Let me see that knife," Jupiter demanded.

Ben grinned. "I've seen that look before. I'll just keep it for now." Ben showed Milton how to secure Gino's hands using a belt. "You'd better apply pressure to that wound," he told Venus and pointed at Jupiter's leg.

Chester Bird had seen the cars whiz by and called the sheriff's office. Ben was holding the knife and rifle when Sheriff Dooley and a deputy roared up. Car after car, packed with inebriated, angry Chatter Box customers, lined the narrow road leading back to Colby. Everyone shouted at Gino when the patrol car passed by. Getting caught had probably saved his life.

On the way back to Colby, Milton drove and Venus held pressure on Jupiter's wound.

"Has the bleeding stopped?" Milton asked. He didn't want to look.

Milton and Jupiter exchanged glances through the rearview mirror. As only men can do, they came to a wordless understanding. The Baumgartner ambulance was waiting for them at the edge of town. The ambulance driver, exhausted and running on pure adrenaline, had never seen this much action in one day.

WHILE JUPITER'S WOUND WAS BEING tended to, Milton and Venus told the standing-room-only hospital waiting room crowd how Gino had been chased and apprehended. Ignoring hospital rules, several from Colby had brought food, of course, and even shared it with hospital staff. Finis Pribble had driven some of the ladies from Twin Oaks to the hospital. Everyone returned approving smiles when Venus proudly recounted Milton's catching Gino and throwing him to the ground; they laughed when she told of Jupiter putting Gino into a bear hug. Everyone gasped and the room fell silent when she told about the knife and the standoff.

"What did Mr. Franklin do?" someone asked.

"Did he use wunna'em Special Forces moves?" another asked.

Everyone waited anxiously to hear how Mr. Franklin, rumored to know countless ways to kill with his bare hands, had disarmed the mobster. Venus smiled and said, "He kicked sand in his face and then hit him with a big rock."

"Dad-gum, I could'a did that," Finnis Pribble said.

"He's done and in jail now," Eugene Meisenheimer added.

"Yeah, that's the main thing," someone else added.

The crowd, clearly disappointed in the less-than-extraordinary methods used by Ben to subdue the mobster, began discussing Alison and the witness protection program. A few of the ladies began whispering to each other about various recipes for the fried chicken served by the Baptists. One of the rumors that had been flippantly discussed at Colby Curls was that women had to know a good fried chicken recipe before being allowed to join the church.

Ted Thompson called home. Tommy and Booger were waiting for the call. They particularly liked the part about Mr. Franklin kicking the bad guy's butt.

Word about Alison's previous life had yet to spread, but it would. And it would explain a lot of things. Lives, attitudes, and hearts were being transformed; the little town of Colby was literally changing overnight. "Turn Turn Turn" by the Byrds could be faintly heard playing on the receptionist's transistor radio. Everything happens for a reason.

Kochs Double Team

THE SECOND SATURDAY IN DECEMBER, less than a month away, had been reserved for the Colby Christmas parade. The parade had been on the same day for as long as anyone could remember. Only once had the Christmas Parade been canceled, on December 13, 1941, the Saturday following the attack on Pearl Harbor. The entire country, including Colby, had found it impossible to celebrate. The parade resumed in 1942, but enthusiasm for the parade wasn't fully restored until the war's end and the return of the soldiers.

Once the war finally ended, Mr. Koch suggested that veterans lead the parade and that the grand marshal be a veteran. The parade committee agreed unanimously on Burt Brown, a WWII Army Ranger, as the first Marshal. Burt had served in both the European and Pacific theaters and had earned the Silver Cross. The town had been so proud of Burt that a collection had been taken up to buy a small parcel of ground for him, and everyone pitched in to help build a service station. Those who couldn't afford to donate money had volunteered their time to build the block building that became Burt's Sinclair. Burt had returned the favor many times over by providing no-cost service for many of Colby's civic organizations.

MR. KOCH HAD NEVER MISSED a parade, and since moving to the duplex, the Kochs had been getting out more often. So no one at the Christmas Parade committee meeting was terribly surprised to see Mrs. Koch wheel him through the door, with a goopy eyed Scout seated on his lap. Mr. Koch had been granted an honorary membership on the committee after serving for nearly twenty years, but he hadn't actually attended a meeting for a couple of years. Nobody expected him to have anything specific on his mind, much less a tradition-shattering proposal. The committee had no idea they were about to be double-teamed by the Kochs.

Deep smile wrinkles lined Mr. Koch's rugged face as he looked into the eyes of each person seated in the room. It was clear to all that he wasn't attending the meeting out of curiosity, but he had a pressing issue on his mind. Mr. Westwood, committee chair, yielded the floor to Mr. Koch as the first item of business, even though he wasn't on the agenda.

Burt Brown had been an easy choice as the first grand marshal. Since then, however, the choice of grand marshal had never been unanimously agreed upon and generally generated considerable debate. In fact, a special subcommittee had been appointed several years earlier and charged with reducing the nomination to three veterans, one of whom would be chosen by the committee. Mr. Koch had appointed the first grand marshal sub-committee.

Mr. Koch cleared his throat and seeing there were no ashtrays, handed his cigar stub to Mrs. Koch. She put it out in a coffee-can-turned-ashtray, and then wiped her fingers on his pants. "As you know, it was during my tenure as chair of this committee that Colby began the tradition of naming an armed forces veteran as the grand marshal."

All heads nodded, and a few exchanged impatient looks.

Mr. Koch paused long enough to visually sweep the room and make momentary eye contact with each committee member. "Based on what has occurred during the past couple of months ... and I think you know of what I speak." He paused a few seconds and let the words permeate everyone's senses. "I think it would be good for our town if this committee would select a black veteran as grand marshal."

Mr. Westwood was the first committee member to speak. "Mr. Koch, I respect your judgment. But we've always named a WWII veteran as grand marshal, and there are several WWII veterans in Colby who have never been named. I don't think it's appropriate to name a Korean War veteran ahead of them." He paused for effect. "Especially someone who only recently moved to town."

All heads nodded in agreement.

Mr. Koch had expected as much. He surprised them by saying, "I agree." Then he continued. "I'm not talking about Carter Webster."

All faces frowned a question. "Who then?" Mr. Westwood asked.

Mr. Koch coughed and cleared his throat once more, punched his cigar-stained finger into the air, and explained his recommendation.

The committee was clearly stunned. Never before had someone who wasn't a citizen of Colby been chosen grand marshal, let alone a Negro.

Burt Brown had been silent up to this point. "I trained with several Negro soldiers at Fort Benning. They all got assigned to the 555th or the triple nickel; those fellas were fine soldiers." Burt was referring to the all-black paratrooper unit that, in spite of being a top-notch unit, had been relegated to fire jumping and domestic missions.

"Don't forget about the Buffalo Soldiers," Mrs. Koch chimed in, commencing the double-team.

"Buffalo Soldiers?" Mr. Westwood asked, visibly exasperated.

"Yes, the first all-black unit. Shall I explain?"

Mr. Westwood glanced at his watch and the meeting agenda, which hadn't included the Kochs, and rubbed his temples. Impatient looks were exchanged. Everyone knew the potential for Mrs. Koch to carry on endlessly.

"Can you make it quick?" Mr. Westwood asked.

"Certainly," Mrs. Koch replied. But every committee member knew better. She explained the history of the Buffalo Soldiers in vivid detail, beginning with the First Regiment of South Carolina being formed in 1862 all the way through to 1950 when the army was integrated and the Buffalo Soldiers disbanded.

When she finished, the room was silent. The only sound heard was the tinkling of the radiator heater that had just kicked on. Mr. Westwood was the first to speak. "I had no idea."

Mrs. Koch held her hand up, motioning that she wasn't finished. "There's one more thing I should mention. There was even a woman, Cathy Williams, who disguised herself as a man and served as a Buffalo Soldier for two years."

After a short discussion, the committee voted, and for the first time since Burt Brown had been chosen grand marshal, the vote was unanimous. Mr. Koch offered to make the contact and confirm that the committee's new choice would be willing and able to serve as grand marshal.

Mr. Westwood looked at the next agenda item and rubbed his temples. "We need to choose who will depict Mary and Joseph," he said. "As usual, we have a long list of applicants from which to choose."

The issue had been tabled since the previous meeting, as they'd been unable to agree. After the Kochs had made their case for a black grand marshal, the proposed choice for Mary and Joseph didn't seem so controversial. And in light of all that had occurred, the choice seemed most fitting. The motion passed without further discussion.

MR. KOCH DIALED THE NUMBER to a friend he hadn't seen or spoken to for several years. He'd been meaning to make the call since having lunch on his porch with Carter. And then the telling of his story to Tommy had increased the urge, but he'd put it off. The voice that answered had aged but was easily recognizable. The two seasoned gentlemen spent several minutes catching up before Mr. Koch got around to the purpose of the call.

"Yes, the vote was unanimous," Mr. Koch assured him. "It didn't surprise me one bit."

"It surprises me a little," Washington said. "Carter says he's still getting odd looks."

"That has more to do with him being new and the fact that he's the factory manager. Half the town reports to him," George assured him.

"Yeah, you might be right," Washington replied. George knew he was half right. The two continued to visit and catch up for nearly an hour, forgetting that it was a long-distance call.

"I'll let the committee know," he said. "And I look forward to seeing you." After hanging up, Mr. Koch stared at the X608 plaque and reminisced. Hearing Washington's voice had taken him back nearly thirty years. Development of the P-38 played a pivotal role in battle for control of the air during WWII. The test pilots were vital to the expeditious development of the P-38 Lightning. Washington Webster had been one of the best, but because of his skin color, little was made of it.

Mr. Koch was still flying during those years, but he lacked the critical reflexes necessary to take a fighter plane to its limits. He could still remember being envious of the young pilots who got to fly the latest technology. In particular, he remembered Washington Webster, the best of the best. He sunk back into his recliner and revisited the pleasant memory before peacefully dozing off.

THAT SAME EVENING, AS PART of their public service commitment from allegedly nearly burning down the football shed, Tommy and Booger were busy imprinting Ping-Pong balls. Knowing the Letter Jackets had gotten their due made the public service work easier to take. Mr. Gooche traditionally enlisted Colby merchants' participation in the Ping-Pong ball drop. The discounts were printed on Ping-Pong balls and dropped from an airplane during the parade.

The tradition had begun as a way to promote the Fairview airport and generate Christmas parade attendance. Colby had too many parades, but each parade had a cadre of supporters. The Christmas parade followed less than a month after the Veterans Day parade, and folks needed something extra to motivate them to stand on the street in cold December weather and watch the same groups trudge along. So, as an added attraction, an airplane would buzz the parade route and drop Ping-Pong balls emblazoned with discounts good only for the day of the parade.

"How many do we need?" Booger asked. Since Booger and Tommy worked for Mr. Gooche, it made it handy for them to imprint Ping-Pong balls.

Mr. Gooche pointed to several mesh bags of balls. "Five hundred."

The equipment for printing Ping-Pong balls was owned by the Chamber of Commerce but kept in Mr. Gooche's storeroom. He showed the boys how to imprint the balls and gave them the list of stores and the amount of discount to be imprinted on each one.

Tommy couldn't help himself. As a joke, and out of boredom, he made a few imprints of his own design, featuring spectacular offers—the amount of the offer limited only by his imagination.

Christmas Lights

CHRISTMAS WAS MRS. KOCH'S FAVORITE time of year. She enjoyed everything about it, the celebration, the lights, but especially the true meaning. The Koch's balcony was always tastefully adorned with a Christmas light display. One Christmas while she and Mr. Koch were standing in the courthouse square admiring their lights, she realized that the balcony was a dazzling wonder in a sea of darkness. That's when she applied for and received a grant from the state beautification committee to be used for the Colby Christmas lights, which eventually grew into the Colby Parade of Lights.

Russell Gooche stored the community Christmas lights in a warehouse behind the grocery store. Tommy and Booger had volunteered to help put up the town's Christmas lights, but they had their ulterior motives. They'd enlisted the band of boys to help on the promise of a ride in Gooche's truck. Except for Tommy and Booger, the rest of boys hadn't been near the truck since taking it for an unauthorized midnight joyride the previous summer during a supposed camping trip.

Leon Goolsby checked on them periodically, mostly because he wanted an excuse to stand on the dock and smoke a cigarette. Tommy and Booger had cleverly used twist ties to secure a string of lights along the top rail of the truck bed, and using a discarded electrical cord, they tied a wreath to the front grill. They'd used an entire roll of Scotch tape to attach a silver garland along the top of the windshield. Leon hooked up the wire for the lights to the truck battery.

Mrs. Koch had acquired enough lights to decorate every utility pole in the square. Russell had observed Tommy and Booger driving the truck back and forth to the incinerator and decided to let them drive the truck around the square to deliver the lights to their designated poles. Leon usually drove the truck, but by letting Tommy and Booger have the honor, the store wouldn't be without a butcher. Leon didn't mind—the weather was raw and working with Marie Koch could be tiring.

The boys piled boxes of giant Christmas ornaments onto the truck. Tommy, Booger, Flop, and Caleb squeezed into the cab. Checkers and Everett stood on the rear bumper and hung onto the stock racks. Tommy eased the truck toward the first pole, careful not to lose any boxes or friends along the way.

"Thangs fallin' apart," Flop said when Checkers and Everett started jumping up and down on the rear bumper.

Tommy thumbed over his shoulder. "No, it's just those idgits." He goosed it a little, causing Checkers and Everett to almost fall off. "That'll take care of that," Tommy said.

Mrs. Koch was very particular about which decoration went on each pole. "There's a theme," she explained. The problem was that the theme was never clear to anyone else. "Precise chaos" is how Cletus had once described helping her place the decorations.

"That was on this pole last year," she said, pointing to a pile of decorations. The boys soon realized that was code for "It's not going on that pole this year." Every ornament was therefore handled several times before the man in the utility company bucket was given the go-ahead.

Somebody put a nickel in the jukebox at the Houn-Dawg, and "White Christmas" by Bing Crosby floated all of the way to the square. Mrs. Pope had requested the vending company put some Christmas selections in. "Snoopy's Christmas" by the Royal Guardsmen was the most popular among the after-school crowd.

As the utility company hung the lights, Tommy overheard the crew talking about how the lights hanging near the school seemed to burst more often than those on the square. The crew had written the phenomenon off to a temperature deviation or electricity spikes. The boys could have explained the mystery; it had more to do with BB guns than weather. As they worked their way around the square, the town came alive with the festive display.

Burt was helping Alison hang a sign in front of a small building between the *Colby Telegraph* and Burt's Sinclair. The building had at one time housed a shoe and clock repair shop, until the owner had sold it to Burt before moving to Florida.

In anticipation of coming out of the witness protection program, Alison enrolled in an art academy in Fairview. A couple of evenings each week, she'd slip into her snug-fitting jeans and ratty sweatshirt and escape to Fairview. The art instructor quickly recognized Alison's talent and encouraged her to consider teaching. Alison took the encouragement seriously, and with money from Tippy's trust and help from Burt, she opened the Colby Art Academy. She immediately put several of her paintings on display. The one in the window was of a snowy mountain scene. She'd painted it from a photograph Vince Gambaiana had taken in the Rocky Mountain National Park.

Melody and her mom were spraying artificial snow on the corners of their display window, preparing to begin the tedious chore of assembling Hinkebeins's famous Christmas village. The village featured an electric train and was always a favorite of the kids. Mrs. Hinkebein would soon be seen every morning cleaning nose smudges from the lower part of the giant window, left there the night before by kids mesmerized by the train.

Melody finally noticed Tommy staring at her and looked his way. The cold air made her complexion glow. The exchange warmed Tommy from tip to toe.

Hinkebeins was the headquarters for Operation Christmas, a benevolent organization that provided gifts to families who couldn't afford them. Checkers commented on a family who was delivering several wrapped gifts. "Last year I got wunna 'em transistor radios from Operation Christmas." His comment caused the other boys, especially Tommy, to stop and consider. Tommy had never known for sure who received the gifts. "It had batteries too," Checkers added. "Thangs are better this year," he said after a pause, as his chubby fingers untangled a knotted string of lights. Tommy, however, was more interested in Melody's rosy cheeks than Checkers's Christmas story.

A Salvation Army Santa Claus was ringing a bucket bell in front of Gooche's. Another nickel had been deposited at the Houn Dawg and Nat King Cole crooned "Chestnuts Roasting on an Open Fire."

Everyone's fingers were nearly frozen, and the utility crew was approaching their wit's end when Mrs. Koch stood back and announced. "I think we're finished. It may be perfect." It was the "may be" part that initiated an exchange of looks among those who had actually been doing the work. "Let me go up and take a look from the balcony." She made her way across the street, stopping frequently to chat with folks and observe the square, now abuzz with people.

A few minutes later, Mrs. Koch and Mrs. Webster appeared together on the balcony. Mrs. Webster had her arm around Mrs. Koch. Mrs. Koch at first wore the expression of an inspector. She slowly took in the decorations and smiled proudly. She leaned into the taller Mrs. Webster for a hug. From the Houn-Dawg, Nat King Cole crooned:

And so I'm offering this simple phrase,
To kids from one to ninety-two,
Although its been said many times, many ways,
A very Merry Christmas to you.

One of the utility men, not a Colby resident, had had enough. "What's with this lady?" he asked.

"Relax," the other one said. "It's like this every year. It's Christmas. Giv'r a break."

Mrs. Koch finally returned and congratulated the group on a job well done. Then she surprised everyone by saying, "Mrs. Webster has invited everyone to come up and see the square from the balcony."

The prospect of seeing the lights from the balcony wasn't as appealing as getting out of the cold wind. The utility company men grumbled a little as they ascended the steps; something about the volunteer work already taking longer than expected, but the view from the balcony was spectacular. The thick clouds cast enough of a shadow that every light sparkled. The ringing bell of the Salvation Army Santa crowned the moment. Hot chocolate was served. A Colby Christmas was beginning to take shape.

Spirit of Colby

WASHINGTON WEBSTER ARRIVED IN COLBY the afternoon before the parade. The Websters hosted a reunion dinner. The Kochs enjoyed being back in the loft apartment and seated at "their" formal dining table. George and Washington reminisced, telling stories that, because of their classification, neither of them had spoken of since the war. During dinner, Washington had conspiratorially told Marie of a parade maneuver he had in mind. She'd already shown him the stone and let him know where they'd be sitting.

Parade day weather was typical December—cold and cloudy. Eugene Meisenheimer and Finis Pribble (Done and Did), representing the First Baptist Deacons, helped maneuver George to a spot in front of the stone. Marie covered the cold stone with a quilt then took a seat. Done and Did positioned George's wheelchair directly in front of her.

The street was lined two and three deep along the entire parade route. Those without gloves or mittens stuffed their hands into their pockets. The cold temperature, accompanied by a northerly breeze, had everyone's teeth chattering, eyes watering, and noses running.

The parade always started in front of the Methodist church. The beginning of the parade would eventually reach the school, its final destination, before the last float departed the church. The county commissioners had entered a cute but amateur float, a flatbed pickup with a silver artificial tree and a bench with the Codgers sitting on it. Rabbit had donned an elf hat.

Gooche's Grocery's had hired a lady from Fairview to dress up like Aunt Jemima and cook and serve pancakes. She looked eerily like the cardboard cutout in Gooche's window and, judging by the line of people waiting to be served, was very popular. Her warm, toothy smile indicated she enjoyed her job. While the Websters had been viewed with suspicion because of their race, the Aunt Jemima look-alike had been judged on her pancakes rather than her skin color.

Members of the marching band stomped their feet, trying to keep warm—there were only so many layers that could be worn under properly fitting uniforms. Tommy and Melody were warm; their uniforms were so large that they were able to stuff several layers underneath.

A short siren burst from the fire truck signaled the start of the parade. Booger, his dad, and Miss Anderson were circling overhead in a Cessna. In an effort to gauge wind drift, they'd already dropped several rolls of toilet paper over the football field.

An overcast sky with occasional sleet had threatened the Ping-Pong ball drop. Miss Anderson, an experienced pilot, had explained to Booger and his dad that they'd return to the airport at the first sign of ice accumulating on the wing.

"Fire truck's in position," Booger shouted. The moving fire truck meant the parade was underway. The engine noise and the wind rushing past the open baggage door of the airplane made it difficult to hear. Miss Anderson gave the thumbs-up signal and maneuvered into a position upwind of the parade route. The plan was to drop the balls well ahead of the parade. One year the balls had been dropped too near the parade, and a few band members had been trampled by overzealous Ping-Pong ball retrievers.

Booger's dad was on his knees in the back of the plane wrestling with the mesh bags filled with Ping-Pong balls. Miss Anderson put the Cessna 172 into a slip, dipping one side of the plane toward the ground while using opposite rudder to keep the plane from turning. Jack Burger emptied the first bag through the baggage compartment door.

He held up an empty Ping-Pong ball bag and shouted, "All out."

"All out," Booger repeated to Miss Anderson. Another thumbs-up signal and she maneuvered the plane so they could see where the Ping-Pong balls were landing. It was impossible to see the small balls, but they could see the mad scramble of people. The absurdity of it all struck Booger as he watched people chasing the elusive airborne Ping-Pong coupons.

People on the ground watched as the plane circled for the second drop. Skyward-looking eyes blinked to avoid small slivers of piercing sleet. A tight wad of balls spilled from the rear of the plane, quickly scattered, and slowly drifted to the ground.

People scurried about grabbing balls as they scattered with each gust. Close scrutiny of Ping-Pong balls was taking place as the plane circled for another pass. Many shouted joyfully the discount offered on the ball they'd recovered.

"Mine says five hundred dollars off," one lady shouted. This instantly drew a crowd since the most anyone had seen was twenty-five dollars.

"I got a five hun'ert dollar wun too," an older man yelled, waving his Ping-Pong ball.

The fire truck cycled its siren and people cleared the street to make way for the parade. The news of the prized balls spread quickly. Knowing that the plane was about to let go another batch, what seemed like half the crowd ran down the street ahead of the fire truck and parade.

Tommy and Melody, still ostracized from the rest of the marching band, were standing together, both shivering. Both were blowing through their mouthpieces in an effort to keep their lips warm. Tommy pulled Melody close and began to rub her back vigorously. She did the same for him. Tommy realized the two of them must have looked odd, both rubbing the other's back, their chins resting on the other's shoulder, and both blowing through their mouthpieces. He didn't care.

Tommy watched people chasing the Ping-Pong balls and grinned, remembering the gag imprints. He recalled vividly the hours of work he and Booger had volunteered imprinting. He reassured himself that the gag was pay back for punishment he'd received for something he hadn't done.

Tommy watched the Cessna circle for another drop and chuckled. He resumed blowing through his mouthpiece to keep his lips warm. He and Melody joined other band members who were huddled together. Everyone was doing heel-raises trying to keep their feet and toes warm.

Coach Bodenschatz, dressed as Santa from the waist down, ran around getting everyone organized. Occasionally he'd blow his whistle to get everyone's attention, causing the horses to jump with each shrill. Only those people standing near Coach paid attention. Most generally knew what they were supposed to do and were anxious to get moving so they could warm up.

Coach removed his heavy parka and put on the rest of his Santa suit and a fake beard that looked more like a cheap quilt than facial hair. To most parade veterans, this was the official starting signal. He hopped onto the back of the fire truck, the driver cycled the siren once more, turned on the red light, and the parade was officially underway.

An announcement the previous week in the *Colby Telegraph* had revealed who had been chosen as grand marshal and his relation to Carter Webster. The article had mentioned that Washington Webster, Carter's brother, was a WWII veteran and went into great detail regarding Washington's relationship to Mr. Koch.

Miss Anderson had submitted the boy's essays to the *Telegraph*. Tommy's had been published first. Many in Colby were surprised to learn of Mr. Koch's esteemed WWI aviation career. Most knew he'd been in WWI, but few, if any, had known of his meritorious service as a fighter pilot. Until Tommy's essay appeared, Mr. Koch had been known primarily as a banker—and that position had been gained by marriage.

"I'll be gosh dog," Tommy had heard one of the Codgers comment while reading the article. They'd be even more surprised if they knew about the X608 program, Tommy thought. He wanted desperately to tell them, but he kept his promise.

EVEN THOUGH WASHINGTON WEBSTER'S FACE and neck told his age, he looked to be in excellent shape. His WWII uniform still fit. He led the color guard, setting the example with a crisp military marching style that hadn't been seen for several years. The others, all WWII or Korean veterans, took his lead and snapped to. Heels clicked in perfect unison as the color guard moved out. Frank Fritz, who had never missed marching in the color guard since WWII, claimed he caught the flu.

Al Tatum was watching the filling station while Burt marched in the parade. It had only taken a couple of hours for word of her background to sweep though Colby. It changed the way people looked at her and Tippy. Now she was free to tell Tippy more details of her father and her extended family. With the burden of staying hidden lifted from her, she began to see things from a more pleasant point of view. Feelings and emotions she'd suppressed for years began to surface. She began to ask people to call her Alison. And she'd started using some of Tippy's makeup.

She and Burt made eye contact when the veterans marched by. He and Alison shared more in common than they realized. Burt, too, had been suppressing emotions. He'd lost his wife long ago and had accepted the fact that he'd probably never remarry. The lingering glance stirred sensations that neither had felt for longer than either could remember. And neither felt even a twinge of guilt at the natural desire that pulsated.

Cold lips and fingers caused the practice rendition of "Jingle Bells" to sound flat in some places and sharp in others. Mr. Tobin was somewhat confident that a few hundred feet into the parade, the blood would begin to circulate to all lips and fingers—the music quality, he hoped, would improve dramatically. But that wasn't his biggest concern.

The committee had agreed that, Tippy, clearly showing by then, was the perfect choice for Mary. And as often happens, one thing leads to another, and in this case the 'nother was drafting Dwight to be Joseph.

Mr. Tobin had made it clear that he wasn't happy about the committee allowing a donkey to be in front of the band. A common rule of thumb for the parades was for all livestock to be placed in the rear. Mr. Purdy had offered a donkey he'd recently acquired, and the committee had agreed that a single donkey shouldn't be a problem. Fortunately for those walking behind Mary and Joseph, the donkey had purged itself prior to parade formation. Of course, Mr. Tobin had witnessed the bodily function and spent the next few minutes pacing about and dramatically exhaling.

Dwight was still suffering the effects of being shot—he was supposed to be in a wheelchair, but he had refused, preferring crutches. Chester Bird had offered a hay trailer for Tippy, the donkey, and Dwight. And as was usually the case, Chester was late getting to the parade, and all Mr. Tobin saw was a manure-producing jackass positioned ahead of his band. He looked at the band and saw forty pair of pearly white spats. His blood pressure wouldn't have sky rocketed had someone told him the donkey was to be placed on Chester's trailer.

Chester showed up just before parade time. Mr. Purdy coaxed the donkey up a plank and into the trailer using a bag of oats. Mr. Tobin's blood pressure fell to just below stroke-causing levels, and the weather resumed as his primary concern.

A traditional manger scene followed Mary and Joseph. Since the parade occurred well before Christmas Day, the committee had long ago decided on depicting both the pilgrimage of Mary and Joseph and the nativity of the newborn King. The manger scene float was made up of real people and artificial animals, except for a mangy goat that was supposed to be a lamb. Baby Jesus was a large rubber doll with a round face and eyes that closed when it was laid on its back. Mrs. Hinkebein had taped the eyes open so the baby looked awake, making the doll look a little creepy to the observant onlooker. Soon after the parade began, the tape on one eye lost its tackiness, and the baby looked like it was winking. It went undiscovered until the parade's end.

As in years past, the string of floats was followed by a potpourri of participants in various costumes. The Ducklings pulled a small wagon with a decorated Christmas tree secured with kite string. Leon Goolsby was driving Burt's 396 Chevelle. He'd rev the engine now and then, thrilling the boys and annoying the girls. Buddy Grover drove his '57 Chevy and threw out peppermint candy to the kids. The Goolsby twins took turns driving their riding lawnmower pulling a small garden trailer. One drove while the other rode in the trailer.

Jackman Super Fan was one of the parade's highlights. Chosen by the pep squad and athletes to represent the Colby Fighting Indians, he marched, dressed head to toe as an Indian chief. He marched to the beat of his own sporadic drum, so to speak, completely devoid of rhythm. He'd occasionally get distracted by the cheering crowd and stop to clap his hands in front and back. Once he picked up a piece of peppermint candy, carefully unwrapped it, and then after putting the candy in his mouth, began gagging, convulsing, and spitting. After that, he returned to performing his previous dancing gyrations with the added twist of incessant spitting.

Rosolini's catering van was pulling a flatbed trailer. Flop was standing on one end of the trailer next to a grouping of bowling pins. Checkers and Everett were at the other, wearing bowling shirts, holding pool cues, and leaning against an artificial pool table. Mrs. Rosolini was standing in the middle tossing miniature bread sticks, wrapped in candy cane colored paper, into the crowd.

Dog owners had petitioned to be allowed into the parade, and several people with dogs on leashes showed up with their beloved pets. Most of the dogs were well behaved, but a few hadn't gotten their fill of sniffing. One that looked to be a mix between German shepherd and Doberman pinscher kept sticking his nose into the rear end of a perfectly manicured standard poodle. The poodle yelped and dashed to the end of its leash with each sniff, which was frequent. The German Shepherd's owner found it all amusing. The fleshy lady with the poodle wore a permanent scowl.

The parade committee had grown tired of putting up with the horse people complaining about all of the nonhorse riding animals that were allowed in the parade. So instead of restricting the riding animals to horses, the category was renamed "large animals." They'd chosen to do this after considerable discussion about all the different variations of donkeys, mules, and horses, such as jenny, burro, and all the others. While fixing one problem, another was created. Until then, all riding animals had at least resembled a horse. With the rule changed, people began showing up with Hereford bulls, spitting llamas, alpacas, and this year, for the first time, a camel. The Hereford bulls created no problem; they were docile. Three or four kids could ride one, and the horses didn't mind. The exotic animals were another story. They made the horses skittish, stretched their long necks to bite anyone within reach, and seemed to cause all the large animals to produce record amounts of manure.

BOOGER HAD NEVER SEEN THE parade from above but sensed that a larger-than-normal number of people were chasing ahead of the parade in search of Ping-Pong balls. Thinking about the gag balls caused him to giggle. Miss Anderson gave him a raised-eyebrow look, as if to ask what joke she'd missed. Booger's giggling and rare smile brought tears to her eyes. She was glad to see him enjoying himself. Booger's dad cluelessly scanned the ground, trying to see what was so funny. Seeing Booger giggling brought tears of joy to his eyes as well.

On the ground, Marty Blanken and Wilma Bodenschatz were examining a gag ball.

"Five hun'ert dollars?" Wilma asked suspiciously.

"Yep," Marty replied without taking his eyes off the ball.

"What store?" Wilma asked.

"Don't say."

"Don't make sense," Wilma replied.

"Know what does?" Marty declared.

"What?" Wilma inquired.

"Tommy and Booger done the imprints."

Wilma met Marty's grin with one of her own.

MR. KOCH'S DROOPY EYES WELLED with tears when the parade, led first by the grand marshal, then the color guard, approached. They were in their full military dress uniforms. Parade watchers near the Kochs sensed the weight of the moment and backed up to let them see. Burt was carrying the American flag, and Cletus carried the American Legion flag. Joe-Bill, Arnold, and Jupiter were carrying their vintage military-issue rifles. Carter was carrying a flag never before seen in Colby.

"Is that the gun he did the shootin' with?" one wide-eyed boy asked his mother when Jupiter limped by.

The color guard halted and marched time in front of the Kochs. Washington Webster turned and saluted them. Mr. Koch instinctively began to stand. With the help of Done and Did and Mrs. Koch, Mr. Koch instinctively but slowly stood; while holding Scout he returned the salute. The blankets that had been keeping him warm fell to the ground, revealing his WWI dress uniform. It hung loosely around his shrunken frame. Physically, he resembled a shell of his youth, but in the eyes of most in Colby, he was a giant, especially since Tommy's essay had revealed so much about Mr. Koch's service to the country. Yet, a few remained skeptical that he'd actually accomplished all that Tommy had written, and they didn't know the best part of his story.

Mr. Koch watched the grand marshal, the only veteran pilot in the color guard, turn and approach him. Washington Webster, the former Tuskegee airman, saluted George once again, and then they vigorously shook hands. Marie stepped forward and embraced Washington. It was a pivotal moment, packed with emotion for the hardest of hearts. Even Jupiter Storm wiped tears from his cheeks.

George and the Tuskegee airman exchanged pilot-to-pilot glances. They'd both been a first of their kind. George was among the first Americans to fly in battle, and Washington among the first black Americans to do so. A gust of wind stood straight the flag that Carter carried—the flag of the Tuskegee airmen. For a moment, time stood still.

Marie had just finished getting George and Scout settled back into his wheelchair when Dwight and Tippy's trailer passed by. Tippy's rosy cheeks brought a feeling of warmth to all, and her maternal condition signified the hope of the season.

The band marched time in front of Mr. Koch and played "White Christmas." Mr. Koch's ashen color shook Tommy such that he stopped playing. Mr. Koch saw Tommy looking his way, smiled and slowly raised his hand to wave. Tommy was heartened by Mr. Koch's acknowledgement, but saddened at his failing health. He wanted more than anything to tell the rest of Mr. Koch's story.

Miss Anderson maneuvered the plane so that the last bag of balls landed on the elementary school playground. From the air, it seemed that there were more people in the playground grabbing for Ping-Pong balls than were watching the parade. The parade looked like a giant centipede inching its way through town.

The Christmas parade represented in every way the true spirit of Christmas and nature of Colby. And Tommy, the paperboy, knew that Colby was changing for the better.

Flop's Snow

THAT FOLLOWING SUNDAY, THE EARLY evening news mentioned a good chance for snow, so Tommy's dad let him stay up and watch the late news and weather. A news clip from the central highlands of Vietnam showed helicopters flying in formation near the Cambodian border. Shots taken from a B52 high above the Vietnamese and Laotian border showed enemy troops and trucks moving south along what Walter Cronkite called the "Ho Chi Minh trail." He reported about how the enemy moved supplies through neutral Laos, but American forces weren't allowed to cross the border to attack the enemy supply caravans. By day, the North Vietnamese moved along the Laotian border at will, and during the night crossed into the Vietnamese jungle at a thousand different spots. It was impossible to defend and frustrating to watch, knowing our B52 bombers could have put a stop to it almost immediately.

"That's about the dumbest thing I've heard in my entire life," Ted Thompson shouted at the TV.

Tommy didn't respond because he knew his dad was talking to the TV, a common practice during the news, particularly when it was about government rules that tied the hands of the troops. Tommy had been paying more attention to the footage than the commentary; he considered the news something to endure until the weather report.

"Snow in the forecast," the giddy anchorman said just before a commercial break. Marsha finished in the bathroom, so Tommy took his turn while a cartoon rooster resembling Foghorn Leghorn strutted around a barnyard announcing the attributes of Gristo Feed. While brushing his teeth, Tommy heard a familiar furniture store commercial. It was the one where the owner of the furniture store cuts a mattress in half with a chainsaw and yells into the camera all the particulars concerning a half-price bedding sale.

Finally, a weather map of the entire USA appeared on the screen. It was a most excruciating wait as the weatherman reported about significant weather, high and low pressure systems, and temperature records set at various places across the country. He talked ad nauseam about converging systems. Tommy was becoming frustrated until he figured out that converging systems increased the chance for snow, which could result in school being cancelled. Sleeping in wasn't what he was looking forward to. Snow in the forecast meant plans had to be made—just in case.

"Yes!" Tommy shouted when Mr. Ad Nauseam finally announced a forecast for up to eight inches of snow for the Colby area.

"Time for bed, Mr. Man," Ted Thompson said. "It's way past your bedtime."

Tommy, energized by the forecast, shot off the couch and ran to his bedroom. He looked out his bedroom window toward the streetlight. A few fat flakes had already begun to fall.

WITH HIS BEDROOM WINDOW PARTIALLY open, he could hear the sound of snowflakes the size of quarters landing gently on the windowsill. The softest sound in the world is that of snowflakes landing on a windless night. Tommy drifted in and out of a fitful sleep. He peeked outside, the illuminated hands on his watch indicated it was only 4 AM and nearly two inches had already accumulated. He slipped back into the warmth of his covers, turned the pillow over to the cool side, and started planning the day. He contemplated sanding the sled runners, rubbing them down with paraffin, and wondered if last year's snow boots still fit. Just before dozing off, he remembered the old truck hood.

Tommy awoke to the sound of his dad's truck starting, followed by the opening and closing of the front door. His dad's winter morning ritual was breakfast, start the truck, and while it warmed, get Tommy and Marsha out of bed for school. He would soon be at the door with the wake-up call. Tommy remained cocooned in the warm blankets and mentally scanned the basement for a rope that would make pulling the hood up the hill easier. Sometime during the night, he scrapped the idea of sanding the runners on the sled—too much work.

He waited for the wake-up call—nothing. Silence confirmed his hope that school had been called off. He fought off the urge to get up and ask. To do so before his dad left increased the risk of getting assigned a chore that would need to be done before going out into the snow. Tommy patiently lay in the warmth of his bed and listened to the snow. The cold air rushing in through the open window froze the hair in his nostrils.

He heard his mom and dad talking, but he couldn't make out what they were saying. Tommy's dad flushed the toilet, and the sound of running water increased Tommy's urge to pee.

Finally, he heard the sound of the truck leaving. The tires made that unmistakable crunching sound as they carved the first tracks in the snow. Tommy bolted for the bathroom.

"Hey, I need in there," Marsha yelled as he flew past her door. Tommy held himself with one hand and locked the door with the other.

Marsha banged on the door. "Thomas! You've got one minute."

The relief was sensational. He returned the toilet seat to the down position, flushed, and waited for Marsha to beg. Marsha pecked on the door as soon as the toilet bowl water stopped running.

He opened the door. Marsha gave him a predatory look and brushed past him. "You're in big trouble if there's any pee on the seat." She slammed the door and locked it before Tommy could respond, not that he'd intended to. There was no need to get into any unnecessary trouble on a snow day. He returned to his room and dug through his drawer for long underwear.

The phone rang. "Tommy, it's for you. It's Booger," his mom yelled from the kitchen. He raced to the phone—the snow day had begun.

"Church Hill," Tommy announced into the phone.

"Stop by my house on the way?" Booger asked.

"Yeah. You call Flop?" Tommy asked.

"He called me. Can you believe it?"

"After all, he did move here from Chicago. But that's still surprising," Tommy agreed.

Booger giggled. "I didn't tell him about the truck hood."

Tommy contemplated Booger's delightful giggle—they'd become more frequent.

THE BOYS PUT THEIR SLEDS on the hood that Burt had given them, tied the rope Tommy had found, and headed toward the hill. To their surprise,

Flop was waiting at the base of the hill. He was wearing so many clothes that his arms and legs could barely bend at the joints. His head was covered with a multicolored sock hat and girly looking earmuffs. Tommy and Booger had long since stopped laughing at the way Flop's mom sometimes dressed him and just let the matter go without comment. Flop had brought a large odd-shaped thing, flat on the bottom, long, and without runners.

"What's 'at thing?" Booger asked.

"Toboggan," Flop answered condescendingly.

Flop looked at the hood. "Is that a car hood?" he asked.

Booger grinned. "Nope, truck hood. Shows what you know."

"I'm sure that makes all the difference," mocked Flop, his Chicago accent making him sound doubly sarcastic. "Where'd you get it?" And before Flop or Tommy could answer Flop fired off another question. "How do you guide it?" Normally, that time of day would have been too early for rapid-fire questions, but the cold and bright sun reflecting off the snow, and the anticipation of a fun day of sledding, had everyone awake and alert.

"Burt gave it to us, and it's easy to guide," Booger answered.

Tommy listened to the exchange and was struck with the notion that neither he nor Booger had given any thought regarding how to control the hood. He was contemplating that thought until he saw Melody approaching. Seeing her rosy cheeks and engaging smile gave Tommy a familiar dizzying sensation—he was glad he'd called her. Worrying about how to guide the hood instantly became the last thing on his mind.

Caleb, Checkers, and Everett arrived and contributed their two cents on how to guide a hood and toboggan. Flop was the only one among them with any experience riding a runner-free contraption, but his opinion didn't count for much; he was still the new kid. And his goofy wardrobe hadn't improved his credentials.

A consensus was finally reached. They'd ride their sleds until a defined track was developed. Then they'd ride the hood and toboggan.

That settled, the group began their ascent of the steep gravel hill known as Church Hill, aptly named because of the crumbling remains of a church that graced the crest.

One of the cool things about getting out early on a snow day is being the first to make tracks. It's as if you're going where no one has gone before. Clearly this wasn't the case since they were in the middle of a road, but the sensation, real or imagined, was energizing. Chester Bird, who lived at the end of the road, hadn't driven to town and probably wouldn't until the snow melted. Melody put her sled on the hood with the others. She and the boys slowly slogged their way toward the top of the steep hill, each taking a turn pulling the hood and the toboggan.

After reaching the top, they took in the snow-drenched view while catching their breath. The snow silenced any sound made by the few cars and trucks that could be seen slowly moving about way down in Colby. Tommy noticed the Ducklings making a trip through the snow to their outhouse; he kept the observation to himself. Church Hill road made a sharp turn a hundred yards or so after leveling out. If the curve hadn't been there, the road would have cut right through the middle of the Duckling's house.

Tommy and Melody first rode separately, then together on one sled. Their extra weight caused them to pick up additional speed, so they always went further and faster than the others. The other boys refused to pile on top of each other onto a single sled. The tracks got more packed with each trip down the hill and the cold and long walk back up the hill depleted everyone's energy.

Flop keeled over into a snow bank. "Lets try 'at toboggan before we all freeze t' death," he moaned. "'At dang track is as good as it's gonna get."

Everyone was cold, hungry, and tired, but they weren't going to admit it. No one argued with Flop; they all moved toward the toboggan and hood. Melody sat in front, then Tommy, Flop, and finally Booger, and they pushed off down the hill on the toboggan. Caleb, Checkers, and Everett rode the hood and launched slightly behind them.

The toboggan riders each had their legs wrapped around the person in front of them. Melody locked her arms around Tommy's knees. They gradually picked up speed just as Flop had said it would and tracked perfectly in the channel the sleds had made. The wind peeled Flop's goofy sock hat off as the four of them screamed down the hill.

The toboggan reached the end of the track with a good head of steam and continued into the fresh trackless snow. Tommy fully expected the fresh deep snow would stop them before Duckling's curve, but the toboggan, with enough momentum to plane out on top, seemed to gain speed.

With no track to guide it, the toboggan continued straight ahead and left the road at the curve. All eyes were wide open; Melody was scream-ing. The toboggan continued down the steep slope on the back side of the curve and the Duckling's house was coming up fast. At the last second, Tommy peeled off and dragged Melody with him. Flop and Booger made no such maneuver.

Flop, oblivious to the peril, had been craning his head back and forth trying to keep an eye on the sock hat, and in the process, he blocked Booger's view. Flop turned his head around just in time to see the tobog-gan slam into the heavy shrubs along the side of the house, sending him and Booger airborne. Flop's scream was instantly muffled when Booger sandwiched him against the shingle-sided house. The impact sounded loud enough to knock the house off its rock foundation, but of course it didn't. Flop's body had cushioned Booger's impact—a good deal for Booger, but not so hot for Flop.

Tommy and Melody witnessed the spectacle. They ran over and at first couldn't tell if Booger was laughing or crying. Then they thought Booger had killed Flop, but after a few very long moments, Flop got his breath and started moving. They all expected Flop to have broken every bone in his body and swallowed his tongue to boot. Melody brushed the pieces of asphalt siding off Flop's face while he caught his breath.

Flop was sitting up but not speaking when Everett, Checkers, and Caleb came running through the snow. They stopped when Erma Duke stuck her head around the corner of the house. She had her coat shut with one hand and a baseball bat in the other.

"What-a-you'unses think yer doin'?" she yelled.

"Leavin'!" Checkers's responded instantaneously. Everett grabbed the toboggan, Caleb and Tommy helped Flop, and they all ran to the safety of the road. Once safely out of the Duckling's yard they all plopped down into the snow. While sitting in a snow bank on the edge of the curve, Caleb stuck Flop's lost sock hat on his bulbous head and patted him on the shoulder. Nothing was said and there was no celebration, just heavy panting and visible breaths. It was that precise moment when Flop was no longer considered a new guy—he'd paid his dues.

For a minute, the only sound was that of heavy breathing and sniffling. Of course everyone could hear the sound of their own heartbeat. Flop was the first to speak. "You'd think we could have missed a house. Dang!" The rest considered him healed and pelted him with snowballs.

During the snowball melee, a small miracle occurred—Booger began to laugh uncontrollably. He fell to his knees belly-laughing and then toppled over onto his side into the snow, laughing and snorting. His face was a snotty mess. Melody gave him a hug, and Tommy didn't mind.

Flop was clutching his side. Caleb whispered to him. "I know it hurts, but seeing Booger laughin' feels good. Doesn't it?"

A simple nod caused Flop to wince in pain. "Guess so," he answered.

Seeing Booger belly laugh was like an early Christmas gift for Tommy. In later years, the boys would refer to that day as Flop's Snow, but their lasting visual was of Booger's laugh.

A National Treasure

THE BAPTIST MEN'S GROUP HOSTED a father and son pancake and sausage breakfast in an effort to attract more helpers to shovel snow off the church parking lot. Burt Brown made his famous chocolate gravy; that drew a good crowd. Carter Webster brought George Koch and, of course, Scout. After breakfast, most of the men hung around inside, saying they were helping clean up the kitchen. Those who had done most of the work fixing breakfast continued their service and moved out onto the cold, snow-covered parking lot.

The frugal Baptists had never budgeted for more than one shovel, and the deacons bragged about the one they had having lasted several decades. No one stopped to think that the handle had been replaced several times after being broken by nitwits who didn't know how to use a shovel, or that the spade had been replaced twice. So, in fact, the famous triple-decade shovel had no original parts.

Burt, Cletus, Jupiter, and George brought shovels. George had bought a shovel after moving to the duplex; it still had the label glued to the spade. There were more men than shovels, so when one stopped for a break, another would take over. The boys gradually turned the event into a competition. First there was the competition among the boys to see who could shovel the most without taking a break. The men found it amusing that the boys had found entertainment in what the adults considered hard work.

At one point during the shovel exchanges, every boy had a shovel while nearly half of the men were taking a so-called break. That's when the competition expanded; the boys challenged the men to see who could clear the biggest area.

George, with Scout on his lap, rolled himself into position between the boys and the men and cheered on both groups. At one point, George stood and his cheering became uncharacteristically animated. His yelling eventually led to a coughing fit, causing him to collapse back into his wheelchair. Once recovered, he'd jab a victory fist into the air any time one of the men made eye contact with him. The boys were winning; George winked at Tommy.

One of Mrs. Crawford's cats was slinking around the church while they shoveled. It stuck its head around the corner of the church foundation and watched. Everett threw a snowball at it. Several minutes later, it was sitting on top of a tall headstone in the church cemetery. Scout spotted it first. He jumped down off of George's lap and gave chase. The cat ran several yards and then jumped up onto another headstone and licked its paws until Scout almost caught up, and then it leapt down and ran to another headstone. This went on for a minute or so until Scout began coughing, sounding eerily similar to George. He was too fatigued to make his way through the snow back to George's lap. Everett, the big softie, trudged through the snow and rescued Scout. For that, he got applause.

He placed Scout back on George's lap and rejoined the boys. "That dog's spitting up blood," he whispered to Tommy. Tommy looked in Mr. Koch's direction. Both Mr. Koch and Scout were still coughing intermittently. The parking lot was nearly finished and since Burt had rallied the men, the competition was going to be close. Tommy got back to work and didn't give Everett's comment any further thought.

The men had the boys outnumbered, but the boys had youth and stamina. In less than two hours, the parking lot was cleared. The boys won and were declared the winners by George. The men headed slump-shouldered for their cars.

If ever there was a case to be made for mental telepathy, it was that day. The boys, with no exchange of words, raced to the giant pile of snow they'd just made. Burt and Jupiter got the brunt of it, but volley after volley of snowballs rained down on the men as they scurried for their cars. Scout, sensing George may have been in danger, jumped off his lap, took up a position next to the wheelchair, and began yapping until he succumbed to another coughing fit.

George, muffling coughs, eased out of his wheelchair, knelt next to the parked car, and made a snowball. Burt offered to help him back to his wheelchair, but he refused the offer. He laughed, yelled an expletive, reared back, threw the ball toward the boys and then climbed, unassisted, into Carter's car. Everyone was amazed by his sudden ambulatory ability.

George was still coughing and laughing when they got to the duplex. By then the adrenaline rush had subsided, and he needed help getting out of the car. He had to stop several times to catch his breath while telling Marie about the fun. She listened as she wheeled him along toward the bedroom.

Scout made no effort to get out of the car and follow George. He lay on the seat, moving only his eyes. Carter carried him into the duplex and set him on a pillow next to the fireplace. He knelt and stroked Scout's head slowly, noticing his shallow and rapid breathing. He waited until Marie returned from getting George settled in the bedroom. "Scout isn't doing so well," he told her.

"Neither is George," she replied. "His coughing will subside once he stops trying to talk." She assured Carter. "I think he enjoyed himself to-day."

After Carter left, Marie helped an animated but exhausted George into warm, dry clothes and then got him settled into his favorite chair. "How about you rest a few minutes?" she said, covering him. "I'll fix us some hot chocolate and you can tell me all about your exciting day." She checked on Scout before going to the kitchen.

George saw her worried look. "How's Scout?" he asked.

"He's resting," she obfuscated. George fell asleep before the hot choco-late was ready.

Marie knew that moving to the duplex had been the right thing to do. George lived for the community, and now he was able to attend more functions. Careful not to wake him, she gently kissed him on the forehead and tucked the blanket snugly around him.

THE METHODISTS HAD NEVER BUILT a parking lot, and since the streets still had snow piled along the sides, there was no place for them to park. Because Colby First Baptist had a cleared parking lot, several Methodist families decided to worship with the Baptists.

The First Baptist choir loft had been converted to a stage for the Christmas play, and attendance in December was well above average— the Christmas effect, Brother Baker called it. The deacons were taking

folding chairs from Sunday school rooms and putting them in the sanctuary at the ends of each aisle.

To make room for the Christmas play props, the choir had moved to
the first three rows. Those who normally sat in the first three rows had
moved in order to make room for the choir. Regulars at First Baptist knew
who the displaced people were and accommodated them; it happened
every Christmas. The displaced people scattered about and squeezed in
wherever they could. Members who attended only on Christmas and Eas-
ter were greeted heartily and told they'd been missed.

The Methodists were another story. When a regular at Colby First
Baptist found a Methodist in their spot, it ignited feelings of sharp contempt. Rather than receive a friendly greeting, as was the custom for unknown visitors, the Methodists were usually greeted with a forced smile
and a rhetorical question regarding their parking lot fund. The exchange
only served to confirm the contempt that each denomination had for the
other—a John Wesley versus John Calvin debate.

Brother Baker's December sermons were always the best of the year.
He knew that December was his only chance to get the Gospel message
to those who only attended once or twice a year. He sat behind the make-
shift pulpit among the Christmas play props and scanned the audience
for unfamiliar faces while Mrs. Enderle led the congregation in a medley
of Christmas carols.

It was the familiar faces that brought joy to Brother Baker's heart. Al,
now Alison, had recently begun to attend regularly with Tippy. Alison
had in turn brought Burt Brown. They were sitting with Dwight Seabaugh and holding a spot for Tippy, who was playing the piano. Dwight
was technically a Methodist, but due to his recent injury and the fact
that he was married to Tippy, the pianist, and he was in uniform and on
crutches, he received warm smiles from the women and approving nods
from the men.

There was only a small problem, and Brother Baker noticed it. He held
back a chuckle when he realized that Dwight was sitting in Mrs. Whitener's spot. Alison Tatum was probably the only person in town with
enough gall to ask Mrs. Whitener to scoot over. The two seemed to be
hitting it off. What most didn't know is that once Alison's story had been
told, Mrs. Whitener had invited her over. The two had shared their life's
journey and bonded over scones and sassafras tea.

The Websters had officially joined the church a week earlier. They had been accepted unanimously by acclamation, but the vote probably would have been different had it been a secret ballot. People were courteous, but still treated them differently. Gloria and Carter continually assured each other that the distant treatment was because they were new, not because of their color. They were sitting behind the Tatums, where the Ducklings usually sat. Brother Baker worried a bit about the Ducklings. They hadn't returned since it had been revealed that Emma was the underwear culprit. He made a mental note to visit them.

Gloria tapped Alison on the shoulder and told her Marie had called— George wasn't feeling well. She'd miss church but planned to make it for the Christmas play.

Mrs. Enderle cleared her throat until she was able to break Brother Baker's trance. Visitors mistakenly thought Brother Baker to be spaced out, but in fact he spent the last stanza so focused on his sermon that he'd completely blocked everything except God's word from his mind. He was praying with his eyes open.

He'd begun working on this particular sermon months earlier and had studied it and refined it many times. This was the day he felt moved to deliver it. He stepped to the pulpit and enthusiastically welcomed the packed crowd. He prayerfully glanced across the congregation, opened his Bible, and commenced.

"What is evil?" he asked the crowd, then paused and scanned the faces. Each person felt like he was speaking to them. "Who is God?" he asked, and then he paused and scanned the congregation, giving the Methodists a particularly menacing look. "What is the pernicious lie?" he asked. Few knew exactly what pernicious meant, but they figured it was bad.

He passionately answered each of his rhetorical questions. Carter Webster was furiously taking notes. His note-taking had at first seemed strange, but then it had caught on. Now, nearly half the congregation was bringing notepads to worship service.

"Please turn in your Bibles to Galatians 5:16," Brother Baker said. He listened to the sound of flipping pages and saw a sea of Baptist heads looking down at their Bibles. The Methodists looked bewildered—few had Bibles with them.

Brother Baker began and ended his sermon from the pulpit, but the forty-five minutes in between, belaboring his three points, were spent pac-

ing up and down the aisle and back and forth across the part of the stage
not taken over by the Christmas play props. His long, wispy body and one
pencil-thin arm swayed back and forth as he accentuated each point. He
closed the sermon with a ten-minute dissertation on the three modes of
man: innocent man, fallen man, and redeemed man.

On the way out, Bem was heard saying, "You'd think he'd lighten up a
bit on Christmas play day, don't cha know."

"Know what cha mean," Rabbit said. "Not sure I need to come back for
that play." He got a look from his wife. "I'm just sayin'," he added. "I'm all
preached out." And for that he got an elbow in the ribs.

MARIE HAD GONE BACK TO bed after calling Gloria. She'd been up several
times that night checking on Scout and getting cough syrup for George.
Each time she'd checked on Scout, his breathing had been shallower, and
he'd stopped moving his head to look at her.

Late in the morning, George woke her with a coughing fit. She helped
him up, and he insisted on shaving even if they weren't going to church.
"Just can't let myself go to pot," he said. Since he'd skipped dinner the
night before, and they'd both slept through breakfast, he was starving.
Marie fixed him pancakes, something that wouldn't be difficult for him
to digest. He ate six pancakes instead of the normal three, settled into his
chair, and then asked about Scout.

Marie got him settled then went to check. Scout hadn't moved—his
breathing had completely stopped, and his open eyes were lifeless. She
covered him with a small blanket and hid her tears.

George reclined his chair and rested his eyes. "How is he?" He asked.

"Resting," is all she could say without breaking down. She had transi-
tioned from obfuscation to flat-out lying—and on a Sunday, no less. For
more than a year, the vet had been telling them to expect this day. She
dried her tears, hid her grief, and decided to wait until later to tell George.
His coughing had subsided, and his color had improved.

She plopped into the sofa near George's chair. "I may not go to the
Christmas play," she lamented.

"You should go," George told her. "I'll be fine." He said through a cough.

She insisted, saying, "I should stay here and watch Scout." She dreaded
having to tell him. There was no way she could tell him and then go to the
play. George seemed to be doing better, so she decided to wait.

While stewing, she thought of a plan. "I'll ask the Websters to take him by the vet," she said.

"Vet?" he asked.

"He was coughing a lot last night. It might be a good idea for the vet to take a look at him." By getting Scout out of the house under the guise of going to the vet, she'd be able to wait until George was feeling better before breaking the news.

She called the Websters, who assured her that taking Scout to the vet wouldn't be any trouble. She then called the vet. The trick would be letting Carter know that Scout was dead without George overhearing. Then she'd have to explain to the vet. All the thinking had taken her mind off of the grief she felt after first realizing that, after fifteen years, Scout was gone.

She started getting ready for the Christmas play more than two hours before the Websters were scheduled to arrive. A good portion of the time was spent crying over Scout, George's faithful companion for more than fifteen years. She dreaded having to tell George—tomorrow, she decided.

During the move, she'd found a Christmas dress that George had bought her long ago. He smiled when she came out of the bedroom. "I'd forgotten all about that dress." He paused and coughed. "I remember seeing it in the catalog and having Hinkebein order it special." She smiled. It had been years since she'd been able to wear it, but giving it away had never been an option. She'd recently lost weight, and it once again fit. George's compliments made her feel younger.

She saw the Websters pull up and went to the door. She stepped onto the porch to explain the situation; Carter understood and played along. He'd seen George interact with Scout and realized the gravity of the situation.

"Under the weather a little?" Carter asked George.

"Just a little tired is all," George replied.

"I'm sure that's right," Carter lied. George's appearance indicated his problems were more than fatigue.

Carter then lifted Scout, pillow and all. "He'll be more comfortable at the vet on his own pillow," Carter told George. The words had no sooner left Carter's mouth than he began worrying about owning up to the lie. He decided he'd deal with that later.

Marie leaned over and kissed George on the cheek. "Chanel No. 5," he said. Marie smiled. "Lean over—let me smell you again." When she did, he swatted her gently on the rear, but the exertion made him cough.

Marie cried all of the way to the vet. Carter explained to the vet what had happened, then got Scout out of the car. The vet agreed to keep Scout's body until the Kochs decided what to do with him.

THE CHRISTMAS PLAY WAS A spectacular affair—it always was. There was snow on the ground and more on the way. It looked like Colby was about to have a white Christmas. To top it off, there was Dwight as Joseph and Tippy as Mary. Marie's emotions stormed. She couldn't keep from thinking about all of the things she and George had been a part of in Colby. She wondered how Colby would have accepted the Websters had she and George not embraced them. She had to believe that everything would have worked out. That's what she decided to believe.

She was settling in when a pang of guilt flooded her mind at not being truthful with George about Scout. She couldn't remember lying to him about anything more serious than the temperature on the thermostat or the cost of her preferred toilet paper. A tear ran down her cheek; she dabbed at it before it ruined her makeup.

After the play, everyone assembled in the basement of the church for refreshments. During that time, a peaceful feeling enveloped Marie. The guilt pangs suddenly subsided, and the realization that George would understand swept over her. Regardless, she asked the Websters to take her home right away.

George was still in his chair and seemed to be resting peacefully. She covered her dress with dry-cleaners plastic and hung it in the main closet. Wearing the dress seemed to have pleased George. She decided to wear it again on Christmas Day.

She gradually stopped tiptoeing; George needed to wake up so he could move to the bedroom. After straightening up in the kitchen and making considerable noise putting pans away, she thought it curious that he hadn't woken. She went to his side and shook him. Her heart sank, and her lips began to tremble. She realized she'd never have to break the news of Scout to him; there'd be no more "one more day" toasts. Worst of all, her last conversation with him had included a lie.

Overcome with emotion, she collapsed beside George's chair. She clung to his still-warm body for more than an hour. Memories of a life spent with a man she considered a national treasure flooded her mind. She finally reached for the phone and called her son.

Jackson could tell his mother had been crying when he first heard her voice. And judging by the time of her call, he surmised the reason. As an adult, he hadn't been close to his parents, but the news of his father's death stirred more emotions than he could control. He and his mother cried, reminisced, and shared tears well into the night. Several moments were spent saying nothing, just clinging to the phone and wishing they were together. Jackson regretted the hippie era he'd put his parents through. He teared up when his mother told him how proud she and his father had become of him. "I'll make the arrangements," he said before slowly returning the phone receiver to its cradle.

Jackson's phone call got Heinz Baumgartner out of bed. Soon the Greystone hearse was in front of the Koch's duplex. Word spread instantly: a patriarch had passed.

Together They Go

Mr. Baumgartner, or Mr. B, had recently attended a funeral director's seminar. Mrs. B always dreaded his return from the annual meeting—he usually returned with an idea for a nonfunctional, aesthetic, improvement. Funeral directors are all about creating a comforting scene. The two of them usually discussed the idea until Mr. B forgot about it or something else came along to occupy his mind.

This year was no different, he'd returned with an idea for a garden feature. But for once, this was an idea that appealed to Mrs. B. The only point of contention was a park bench that Mr. B had seen in the display garden at the seminar. "It sets it off," he'd said. Mrs. B liked the idea of the garden so much that she quickly gave in to her husband's wishes. She hired a nursery from Fairview to install a scheme of evergreens they called a winter themed meditation collection. They too recommended a bench.

Earlier that year, the county commissioners decided to replace the old wooden courthouse bench with a new aluminum affair. The Codgers thought the idea ludicrous, but few others cared, or even noticed. The wooden bench was supposed to be painted each year, but that hadn't happened and the old paint was peeling away. A few of the boards were soft and needed replacement.

The local VFW, along with every civic organization in Colby, had raised the funds to purchase a monument with the names of those who'd served in foreign wars. It was a huge monument; the list was long. At the top of the list were those who'd made the ultimate sacrifice, followed by those who'd received the Purple Heart. Greystone Monument had agreed to provide the stone and the labor at a significantly reduced price. Toward the end of the summer, Mr. B had been supervising the setting of the monument on the courthouse lawn when the new bench was being delivered. Since nobody had given any thought as to what should happen with the old bench, Mr. B had his crew put it onto the bed of the monument truck. Since then, the bench had been sitting behind his shed, hidden from Mrs. B's view.

Mrs. B reluctantly agreed to allow the courthouse bench in the meditation garden so long as it received a fresh coat of paint. "Cover up those tacky ads," she'd said. "We don't want to be advertising for Rexall Drug or Ex-Lax."

Funeral visitations in Colby tended to become a social event. Some people stayed for hours; some, mostly widows, attended every funeral visitation even if they didn't know the deceased or their family. It's not as if they were professional mourners as in Biblical times—they simply enjoyed being where the crowd was. George Koch had touched countless lives, not only in the county but elsewhere too. His visitation was bound to be a doozy.

JACKSON KOCH ARRIVED THE DAY after his father's death and spent the first few days helping his mother sort through his father's items. As a pre-adolescent he'd listened as others told of what their fathers did during the war. He'd always been forbidden to ask his own father about the war, and that was the foundation of the emotional barrier that began to form between George and his only son.

Jackson had inherited at least one remarkable trait from George, a strong work ethic. He'd eventually gotten his act straight and chosen a career that made his parents proud. The FBI had always intrigued him and the FBI academy seemed a patriotic alternative to getting drafted. He spent most of his career working undercover and most recently on race-related organized crime.

Few in Colby had seen Jackson since he'd left for college. Nobody recognized him; he'd shaved and cut his hair. The inside-out sweatshirt and ratty jeans had been replaced by a dark, three-piece suit. He'd made the change after deciding to earn the respect of his parents and pursue a career with the FBI. Mr. Koch's connections had helped in getting Jackson accepted at the FBI academy. He didn't have any friends he wished to see, but he did have some business to attend to. He drove to Frank Fritz's, hoping to catch Fritz alone.

Frank Fritz was standing in the doorway of his garage, deep in thought, when the dark sedan started up his lane. He watched the strange car approach while contemplating which vehicle to drive to the visitation. Fritz moved a little further into the shadow and watched the car roll to a stop. The driver, well-dressed, middle aged, seemed vaguely familiar, but Fritz couldn't place him. He reached into his pocket and felt the revolver he'd been carrying since the Carters had moved to town.

Jackson Koch had known Fritz, or at least about him, for all of his life. He'd always considered him peculiar but harmless. Fritz's appearance hadn't changed—his thick frameless spectacles weighed heavily on his bulbous-tipped nose and magnified his beady blue eyes.

Jackson was part of a team of agents in the FBI's Atlanta office. They were hot on the trail of a KKK grand dragon from Mississippi who they suspected was involved in a long list of racially motivated crimes. Jackson had immediately recognized Fritz in a couple of agency surveillance photos taken less than a month earlier. This was not a social visit. Fritz was an FBI suspect. Jackson hadn't acknowledged that he'd recognized anyone in the photos. For a few days, he wrestled with how to approach Fritz. He had contacted his parents to let them know he was coming to Colby and had talked to his dad about Fritz and the photos. The very next day, he got the late night call from his mother.

Jackson extended his hand. "Hi, Mr. Fritz, I'm Jackson Koch, George's son." Jackson got straight to the point. "I'm in town for my dad's funeral."

Fritz returned a half-understanding nod. "I was sorry to hear about your Pop."

"Yes, thanks, but that's not why I'm here." He withdrew his ID and offered it to Fritz. "I'm with the FBI," he said, and then waited for a response. He got none.

Fritz gave Jackson a suspicious once-over, and then he said, "I thought you ran off and joined the hippies."

Jackson got Fritz's attention by opening a photo folder. "I recognized you in these photos and asked for the assignment to investigate and identify you." Jackson showed him the photos. Fritz examined them closely and rubbed his chin. Jackson continued, "In a sense, I'm doing you a favor. The good news is these photos put you in Laurel, Mississippi, on the night of Tatum's shed fire, sort of. And," he continued, "no one at the FBI knows that I already know you."

Fritz had stiffened when Jackson qualified his remark with "sort of." Jackson recognized the defensive posture. "I haven't done anything illegal," Fritz said. He avoided eye contact, which told Jackson he was lying.

"Maybe, or at least not with this organization," Jackson responded. "But these men aren't Rotary or Optimist Club delegates. You and I both know what they're up to." Jackson let his words soak in.

After a few moments, Fritz looked directly into Jackson's eyes. In a strained voice, he asked, "Doesn't it bother you that those," he paused in search of a word less caustic than what came naturally, "those *people* moved into your parent's home?"

"Not in the least," he said. "My father considered it an honor that the Websters wanted to move into their apartment. He'd grown quite fond of them."

"I don't understand," Fritz said.

"You don't need to," Jackson responded. He gave Fritz a few more moments to think. "You're being watched. It would be in your best interest to avoid any further contact with these KKK types, they're known criminals." Fritz looked off into the distance. Jackson asked, "Have you even spoken to the Websters?"

Fritz shook his head. "I let the ni—" then caught himself, "man ride in my truck in the parade, but I didn't talk to him."

"Here's what I'm going to do," Jackson continued. "I have to make a report. I'll report what I know—your name and where you live." Fritz frowned. Jackson continued. "The agency is bound to find out anyway. I've already done a background check. You're clean for now."

"It's just as well," Fritz said.

"How's that?" Jackson asked.

"They said that Missouri was too sympathetic with the blacks." He paused. "There's just not enough support to get a KKK chapter established."

"You need two things to start a KKK chapter," Jackson said.

"What's that?" Fritz asked.

"First you need people filled with hatred, and second you need people to hate." Jackson squared off with Fritz for effect. "I think that there's a shortage of both here in Colby."

"I don't reckon I hate 'em," Fritz said.

"Then you'd make a lousy Klan member," Jackson responded.

Fritz extended his hand. The two men shook. Fritz said, "You won't be getting anymore pictures of me unless they're taken here in Colby."

Jackson smiled. "That would make life less complicated for both of us." Jackson stood there, tapping the palm of one hand with his badge holder. "There's one more thing," he said. "I'd like to see those receipts you showed Sheriff Dooley."

Fritz pulled a cigar box from the cabinet and produced the receipts. With a trained eye, Jackson looked at the two restaurant receipts; he grinned. Fritz snatched the two receipts and looked for himself. "What?" he asked.

"Look at the sequence numbers," Jackson told him. "The number for the breakfast, supposedly after the fire, is smaller than the one dated for the evening before the fire."

"So?" Fritz said, putting the receipts back into the cigar box.

"That means you tipped the waitress and convinced her to put the wrong date on the breakfast receipt." Jackson pointed at the sequence number. "This receipt is for a meal that occurred before the fire."

By now Fritz's nervous twitch made him look like he was either dancing or getting electrocuted. "Not necessarily," replied Fritz. "She could have had more than one book."

"That's true," Jackson agreed. Fritz's jitter calmed a tad until Jackson continued. "But that doesn't explain a record of you having spent the night in one of those flea bag hotels across the river from Fairview the night of the fire." Fritz was too shocked to respond. "Remember, I work for the FBI. Investigation is my business."

"That still doesn't prove I started the shed fire," Fritz answered.

"That's right. But then there's the eyewitness who saw a VW similar to yours in town that night." Fritz swallowed hard. Jackson knew he had him on the ropes. "We'll just keep this between us chickens. The eyewitness had no business being out that night and doesn't know what I know. In fact, nobody has it all put together except me." Jackson sensed that Fritz realized he'd been caught. "If there's no more trouble, then there's no need for anyone to find out."

"That shed needed to go anyway," Fritz said, as much as confessing guilt.

"That's probably true," Jackson said and smiled. The two shook again. Jackson gave Fritz an "I gotcha" grin.

Euphoria swept over Jackson on the way back to his mom's duplex. He'd left Colby as a troublemaker with no sense of direction. He'd just proven to himself that he'd changed. He was saddened he wouldn't be able to share the Fritz encounter with his dad.

JACKSON AND HIS MOTHER ARRIVED at Greystone thirty minutes before visitation was to begin, and the parking lot was already full. They parked in the rear in a space reserved for family. Mr. B, wringing his hands, met them at the door. He was visibly distraught. He noticed that the parking had already spilled into the surrounding neighborhood and knew there'd be complaints.

He'd been watching for them, and when he saw Mrs. Koch get out of the car and saw what she was wearing, said to himself, "Oh my." Rather than a traditional black dress, Marie had chosen to wear the red dress she'd worn to the Christmas play. It was George's favorite dress and the one she'd been wearing when he'd last seen her. But the main cause for Mr. B's nervous sweat was the phone call he'd just gotten.

He opened the door for them and said. "I received a call from a Clarence Johnson."

Mrs. Koch thought for second. "You mean Kelly?"

"He just said Clarence, but said he would be attending the funeral with 'other' dignitaries."

"We haven't heard from Kelly for years," she said.

Mrs. Koch's calm only made Mr. B more nervous. "So what does he mean by dignitaries?" Before she could answer he continued. "And he asked if there'd be special seating."

She smiled. "That's the Kelly I know." A bittersweet notion struck her: the entire town would now learn what George had been reluctant to share.

Bridgette had seen the Kochs arrive and had threaded her way to the rear entrance where she hoped to catch them ahead of the crowd. She had papers to grade and wanted to offer her condolences, and then head home.

"What does he mean by dignitaries?"

"That's anybody's guess," Mrs. Koch replied, which didn't help the matter. "Could be government people, could be people from Lockheed."

Bridgette Anderson heard the tail-end of the conversation. "You don't know who Kelly Johnson is?" she asked Mr. B. Her face wore an expression of shock. By this time Mr. B was nearly beside himself, and he began to twist and turn. First the town patriarch passes away, meaning a record turnout, and then this!

Jackson took his mother's arm. "Mother, there are people waiting." He was leading her toward the viewing room when Bridgette touched his forearm. He introduced himself. Bridgette shook his hand, gave Marie a hug, and then offered them her condolences.

"Look," Jackson said. "You seem to know a little about Kelly. Would you mind explaining him to Baumgartner?"

Mr. Baumgartner was rubbing his temples when she began to explain. "I guess you read Tommy Thompson's essay about Mr. Koch, it was in the paper?"

Mr. B nodded impatiently. "Oh sure. I'd never heard of the Lafayette Escadrille until then. So is this guy another WWI pilot?" He pictured a crusty old man on the verge of death.

Bridgette shook her head and grinned. "Kelly Johnson was the lead engineer for the P-38."

"That's one of the airplane models on display next to the urn?" he asked. Bridgette nodded.

"Oh, so this Clarence Kelly guy helped build WWII planes?" Mr. B asked.

Bridgette corrected him. "It's Clarence Johnson, but he goes by Kelly instead of Clarence." She quickly listed the planes that Kelly Johnson had designed, including the F-104, U2, and SR71. The phone rang. Mrs. B came out of the funeral home office and told Mr. B it was for him. He excused himself. Bridgette went home to grade papers, energized by the notion that she might get to meet Kelly Johnson.

MONKEY PICKED UP THE OTHER Codgers and they rode together on the golf cart. He'd recently put snow tires on it and was anxious to test them. He nosed it into a small spot between two cars. "Best thing about it is it's easy to park," he bragged. The others rolled their eyes and shuffled toward Greystone.

Seeing their old bench drew their attention to the serenity garden. Not that they were bent on introspection, but more an inspection of the paint job of the courthouse bench on which they'd spent every afternoon for the past decade. The inspection led to them taking a seat. The Codgers were an island unto themselves, sitting on the bench surrounded by recently planted snow-covered shrubs and ornamental trees. The shrubs were green, but everything else was dormant and looked dead. The Codgers, as was the case with most people, had no idea the bench was meant for decoration. Nonfunctional yard furniture, popular in Fairview, hadn't caught on in Colby.

Although it wasn't Mr. B's intention that people sit on the bench, the Codgers were a natural addition to the tranquil setting. Since the garden was only a few feet from the entrance, they greeted everyone. Many thought their placement intentional and thanked them for taking the time to help with the visitation.

Most of the town had shown up well before the posted time for the visitation. The Codgers were enjoying their seat in the serenity garden while everyone else stood in line waiting for the doors to open. Each time a new couple arrived, women opened their compacts for a last look and men renewed their efforts at sucking in their bellies. The men, not knowing what to do with their hands, put them in their pockets when speaking and used their elbows and shoulders to accentuate.

Fritz saw where Monkey had parked his golf cart, pushed it into the adjacent yard, and parked his Volkswagen where the cart had been. He thought it ridiculous that Monkey would be driving the stupid thing in the dead of winter.

"Say now," Fish said. "Did you read the essay that the Thompson boy did about George?"

Bem spit before saying, "It said that old man Koch was a WWI pilot, don't cha know."

"I knew that," Fish replied.

"What in the heck was the Lafayette Escadrille?" Joe-Bill asked. He, too, had read the article. They speculated endlessly about the Escadrille. None of them, it turned out, added anything that hadn't been mentioned in the paper.

The band of boys arrived en masse. They'd ridden with their parents and had loafed in the parking lot until time for the visitation. Since the publication of the essays, they'd become popular with the veterans.

Marie and Jackson were given a few minutes alone in the viewing room.

She gently stroked the urn. Heinz Baumgartner had tried to talk them out of cremation, mostly likely because Greystone didn't have a crematorium. Jackson and Marie spent several moments looking at the display of photos and old newspaper clippings with the flowers and urn at the center.

During the move, she'd boxed up collections of old photos. She surveyed the room and read aloud a few of the notes attached to the floral arrangements. She steeled herself and tugged gently on Jackson's sleeve, and then he nodded to the attendants to open the door.

People expecting a weeping widow standing next to an open casket with a corpse made to look like a sleeping likeness of the deceased were surprised. The place had been transformed into a museum. Placed throughout the room were large photo boards. They were divided into categories. There was a section from WWI, another for photos depicting his time on the X608 project, several showing him with Scout as a puppy, wedding photos, and several with Jackson as a youngster.

Scale replicas of the WWII P-38 and a WWI Spad S.XIII, and photos of Mr. Koch flying, lined a long table that sat where the casket would normally be. There was a photo of Mr. Koch standing next to Eddie Rickenbacker, and another of him with Gene Bullard. One would think the photo of Mr. Koch standing next to Rickenbacker, the famous WWI ace, would have drawn the most attention. But it was the other photo that drew the most attention.

Eugene Jacques Bullard was from Georgia, fluent in French, and officially the first black fighter pilot. Frank Fritz flinched when he saw the photo and realized that George had had a deep relationship with a Negro, which explained his compassion for the Websters.

In the center of the long table, next to Mr. Koch's urn, was a silver framed photo of the Kochs on their wedding day. Next to their photo was a smaller urn, accompanied by a photo of Scout. A small card between the urns read "Together They Go."

The doors had opened to the playing of "Eine Kleine Nachtmusik," a lively beginning. A potpourri of Mozart, Brahms, and Chopin, George's favorites, played during the remainder of the visitation.

Marie was standing next to the photos of her and George. Jackson stood a few feet away. This confused the crowd. Normally, a line would form and wind its way from the coffin to however far it needed to go. And the survivors would stand in line and greet each person. Mrs. Koch chose to work the crowd. A few made their way to the front and visited with themselves as they viewed the display.

Eventually a line began forming at Mrs. Koch. As soon as it did, she'd whisper something to Jackson and move to another photo poster. Then when the line began to form there, the two of them moved again. They repeated this throughout the evening. On seeing a dear friend in the crowd, she'd go directly to them. Men thought it made sense; just sign the book, look at a few photos, and get the heck out of there. Some mourners became frustrated at the nontraditional setting. Women began to talk. The Colby Curls crowd thought the red dress scandalous. But all the women were interested in the tall, dark, handsome FBI agent.

Jackson felt the most comfortable when speaking to his former teachers. It was no surprise to them that he'd done well; he'd always been an outstanding student. The fact that he'd joined the FBI was a surprise. They'd expected him to land a position in academia. To others, seeing Jackson was confirmation of the Koch's claim that he'd "come around." To Brother Baker, seeing Jackson confirmed the teaching of Proverbs 22:6: "Train up a child in the way he should go and when he is old he will not depart from it."

Mr. B made his way through the crowd, forcing a smile only when necessary. The unorthodox way in which Mrs. Koch was receiving guests had him stressed beyond measure, and then the phone call had compounded his anxiety.

He touched Jackson on the elbow. "I need to speak to you."

Jackson was just getting comfortable speaking to those he hadn't seen since high school. "Can it wait?" he asked.

Mr. B wiped sweat from his forehead and replied, "No." Jackson followed him to his office.

"Who is this Clarence Kelly fellow?" Mr. B asked.

Jackson grinned. "It's Kelly Johnson. I've never met him, but Dad used to speak to him on the phone from time to time."

"Do you have any idea what he's planning for tomorrow?"

Jackson recalled a few of the stories he'd heard about the man who was the brains behind the world's most remarkable aircraft. "Nothing would surprise me," Jackson replied, after Mr. B explained Kelly's plan.

"I see," Jackson said. "Well, he's probably the only person who could pull something like that off." While growing up, Jackson had pried information from his dad about the legends with whom he'd served. Stories about Kelly had been the most interesting.

With that, Mr. B became even more agitated. "Yes, and that's another thing. He's asked for reserved seats for four. Can you imagine?" Jackson grinned and nodded that yes, he could.

Mr. B took a seat while Jackson gave him the short bio on each and his dad's connection. Ben Kelsey had designed the P-38, Tony Levier had been the primary test pilot, and Hall Hibbard had been the Lockheed executive who oversaw the project.

"I've never had celebrities attend a funeral," Mr. B said.

"These men aren't celebrities," Jackson said. "They're legends. There's a difference." He gave Mr. B a comforting pat on the shoulder. "They don't need to be pampered, just respected," he said and then returned to the parlor. He spoke to people as he made his way to his mother and let her know.

Mr. B remained in a stupor for a few seconds, thinking that legends probably trumped celebrities. He gradually returned to the present and began planning the funeral service.

While Jackson was filling Mr. B in on the legendary status of the men, Tommy was looking at the photo display. He zeroed in on the X608 plaque and the photos surrounding it. He'd yet to tell a single soul what George had shared. The urge to tell someone, anyone, especially his friends, the significance of the plaque disturbed him beyond measure.

He noticed Mrs. Crawford enter the room. Mrs. Koch went to her immediately and the two embraced; they took a seat and held each other for several minutes. Tommy wondered if Mrs. Koch's red dress would get covered with cat hair.

So, You're a Paperboy?

MR. B HAD TOLD ONE friend of his conversations with the "famous guy." The word spread quickly.

Realizing the Greystone facility wasn't sufficient to seat the number of people sure to attend the funeral, Mr. B made arrangements to move it to the high school gymnasium.

The famous four and the pallbearers, Burt Brown, Jupiter Storm, Washington Webster, Tommy Thompson, Cletus Thornton, and Russell Gooche, were invited to a private reception that took place just before the memorial service. Newt Thorpe was allowed in to snap a few photos for the paper.

Tommy moved about knowing he was in the presence of giants. He was so nervous that he itched all over. Tony Levier had a swagger, and of the famous four was the only one who didn't wear a tie. He sported an ascot. He picked Tommy out of the crowd. "So why'd you get chosen to be a pallbearer?" Tommy's mind blanked, his mouth dried, and he nearly swallowed his tongue.

Marie answered for him. "He interviewed George and wrote a very nice essay about him. And," she continued with emphasis, "He's our paperboy."

"That so?" the legendary test pilot said. "So why'd you write an essay about George?"

Marie interceded again. "He had to write an essay as punishment for shooting at some high school kids with a potato gun." She gave Tony a grin, knowing he'd understand such behavior.

"Did you hit 'em?" Tony asked.

"No," Tommy stuttered, and quickly followed up with, "I wasn't aiming at them, just trying to scare 'em." Tommy was still taken aback at Mrs.

Koch's apparent approval of the potato gun episode. He was reminded of the encounter she'd had with Jupiter.

Tony winked at Marie and turned to Tommy. "But why'd you choose George?"

"Actually, Miss Anderson assigned him to me," he said. "I'd asked her about the X608 program."

She turned to Tony. "He noticed the plaque when he was collecting for the newspaper."

Tony grinned. "You learn a lot about people when you're their paper boy. Don't 'cha?"

"Yes, sir," Tommy replied.

"I was a paperboy," Tony said. "Everyday I'd ride my bicycle by the airport. That's what got me interested in flying. In fact, I used my route money to pay for flying lessons." Tommy couldn't believe he was having a conversation with a legend, and that they had something in common! Wow!

Tony had been looking around the concession stand area while he and Tommy visited. He noticed Randy Burger's retired jersey and the 1966 All-State plaque beside it. "This Randy Burger must have been a real stand-out," Tony said. "All-State, jersey retired. Is he playing college ball?"

Tommy shook his head no. "He was a great football player. He had football scholarship offers but chose to join the Marines instead." Tommy swallowed the lump in his throat. "He got killed in Vietnam."

Their conversation was interrupted when Kelly Johnson whistled to get their attention. "Gentlemen," he said.

Tony winked at Tommy. "Watch this—bet he says something about being quiet, quick, and on time. He always works that saying in somehow." The men huddled around Kelly Johnson, Tommy stood motionless.

"You too, young Mr. Thompson," Kelly Johnson said. At first Tommy thought Mr. Johnson was addressing his dad. Then he nearly lost control of his bodily functions after realizing he was being singled out by the Mr. Kelly Johnson. Tony was grinning. Tommy nervously joined the huddle of men surrounding Mr. Johnson and Mrs. Koch.

"Here's how it's going to work," he began. He explained how the service would occur, where they'd be sitting, who would be speaking, and then how everyone would be invited to gather on the football field for a farewell salute. A question that had been looming in Tommy's mind since being asked to be a pallbearer was answered. What do pallbearers do when there's no casket? Kelly Johnson looked at his watch and said, "It's time—quickly and quietly, let's join the rest." Tommy looked at Tony and got a told-you-so shrug.

Mrs. Koch and Jackson went first, followed by the famous four. The gymnasium was packed. All of the items that had been on display at Greystone had been moved to the stage. The pallbearers were seated on the left side of the stage. Brother Baker and Mrs. Enderle were on the other side. Mrs. Koch and Jackson were seated just left of center stage, next to the urns.

After being seated, Tommy scanned the crowd for the rest of the boys and Melody. They were looking at him when he spotted them, Melody gave him a wiggly finger wave—he blushed. He couldn't see, but he imagined that she was wearing the sparkly lipstick. He concealed a smile when he saw his Uncle Cletus and Penny sitting together. Next to them were Booger's dad and Miss Anderson.

A smugness fell over Tommy as he contemplated being chosen as a pallbearer and having privileged knowledge of the details of the farewell ceremony. The chance to be considered in the same light as the other pall-bearers, and simply being in the same room with the famous four, was surreal. He was filled with a Christmas morning joy upon learning that Mr. Koch's participation in the X608 program was going to be made public.

A sudden, uncontrollable burp-hiccup snapped him back to reality. He got a look from his dad. He continued to scan the crowd and tasted the breakfast bacon Marsha had fried for him.

He spotted Mr. and Mrs. Dwight Seabaugh, as they were now known. Dwight was in uniform—his medical discharge wasn't official until the end of the month. Velma and Alison were there too. Velma looked proud, a new look for her. Alison was wearing a dress, a new look for her as well. She'd surprised everyone by showing up in a black dress with her thick, golden hair arranged in an up-do.

Next to Alison were the men Tommy had seen driving the car with the shotgun mounted on the dash. He had since learned they were U.S. Marshals assigned to the Tatum witness protection program.

Mrs. Enderle sang "Heaven Came Down." The speakers in the gym worked fine for announcements, but not so much for singing. The words bounced off the walls and sounded like an infinite echo. People cried, some due to emotion, some because their ears were hurting.

Brother Baker read the obituary. It was a long one. Hearing the accomplishments read aloud seemed to bring them to life. No doubt many regretted not getting to know more about George Koch while he was living. Everyone was filled with a new respect for the many veterans in attendance.

Burt Brown spoke next. Tommy saw him glance up at Alison before he began. He went into detail on Mr. Koch's civic involvement. Burt fought back tears while he told of how grateful he was for Mr. Koch's leadership role in getting the service station built. Tommy saw him glance up into the stands again, but this time he was looking at Dwight and Tippy. Tommy knew what Burt was thinking. He'd asked Dwight to join him as a partner. Tippy had eagerly agreed to use part of her trust money to finance an additional bay for the filling station.

Kelly Johnson spoke next. It was immediately clear that he was an experienced public speaker. He confessed something to the crowd he claimed to have never told anyone. "I've been given credit for a phrase," he said. "A phrase, which by the way, I didn't coin." He looked back at Jackson and Mrs. Koch. "The phrase 'Be quick, be quiet, be on time' was first used by George." He explained how he'd picked up on the phrase, began to use it, and had been given credit for it. "It's just one example of the many accomplishments of others in which George Koch was instrumental."

He panned the crowd. "Ever since George moved here, I've wanted to visit Colby. Most of you probably know your native son, Ira Biffle, who taught Charles Lindbergh how to fly." He composed himself. "Knowing George, I'm sure he never told anyone that it was George who taught Ira to fly." He let that soak in. "Is that coincidence or providence?"

The sad fact was, until Bridgette Anderson moved to town, few had heard of Ira Biffle; he'd left the area fifty years earlier. Kelly then began introducing the rest of the famous four.

Hal Hibbard told of how George Koch's name was repeatedly mentioned when the X608 team was being assembled. "We knew there'd be conflict," he said. "And Mr. Koch was our resolution general. He knew how to deal with people." He glanced toward Tony Levier, and then continued, "And as a fighter pilot, he knew how to deal with inflated egos."

"I'm the guy with the inflated ego," Tony Levier said after being introduced by Hal Hibbard; the crowd returned a reserved laughter. "But in the presence of those who knew General George, as we used to call him, I'm awash with humility." Tony took a few seconds to fight back tears and get control of his emotions. "You knew him, he lived among you. There's very little that I can add, except," he paused, "George Koch was a national treasure." With those words, the tears Marie had been trying so hard to hold back so as not to mess up her makeup streamed down her cheeks.

Tommy had never seen so many people crying at the same time. By then, he'd found the Colby Curls crew. He could see the mascara running from across the gym. The previous day, they'd been talking about Alison Tatum. Through hard work at the filling station, she'd kept a taut figure. After a couple of visits, the Avon lady confessed that Alison's natural beauty was such that she needed little makeup. The Curls crew found all of that disgusting. Jealousy prevailed.

Ben Kelsey began by saying, "While my official rank was always superior to George Koch, there was never any doubt that George's emotional and functional rank was superior to anyone on the X608 team." Tommy noticed how Gen. Kelsey spoke in sharp phrases. His sentences ended with a snap. The crowd began to get restless. Tommy noticed people squirming in their seats like they did in that TV commercial for Preparation H.

Then Kelsey asked. "How many of you played the 'who's your favorite American hero' game with George?" Several heads nodded. Tommy remembered Mr. Koch asking him that question during the interview. Kelsey watched as heads bobbed. "Okay," he continued. "Let me ask this, how many of you know who George Koch's favorite hero was?" Tommy didn't understand the hush that fell upon the room.

Kelsey looked over at Tommy and winked. The two of them had talked about Mr. Koch. Kelsey had asked him the question and was surprised that Tommy knew. Kelsey continued. "George always thought it said lot about a person when you knew who their favorite hero was." Tommy felt a sense of pride for knowing the answer was George Washington.

Tommy located Mrs. Whitener. Just as in church, she'd maintained a space on each side. She was an island of sorts. Tommy wondered how many people knew her background as he and Booger did. He was sure that most saw her as he once had, a short, globe-shaped simple lady. He made a mental note to ask Miss Anderson about doing an essay on her.

Then it dawned on Tommy that several of his customers had a side that wasn't well known.

Those gathered had already received a big surprise to learn about George's critical involvement in the X608 program, which was instrumental in winning WWII. Gen. Kelsey stunned the crowd when he introduced the last speaker, Washington Webster.

Just as it did anytime there was a crowd, the gym had gotten hot. "George Koch was at first a friend," he began with a quivering voice. A hush fell upon an already quiet crowd. Tommy had spotted the Codgers; Frank Fritz was sitting with them. Fritz seemed to be hanging on Washington's each and every word. "George introduced me to Gene Bullard." The faces of the famous four indicated they were accessing a long-forgotten memory. Gen. Kelsey nodded approvingly. "For those of you who might not know," Washington said, "Gene Bullard was the first black fighter pilot. He flew with George in the Lafayette Escadrille." A murmur swept the room. Fritz was so focused he'd stopped blinking. He visualized the photo he'd seen the night before of George with this Gene. Washington surveyed the crowd. "George Koch believed in me." He continued for nearly twenty minutes about George Koch, the man. The crowd that had grown weary of sitting on bleachers and listening to too many speakers stopped squirming and drank in every word. When Washington finished, the gymnasium exploded in a thunderous applause. But the best was yet to come.

Brother Baker approached the lectern and asked everyone to move to the football field for a final salute. The pallbearers led the way, followed by Jackson, Mrs. Koch, and then the famous four. They assembled inside a roped-off area in the center of the field. The rest of Colby scattered across the pit.

The famous four were looking skyward, so everyone else did the same. Four F-100D Super Sabres, the USAF Thunderbirds, came into sight just seconds before the deafening sound filled the pit. The fighters split their formation and departed in four different directions. The sound of their jet engines lingered.

The sound of the next plane reached the crowd before coming into sight. It was moving much slower than the Thunderbirds. A Sopwith Strutter, similar to the one George Koch had flown in WWI, approached the football field and began circling. It made one circle, and then was joined by a P-38. The sight and the sound of the two legendary planes was mesmerizing. The antique planes belonged to Kelly Johnson. He'd made all arrangements and taken care of the expense for the impressive flyover.

While the Sopwith and P-38 were circling at low level, the four F-100D Thunderbirds returned, this time flying much slower and a little higher. When the Thunderbirds were directly overhead, one wingman added full power and climbed straight up. Once again, the sound was deafening. The Sopwith and P-38 peeled off and departed the area as the lone Thunderbird roared away into the heavens. The three remaining Thunderbirds returned less than a minute later and made one last high-speed pass.

Sobbing men held their wives, mothers held their children. The children were moved by their parents' reactions to the symbolism. The astonishing sound of the jets touched a nerve inside everyone. Unfamiliar emotions were unleashed. A feeling of awe, pride, strength, and patriotism were wrapped into a single, focused moment. Goose bumps, tears, and smiles prevailed.

The smell of jet fueled wafted upon the crowd. Nobody stirred. Chins were trembling and all eyes were filled with tears. During the flyover, an Air Force color guard had taken position on the hill. "Taps" began sorrowfully. It was a fitting final tribute to an American treasure.

Seeing the planes together in the sky demonstrated how far flight had progressed during a single generation. The full realization that George Koch had been a fighter pilot instructor sent a tremor through Tommy. He realized that if a man was to make it to the moon, it would be a fighter pilot. Fighter pilots are the true pioneers in manned flight. As one of the original instructors, a thread of George Koch's legacy was laced into every cutting-edge fighter plane. In medieval times there were the Knights of the Round Table, Tommy was thinking, but today there are the fighter pilots. Tommy stretched the parallel logic a tad and concluded that Mr. Koch had been not only akin to a Knight, but possibly a King Arthur.

THE BOYS FOUND THEIR WAY to Tommy in hopes of getting to meet one of the legends. Tommy saw them coming and tapped Kelly Johnson on the arm, warning him. "I think my friends want to meet you, sir."

The story of Johnny Burger had spread among the four. "Which one is Booger?" Kelly Johnson asked after the boys approached. The boys all pointed to Booger, and then hung tight as the famous four stood in line to shake hands with him.

"So you're Randy Burger's brother?" Tony Levier asked. He knuckled Booger in the shoulder. "You must be proud of him." Booger nodded his head in agreement—his chin was quivering. "Paperboy too?" he asked Booger. Booger nodded. Tony squeezed Booger's shoulder as bonding men do. "I was a paperboy." He said it in such a way as to be looking for approval.

Flop and the rest of the band were huddled behind Booger. "We help too," Flop said.

Tony looked at Flop and the others and snickered. "Fair weather helpers?"

Tommy chuckled and nodded. He was amazed that Tony's experience as a paperboy was so similar to his. The other boys looked at each other sheepishly.

Tommy and Booger stood shoulder to shoulder, the rest of the band behind them. Tommy looked at the famous four and particularly Tony Levier, and he realized they had all come from humble beginnings and one of them had even been a paperboy.

Fritz looked disturbed while making his way through the crowd. He found Jackson and handed him a small notebook. "Look that over and then stop by," Fritz said.

Jackson looked at him suspiciously. "What is it?" Jackson asked.

Fritz pointed at the notebook. "There's information in there that can help your investigation."

"I'll stop by tomorrow," Jackson said.

Fritz nodded, and then looked around as if he suspected he was being watched.

ALISON INTRODUCED JACKSON TO THE Chicago-based U.S. Marshals. They filled him in on his dad's role in the witness protection program.

"I had no idea," Jackson said.

"It's no surprise," Vince Gambaiana said. "He only told those who needed to know."

"I should have seen it," Jackson said.

"How's that?" Vince asked.

"He paid way too much attention to Al Tatum. When the whole town was talking trash about her, Dad always came to her defense, her right to be different." He paused. "Looking back, it's clear."

Several people were waiting to speak to Jackson. "We're going to try that Italian place, Rosolini's," Vince said. "Why don't we meet there later on and continue the conversation?"

Jackson agreed, and then he caught up with Tommy. "Nice essay on Dad," he said.

"Thanks," Tommy replied. Tommy felt uneasy. He looked curiously at Jackson. The ladies at Colby Curls had gone on and on about how good-looking Jackson was. Tommy wasn't sure what it was the ladies were excited about, but for once they'd had something good to say about someone.

"I talked to Mom," Jackson said. "We'd like you to have the plaque."

Tommy was almost speechless. "You mean the X608 plaque?" he asked.

Jackson grinned. "Of course."

At first Tommy couldn't get his mouth to work. "I don't know what to say," Tommy managed to stutter.

Jackson's smile broadened, revealing the perfect teeth the Colby Curls crew had spoken of. "Thanks would be a start," he said.

"Thanks!" Tommy said. "I mean, thanks a lot!"

THE HAT FACTORY SNOOP MADE what he hoped would be his final road report. This time, he used a Colby phone booth. It no longer mattered if his cover was blown. The president of the board of International Hat took the call. "There's not going to be a problem," the caller said. "Even with George Koch gone, there's not going to be a racial problem."

"Are you sure?" the chairman asked.

"I just left the memorial service," he replied. "One of the speakers was Carter's brother; he was a pilot in WWII. It turns out he and the deceased knew each other way back when. Anyway, judging from the way people responded to his speech, I'd say Carter is in like flint."

"I'll need a full report, just the same," the president replied.

"You'll have it first thing Monday morning," the caller assured him.

"Have a safe trip home," the president said. "It's cloudy and they're calling for snow here in St. Louis."

"Will do," the caller said, and then he hung up. He stepped outside the phone booth and took in a deep breath of pollution-free air. During his trips to Colby, he'd kept his conversations with people superficial since his primary objective was observation of the town's reaction to Carter Webster. In that time, he'd observed so much more. He'd seen a culture that, having grown up in the inner city, he never knew existed. A culture in which, when the chips were down, everyone pulled together, regardless of religion or social status. He had never met George Koch, but he had been deeply touched by the memorial service. As he left town, he caught himself focusing more on the rearview mirror than the windy road ahead.

The president of the board leaned back into his chair and smiled. While the media was plying the country with news of racial unrest, a small town in Missouri had demonstrated that given a chance, good could prevail. For once, the president was happy to be wrong.

ALISON SLIPPED OFF THE DRESS she'd worn to the funeral. Rather than return it to the trunk, where it had been stored for years, she hung it in her closet. She'd received several compliments at the funeral, the most prized of which had come from Burt. It was time to start wearing it again.

Magical Moments

TOMMY SPENT THE REMAINDER OF Saturday and most of Sunday on a natural high, induced by the exhilaration of meeting the legends behind the X608 project. He came crashing down on the way to school on Monday morning when the weather began to deteriorate. Sitting on the bus on the way home watching the drizzle begin to freeze on the window caused him to face reality—he and Booger still had the paper to deliver. It was shaping up to be another glamour-free day to be a paperboy.

He and Booger decided to walk the route. Customers didn't like bicycles ridden across their lawns when it rained, but they still wanted the paper thrown to a dry place on their porches. Plus, it was the last week before Christmas. Several customers had begun to give them small gifts. They'd watch for the boys, call them to the door, and give them a present.

Tommy and Booger were sitting back to back on the stone waiting for the paper drop and laughing about the gifts they'd received the week before. Mrs. Whitener had given them scones. Neither had had them before or intended to have them again. She was proud to serve them something from her homeland. Both boys had forced the bone-dry British biscuit down and lied how about how good they were. They'd taken the second serving with them and dispatched them less than a block away—into Venus Storm's flower bed. They'd justified the lie since it had been told to keep from hurting Mrs. Whitener's feelings. They'd agreed that the scones tasted good to somebody somewhere, so saying they were good wasn't lying.

Mrs. Gooche had given them peanut brittle. Booger lost a filling eating his and had yet to tell his dad. The dentist was something to be avoided at all costs. He planned to tell Miss Anderson first.

Mrs. Crawford gave them each a pair of dress socks. They'd been worn, probably by her late husband. Since they were free of cat hair, the boys knew she'd gone to some extra effort and washed them.

Another widow had given them a baby-food jar full of pennies. She'd tied a thin ribbon around the neck of each jar, making them look festive—sort of.

Tommy and Booger were discussing what to do with the tiny jar of pennies when Mrs. Webster came out of the post office. She'd asked the boys what could possibly be so amusing when they were sitting on a cold stone and faced with having to deliver the paper in the winter drizzle. She laughed when they told her. "I'll be right back," she said; then she ran up the stairs and returned with two cups of hot chocolate. "You can return the cups when you bring the paper," she said. They sat on the cold stone, sipped the hot chocolate, and waited for the paper. Tommy glanced at the bank thermometer and saw that the temperature had dropped to thirty-one degrees. The sidewalks would soon be covered with a thin sheet of ice.

The papers arrived—Tommy and Booger both climbed the stairs to deliver Mrs. Webster's *Colby Telegraph* and return the cups. The dank odor had been replaced by the smell of three coats of paint.

"You're going to get wet today," she said.

"Yes, ma'am," Booger replied with a hot chocolate mustache.

She smiled consolingly. "Guess that's part of being a paperboy."

"We better get going," Tommy said with zero enthusiasm. "It's only going to get colder and darker."

The two of them walked, slump-shouldered, slowly down the warm stairway, the last warmth they'd enjoy until the papers got delivered. They stepped out of the stairwell to a welcome surprise. Flop, Checkers, Caleb, and Everett were waiting by the stone. Melody was standing on the stone, rocking back and forth heel to toe. She'd been helping at the store and had gotten permission to tag along.

Flop wore a pained expression, or it may have been that the two sock hats had compressed his face. "That Tony guy is full of baloney," he said.

"Yeah," Checkers agreed. "We ain't fair-weather helpers."

They divided the papers equally. It took less than thirty minutes to deliver every paper. While Melody walked with Tommy, the heavy drizzle slowly turned into large, half-dollar sized snowflakes.

SOON AFTER TOMMY AND BOOGER left, the Websters' phone rang. "Mrs. Webster?" Gloria's caller asked.

"Yes, this is she," replied Gloria.

"This is Mable Sapington. The ladies are having a tea tomorrow," Mable continued. "We'd be delighted if you could join us." Gloria's legs became wobbly.

She gathered her composure, tried not to sound shocked, and replied. "Why, I'd love that." After getting the particulars she thanked Mable for calling and sank into Carter's favorite chair; her eyes welled with tears of joy.

Across town, the Tatums' phone rang too, and Alison picked up. "Alison?" Burt asked.

"Yes?" Alison replied. She was fairly certain it was Burt.

"Ah, well the thing is," he stuttered. "Would you like to go to dinner at Rosolini's?"

The door to a room in Alison's heart that had been closed for years swung wide open. She swallowed and regained her composure. "Burt, are you asking me out?" She was being coy and knew it.

"Is that what they call it now?" he asked. Burt sensed Alison's smile.

"So long as you don't drive the wrecker," she replied.

"Deal," he said.

It was a moment Alison would remember for many years.

CAMARADERIE HAD KEPT THE BAND of boys and Melody warm. After delivering the papers in record time, they'd gone traipsing around in the fresh snow. While their parents worried why they hadn't come home, the friends for life were lying on the fifty-yard line in rapidly accumulating snow. They were catching giant snowflakes with their mouths and making plans for the next day—a snow day.

Tommy was lying beside Melody. He was sneaking peeks at her and could see the silhouette of her angelic face, even her eyelashes, against a distant streetlight. He watched a snowflake land on the tip of her waiting tongue.

It was a magical moment until Checkers blurted out, "Dang, one of 'em snowflakes hit me square in th' eye." A gang-tackling melee of Checkers ensued.

Exhausted, they called it a day and went their separate ways, except Tommy and Melody, who walked home together. Christmas shoppers were milling about the square, admiring the Christmas lights. Melody insisted on going past the stone. She was brushing the snow off of the top of the stone when the Websters stepped out.

Gloria saw Melody wearing Tommy's paper bag and smiled. "Oh, I see how it is," she said.

Carter winked. "Smart man." Tommy was embarrassed. Melody patted the bag with pride. She'd only been wearing it since they warmed up at Mrs. Whitener's.

The Websters were on their way to Rosolini's. Burt and Alison had walked, too. They'd just been seated and were looking at the "Ini" menu when the Websters arrived. "Hey, Carter," Burt said, as if the two had known each other for years. "Would you like to join us?" A month earlier, Burt's invitation would have caused a stir. As it was, the four of them having dinner together didn't merit a single call, not even a passing mention at Colby Curls.

"Mele Kalikimaka" by Bing Crosby began playing at the Houn-Dawg. The snow created an acoustic that made the outdoor speakers sound rich. Melody sat on the stone and took Tommy's hand. They were wearing gloves so her touch wasn't as romantic, but Tommy considered it a hopeful gesture.

Since the football field, he'd been working up the nerve to kiss her and had figured out a strategy. The plan was to move in close as he was taking the paper bag off her shoulder, and while there, he'd go for the kiss. Time stood still.

Using the toe of her boot, she carved '831' into the virgin snow. Tommy mustered the nerve to ask, "What does 831 mean?"

"Eight letters, three words, one meaning," she replied. Tommy was too dull to connect the proverbial dots. Melody glowed when she explained. "I like you."

All the places he'd seen '831' swept through his mind. It was now or never, but he didn't count on her ducking her head to let the bag strap pass over. He missed her mouth and got her nose—it was cold and damp. Before he had a chance to become flustered or embarrassed, she adjusted and they kissed. The moment was infinitely more magical than he'd imagined.

With a frozen mitten, Tommy gently wrote '831' onto Melody's forehead, paused in thought a split second, and then cleverly stroked the shape of a '2.' He and Melody now had a stone story of their own.

STAN AND HIS WIFE DEBBIE live in Southern Missouri where they raised three boys and a golden retriever.

WWW.STANCRADER.COM

CPSIA information can be obtained at www.ICGtesting.com
Printed in the USA
LVOW041339271012

304695LV00002B/2/P